Fireside Ghost Stories for

CHRISTMAS EVE

AN ANTHOLOGY *of*
WINTER HORROR TALES

Edited and Illustrated By

M. GRANT KELLERMEYER, M.A.

☙

{5}

OLDSTYLE TALES PRESS
Supernatural, Weird, & Horror Fiction

This edition published 2015 by
Oldstyle Tales Press

Notes, Introductions, and Illustrations
Copyright © 2015 by Michael Grant Kellermeyer

**Readers who are interested in further titles from
Oldstyle Tales Press are invited to visit our website at
WWW.OLDSTYLETALES.COM**

ANNOTATIONS AND INTRODUCTORY NOTES
The greatest care is made to ensure that accurate, detailed, and helpful critical material accompanies the fiction included in this volume. Annotations and introductory notes are created using peer-reviewed scholarly articles accessed from JSTOR, Project MUSE, EBSCO Host, and bound collections of criticism accessed at Indiana University, Ball State University, Purdue University, and through interlibrary loans. Definitions and references are informed by the Oxford English Dictionary, the Dictionary of English Nautical Language, the Encyclopædia Britannica, Grolier Online, and credible online databases. Foreign translations are only released after comparing the results of several books of grammar pertaining to the source language. Biographical, critical, and contextual information regarding the writer, their work, and their world are generated after consulting peer-reviewed biographies, reference works, compendiums, collected correspondences, histories, and literary criticism.

OLDSTYLE TALES PRESS
Founded in 2013, Oldstyle Tales Press is committed to producing affordable editions of the best supernatural, weird, and horror fiction produced in the English-speaking world before World War Two. While most anthologies and editions of horror fiction are either entirely lacking (or notably sparse) in their critical material or designed for professional use by literary scholars, Oldstyle Press strives to offer quality editions with informative-but-accessible critical material, an attractive horror aesthetic, and a guided narrative at an affordable price designed to attract and encourage readership.

— TABLE *of* CONTENTS —

— CHRISTMAS MESSENGERS —
TALES OF SPECTRES ON A MISSION

— WINTRY VISITORS —
TALES OF WANDERING SPIRITS AND SHADES

— CHILDREN IN DANGER —
TALES OF HAUNTED NURSERIES AND TOYS

— SNOW DEMONS —
TALES OF MONSTERS AND SHAPESHIFTERS

— HAUNTED HOUSES —
TALES OF TROUBLED HOMES AND ROOMS

— DEATH IN THE SNOW —
TALES OF TRECHEROUS LANDSCAPES AND MEN

"My father used to declare positively that the last time he slept here the ghost ... lowered itself from the top of his bed and tried to strangle him..."

— *"JERRY BUNDLER"* —

YULE HORROR

H. P. Lovecraft

There is snow on the ground,
      And the valleys are cold,
   And a midnight profound
      Blackly squats o'er the wold;
But a light on the hilltops half-seen hints of feastings unhallow'd and old.

   There is death in the clouds,
      There is fear in the night,
For the dead in their shrouds
      Hail the sun's turning flight,
And chant wild in the woods as they dance round a Yule-altar fungous and white.

   To no gale of earth's kind
      Sways the forest of oak,
Where the sick boughs entwin'd
      By mad mistletoes choke,
For these pow'rs are the pow'rs of the dark, from the graves of the lost Druid-folk.

   And mayst thou to such deeds
      Be an abbot and priest,
Singing cannibal greeds
      At each devil-wrought feast,
And to all the incredulous world shewing dimly the sign of the beast.

— CONCERNING WHAT —
YOU ARE ABOUT TO READ

"Among the terms in circulation in the period for far-fetched narratives and improbable fables, one favorite was "a winter's tale." In the long, cold evenings, when the soil had been tilled to the extent that climatic conditions permitted, the still predominantly agricultural community of early modern England would sit and while away the hours of darkness with fireside pastimes, among them old wives' tales designed to enthrall young and old alike."

Catherine Belsey,
'Hamlet' and the Tradition of the Fireside Ghost Story

"A sad tale's best for winter: I have one of sprites and goblins..."

William Shakespeare
A Winter's Tale

"There'll be scary ghost stories and tales of the glories of Christmases long, long ago.."

OR so the carol tells us. To most Americans, this snippet from the Andy Williams classic has remained an anachronistic – even disturbing – oddity. Who tells scary stories at Christmas? That's Halloween, right? Many have assumed that it is "merely referring solely, in a hap-hazard fashion, to Dickens' *A Christmas Carol.*" As most Britons will be able to attest, however, ghost stories (such as those related in the BBC's "A Ghost Story for Christmas" franchise, spreading holiday fear throughout the 1970s and 2010s) are part and parcel of the Season, though the oral tradition of spending windy, winter nights listening to grandma's gory folklore has long since been resigned to the past. Ghost stories, besides providing a fantastic means of family bonding and entertainment for kids cooped up on frigid days, offer ethical dilemmas, moral quandaries, and social criticisms that go hand in hand with the season of introspection, repentance, forgiveness, and resolutions.

Ghost stories at Christmas can be traced back to pagan times – Yule and Saturnalia – when the Winter Solstice (like Hallowe'en and Wulpurgis Night) was viewed as a moment in space and time where the thinness of the boundaries between the supernatural and human worlds became remarkably plastic, and all manner of strange things were said to be seen and heard in the winter air.

One of my most prized Christmas possessions is a book called Christmas Curiosities: Odd, Dark, and Forgotten Christmas. A catalog of Victorian and Edwardian Christmas cards and trivia, it gives a glimpse of a Christmas long forgotten – one morbid, spectral, and macabre. John Grossman, the author, explains the way that Britons and Americans viewed Christmas before its commercialization in the flourishing 1920s:

"This was the Christmas season in early America around 1800, before Santa Claus, before decorating Christmas trees, Christmas shopping, family gift giving, and all other familiar activities now associated with Christmas... The winter nights were long and dark. Oil lamps, candles, torches, and the fireplace were the only sources of light to keep back the shifting shadows. In many parts of Europe, those shadows were believed to include malicious spirits, demons, and other threatening entities. These had to be appeased by gifts, and precautions had to be taken to drive them off... Venturing into the night was frightening and to be avoided at all costs, since folk beliefs in parts of northern Europe claimed that bears, werewolves, and trolls were out and about.

"The Twelve Days of Christmas, Decmeber 25 to January 6 (Epiphany), declared a sacred season of celebration [by the Church], had become in the minds of the ordinary people a period during which spirits and supernatural forces roamed the earth. The old pagan gods seemed never far off..."

Far more reminiscent of our modern Hallowe'en than modern Christmas, and yet, the time of year welcomes such traditions: it is darker, colder, more bitter; life is more fragile now, and after the family gatherings for the Christ Mass, there is a keen chance that it will be the last time that many of them see one another before sickness, feminine, and plague carry the weaker ones away before the warmth of spring returns. Death and birth are comingled in these agrarian, pre-industrial communities: the coming of the Savior is on the lips of the ministers, but the promise of the grave is in the shrill whispers of the frosty wind outside the stained-glass windows. Nearly a fortnight of local festivities would follow the Christ Mass, and the cold winters (mini ice ages, we now know) that lashed the 17th and 18th century countryside forced friends and family to cram indoors around snapping fires. Here the old dames held center stage. Their domestic lives had been spent inside: spinning wool, cooking food, sewing clothes, caring for the sick, and nursing babies, usually in the company of other women, and as a result they were excellent story tellers, using the old tales and traditions to banish mental boredom. In these days before iPhones, television, radios, or mass literacy, the oral terrors these women wove were galvanizing, and fearful was the journey home for the youngsters who had been spell-bound by tales of witches, trolls, goblins, demons, vampires, and skeletons.

And so, while we no longer have the old stories spoken in the old homes around the old fires by the old myth-keepers, let us sit around and enjoy some of the stories that would have sent shivers up the great-great-grandchildren of those little ones sitting around the Yule fire – the supernatural literature of the Victorians and Edwardians. Enclosed in this volume are tales of dark winter nights and harrowing encounters between the worlds of Man and the Hereafter. Not all of the stories occur in Christmastide – not all are even set in December, though the vast majority are – but all escort you into a chilled, winter world of open, watchful skies, brittle snow underfoot, and strange shadows that bend and bleed across the white expanses. Naturally we have selections from Dickens, including the first Stave of *A Christmas Carol*, as well as the most prolific of Christmas ghost story writers, E. F. Benson, who writes of suicide-inducing phantoms in haunted hotels, elementals that barrel into English gardens, and unevolved monsters stalking the Alps. M. R. James is renowned for his spectral Christmas readings, and here you will find the only ghost story that he set during that season. Amelia B. Edwards, Mrs Oliphant, E. Nesbit, and Elizabeth Gaskell – four of the most excellent writers of ghost stories (among the Victorians, women unquestionably reigned as writers of the supernatural) – each off up some snow-swept fantasias drenched in feminine elegance, moral complexity, and wrenching pathos. There are tales of cursed antiquities (The Silver Hatchet), otherworldly toy stores (The Magic Shop), possessed dolls (The Wondersmith), deals with the devil (The Dead Sexton), and murderous cabin fever (The Hostel). I hope your Christmas is – as M. R. James put it "may be the cheerfuller for a story-book" which takes you back to a different world – one not mapped out, trending, or tweeted about, one dark, forbidding, and evocative. Perhaps I may be a luddite for saying it, but I find something strangely comforting in that. Something consoling and hushing and chilling. Perhaps you will, too.

M. Grant Kellermeyer
Fort Wayne, St Nicholas Day, December 2015

A Christmas Tree
Charles Dickens

THERE is probably a smell of roasted chestnuts and other good comfortable things all the time, for we are telling Winter Stories — Ghost Stories, or more shame for us — round the Christmas fire; and we have never stirred, except to draw a little nearer to it. But, no matter for that. We came to the house, and it is an old house, full of great chimneys where wood is burnt on ancient dogs upon the hearth, and grim portraits (some of them with grim legends, too) lower distrustfully from the oaken panels of the walls. We are a middle-aged nobleman, and we make a generous supper with our host and hostess and their guests — it being Christmas-time, and the old house full of company — and then we go to bed. Our room is a very old room. It is hung with tapestry. We don't like the portrait of a cavalier in green, over the fireplace. There are great black beams in the ceiling, and there is a great black bedstead, supported at the foot by two great black figures, who seem to have come off a couple of tombs in the old baronial church in the park, for our particular accommodation. But, we are not a superstitious nobleman, and we don't mind. Well! we dismiss our servant, lock the door, and sit before the fire in our dressing-gown, musing about a great many things. At length we go to bed. Well! we can't sleep. We toss and tumble, and can't sleep. The embers on the hearth burn fitfully and make the room look ghostly. We can't help peeping out over the counterpane, at the two black figures and the cavalier — that wicked- looking cavalier — in green. In the flickering light they seem to advance and retire: which, though we are not by any means a superstitious nobleman, is not agreeable. Well! we get nervous — more and more nervous. We say "This is very foolish, but we can't stand this; we'll pretend to be ill, and knock up somebody." Well! we are just going to do it, when the locked door opens, and there comes in a young woman, deadly pale, and with long fair hair, who glides to the fire, and sits down in the chair we have left there, wringing her hands. Then, we notice that her clothes are wet. Our tongue cleaves to the roof of our mouth, and we can't speak; but, we observe her accurately. Her clothes are wet; her long hair is dabbled with moist mud; she is dressed in the fashion of two hundred years ago; and she has at her girdle a bunch of rusty keys. Well! there she sits, and we can't even faint, we are in such a state about it. Presently she gets up, and tries all the locks in the room with the rusty keys, which won't fit one of them; then, she fixes her eyes on the portrait of the cavalier in green, and says, in a low, terrible voice, "The stags know it!" After that, she wrings her hands again, passes the bedside, and goes out at the door. We hurry on our dressing-gown, seize our pistols (we always travel with pistols), and are following, when we find the door locked. We turn the key, look out into the dark gallery; no one there. We wander away, and try to find our servant. Can't be done. We pace the gallery till daybreak; then return to our deserted room, fall asleep, and are awakened by our servant (nothing ever haunts him) and the shining sun. Well! we make a wretched breakfast, and all the company say we look queer. After breakfast, we go over the house with our host, and then we take him to the portrait of the cavalier in green, and then it all comes out. He was false to a young housekeeper once attached to that family, and famous for her beauty, who drowned herself in a pond, and whose body was discovered, after a long time, because the stags refused to drink of the water. Since which, it has been whispered that she traverses the house at midnight (but goes especially to that room where the cavalier in green was wont to sleep), trying the old locks with the rusty keys. Well! we tell our host of what we have seen, and a shade comes over his features, and he begs it may be hushed up; and so it is. But, it's all true; and we said so, before we died (we are dead now) to many responsible people.

There is no end to the old houses, with resounding galleries, and dismal state-bedchambers, and haunted wings shut up for many years, through which we may ramble, with an agreeable creeping up our back, and encounter any number of ghosts, but (it is worthy of remark perhaps) reducible to a very few general types and classes; for, ghosts have little originality, and "walk" in a beaten track. Thus, it comes to pass, that a certain room in a certain old hall, where a certain bad lord, baronet, knight, or gentleman, shot himself, has certain planks in the floor from which the blood WILL NOT be taken out. You may scrape and scrape, as the present owner has done, or plane and plane, as his father did, or scrub and scrub, as his grandfather did, or burn and burn with strong acids, as his great- grandfather did, but, there the blood will still be — no redder and no paler — no more and no less — always just the same. Thus, in such another house there is a haunted door, that never will keep open; or another door that never will keep shut, or a haunted sound of a spinning-wheel, or a hammer, or a footstep, or a cry, or a sigh, or a horse's tramp, or the rattling of a chain. Or else, there is a turret-clock, which, at the midnight hour, strikes thirteen when the head of the family is going to die; or a shadowy, immovable black carriage which at such a time is always seen by somebody, waiting near the great gates in the stable-yard. Or thus, it came to pass how Lady Mary went to pay a visit at a large wild house in the Scottish Highlands, and, being fatigued with her long journey, retired to bed early, and innocently said, next morning, at the breakfast-table, "How odd, to have so late a party last night, in this remote place, and not to tell me of it, before I went to bed!" Then, every one asked Lady Mary what she meant? Then, Lady Mary replied, "Why, all night long, the carriages were driving round and round the terrace, underneath my window!" Then, the owner of the house turned pale, and so did his Lady, and Charles Macdoodle of Macdoodle signed to Lady Mary to say no more, and every one was silent. After breakfast, Charles Macdoodle told Lady Mary that it was a tradition in the family that those rumbling carriages on the terrace betokened death. And so it proved, for, two months afterwards, the Lady of the mansion died. And Lady Mary, who was a Maid of Honour at Court, often told this story to the old Queen Charlotte; by this token that the old King always said, "Eh, eh? What, what? Ghosts, ghosts? No such thing, no such thing!" And never left off saying so, until he went to bed.

Or, a friend of somebody's whom most of us know, when he was a young man at college, had a particular friend, with whom he made the compact that, if it were possible for the Spirit to return to this earth after its separation from the body, he of the twain who first died, should reappear to the other. In course of time, this compact was forgotten by our friend; the two young men having progressed in life, and taken diverging paths that were wide asunder. But, one night, many years afterwards, our friend being in the North of England, and staying for the night in an inn, on the Yorkshire Moors, happened to look out of bed; and there, in the moonlight, leaning on a bureau near the window, steadfastly regarding him, saw his old college friend! The appearance being solemnly addressed, replied, in a kind of whisper, but very audibly,

"Do not come near me. I am dead. I am here to redeem my promise. I come from another world, but may not disclose its secrets!" Then, the whole form becoming paler, melted, as it were, into the moonlight, and faded away.

Or, there was the daughter of the first occupier of the picturesque Elizabethan house, so famous in our neighbourhood. You have heard about her? No! Why, SHE went out one summer evening at twilight, when she was a beautiful girl, just seventeen years of age, to gather flowers in the garden; and presently came running, terrified, into the hall to her father, saying, "Oh, dear father, I have met myself!" He took her in his arms, and told her it was fancy, but she said, "Oh no! I met myself in the broad walk, and I was pale and gathering withered flowers, and I turned my head, and held them up!" And, that night, she died; and a picture of her story was begun, though never finished, and they say it is somewhere in the house to this day, with its face to the wall.

Or, the uncle of my brother's wife was riding home on horseback, one mellow evening at sunset, when, in a green lane close to his own house, he saw a man standing before him, in the very centre of a narrow way. "Why does that man in the cloak stand there!" he thought. "Does he want me to ride over him?" But the figure never moved. He felt a strange sensation at seeing it so still, but slackened his trot and rode forward. When he was so close to it, as almost to touch it with his stirrup, his horse shied, and the figure glided up the bank, in a curious, unearthly manner — backward, and without seeming to use its feet — and was gone. The uncle of my brother's wife, exclaiming, "Good Heaven! It's my cousin Harry, from Bombay!" put spurs to his horse, which was suddenly in a profuse sweat, and, wondering at such strange behaviour, dashed round to the front of his house. There, he saw the same figure, just passing in at the long French window of the drawing-room, opening on the ground. He threw his bridle to a servant, and hastened in after it. His sister was sitting there, alone. "Alice, where's my cousin Harry?" "Your cousin Harry, John?" "Yes. From Bombay. I met him in the lane just now, and saw him enter here, this instant." Not a creature had been seen by any one; and in that hour and minute, as it afterwards appeared, this cousin died in India.

Or, it was a certain sensible old maiden lady, who died at ninety- nine, and retained her faculties to the last, who really did see the Orphan Boy; a story which has often been incorrectly told, but, of which the real truth is this — because it is, in fact, a story belonging to our family — and she was a connexion of our family. When she was about forty years of age, and still an uncommonly fine woman (her lover died young, which was the reason why she never married, though she had many offers), she went to stay at a place in Kent, which her brother, an Indian-Merchant, had newly bought. There was a story that this place had once been held in trust by the guardian of a young boy; who was himself the next heir, and who killed the young boy by harsh and cruel treatment. She knew nothing of that. It has been said that there was a Cage in her bedroom in which the guardian used to put the boy. There was no such thing. There was only a closet. She went to bed, made no alarm whatever in the night, and in the morning said composedly to her maid when she came in, "Who is the pretty forlorn-looking child who has been peeping out of that closet all night?" The maid replied by giving a loud scream, and instantly decamping. She was surprised; but she was a woman of remarkable strength of mind, and she dressed herself and went downstairs, and closeted herself with her brother. "Now, Walter," she said, "I have been disturbed all night by a pretty, forlorn-looking boy, who has been constantly peeping out of that closet in my room, which I can't open. This is some trick." "I am afraid not, Charlotte," said he, "for it is the legend of the house. It is the Orphan Boy. What did he do?" "He opened the door softly," said she, "and peeped out. Sometimes, he came a step or two into the room. Then, I called to him, to encourage him, and he shrunk, and shuddered, and crept in again, and shut the door." "The closet has no communication, Charlotte," said her brother, "with any other part of the house, and it's nailed up." This was undeniably true, and it took two carpenters a whole forenoon to get it open, for examination. Then, she was satisfied that she had seen the Orphan Boy. But, the wild and terrible part of the story is, that he was also seen by three of her brother's sons, in succession, who all died young. On the occasion of each child being taken ill, he came home in a heat, twelve hours before, and said, Oh, Mamma, he had been playing under a particular oak-tree, in a certain meadow, with a strange boy — a pretty, forlorn-looking boy, who was very timid, and made signs! From fatal experience, the parents came to know that this was the Orphan Boy, and that the course of that child whom he chose for his little playmate was surely run.

Legion is the name of the German castles, where we sit up alone to wait for the Spectre — where we are shown into a room, made comparatively cheerful for our reception — where we glance round at the shadows, thrown on the blank walls by the crackling fire — where we feel very lonely when the village innkeeper and his pretty daughter have retired, after laying down a fresh store of wood upon the hearth, and setting forth on the small table such supper-cheer as a cold roast capon, bread, grapes, and a flask of old Rhine wine — where the reverberating doors close on their retreat, one after another, like so many peals of sullen thunder — and where, about the small hours of the night, we come into the knowledge of divers supernatural mysteries. Legion is the name of the haunted German students, in whose society we draw yet nearer to the fire, while the schoolboy in the corner opens his eyes wide and round, and flies off the footstool he has chosen for his seat, when the door accidentally blows open. Vast is the crop of such fruit, shining on our Christmas Tree; in blossom, almost at the very top; ripening all down the boughs!

{17}

POLLOCK AND THE PORROH MAN

H. G. Wells

IT was in a swampy village on the lagoon river behind the Turner Peninsula that Pollock's first encounter with the Porroh man occurred. The women of that country are famous for their good looks--they are Gallinas with a dash of European blood that dates from the days of Vasco da Gama and the English slave-traders, and the Porroh man too, was possibly inspired by a faint Caucasian taint in his composition. (It's a curious thing to think that some of us may have distant cousins eating men on Sherboro Island or raiding with the Sofas.) At anyrate, the Porroh man stabbed the woman to the heart as though he had been a mere low-class Italian, and very narrowly missed Pollock. But Pollock, using his revolver to parry the lightning stab which was aimed at his deltoid muscle, sent the iron dagger flying, and firing, hit the man in the hand.

He fired again and missed, knocking a sudden window out of the wall of the hut. The Porroh man stooped in the doorway, glancing under his arm at Pollock. Pollock caught a glimpse of his inverted face in the sunlight, and then the Englishman was alone, sick and trembling with the excitement of the affair, in the twilight of the place. It had all happened in less time than it takes to read about it.

The woman was quite dead, and having ascertained this, Pollock went to the entrance of the hut and looked out. Things outside were dazzling bright. Half a dozen of the porters of the expedition were standing up in a group near the green huts they occupied, and staring towards him, wondering what the shots might signify. Behind the little group of men was the broad stretch of black fetid mud by the river, a green carpet of rafts of papyrus and water-grass, and then the leaden water. The mangroves beyond the stream loomed indistinctly through the blue haze. There were no signs of excitement in the squat village, whose fence was just visible above the cane-grass.

Pollock came out of the hut cautiously and walked towards the river, looking over his shoulder at intervals. But the Porroh man had vanished Pollock clutched his revolver nervously in his hand.

One of his men came to meet him, and as he came, pointed to the bushes behind the hut in which the Porroh man had disappeared. Pollock had an irritating persuasion of having made an absolute fool of himself; he felt bitter, savage, at the turn things had taken. At the same time, he would have to tell Waterhouse--the moral, exemplary, cautious Waterhouse--who would inevitably take the matter seriously. Pollock cursed bitterly at his luck, at Waterhouse, and especially at the West Coast of Africa. He felt consummately sick of the expedition. And in the back of his mind all the time was a speculative doubt where precisely within the visible horizon the Porroh man might be.

It is perhaps rather shocking, but he was not at all upset by the murder that had just happened. He had seen so much brutality during the last three months, so many dead women, burnt huts, drying skeletons, up the Kittam River in the wake

of the Sofa cavalry, that his senses were blunted. What disturbed him was the persuasion that this business was only beginning.

He swore savagely at the black, who ventured to ask a question, and went on into the tent under the orange-trees where Waterhouse was lying, feeling exasperatingly like a boy going into the headmaster's study.

Waterhouse was still sleeping off the effects of his last dose of chlorodyne, and Pollock sat down on a packing-case beside him, and lighting his pipe, waited for him to awake. About him were scattered the pots and weapons Waterhouse had collected from the Mendi people, and which he had been repacking for the canoe voyage to Sulyma.

Presently Waterhouse woke up, and after judicial stretching, decided he was all right again. Pollock got him some tea. Over the tea, the incidents of the afternoon were described by Pollock, after some preliminary beating about the bush. Waterhouse took the matter even more seriously than Pollock had anticipated. He did not simply disapprove, he scolded, he insulted.

"You're one of those infernal fools who think a black man isn't a human being," he said. "I can't be ill a day without you must get into some dirty scrape or other. This is the third time in a month that you have come crossways-on with a native, and this time you're in for it with a vengeance. Porroh, too! They're down upon you enough as it is, about that idol you wrote your silly name on. And they're the most vindictive devils on earth! You make a man ashamed of civilisation. To think you come of a decent family! If ever I cumber myself up with a vicious, stupid young lout like you again--"

"Steady on, now," snarled Pollock, in the tone that always exasperated Waterhouse; "steady on."

At that Waterhouse became speechless. He jumped to his feet.

"Look here, Pollock," he said, after a struggle to control his breath. "You must go home. I won't have you any longer. I'm ill enough as it is, through you--"

"Keep your hair on," said Pollock, staring in front of him. "I'm ready enough to go."

Waterhouse became calmer again. He sat down on the camp-stool. "Very well," he said. "I don't want a row, Pollock you know, but it's confoundedly annoying to have one's plans put out by this kind of thing. I'll come to Sulyma with you, and see you safe aboard--"

"You needn't," said Pollock. "I can go alone. From here."

"Not far," said Waterhouse. "You don't understand this Porroh business."

"How should I know she belonged to a Porroh man?" said Pollock bitterly.

"Well, she did," said Waterhouse; "and you can't undo the thing. Go alone, indeed! I wonder what they'd do to you. You don't seem to understand that this Porroh hokey-pokey rules this country, is its law, religion, constitution, medicine, magic...They appoint the chiefs. The Inquisition, at its best, couldn't hold a candle to these chaps. He will probably set Awajale, the chief here, on to us. It's lucky our porters are Mendis. We shall have to shift this little settlement of ours... Confound you, Pollock! And, of course, you must go and miss him."

He thought, and his thoughts seemed disagreeable. Presently he stood up and took his rifle. "I'd keep close for a bit, if I were you," he said, over his shoulder, as he went out. "I'm going out to see what I can find out about it."

Pollock remained sitting in the tent, meditating. "I was meant for a civilised life," he said to himself, regretfully, as he filled his pipe. "The sooner I get back to London or Paris the better for me."

His eye fell on the sealed case in which Waterhouse had put the featherless poisoned arrows they had bought in the Mendi country. "I wish I had hit the beggar somewhere vital," said Pollock viciously.

Waterhouse came back after a long interval. He was not communicative, though Pollock asked him questions enough. The Porroh man, it seems was a prominent member of that mystical society. The village was interested, but not threatening. No doubt the witch-doctor had gone into the bush. He was a great witch-doctor. "Of course, he's up to something," said Waterhouse, and became silent.

"But what can he do?" asked Pollock, unheeded.

"I must get you out of this. There's something brewing, or things would not be so quiet," said Waterhouse, after a gap of silence. Pollock wanted to know what the brew might be. "Dancing in a circle of skulls", said Waterhouse; "brewing a stink in a copper pot." Pollock wanted particulars. Waterhouse was vague, Pollock pressing. At last Waterhouse lost his temper. "How the devil should I know?" he said to Pollock's twentieth inquiry what the Porroh man would do. "He tried to kill you off-hand in the hut. Now, I fancy he will try something more elaborate. But you'll see fast enough. I don't want to help unnerve you. It's probably all nonsense."

That night, as they were sitting at their fire, Pollock again tried to draw Waterhouse out on the subject of Porroh methods. "Better get to sleep," said Waterhouse, when Pollock's bent became apparent; "we start early to-morrow. You may want all your nerve about you."

"But what line will he take?"

"Can't say. They're versatile people. They know a lot of rum dodges. You'd better get that copper-devil, Shakespear, to talk."

There was a flash and a heavy bang, out of the darkness behind the huts, and a clay bullet came whistling close to Pollock's head. This, at least, was crude enough. The blacks and half-breeds sitting and yarning round their own fire jumped up, and someone fired into the dark.

"Better go into one of the huts," said Waterhouse quietly, still sitting unmoved.

Pollock stood up by the fire and drew his revolver. Fighting, at least, he was not afraid of. But a man in the dark is in the best of armour. Realising the wisdom of Waterhouse's advice, Pollock went into the tent and lay down there.

What little sleep he had was disturbed by dreams, variegated dreams, but chiefly of the Porroh man's face, upside down, as he went out of the hut, and looked up under his arm. It was odd that this transitory impression should have stuck so firmly in Pollock's memory. Moreover, he was troubled by queer pains in his limbs.

{21}

In the white haze of the early morning, as they were loading the canoes, a barbed arrow suddenly appeared quivering in the ground close to Pollock's foot. The boys made a perfunctory effort to clear out the thicket, but it led to no capture.

After these two occurrences, there was a disposition on the part of the expedition to leave Pollock to himself, and Pollock became, for the first time in his life, anxious to mingle with blacks. Waterhouse took one canoe, and Pollock, in spite of a friendly desire to chat with Waterhouse, had to take the other. He was left all alone in the front part of the canoe, and he had the greatest trouble to make the men--who did not love him--keep to the middle of the river, a clear hundred yards or more from either shore. However, he made Shakespear, the Freetown half-breed, come up to his own end of the canoe and tell him about Porroh, which Shakespear, failing in his attempts to leave Pollock alone, presently did with considerable freedom and gusto.

The day passed. The canoe glided swiftly along the ribbon of lagoon water, between the drift of water-figs, fallen trees, papyrus, and palm-wine palms, and with the dark mangrove swamp to the left, through which one could hear now and then the roar of the Atlantic surf. Shakespear told in his soft, blurred English of how the Porroh could cast spells; how men withered up under their malice; how they could send dreams and devils; how they tormented and killed the sons of Ijibu; how they kidnapped a white trader from Sulyma who had maltreated one of the sect, and how his body looked when it was found. And Pollock after each narrative cursed under his breath at the want of missionary enterprise that allowed such things to be, and at the inert British Government that ruled over this dark heathendom of Sierra Leone. In the evening they came to the Kasi Lake, and sent a score of crocodiles lumbering off the island on which the expedition camped for the night.

The next day they reached Sulyma, and smelt the sea breeze, but Pollock had to put up there for five days before he could get on to Freetown. Waterhouse, considering him to be comparatively safe here, and within the pale of Freetown influence, left him and went back with the expedition to Gbemma, and Pollock became very friendly with Perera, the only resident white trader at Sulyma--so friendly, indeed, that he went about with him everywhere. Perera was a little Portuguese Jew, who had lived in England, and he appreciated the Englishman's friendliness as a great compliment.

For two days nothing happened out of the ordinary; for the most part Pollock and Perera played Nap--the only game they had in common--and Pollock got into debt. Then, on the second evening, Pollock had a disagreeable intimation of the arrival of the Porroh man in Sulyma by getting a flesh-wound in the shoulder from a lump of filed iron. It was a long shot, and the missile had nearly spent its force when it hit him. Still it conveyed its message plainly enough. Pollock sat up in his hammock, revolver in hand, all that night, and next morning confided, to some extent, in the Anglo-Portuguese.

Perera took the matter seriously. He knew the local customs pretty thoroughly. "It is a personal question, you must know. It is revenge. And of course he is hurried

{22}

by your leaving de country. None of de natives or half-breeds will interfere wid him very much--unless you make it wort deir while. If you come upon him suddenly, you might shoot him. But den he might shoot you.

"Den dere's dis--infernal magic," said Perera. "Of course, I don't believe in it--superstition--but still it's not nice to tink dat wherever you are, dere is a black man, who spends a moonlight night now and den a-dancing about a fire to send you bad dreams...Had any bad dreams?"

"Rather," said Pollock. "I keep on seeing the beggar's head upside down grinning at me and showing all his teeth as he did in the hut, and coming close up to me, and then going ever so far off, and coming back. It's nothing to be afraid of, but somehow it simply paralyses me with terror in my sleep. Queer things--dreams. I know it's a dream all the time, and I can't wake up from it."

"It's probably only fancy," said Perera. "Den my niggers say Porroh men can send snakes. Seen any snakes lately?"

"Only one. I killed him this morning, on the floor near my hammock. Almost trod on him as I got up."

"Ah!" said Perera, and then, reassuringly, "Of course it is a--coincidence. Still I would keep my eyes open. Den dere's pains in de bones."

"I thought they were due to miasma," said Pollock.

"Probably dey are. When did dey begin?"

Then Pollock remembered that he first noticed them the night after the fight in the hut. "It's my opinion he don't want to kill you," said Perera--"at least not yet. I've heard deir idea is to scare and worry a man wid deir spells, and narrow misses, and rheumatic pains, and bad dreams, and all dat, until he's sick of life. Of course, it's all talk, you know. You mustn't worry about it...But I wonder what he'll be up to next."

"I shall have to be up to something first," said Pollock, staring gloomily at the greasy cards that Perera was putting on the table. "It don't suit my dignity to be followed about, and shot at, and blighted in this way. I wonder if Porroh hokey-pokey upsets your luck at cards."

He looked at Perera suspiciously.

"Very likely it does," said Perera warmly, shuffling. "Dey are wonderful people."

That afternoon Pollock killed two snakes in his hammock, and there was also an extraordinary increase in the number of red ants that swarmed over the place; and these annoyances put him in a fit temper to talk over business with a certain Mendi rough he had interviewed before. The Mendi rough showed Pollock a little iron dagger, and demonstrated where one struck in the neck, in a way that made Pollock shiver, and in return for certain considerations Pollock promised him a double-barrelled gun with an ornamental lock.

In the evening, as Pollock and Perera were playing cards, the Mendi rough came in through the doorway, carrying something in a blood-soaked piece of native cloth.

"Not here!" said Pollock very hurriedly. "Not here!"

{23}

But he was not quick enough to prevent the man, who was anxious to get to Pollock's side of the bargain, from opening the cloth and throwing the head of the Porroh man upon the table. It bounded from there on to the floor, leaving a red trail on the cards, and rolled into the corner, where it came to rest upside down, but glaring hard at Pollock.

Perera jumped up as the thing fell among the cards, and began in his excitement to gabble in Portuguese. The Mendi was bowing, with the red cloth in his hand. "De gun!" he cried. Pollock stared back at the head in the corner. It bore exactly the expression it had in his dreams. Something seemed to snap in his own brain as he looked at it.

Then Perera found his English again.

"You got him killed?" he said. "You did not kill him yourself?"

"Why should I?" said Pollock.

"But he will not be able to take it off now!"

"Take what off?" said Pollock.

"And all dese cards are spoiled!"

"What do you mean by taking off?" said Pollock.

"You must send me a new pack from Freetown. You can buy dem dere."

"But--'take it off'?"

"It is only superstition. I forgot. De niggers say dat if de witches--he was a witch-- But it is rubbish...You must make de Porroh man take it off, or kill him yourself...It is very silly."

Pollock swore under his breath, still staring hard at the head in the corner.

"I can't stand that glare," he said. Then suddenly he rushed at the thing and kicked it. It rolled some yards or so, and came to rest in the same position as before, upside down, and looking at him.

"He is ugly," said the Anglo-Portuguese. "Very ugly. Dey do it on deir faces with little knives."

Pollock would have kicked the head again, but the Mendi man touched him on the arm. "De gun?" he said, looking nervously at the head.

"Two--if you will take that beastly thing away," said Pollock.

The Mendi shook his head, and intimated that he only wanted one gun now due to him, and for which he would be obliged. Pollock found neither cajolery nor bullying any good with him. Perera had a gun to sell (at a profit of three hundred per cent), and with that the man presently departed. Then Pollock's eyes, against his will, were recalled to the thing on the floor.

"It is funny dat his head keeps upside down," said Perera, with an uneasy laugh. "His brains must be heavy, like de weight in de little images one sees dat keep always upright wid lead in dem. You will take him wiv you when you go presently. You might take him now. De cards are all spoilt. Dere is a man sell dem in Freetown. De room is in a filthy mess as it is. You should have killed him yourself."

Pollock pulled himself together, and went and picked up the head. He would hang it up by the lamp-hook in the middle of the ceiling of his room, and dig a grave for it at once. He was under the impression that he hung it up by the hair, but that must have been wrong, for when he returned for it, it was hanging by the neck upside down.

He buried it before sunset on the north side of the shed he occupied, so that he should not have to pass the grave after dark when he was returning from Perera's. He killed two snakes before he went to sleep. In the darkest part of the night he awoke with a start, and heard a pattering sound and something scraping on the floor. He sat up noiselessly, and felt under his pillow for his revolver. A mumbling growl followed, and Pollock fired at the sound. There was a yelp, and something dark passed for a moment across the hazy blue of the doorway. "A dog!" said Pollock, lying down again.

In the early dawn he awoke again with a peculiar sense of unrest. The vague pain in his bones had returned. For some time he lay watching the red ants that were swarming over the ceiling, and then, as the light grew brighter, he looked over the edge of his hammock and saw something dark on the floor. He gave such a violent start that the hammock overset and flung him out.

He found himself lying, perhaps, a yard away from the head of the Porroh man. It had been disinterred by the dog, and the nose was grievously battered. Ants and flies swarmed over it. By an odd coincidence, it was still upside down, and with the same diabolical expression in the inverted eyes.

Pollock sat paralysed, and stared at the horror for some time. Then he got up and walked round it--giving it a wide berth--and out of the shed. The clear light of the sunrise, the living stir of vegetation before the breath of the dying land-breeze, and the empty grave with the marks of the dog's paws, lightened the weight upon his mind a little.

He told Perera of the business as though it was a jest--a jest to be told with white lips. "You should not have frighten de dog," said Perera, with poorly simulated hilarity.

The next two days, until the steamer came, were spent by Pollock in making a more effectual disposition of his possession. Overcoming his aversion to handling the thing, he went down to the river mouth and threw it into the sea-water, but by some miracle it escaped the crocodiles, and was cast up by the tide on the mud a little way up the river, to be found by an intelligent Arab half-breed, and offered for sale to Pollock and Perera as a curiosity, just on the edge of night. The native hung about in the brief twilight, making lower and lower offers, and at last, getting scared in some way by the evident dread these wise white men had for the thing, went off, and passing Pollock's shed, threw his burden in there for Pollock to discover in the morning.

At this Pollock got into a kind of frenzy. He would burn the thing. He went out straightway into the dawn, and had constructed a big pyre of brushwood before he heat of the day. He was interrupted by the hooter of the little paddle steamer from Monrovia to Bathurst, which was coming through the gap in the bar. "Thank Heaven!" said Pollock, with infinite piety, when the meaning of the sound dawned upon him. With trembling hands he lit his pile of wood hastily, threw the head upon it, and went away to pack his portmanteau and make his adieux to Perera.

That afternoon, with a sense of infinite relief, Pollock watched the flat swampy foreshore of Sulyma grow small in the distance. The gap in the long line of white surge became narrower and narrower. It seemed to be closing in and cutting him off from his trouble. The feeling of dread and worry began to slip from him bit by bit. At Sulyma belief in Porroh malignity and Porroh magic had been in the air, his sense of Porroh had been vast, pervading, threatening, dreadful. Now manifestly the domain of Porroh was only a little place, a little black band between the sea and the blue cloudy Mendi uplands.

"Good-bye, Porroh!" said Pollock. "Good-bye--certainly not au revoir."

The captain of the steamer came and leant over the rail beside him, and wished him good-evening, and spat at the froth of the wake in token of friendly ease.

"I picked up a rummy curio on the beach this go," said the captain. "It's a thing I never saw done this side of Indy before."

"What might that be?" said Pollock.

"Pickled 'ed," said the captain.

"What!" said Pollock.

"'Ed--smoked. 'Ed of one of those Porroh chaps, all ornamented with knife-cuts. Why! What's up? Nothing? I shouldn't have took you for a nervous chap. Green in the face. By gosh! You're a bad sailor. All right, eh? Lord, how funny you went...! Well, this 'ed I was telling you of is a bit rum in a way. I've got it, along with some snakes, in a jar of spirit in my cabin what I keeps for such curios, and I'm hanged if it don't float upsy down. Hullo!"

Pollock had given an incoherent cry, and had his hands in his hair. He ran towards the paddle-boxes with a half-formed idea of jumping into the sea, and then he realised his position and turned back towards the captain.

"Here!" said the captain. "Jack Philips, just keep him off me! Stand off! No nearer, mister! What's the matter with you? Are you mad?"

Pollock put his hand to his head. It was no good explaining. "I believe I am pretty nearly mad at times," he said. "It's a pain I have here. Comes suddenly. You'll excuse me, I hope."

He was white and in a perspiration. He saw suddenly very clearly all the danger he ran of having his sanity doubted. He forced himself to restore the captain's confidence, by answering his sympathetic inquiries, noting his suggestions, even trying a spoonful of neat brandy in his cheek, and that matter settled, asking a number of questions about the captain's private trade in curiosities. The captain described the head in detail. All the while Pollock was struggling to keep under a preposterous persuasion that the ship was as transparent as glass, and that he could distinctly see the inverted face looking at him from the cabin beneath his feet.

Pollock had a worse time almost on the steamer than he had at Sulyma. All day he had to control himself in spite of his intense perception of the imminent presence of that horrible head that was overshadowing his mind. At night his old nightmare returned, until, with a violent effort, he would force himself awake, rigid with the horror of it, and with the ghost of a hoarse scream in his throat.

He left the actual head behind at Bathurst, where he changed ship for Teneriffe, but not his dreams nor the dull ache in his bones. At Teneriffe, Pollock transferred to a Cape liner, but the head followed him. He gambled, he tried chess, he even read books, but he knew the danger of drink. Yet whenever a round black shadow, a round black object came into his range, there he looked for the head, and--saw it. He knew clearly enough that his imagination was growing traitor to him, and yet at times it seemed the ship he sailed in, his fellow-passengers, the sailors, the wide sea, was all part of a filmy phantasmagoria that hung, scarcely veiling it, between him and a horrible real world. Then the Porroh man, thrusting his diabolical face through that curtain, was the one real and undeniable thing. At that he would get up and touch things, taste something, gnaw something, burn his hand with a match, or run a needle into himself.

So, struggling grimly and silently with his excited imagination, Pollock reached England. He landed at Southampton, and went on straight from Waterloo to his banker's in Cornhill in a cab. There he transacted some business with the manager in a private room, and all the while the head hung like an ornament under the black marble mantel and dripped upon the fender. He could hear the drops fall, and see the red on the fender.

"A pretty fern," said the manager, following his eyes. "But it makes the fender rusty."

"Very," said Pollock; "a very pretty fern. And that reminds me. Can you recommend me a physician for mind troubles? I've got a little--what is it--? Hallucination."

The head laughed savagely, wildly. Pollock was surprised the manager did not notice it. But the manager only stared at his face.

With the address of a doctor, Pollock presently emerged in Cornhill. There was no cab in sight, and so he went on down to the western end of the street, and essayed the crossing opposite the Mansion House. The crossing is hardly easy even for the expert Londoner; cabs, vans, carriages, mail-carts, omnibuses go by in one incessant stream; to anyone fresh from the malarious solitudes of Sierra Leone it is a boiling, maddening confusion. But when an inverted head suddenly comes bouncing, like an indiarubber ball, between your legs, leaving distinct smears of blood every time it touches the ground, you can scarcely hope to avoid an accident. Pollock lifted his feet convulsively to avoid it, and then kicked at the thing furiously. Then something hit him violently in the back, and a hot pain ran up his arm.

He had been hit by the pole of an omnibus, and three of the fingers of his left hand smashed by the hoof of one of the horses--the very fingers, as it happened, that he shot from the Porroh man. They pulled him out from between the horse's legs, and found the address of the physician, in his crushed hand.

For a couple of days Pollock's sensations were full of the sweet, pungent smell of chloroform, of painful operations that caused him no pain, of lying still and being given food and drink. Then he had a slight fever, and was very thirsty, and his old nightmare came back. It was only when it returned that he noticed it had left him for a day.

"If my skull had been smashed instead of my fingers, it might have gone altogether," said Pollock, staring thoughtfully at the dark cushion that had taken on for the time the shape of the head.

Pollock at the first opportunity told the physician of his mind trouble. He knew clearly that he must go mad unless something should intervene to save him. He explained that he had witnessed a decapitation in Dahomey, and was haunted by one of the heads. Naturally, he did not care to state the actual facts. The physician looked grave.

Presently he spoke hesitatingly. "As a child, did you get very much religious training?"

"Very little," said Pollock.

A shade passed over the physician's face. "I don't know if you have heard of the miraculous cures--it may be, of course, they are not miraculous--at Lourdes."

"Faith-healing will hardly suit me, I am afraid," said Pollock, with his eye on the dark cushion.

The head distorted its scarred features in an abominable grimace. The physician went upon a new track. "It's all imagination," he said, speaking with sudden briskness. "A fair case for faith-healing, anyhow. Your nervous system has run down, you're in that twilight state of health when the bogles come easiest. The strong impression was too much for you. I must make you up a little mixture that will strengthen your nervous system--especially your brain. And you must take exercise."

"I'm no good for faith-healing," said Pollock.

"And therefore we must restore tone. Go in search of stimulating air--Scotland, Norway, the Alps--"

"Jericho, if you like," said Pollock--"where Naaman went."

However, so soon as his fingers would let him, Pollock made a gallant attempt to follow out the doctor's suggestion. It was now November. He tried football, but to Pollock the game consisted in kicking a furious inverted head about a field. He was no good at the game. He kicked blindly, with a kind of horror, and when they put him back into goal, and the ball came swooping down upon him, he suddenly yelled and got out of its way. The discreditable stories that had driven him from England to wander in the tropics shut him off from any but men's society, and now his increasingly strange behaviour made even his man friends avoid him. The thing was no longer a thing of the eye merely; it gibbered at him, spoke to him. A horrible fear came upon him that presently, when he took hold of the apparition, it would no longer become some mere article of furniture, but would feel like a real dissevered head. Alone, he would curse at the thing, defy it, entreat it; once or twice, in spite of his grim self-control, he addressed it in the presence of others. He felt the growing suspicion in the eyes of the people that watched him--his landlady, the servant, his man.

{28}

One day early in December his cousin Arnold--his next of kin--came to see him and draw him out, and watch his sunken yellow face with narrow eager eyes. And it seemed to Pollock that the hat his cousin carried in his hand was no hat at all, but a Gorgon head that glared at him upside down, and fought with its eyes against his reason. However, he was still resolute to see the matter out. He got a bicycle, and, riding over the frosty road from Wandsworth to Kingston, found the thing rolling along at his side, and leaving a dark trail behind it. He set his teeth and rode faster. Then suddenly, as he came down the hill towards Richmond Park, the apparition rolled in front of him and under his wheel, so quickly that he had no time for thought, and, turning quickly to avoid it, was flung violently against a heap of stones and broke his left wrist.

The end came on Christmas morning. All night he had been in a fever, the bandages encircling his wrist like a band of fire, his dreams more vivid and terrible than ever. In the cold, colourless, uncertain light that came before the sunrise, he sat up in his bed, and saw the head upon the bracket in the place of the bronze jar that had stood there overnight.

"I know that is a bronze jar," he said, with a chill doubt at his heart. Presently the doubt was irresistible. He got out of bed slowly, shivering, and advanced to the jar with his hand raised. Surely he would see now his imagination had deceived him, recognise the distinctive sheen of bronze. At last, after an age of hesitation, his fingers came down on the patterned cheek of the head. He withdrew them spasmodically. The last stage was reached. His sense of touch had betrayed him.

Trembling, stumbling against the bed, kicking against his shoes with his bare feet, a dark confusion eddying round him, he groped his way to the dressing-table, took his razor from the drawer, and sat down on the bed with this in his hand. In the looking-glass he saw his own face, colourless, haggard, full of the ultimate bitterness of despair.

He beheld in swift succession the incidents in the brief tale of his experience. His wretched home, his still more wretched schooldays, the years of vicious life he had led since then, one act of selfish dishonour leading to another; it was all clear and pitiless now, all its squalid folly, in the cold light of the dawn. He came to the hut, to the fight with the Porroh man, to the retreat down the river to Sulyma, to the Mendi assassin and his red parcel, to his frantic endeavours to destroy the head, to the growth of his hallucination. It was a hallucination! He knew it was. A hallucination merely. For a moment he snatched at hope. He looked away from the glass, and on the bracket, the inverted head grinned and grimaced at him...With the stiff fingers of his bandaged hand he felt at his neck for the throb of his arteries. The morning was very cold, the steel blade felt like ice.

{29}

THE SHADOW
E. Nesbit

THIS is not an artistically rounded-off ghost story, and nothing is explained in it, and there seems to be no reason why any of it should have happened. But that is no reason why it should not be told. You must have noticed that all the real ghost stories you have ever come close to, are like this in these respects --no explanation, no logical coherence. Here is the story.

There were three of us and another, but she had fainted suddenly at the second extra of the Christmas dance, and had been put to bed in the dressing room next to the room which we three shared. It had been one of those jolly, old-fashioned dances where nearly everybody stays the night, and the big country house is stretched to its utmost containing --guests harbouring on sofas, couches, settles and even mattresses on floors. Some of the young men actually, I believe, slept on the great dining table. We had talked of our partners, as girls will, and then the stillness of the manor house, broken only by the whisper of the wind in the cedar branches, and the scraping of their harsh fingers against our windowpanes, had pricked us to such luxurious confidence in our surroundings of bright chintz and candle-flame and firelight, that we had dared to talk of ghosts – in which, we all said, we did not believe one bit. We had told the story of the phantom coach, and the horribly strange bed, and the lady in the sacque, and the house in Berkeley Square.

We none of us believed in ghosts, but my heart, at least, seemed to leap to my throat and choke me there when a tap came to our door --a tap faint, not to be mistaken.

'Who's there?' said the youngest of us, craning a lean neck towards the door. It opened slowly, and I give you my word the instant of suspense that followed is still reckoned among my life's least confident moments. Almost at once the door opened fully, and Miss Eastwich, my aunt's housekeeper, companion and general stand-by, looked in on us.

We all said, 'Come in,' but she stood there. She was, at all normal hours, the most silent woman I have ever known. She stood and looked at us, and shivered a little. So did we --for in those days corridors were not warmed by hot-water pipes and the air from the door was keen.

'I saw your light,' she said at last, 'and I thought it was late for you to be up --after all this gaiety. I thought perhaps—' her glance turned towards the door of the dressing room.

'No,' I said, 'she's fast asleep.' I should have added a goodnight, but the youngest of us forestalled my speech. She did not know Miss Eastwich as we others did; did not know how her persistent silence had built a wall round her --a wall that no one dared to break down with the commonplaces of talk, or the littlenesses of mere human relationship. Miss Eastwich's silence had taught us to treat her as a machine; and as other than a machine we never dreamed of treating her. But the youngest of us had seen Miss Eastwich for the first time that day. She was young, crude, ill-balanced, subject to blind, calf-like impulses. She was also the heiress of

a rich tallow-chandler, but that has nothing to do with this part of the story. She jumped up from the hearth rug, her unsuitably rich silk lace-trimmed dressing gown falling back from her thin collarbones, and ran to the door and put an arm round Miss Eastwich's prim, lisse-encircled neck. I gasped. I should as soon have dared to embrace Cleopatra's Needle. 'Come in,' said the youngest of us --'come in and get warm. There's lots of cocoa left.' She drew Miss Eastwich in and shut the door.

The vivid light of pleasure in the housekeeper's pale eyes went through my heart like a knife. It would have been so easy to put an arm round her neck, if one had only thought she wanted an arm there. But it was not I who had thought that --and indeed, my arm might not have brought the light evoked by the thin arm of the youngest of us.

'Now,' the youngest went on eagerly, 'you shall have the very biggest, nicest chair, and the cocoa pot's here on the hob as hot as hot --and we've all been telling ghost stories, only we don't believe in them a bit; and when you get warm you ought to tell one too.'

Miss Eastwich --that model of decorum and decently done duties --tell a ghost story!

'You're sure I'm not in your way,' Miss Eastwich said, stretching her hands to the blaze. I wondered whether housekeepers have fires in their rooms even at Christmas time. 'Not a bit,' I said it, and I hope I said it as warmly as I felt it. 'I --Miss Eastwich --I'd have asked you to come in other times --only I didn't think you'd care for girls' chatter.'

The third girl, who was really of no account, and that's why I have not said anything about her before, poured cocoa for our guest. I put my fleecy Madeira shawl round her shoulders. I could not think of anything else to do for her and I found myself wishing desperately to do something. The smiles she gave us were quite pretty. People can smile prettily at forty or fifty, or even later, though girls don't realise this. It occurred to me, and this was another knife thrust, that I had never seen Miss Eastwich smile --a real smile --before. The pale smiles of dutiful acquiescence were not of the same blood as this dimpling, happy, transfiguring look.

'This is very pleasant,' she said, and it seemed to me that I had never before heard her real voice. It did not please me to think that at the cost of cocoa, a fire, and my arm round her neck, I might have heard this new voice any time these six years.

'We've been telling ghost stories,' I said. 'The worst of it is, we don't believe in ghosts. No one we know has ever seen one.'

'It's always what somebody told somebody, who told somebody you know,' said the youngest of us, 'and you can't believe that, can you?'

'What the soldier said is not evidence,' said Miss Eastwich. Will it be believed that the little Dickens quotation pierced one more keenly than the new smile or the new voice?

'And all the ghost stories are so beautifully rounded off -- a murder committed on the spot --or a hidden treasure, or a warning -- I think that makes them harder to believe. The most horrid ghost story I ever heard was one that was quite silly.'

'Tell it.'

'I can't --it doesn't sound anything to tell. Miss Eastwich ought to tell one.'

'Oh, do,' said the youngest of us, and her salt cellars loomed dark, as she stretched her neck eagerly and laid an entreating arm on our guest's knee.

'The only thing that I ever knew of was --was hearsay,' she said slowly, 'till just the end.'

I knew she would tell her story, and I knew she had never before told it, and I knew she was only telling it now because she was proud, and this seemed the only way to pay for the fire and the cocoa and the laying of that arm round her neck.

'Don't tell it,' I said suddenly. 'I know you'd rather not.'

'I dare say it would bore you,' she said meekly, and the youngest of us, who, after all, did not understand everything, glared resentfully at me.

'We should just *love* it,' she said. '*Do* tell us. Never mind if it isn't a real, proper, fixed-up story. I'm certain anything *you* think ghostly would be quite too beautifully horrid for anything.'

Miss Eastwich finished her cocoa and reached up to set the cup on the mantelpiece.

'I can't do any harm,' she said half to herself, 'they don't believe in ghosts, and it wasn't exactly a ghost either. And they're all over twenty --they're not babies.'

There was a breathing time of hush and expectancy. The fire crackled and the gas suddenly glared higher because the billiard lights had been put out. We heard the steps and voices of the men going along the corridors.

'It is really hardly worth telling,' Miss Eastwich said doubtfully, shading her faded face from the fire with her thin hand.

We all said, 'Go on --oh, go on --do!'

'Well,' she said, 'twenty years ago --and more than that --I had two friends, and I loved them more than anything in the world. And they married each other—'

She paused, and I knew just in what way she had loved each of them. The youngest of us said, 'How awfully nice for you. Do go on.'

She patted the youngest's shoulder, and I was glad that I had understood, and that the youngest of all hadn't. She went on.

'Well, after they were married, I did not see much of them for a year or two; and then he wrote and asked me to come and stay, because his wife was ill, and I should cheer her up, and cheer him up as well; for it was a gloomy house, and he himself was growing gloomy too.'

I knew, as she spoke, that she had every line of that letter by heart.

'Well, I went. The address was in Lee, near London; in those days there were streets and streets of new villa houses growing up round old brick mansions standing in their own grounds, with red walls round, you know, and a sort of flavour of coaching days, and post-chaises, and Blackheath highwaymen about them. He had said the house was gloomy, and it was called The Firs, and I imagined my cab going through a dark, winding shrubbery, and drawing up in front of one of these sedate, old, square houses. Instead, we drew up in front of a large, smart villa, with iron railings, gay encaustic tiles leading from the iron gate to the stained-glass-panelled door, and for shrubbery only a few stunted cypresses and aucubas in the tiny front garden. But inside it was all warm and welcoming. He met me at the door.'

She was gazing into the fire and I knew she had forgotten us. But the youngest girl of all still thought it was to us she was telling her story.

'He met me at the door,' she said again, 'and thanked me for coming, and asked me to forgive the past.'

'What past?' said that high priestess of the *inapropos*, the youngest of all.

'Oh --I suppose he meant because they hadn't invited me before, or something,' said Miss Eastwich worriedly, 'but it's a very dull story, I find, after all, and – '

'Do go on,' I said --then I kicked the youngest of us, and got up to rearrange Miss Eastwich's shawl, and said in blatant dumb show, over the shawled shoulder, 'Shut up, you little idiot!'

After another silence, the housekeeper's new voice went on.

'They were very glad to see me and I was very glad to be there. You girls, now, have such troops of friends, but these two were all I had --all I had ever had. Mabel wasn't exactly ill, only weak and excitable. I thought he seemed more ill than she did. She went to bed early and before she went, she asked me to keep him company through his last pipe, so we went into the dining room and sat in the two armchairs on each side of the fireplace. They were covered with green leather, I remember. There were bronze groups of horses and a black marble clock on the mantelpiece --all wedding presents. He poured out some whisky for himself, but he hardly touched it. He sat looking into the fire.

At last I said, "What's wrong? Mabel looks as well as you could expect."

'He said, "Yes --but I don't know from one day to another that she won't begin to notice something wrong. That's why I wanted you to come. You were always so sensible and strong-minded, and Mabel's like a little bird on a flower."

'I said yes, of course, and waited for him to go on. I thought he must be in debt, or in trouble of some sort. So I just waited. Presently he said, "Margaret, this is a very peculiar house – " He always called me Margaret. You see, we'd been such old friends. I told him I thought the house was very pretty, and fresh, and home-like -- only a little too new --but that fault would mend with time. He said, "It *is* new: that's just it. We're the first people who've ever lived in it. If it were an old house, Margaret, I should think it was haunted."

'I asked if he had seen anything. "No," he said, "not yet."

'"Heard then?" said I.

'"No --not heard either," he said, "but there's a sort of feeling: I can't describe it --I've seen nothing and I've heard nothing, but I've been so near to seeing and hearing, just near, that's all. And something follows me about --only when I turn round, there's never anything, only my shadow. And I always feel that I *shall* see the thing next minute --but I never do --not quite --it's always just not visible."

{34}

'I thought he'd been working rather hard --and tried to cheer him up by making light of all this. It was just nerves, I said. Then he said he had thought I could help him, and did I think anyone he had wronged could have laid a curse on him, and did I believe in curses. I said I didn't --and the only person anyone could have said he had wronged forgave him freely, I knew, if there was anything to forgive. So I told him this too.'

It was I, not the youngest of us, who knew the name of that person, wronged and forgiving.

'So then I said he ought to take Mabel away from the house and have a complete change. But he said no; Mabel had got everything in order, and he could never manage to get her away just now without explaining everything --"and, above all," he said, "she mustn't guess there's anything wrong. I dare say I shan't feel quite such a lunatic now you're here."

'So we said goodnight.'

'Is that all the story!' said the third girl, striving to convey that even as it stood it was a good story.

'That's only the beginning,' said Miss Eastwich. 'Whenever I was alone with him he used to tell me the same thing over and over again, and at first when I began to notice things, I tried to think that it was his talk that had upset my nerves. The odd thing was that it wasn't only at night --but in broad daylight --and particularly on the stairs and passages. On the staircase the feeling used to be so awful that I have had to bite my lips till they bled to keep myself from running upstairs at full speed. Only I knew if I did I should go mad at the top. There was always something behind me --exactly as he had said --something that one could just not see. And a sound that one could just not hear. There was a long corridor at the top of the house. I have sometimes almost seen something --you know how one sees things without looking --but if I turned round, it seemed as if the thing drooped and melted into my shadow. There was a little window at the end of the corridor.

'Downstairs there was another corridor, something like it, with a cupboard at one end and the kitchen at the other. One night I went down into the kitchen to heat some milk for Mabel. The servants had gone to bed. As I stood by the fire, waiting for the milk to boil, I glanced through the open door and along the passage. I never could keep my eyes on what I was doing in that house. The cupboard door was partly open; they used to keep empty boxes and things in it. And, as I looked, I knew that now it was not going to be "almost" any more. Yet I said, "Mabel?" not because I thought it could be Mabel who was crouching down there, half in and half out of the cupboard. The thing was grey at first, and then it was black. And when I whispered, "Mabel", it seemed to sink down till it lay like a pool of ink on the floor, and then its edges drew in, and it seemed to flow, like ink when you tilt up the paper you have spilt it on, and it flowed into the cupboard till it was all gathered into the shadow there. I saw it go quite plainly. The gas was full on in the kitchen. I screamed aloud, but even then, I'm thankful to say, I had enough sense to upset the boiling milk, so that when he came downstairs three steps at a time, I had the excuse for my scream of a scalded hand. The explanation satisfied Mabel, but next night he said, "Why didn't you tell me? It was that cupboard. All the horror of the house comes out of that. Tell me --have you seen anything yet? Or is it only the nearly seeing and nearly hearing still?"

'I said, "You must tell me first what you've seen." He told me, and his eyes wandered, as he spoke, to the shadows by the curtains, and I turned up all three gas lights, and lit the candles on the mantelpiece. Then we looked at each other and said we were both mad, and thanked God that Mabel at least was sane. For what he had seen was what I had seen.

'After that I hated to be alone with a shadow, because at any moment I might see something that would crouch, and sink, and lie like a black pool, and then slowly draw itself into the shadow that was nearest. Often that shadow was my own. The thing came first at night, but afterwards there was no hour safe from it. I saw it at dawn and at noon, in the dusk and in the firelight, and always it crouched and sank, and was a pool that flowed into some shadow and became part of it. And always I saw it with a straining of the eyes --a pricking and aching. It seemed as though I could only just see it, as if my sight, to see it, had to be strained to the uttermost. And still the sound was in the house --the sound that I could just not hear. At last, one morning early, I did hear it. It was close behind me, and it was only a sigh. It was worse than the thing that crept into the shadows.

'I don't know how I bore it. I couldn't have borne it, if I hadn't been so fond of them both. But I knew in my heart that, if he had no one to whom he could speak openly, he would go mad, or tell Mabel. His was not a very strong character; very sweet, and kind, and gentle, but not strong. He was always easily led. So I stayed on and bore up, and we were very cheerful, and made little jokes, and tried to be amusing when Mabel was with us. But when we were alone, we did not try to be amusing. And sometimes a day or two would go by without our seeing or hearing anything, and we should perhaps have fancied that we had fancied what we had seen and heard --only there was always the feeling of there being something about the house, that one could just not hear and not see. Sometimes we used to try not to talk about it, but generally we talked of nothing else at all. And the weeks went by, and Mabel's baby was born. The nurse and the doctor said that both mother and child were doing well. He and I sat late in the dining room that night. We had neither of us seen or heard anything for three days; our anxiety about Mabel was lessened. We talked of the future --it seemed then so much brighter than the past. We arranged that, the moment she was fit to be moved, he should take her away to the sea, and I should superintend the moving of their furniture into the new house he had already chosen. He was gayer than I had seen him since his marriage --almost like his old self. When I said goodnight to him, he said a lot of things about my having been a comfort to them both. I hadn't done anything much, of course, but still I am glad he said them.

'Then I went upstairs, almost for the first time without that feeling of something following me. I listened at Mabel's door. Everything was quiet. I went on towards my own room, and in an instant I felt that there *was* something behind me. I turned. It was crouching there; it sank, and the black fluidness of it seemed to be sucked under the door of Mabel's room.

{36}

'I went back. I opened the door a listening inch. All was still. And then I heard a sigh close behind me. I opened the door and went in. The nurse and the baby were asleep. Mabel was asleep too --she looked so pretty --like a tired child --the baby was cuddled up into one of her arms with its tiny head against her side. I prayed then that Mabel might never know the terrors that he and I had known. That those little ears might never hear any but pretty sounds, those clear eyes never see any but pretty sights. I did not dare to pray for a long time after that. Because my prayer was answered. She never saw, never heard anything more in this world. And now I could do nothing more for him or for her.

'When they had put her in her coffin, I lighted wax candles round her, and laid the horrible white flowers that people will send near her, and then I saw he had followed me. I took his hand to lead him away.

'At the door we both turned. It seemed to us that we heard a sigh. He would have sprung to her side in I don't know what mad, glad hope. But at that instant we both saw it. Between us and the coffin, first grey, then black, it crouched an instant, then sank and liquefied --and was gathered together and drawn till it ran into the nearest shadow. And the nearest shadow was the shadow of Mabel's coffin. I left the next day. His mother came. She had never liked me.'

Miss Eastwich paused. I think she had quite forgotten us.

'Didn't you see him again?' asked the youngest of us all.

'Only once,' Miss Eastwich answered, 'and something black crouched then between him and me. But it was only his second wife, crying beside his coffin. It's not a cheerful story, is it? And it doesn't lead anywhere. I've never told anyone else. I think it was seeing his daughter that brought it all back.'

She looked towards the dressing-room door.

'Mabel's baby?'

'Yes --and exactly like Mabel, only with his eyes.'

The youngest of all had Miss Eastwich's hands and was petting them.

Suddenly the woman wrenched her hands away and stood at her gaunt height, her hands clenched, eyes straining. She was looking at something that we could not see, and I know what the man in the Bible meant when he said, 'The hair of my flesh stood up.'

What she saw seemed not quite to reach the height of the dressing-room door handle. Her eyes followed it down, down --widening and widening. Mine followed them --all the nerves of them seemed strained to the uttermost --and I almost saw --or did I quite see? I can't be certain. But we all heard the long-drawn, quivering sigh. And to each of us it seemed to be breathed just behind us.

It was I who caught up the candle --it dripped all over my trembling hand --and was dragged by Miss Eastwich to the girl who had fainted during the second extra. But it was the youngest of all whose lean arms were round the housekeeper when we turned away, and that have been round her many a time since, in the new home where she keeps house for the youngest of us.

The doctor who came in the morning said that Mabel's daughter had died of heart disease --which she had inherited from her mother. It was that that had made her faint during the second extra. But I have sometimes wondered whether she may not have inherited something from her father. I had never been able to forget the look on her dead face.

{37}

MARLEY'S GHOST
Charles Dickens

MARLEY was dead: to begin with. There is no doubt whatever about that. The register of his burial was signed by the clergyman, the clerk, the undertaker, and the chief mourner. Scrooge signed it: and Scrooge's name was good upon 'Change, for anything he chose to put his hand to. Old Marley was as dead as a door-nail.

Mind! I don't mean to say that I know, of my own knowledge, what there is particularly dead about a door-nail. I might have been inclined, myself, to regard a coffin-nail as the deadest piece of ironmongery in the trade. But the wisdom of our ancestors is in the simile; and my unhallowed hands shall not disturb it, or the Country's done for. You will therefore permit me to repeat, emphatically, that Marley was as dead as a door-nail.

Scrooge knew he was dead? Of course he did. How could it be otherwise? Scrooge and he were partners for I don't know how many years. Scrooge was his sole executor, his sole administrator, his sole assign, his sole residuary legatee, his sole friend, and sole mourner. And even Scrooge was not so dreadfully cut up by the sad event, but that he was an excellent man of business on the very day of the funeral, and solemnised it with an undoubted bargain.

The mention of Marley's funeral brings me back to the point I started from. There is no doubt that Marley was dead. This must be distinctly understood, or nothing wonderful can come of the story I am going to relate. If we were not perfectly convinced that Hamlet's Father died before the play began, there would be nothing more remarkable in his taking a stroll at night, in an easterly wind, upon his own ramparts, than there would be in any other middle-aged gentleman rashly turning out after dark in a breezy spot—say Saint Paul's Churchyard for instance—literally to astonish his son's weak mind.

Scrooge never painted out Old Marley's name. There it stood, years afterwards, above the warehouse door: Scrooge and Marley. The firm was known as Scrooge and Marley. Sometimes people new to the business called Scrooge Scrooge, and sometimes Marley, but he answered to both names. It was all the same to him.

Oh! But he was a tight-fisted hand at the grindstone, Scrooge! a squeezing, wrenching, grasping, scraping, clutching, covetous, old sinner! Hard and sharp as flint, from which no steel had ever struck out generous fire; secret, and self-contained, and solitary as an oyster. The cold within him froze his old features, nipped his pointed nose, shrivelled his cheek, stiffened his gait; made his eyes red, his thin lips blue; and spoke out shrewdly in his grating voice. A frosty rime was on his head, and on his eyebrows, and his wiry chin. He carried his own low temperature always about with him; he iced his office in the dog-days; and didn't thaw it one degree at Christmas.

External heat and cold had little influence on Scrooge. No warmth could warm, no wintry weather chill him. No wind that blew was bitterer than he, no falling snow was more intent upon its purpose, no pelting rain less open to entreaty. Foul

weather didn't know where to have him. The heaviest rain, and snow, and hail, and sleet, could boast of the advantage over him in only one respect. They often "came down" handsomely, and Scrooge never did.

Nobody ever stopped him in the street to say, with gladsome looks, "My dear Scrooge, how are you? When will you come to see me?" No beggars implored him to bestow a trifle, no children asked him what it was o'clock, no man or woman ever once in all his life inquired the way to such and such a place, of Scrooge. Even the blind men's dogs appeared to know him; and when they saw him coming on, would tug their owners into doorways and up courts; and then would wag their tails as though they said, "No eye at all is better than an evil eye, dark master!"

But what did Scrooge care! It was the very thing he liked. To edge his way along the crowded paths of life, warning all human sympathy to keep its distance, was what the knowing ones call "nuts" to Scrooge.

Once upon a time—of all the good days in the year, on Christmas Eve—old Scrooge sat busy in his counting-house. It was cold, bleak, biting weather: foggy withal: and he could hear the people in the court outside, go wheezing up and down, beating their hands upon their breasts, and stamping their feet upon the pavement stones to warm them. The city clocks had only just gone three, but it was quite dark already—it had not been light all day—and candles were flaring in the windows of the neighbouring offices, like ruddy smears upon the palpable brown air. The fog came pouring in at every chink and keyhole, and was so dense without, that although the court was of the narrowest, the houses opposite were mere phantoms. To see the dingy cloud come drooping down, obscuring everything, one might have thought that Nature lived hard by, and was brewing on a large scale.

The door of Scrooge's counting-house was open that he might keep his eye upon his clerk, who in a dismal little cell beyond, a sort of tank, was copying letters. Scrooge had a very small fire, but the clerk's fire was so very much smaller that it looked like one coal. But he couldn't replenish it, for Scrooge kept the coal-box in his own room; and so surely as the clerk came in with the shovel, the master predicted that it would be necessary for them to part. Wherefore the clerk put on his white comforter, and tried to warm himself at the candle; in which effort, not being a man of a strong imagination, he failed.

"A merry Christmas, uncle! God save you!" cried a cheerful voice. It was the voice of Scrooge's nephew, who came upon him so quickly that this was the first intimation he had of his approach.

"Bah!" said Scrooge, "Humbug!"

He had so heated himself with rapid walking in the fog and frost, this nephew of Scrooge's, that he was all in a glow; his face was ruddy and handsome; his eyes sparkled, and his breath smoked again.

"Christmas a humbug, uncle!" said Scrooge's nephew. "You don't mean that, I am sure?"

"I do," said Scrooge. "Merry Christmas! What right have you to be merry? What reason have you to be merry? You're poor enough."

{40}

"Come, then," returned the nephew gaily. "What right have you to be dismal? What reason have you to be morose? You're rich enough."

Scrooge having no better answer ready on the spur of the moment, said, "Bah!" again; and followed it up with "Humbug."

"Don't be cross, uncle!" said the nephew.

"What else can I be," returned the uncle, "when I live in such a world of fools as this? Merry Christmas! Out upon merry Christmas! What's Christmas time to you but a time for paying bills without money; a time for finding yourself a year older, but not an hour richer; a time for balancing your books and having every item in 'em through a round dozen of months presented dead against you? If I could work my will," said Scrooge indignantly, "every idiot who goes about with 'Merry Christmas' on his lips, should be boiled with his own pudding, and buried with a stake of holly through his heart. He should!"

"Uncle!" pleaded the nephew.

"Nephew!" returned the uncle sternly, "keep Christmas in your own way, and let me keep it in mine."

"Keep it!" repeated Scrooge's nephew. "But you don't keep it."

"Let me leave it alone, then," said Scrooge. "Much good may it do you! Much good it has ever done you!"

"There are many things from which I might have derived good, by which I have not profited, I dare say," returned the nephew. "Christmas among the rest. But I am sure I have always thought of Christmas time, when it has come round—apart from the veneration due to its sacred name and origin, if anything belonging to it can be apart from that—as a good time; a kind, forgiving, charitable, pleasant time; the only time I know of, in the long calendar of the year, when men and women seem by one consent to open their shut-up hearts freely, and to think of people below them as if they really were fellow-passengers to the grave, and not another race of creatures bound on other journeys. And therefore, uncle, though it has never put a scrap of gold or silver in my pocket, I believe that it has done me good, and will do me good; and I say, God bless it!"

The clerk in the Tank involuntarily applauded. Becoming immediately sensible of the impropriety, he poked the fire, and extinguished the last frail spark for ever.

"Let me hear another sound from you," said Scrooge, "and you'll keep your Christmas by losing your situation! You're quite a powerful speaker, sir," he added, turning to his nephew. "I wonder you don't go into Parliament."

"Don't be angry, uncle. Come! Dine with us to-morrow."

Scrooge said that he would see him—yes, indeed he did. He went the whole length of the expression, and said that he would see him in that extremity first.

"But why?" cried Scrooge's nephew. "Why?"

"Why did you get married?" said Scrooge.

"Because I fell in love."

"Because you fell in love!" growled Scrooge, as if that were the only one thing in the world more ridiculous than a merry Christmas. "Good afternoon!"

"Nay, uncle, but you never came to see me before that happened. Why give it as a reason for not coming now?"

"Good afternoon," said Scrooge.

"I want nothing from you; I ask nothing of you; why cannot we be friends?"

"Good afternoon," said Scrooge.

"I am sorry, with all my heart, to find you so resolute. We have never had any quarrel, to which I have been a party. But I have made the trial in homage to Christmas, and I'll keep my Christmas humour to the last. So A Merry Christmas, uncle!"

"Good afternoon!" said Scrooge.

"And A Happy New Year!"

"Good afternoon!" said Scrooge.

His nephew left the room without an angry word, notwithstanding. He stopped at the outer door to bestow the greetings of the season on the clerk, who, cold as he was, was warmer than Scrooge; for he returned them cordially.

"There's another fellow," muttered Scrooge; who overheard him: "my clerk, with fifteen shillings a week, and a wife and family, talking about a merry Christmas. I'll retire to Bedlam."

This lunatic, in letting Scrooge's nephew out, had let two other people in. They were portly gentlemen, pleasant to behold, and now stood, with their hats off, in Scrooge's office. They had books and papers in their hands, and bowed to him.

"Scrooge and Marley's, I believe," said one of the gentlemen, referring to his list. "Have I the pleasure of addressing Mr. Scrooge, or Mr. Marley?"

"Mr. Marley has been dead these seven years," Scrooge replied. "He died seven years ago, this very night."

"We have no doubt his liberality is well represented by his surviving partner," said the gentleman, presenting his credentials.

It certainly was; for they had been two kindred spirits. At the ominous word "liberality," Scrooge frowned, and shook his head, and handed the credentials back.

"At this festive season of the year, Mr. Scrooge," said the gentleman, taking up a pen, "it is more than usually desirable that we should make some slight provision for the Poor and destitute, who suffer greatly at the present time. Many thousands are in want of common necessaries; hundreds of thousands are in want of common comforts, sir."

"Are there no prisons?" asked Scrooge.

"Plenty of prisons," said the gentleman, laying down the pen again.

"And the Union workhouses?" demanded Scrooge. "Are they still in operation?"

"They are. Still," returned the gentleman, "I wish I could say they were not."

"The Treadmill and the Poor Law are in full vigour, then?" said Scrooge.

"Both very busy, sir."

"Oh! I was afraid, from what you said at first, that something had occurred to stop them in their useful course," said Scrooge. "I'm very glad to hear it."

"Under the impression that they scarcely furnish Christian cheer of mind or body to the multitude," returned the gentleman, "a few of us are endeavouring to raise a fund to buy the Poor some meat and drink, and means of warmth. We choose this time, because it is a time, of all others, when Want is keenly felt, and Abundance rejoices. What shall I put you down for?"

"Nothing!" Scrooge replied.

"You wish to be anonymous?"

"I wish to be left alone," said Scrooge. "Since you ask me what I wish, gentlemen, that is my answer. I don't make merry myself at Christmas and I can't afford to make idle people merry. I help to support the establishments I have mentioned—they cost enough; and those who are badly off must go there."

"Many can't go there; and many would rather die."

"If they would rather die," said Scrooge, "they had better do it, and decrease the surplus population. Besides—excuse me—I don't know that."

"But you might know it," observed the gentleman.

"It's not my business," Scrooge returned. "It's enough for a man to understand his own business, and not to interfere with other people's. Mine occupies me constantly. Good afternoon, gentlemen!"

Seeing clearly that it would be useless to pursue their point, the gentlemen withdrew. Scrooge resumed his labours with an improved opinion of himself, and in a more facetious temper than was usual with him.

Meanwhile the fog and darkness thickened so, that people ran about with flaring links, proffering their services to go before horses in carriages, and conduct them on their way. The ancient tower of a church, whose gruff old bell was always peeping slily down at Scrooge out of a Gothic window in the wall, became invisible, and struck the hours and quarters in the clouds, with tremulous vibrations afterwards as if its teeth were chattering in its frozen head up there. The cold became intense. In the main street, at the corner of the court, some labourers were repairing the gas-pipes, and had lighted a great fire in a brazier, round which a party of ragged men and boys were gathered: warming their hands and winking their eyes before the blaze in rapture. The water-plug being left in solitude, its overflowings sullenly congealed, and turned to misanthropic ice. The brightness of the shops where holly sprigs and berries crackled in the lamp heat of the windows, made pale faces ruddy as they passed. Poulterers' and grocers' trades became a splendid joke: a glorious pageant, with which it was next to impossible to believe that such dull principles as bargain and sale had anything to do. The Lord Mayor, in the stronghold of the mighty Mansion House, gave orders to his fifty cooks and butlers to keep Christmas as a Lord Mayor's household should; and even the little tailor, whom he had fined five shillings on the previous Monday for being drunk and bloodthirsty in the streets, stirred up to-morrow's pudding in his garret, while his lean wife and the baby sallied out to buy the beef.

Foggier yet, and colder. Piercing, searching, biting cold. If the good Saint Dunstan had but nipped the Evil Spirit's nose with a touch of such weather as that, instead of using his familiar weapons, then indeed he would have roared to lusty purpose. The owner of one scant young nose, gnawed and mumbled by the hungry cold as bones are gnawed by dogs, stooped down at Scrooge's keyhole to regale him with a Christmas carol: but at the first sound of

"God bless you, merry gentleman!
May nothing you dismay!"

Scrooge seized the ruler with such energy of action, that the singer fled in terror, leaving the keyhole to the fog and even more congenial frost.

At length the hour of shutting up the counting-house arrived. With an ill-will Scrooge dismounted from his stool, and tacitly admitted the fact to the expectant clerk in the Tank, who instantly snuffed his candle out, and put on his hat.

"You'll want all day to-morrow, I suppose?" said Scrooge.

"If quite convenient, sir."

"It's not convenient," said Scrooge, "and it's not fair. If I was to stop half-a-crown for it, you'd think yourself ill-used, I'll be bound?"

The clerk smiled faintly.

"And yet," said Scrooge, "you don't think me ill-used, when I pay a day's wages for no work."

The clerk observed that it was only once a year.

"A poor excuse for picking a man's pocket every twenty-fifth of December!" said Scrooge, buttoning his great-coat to the chin. "But I suppose you must have the whole day. Be here all the earlier next morning."

The clerk promised that he would; and Scrooge walked out with a growl. The office was closed in a twinkling, and the clerk, with the long ends of his white comforter dangling below his waist (for he boasted no great-coat), went down a slide on Cornhill, at the end of a lane of boys, twenty times, in honour of its being Christmas Eve, and then ran home to Camden Town as hard as he could pelt, to play at blindman's-buff.

Scrooge took his melancholy dinner in his usual melancholy tavern; and having read all the newspapers, and beguiled the rest of the evening with his banker's-book, went home to bed. He lived in chambers which had once belonged to his deceased partner. They were a gloomy suite of rooms, in a lowering pile of building up a yard, where it had so little business to be, that one could scarcely help fancying it must have run there when it was a young house, playing at hide-and-seek with other houses, and forgotten the way out again. It was old enough now, and dreary enough, for nobody lived in it but Scrooge, the other rooms being all let out as offices. The yard was so dark that even Scrooge, who knew its every stone, was fain to grope with his hands. The fog and frost so hung about the black old gateway of the house, that it seemed as if the Genius of the Weather sat in mournful meditation on the threshold.

Now, it is a fact, that there was nothing at all particular about the knocker on the door, except that it was very large. It is also a fact, that Scrooge had seen it, night and morning, during his whole residence in that place; also that Scrooge had as little of what is called fancy about him as any man in the city of London, even including—which is a bold word—the corporation, aldermen, and livery. Let it also be borne in mind that Scrooge had not bestowed one thought on Marley, since his last mention of his seven years' dead partner that afternoon. And then let any man explain to me, if he can, how it happened that Scrooge, having his key in the lock of the door, saw in the knocker, without its undergoing any intermediate process of change—not a knocker, but Marley's face.

Marley's face. It was not in impenetrable shadow as the other objects in the yard were, but had a dismal light about it, like a bad lobster in a dark cellar. It was not angry or ferocious, but looked at Scrooge as Marley used to look: with ghostly spectacles turned up on its ghostly forehead. The hair was curiously stirred, as if by breath or hot air; and, though the eyes were wide open, they were perfectly motionless. That, and its livid colour, made it horrible; but its horror seemed to be in spite of the face and beyond its control, rather than a part of its own expression.

As Scrooge looked fixedly at this phenomenon, it was a knocker again.

To say that he was not startled, or that his blood was not conscious of a terrible sensation to which it had been a stranger from infancy, would be untrue. But he put his hand upon the key he had relinquished, turned it sturdily, walked in, and lighted his candle.

He did pause, with a moment's irresolution, before he shut the door; and he did look cautiously behind it first, as if he half expected to be terrified with the sight of Marley's pigtail sticking out into the hall. But there was nothing on the back of the door, except the screws and nuts that held the knocker on, so he said "Pooh, pooh!" and closed it with a bang.

The sound resounded through the house like thunder. Every room above, and every cask in the wine-merchant's cellars below, appeared to have a separate peal of echoes of its own. Scrooge was not a man to be frightened by echoes. He fastened the door, and walked across the hall, and up the stairs; slowly too: trimming his candle as he went.

You may talk vaguely about driving a coach-and-six up a good old flight of stairs, or through a bad young Act of Parliament; but I mean to say you might have got a hearse up that staircase, and taken it broadwise, with the splinter-bar towards the wall and the door towards the balustrades: and done it easy. There was plenty of width for that, and room to spare; which is perhaps the reason why Scrooge thought he saw a locomotive hearse going on before him in the gloom. Half-a-dozen gas-lamps out of the street wouldn't have lighted the entry too well, so you may suppose that it was pretty dark with Scrooge's dip.

Up Scrooge went, not caring a button for that. Darkness is cheap, and Scrooge liked it. But before he shut his heavy door, he walked through his rooms to see that all was right. He had just enough recollection of the face to desire to do that.

Sitting-room, bedroom, lumber-room. All as they should be. Nobody under the table, nobody under the sofa; a small fire in the grate; spoon and basin ready; and the little saucepan of gruel (Scrooge had a cold in his head) upon the hob. Nobody under the bed; nobody in the closet; nobody in his dressing-gown, which was

{45}

hanging up in a suspicious attitude against the wall. Lumber-room as usual. Old fire-guard, old shoes, two fish-baskets, washing-stand on three legs, and a poker.

Quite satisfied, he closed his door, and locked himself in; double-locked himself in, which was not his custom. Thus secured against surprise, he took off his cravat; put on his dressing-gown and slippers, and his nightcap; and sat down before the fire to take his gruel.

It was a very low fire indeed; nothing on such a bitter night. He was obliged to sit close to it, and brood over it, before he could extract the least sensation of warmth from such a handful of fuel. The fireplace was an old one, built by some Dutch merchant long ago, and paved all round with quaint Dutch tiles, designed to illustrate the Scriptures. There were Cains and Abels, Pharaoh's daughters; Queens of Sheba, Angelic messengers descending through the air on clouds like feather-beds, Abrahams, Belshazzars, Apostles putting off to sea in butter-boats, hundreds of figures to attract his thoughts; and yet that face of Marley, seven years dead, came like the ancient Prophet's rod, and swallowed up the whole. If each smooth tile had been a blank at first, with power to shape some picture on its surface from the disjointed fragments of his thoughts, there would have been a copy of old Marley's head on every one.

"Humbug!" said Scrooge; and walked across the room.

After several turns, he sat down again. As he threw his head back in the chair, his glance happened to rest upon a bell, a disused bell, that hung in the room, and communicated for some purpose now forgotten with a chamber in the highest story of the building. It was with great astonishment, and with a strange, inexplicable dread, that as he looked, he saw this bell begin to swing. It swung so softly in the outset that it scarcely made a sound; but soon it rang out loudly, and so did every bell in the house.

This might have lasted half a minute, or a minute, but it seemed an hour. The bells ceased as they had begun, together. They were succeeded by a clanking noise, deep down below; as if some person were dragging a heavy chain over the casks in the wine-merchant's cellar. Scrooge then remembered to have heard that ghosts in haunted houses were described as dragging chains.

The cellar-door flew open with a booming sound, and then he heard the noise much louder, on the floors below; then coming up the stairs; then coming straight towards his door.

"It's humbug still!" said Scrooge. "I won't believe it."

His colour changed though, when, without a pause, it came on through the heavy door, and passed into the room before his eyes. Upon its coming in, the dying flame leaped up, as though it cried, "I know him; Marley's Ghost!" and fell again.

The same face: the very same. Marley in his pigtail, usual waistcoat, tights and boots; the tassels on the latter bristling, like his pigtail, and his coat-skirts, and the hair upon his head. The chain he drew was clasped about his middle. It was long, and wound about him like a tail; and it was made (for Scrooge observed it closely)

{46}

of cash-boxes, keys, padlocks, ledgers, deeds, and heavy purses wrought in steel. His body was transparent; so that Scrooge, observing him, and looking through his waistcoat, could see the two buttons on his coat behind.

Scrooge had often heard it said that Marley had no bowels, but he had never believed it until now.

No, nor did he believe it even now. Though he looked the phantom through and through, and saw it standing before him; though he felt the chilling influence of its death-cold eyes; and marked the very texture of the folded kerchief bound about its head and chin, which wrapper he had not observed before; he was still incredulous, and fought against his senses.

"How now!" said Scrooge, caustic and cold as ever. "What do you want with me?"

"Much!"—Marley's voice, no doubt about it.

"Who are you?"

"Ask me who I was."

"Who were you then?" said Scrooge, raising his voice. "You're particular, for a shade." He was going to say "to a shade," but substituted this, as more appropriate.

"In life I was your partner, Jacob Marley."

"Can you—can you sit down?" asked Scrooge, looking doubtfully at him.

"I can."

"Do it, then."

Scrooge asked the question, because he didn't know whether a ghost so transparent might find himself in a condition to take a chair; and felt that in the event of its being impossible, it might involve the necessity of an embarrassing explanation. But the ghost sat down on the opposite side of the fireplace, as if he were quite used to it.

"You don't believe in me," observed the Ghost.

"I don't," said Scrooge.

"What evidence would you have of my reality beyond that of your senses?"

"I don't know," said Scrooge.

"Why do you doubt your senses?"

"Because," said Scrooge, "a little thing affects them. A slight disorder of the stomach makes them cheats. You may be an undigested bit of beef, a blot of mustard, a crumb of cheese, a fragment of an underdone potato. There's more of gravy than of grave about you, whatever you are!"

Scrooge was not much in the habit of cracking jokes, nor did he feel, in his heart, by any means waggish then. The truth is, that he tried to be smart, as a means of distracting his own attention, and keeping down his terror; for the spectre's voice disturbed the very marrow in his bones.

To sit, staring at those fixed glazed eyes, in silence for a moment, would play, Scrooge felt, the very deuce with him. There was something very awful, too, in the spectre's being provided with an infernal atmosphere of its own. Scrooge could not feel it himself, but this was clearly the case; for though the Ghost sat perfectly motionless, its hair, and skirts, and tassels, were still agitated as by the hot vapour from an oven.

"You see this toothpick?" said Scrooge, returning quickly to the charge, for the reason just assigned; and wishing, though it were only for a second, to divert the vision's stony gaze from himself.

"I do," replied the Ghost.

"You are not looking at it," said Scrooge.

"But I see it," said the Ghost, "notwithstanding."

"Well!" returned Scrooge, "I have but to swallow this, and be for the rest of my days persecuted by a legion of goblins, all of my own creation. Humbug, I tell you! humbug!"

At this the spirit raised a frightful cry, and shook its chain with such a dismal and appalling noise, that Scrooge held on tight to his chair, to save himself from falling in a swoon. But how much greater was his horror, when the phantom taking off the bandage round its head, as if it were too warm to wear indoors, its lower jaw dropped down upon its breast!

Scrooge fell upon his knees, and clasped his hands before his face.

"Mercy!" he said. "Dreadful apparition, why do you trouble me?"

"Man of the worldly mind!" replied the Ghost, "do you believe in me or not?"

"I do," said Scrooge. "I must. But why do spirits walk the earth, and why do they come to me?"

"It is required of every man," the Ghost returned, "that the spirit within him should walk abroad among his fellowmen, and travel far and wide; and if that spirit goes not forth in life, it is condemned to do so after death. It is doomed to wander through the world—oh, woe is me!—and witness what it cannot share, but might have shared on earth, and turned to happiness!"

Again the spectre raised a cry, and shook its chain and wrung its shadowy hands.

"You are fettered," said Scrooge, trembling. "Tell me why?"

"I wear the chain I forged in life," replied the Ghost. "I made it link by link, and yard by yard; I girded it on of my own free will, and of my own free will I wore it. Is its pattern strange to you?"

Scrooge trembled more and more.

"Or would you know," pursued the Ghost, "the weight and length of the strong coil you bear yourself? It was full as heavy and as long as this, seven Christmas Eves ago. You have laboured on it, since. It is a ponderous chain!"

Scrooge glanced about him on the floor, in the expectation of finding himself surrounded by some fifty or sixty fathoms of iron cable: but he could see nothing.

"Jacob," he said, imploringly. "Old Jacob Marley, tell me more. Speak comfort to me, Jacob!"

"I have none to give," the Ghost replied. "It comes from other regions, Ebenezer Scrooge, and is conveyed by other ministers, to other kinds of men. Nor can I tell you what I would. A very little more is all permitted to me. I cannot rest, I cannot stay, I cannot linger anywhere. My spirit never walked beyond our counting-house—mark me!—in life my spirit never roved beyond the narrow limits of our money-changing hole; and weary journeys lie before me!"

It was a habit with Scrooge, whenever he became thoughtful, to put his hands in his breeches pockets. Pondering on what the Ghost had said, he did so now, but without lifting up his eyes, or getting off his knees.

"You must have been very slow about it, Jacob," Scrooge observed, in a business-like manner, though with humility and deference.

"Slow!" the Ghost repeated.

"Seven years dead," mused Scrooge. "And travelling all the time!"

"The whole time," said the Ghost. "No rest, no peace. Incessant torture of remorse."

"You travel fast?" said Scrooge.

"On the wings of the wind," replied the Ghost.

"You might have got over a great quantity of ground in seven years," said Scrooge.

The Ghost, on hearing this, set up another cry, and clanked its chain so hideously in the dead silence of the night, that the Ward would have been justified in indicting it for a nuisance.

"Oh! captive, bound, and double-ironed," cried the phantom, "not to know, that ages of incessant labour by immortal creatures, for this earth must pass into eternity before the good of which it is susceptible is all developed. Not to know that any Christian spirit working kindly in its little sphere, whatever it may be, will find its mortal life too short for its vast means of usefulness. Not to know that no space of regret can make amends for one life's opportunity misused! Yet such was I! Oh! such was I!"

"But you were always a good man of business, Jacob," faltered Scrooge, who now began to apply this to himself.

"Business!" cried the Ghost, wringing its hands again. "Mankind was my business. The common welfare was my business; charity, mercy, forbearance, and benevolence, were, all, my business. The dealings of my trade were but a drop of water in the comprehensive ocean of my business!"

It held up its chain at arm's length, as if that were the cause of all its unavailing grief, and flung it heavily upon the ground again.

"At this time of the rolling year," the spectre said, "I suffer most. Why did I walk through crowds of fellow-beings with my eyes turned down, and never raise them to that blessed Star which led the Wise Men to a poor abode! Were there no poor homes to which its light would have conducted me!"

Scrooge was very much dismayed to hear the spectre going on at this rate, and began to quake exceedingly.

"Hear me!" cried the Ghost. "My time is nearly gone."

"I will," said Scrooge. "But don't be hard upon me! Don't be flowery, Jacob! Pray!"

"How it is that I appear before you in a shape that you can see, I may not tell. I have sat invisible beside you many and many a day."

{49}

It was not an agreeable idea. Scrooge shivered, and wiped the perspiration from his brow.

"That is no light part of my penance," pursued the Ghost. "I am here to-night to warn you, that you have yet a chance and hope of escaping my fate. A chance and hope of my procuring, Ebenezer."

"You were always a good friend to me," said Scrooge. "Thank'ee!"

"You will be haunted," resumed the Ghost, "by Three Spirits."

Scrooge's countenance fell almost as low as the Ghost's had done.

"Is that the chance and hope you mentioned, Jacob?" he demanded, in a faltering voice.

"It is."

"I—I think I'd rather not," said Scrooge.

"Without their visits," said the Ghost, "you cannot hope to shun the path I tread. Expect the first to-morrow, when the bell tolls One."

"Couldn't I take 'em all at once, and have it over, Jacob?" hinted Scrooge.

"Expect the second on the next night at the same hour. The third upon the next night when the last stroke of Twelve has ceased to vibrate. Look to see me no more; and look that, for your own sake, you remember what has passed between us!"

When it had said these words, the spectre took its wrapper from the table, and bound it round its head, as before. Scrooge knew this, by the smart sound its teeth made, when the jaws were brought together by the bandage. He ventured to raise his eyes again, and found his supernatural visitor confronting him in an erect attitude, with its chain wound over and about its arm.

The apparition walked backward from him; and at every step it took, the window raised itself a little, so that when the spectre reached it, it was wide open.

It beckoned Scrooge to approach, which he did. When they were within two paces of each other, Marley's Ghost held up its hand, warning him to come no nearer. Scrooge stopped.

Not so much in obedience, as in surprise and fear: for on the raising of the hand, he became sensible of confused noises in the air; incoherent sounds of lamentation and regret; wailings inexpressibly sorrowful and self-accusatory. The spectre, after listening for a moment, joined in the mournful dirge; and floated out upon the bleak, dark night.

Scrooge followed to the window: desperate in his curiosity. He looked out.

The air was filled with phantoms, wandering hither and thither in restless haste, and moaning as they went. Every one of them wore chains like Marley's Ghost; some few (they might be guilty governments) were linked together; none were free. Many had been personally known to Scrooge in their lives. He had been quite familiar with one old ghost, in a white waistcoat, with a monstrous iron safe attached to its ankle, who cried piteously at being unable to assist a wretched woman with an infant, whom it saw below, upon a door-step. The misery with them all was, clearly, that they sought to interfere, for good, in human matters, and had lost the power for ever.

Whether these creatures faded into mist, or mist enshrouded them, he could not tell. But they and their spirit voices faded together; and the night became as it had been when he walked home.

Scrooge closed the window, and examined the door by which the Ghost had entered. It was double-locked, as he had locked it with his own hands, and the bolts were undisturbed. He tried to say "Humbug!" but stopped at the first syllable. And being, from the emotion he had undergone, or the fatigues of the day, or his glimpse of the Invisible World, or the dull conversation of the Ghost, or the lateness of the hour, much in need of repose; went straight to bed, without undressing, and fell asleep upon the instant.

THE GOBLINS WHO STOLE A SEXTON
Charles Dickens

IN an old abbey town, down in this part of the country, a long, long while ago—so long, that the story must be a true one, because our great-grandfathers implicitly believed it—there officiated as sexton and grave-digger in the churchyard, one Gabriel Grub. It by no means follows that because a man is a sexton, and constantly surrounded by the emblems of mortality, therefore he should be a morose and melancholy man; your undertakers are the merriest fellows in the world; and I once had the honour of being on intimate terms with a mute, who in private life, and off duty, was as comical and jocose a little fellow as ever chirped out a devil-may-care song, without a hitch in his memory, or drained off a good stiff glass without stopping for breath. But notwithstanding these precedents to the contrary, Gabriel Grub was an ill-conditioned, cross-grained, surly fellow—a morose and lonely man, who consorted with nobody but himself, and an old wicker bottle which fitted into his large deep waistcoat pocket—and who eyed each merry face, as it passed him by, with such a deep scowl of malice and ill-humour, as it was difficult to meet without feeling something the worse for.

'A little before twilight, one Christmas Eve, Gabriel shouldered his spade, lighted his lantern, and betook himself towards the old churchyard; for he had got a grave to finish by next morning, and, feeling very low, he thought it might raise his spirits, perhaps, if he went on with his work at once. As he went his way, up the ancient street, he saw the cheerful light of the blazing fires gleam through the old casements, and heard the loud laugh and the cheerful shouts of those who were assembled around them; he marked the bustling preparations for next day's cheer, and smelled the numerous savoury odours consequent thereupon, as they steamed up from the kitchen window in clouds. All this was gall and wormwood to the heart of Gabriel Grub; and when groups of children bounded out of the houses, tripped across the road, and were met, before they could knock at the opposite door, by half a dozen curly-headed little rascals who crowded round them as they flocked upstairs to spend the evening in their Christmas games, Gabriel smiled grimly, and clutched the handle of his spade with a firmer grasp, as he thought of measles, scarlet fever, thrush, whooping-cough, and a good many other sources of consolation besides.

'In this happy frame of mind, Gabriel strode along, returning a short, sullen growl to the good-humoured greetings of such of his neighbours as now and then passed him, until he turned into the dark lane which led to the churchyard. Now, Gabriel had been looking forward to reaching the dark lane, because it was, generally speaking, a nice, gloomy, mournful place, into which the townspeople did not much care to go, except in broad daylight, and when the sun was shining; consequently, he was not a little indignant to hear a young urchin roaring out some jolly song about a merry Christmas, in this very sanctuary which had been

called Coffin Lane ever since the days of the old abbey, and the time of the shaven-headed monks. As Gabriel walked on, and the voice drew nearer, he found it proceeded from a small boy, who was hurrying along, to join one of the little parties in the old street, and who, partly to keep himself company, and partly to prepare himself for the occasion, was shouting out the song at the highest pitch of his lungs. So Gabriel waited until the boy came up, and then dodged him into a corner, and rapped him over the head with his lantern five or six times, just to teach him to modulate his voice. And as the boy hurried away with his hand to his head, singing quite a different sort of tune, Gabriel Grub chuckled very heartily to himself, and entered the churchyard, locking the gate behind him.

'He took off his coat, set down his lantern, and getting into the unfinished grave, worked at it for an hour or so with right good-will. But the earth was hardened with the frost, and it was no very easy matter to break it up, and shovel it out; and although there was a moon, it was a very young one, and shed little light upon the grave, which was in the shadow of the church. At any other time, these obstacles would have made Gabriel Grub very moody and miserable, but he was so well pleased with having stopped the small boy's singing, that he took little heed of the scanty progress he had made, and looked down into the grave, when he had finished work for the night, with grim satisfaction, murmuring as he gathered up his things—

> Brave lodgings for one, brave lodgings for one,
> A few feet of cold earth, when life is done;
> A stone at the head, a stone at the feet,
> A rich, juicy meal for the worms to eat;
> Rank grass overhead, and damp clay around,
> Brave lodgings for one, these, in holy ground!

'"Ho! ho!" laughed Gabriel Grub, as he sat himself down on a flat tombstone which was a favourite resting-place of his, and drew forth his wicker bottle. "A coffin at Christmas! A Christmas box! Ho! ho! ho!"

'"Ho! ho! ho!" repeated a voice which sounded close behind him.

'Gabriel paused, in some alarm, in the act of raising the wicker bottle to his lips, and looked round. The bottom of the oldest grave about him was not more still and quiet than the churchyard in the pale moonlight. The cold hoar frost glistened on the tombstones, and sparkled like rows of gems, among the stone carvings of the old church. The snow lay hard and crisp upon the ground; and spread over the thickly-strewn mounds of earth, so white and smooth a cover that it seemed as if corpses lay there, hidden only by their winding sheets. Not the faintest rustle broke the profound tranquillity of the solemn scene. Sound itself appeared to be frozen up, all was so cold and still.

'"It was the echoes," said Gabriel Grub, raising the bottle to his lips again.

'"It was NOT," said a deep voice.

'Gabriel started up, and stood rooted to the spot with astonishment and terror; for his eyes rested on a form that made his blood run cold.

'Seated on an upright tombstone, close to him, was a strange, unearthly figure, whom Gabriel felt at once, was no being of this world. His long, fantastic legs which might have reached the ground, were cocked up, and crossed after a quaint, fantastic fashion; his sinewy arms were bare; and his hands rested on his knees. On his short, round body, he wore a close covering, ornamented with small slashes; a short cloak dangled at his back; the collar was cut into curious peaks, which served the goblin in lieu of ruff or neckerchief; and his shoes curled up at his toes into long points. On his head, he wore a broad-brimmed sugar-loaf hat, garnished with a single feather. The hat was covered with the white frost; and the goblin looked as if he had sat on the same tombstone very comfortably, for two or three hundred years. He was sitting perfectly still; his tongue was put out, as if in derision; and he was grinning at Gabriel Grub with such a grin as only a goblin could call up.

'"It was NOT the echoes," said the goblin.

'Gabriel Grub was paralysed, and could make no reply.

'"What do you do here on Christmas Eve?" said the goblin sternly. '"I came to dig a grave, Sir," stammered Gabriel Grub.

'"What man wanders among graves and churchyards on such a night as this?" cried the goblin.

'"Gabriel Grub! Gabriel Grub!" screamed a wild chorus of voices that seemed to fill the churchyard. Gabriel looked fearfully round—nothing was to be seen.

'"What have you got in that bottle?" said the goblin.

'"Hollands, sir," replied the sexton, trembling more than ever; for he had bought it of the smugglers, and he thought that perhaps his questioner might be in the excise department of the goblins.

'"Who drinks Hollands alone, and in a churchyard, on such a night as this?" said the goblin.

'"Gabriel Grub! Gabriel Grub!" exclaimed the wild voices again.

'The goblin leered maliciously at the terrified sexton, and then raising his voice, exclaimed—

'"And who, then, is our fair and lawful prize?"

'To this inquiry the invisible chorus replied, in a strain that sounded like the voices of many choristers singing to the mighty swell of the old church organ—a strain that seemed borne to the sexton's ears upon a wild wind, and to die away as it passed onward; but the burden of the reply was still the same, "Gabriel Grub! Gabriel Grub!"

'The goblin grinned a broader grin than before, as he said, "Well, Gabriel, what do you say to this?"

'The sexton gasped for breath. '"What do you think of this, Gabriel?" said the goblin, kicking up his feet in the air on either side of the tombstone, and looking at the turned-up points with as much complacency as if he had been contemplating the most fashionable pair of Wellingtons in all Bond Street.

'"It's—it's—very curious, Sir," replied the sexton, half dead with fright; "very curious, and very pretty, but I think I'll go back and finish my work, Sir, if you please."

'"Work!" said the goblin, "what work?"

'"The grave, Sir; making the grave," stammered the sexton.

'"Oh, the grave, eh?" said the goblin; "who makes graves at a time when all other men are merry, and takes a pleasure in it?"

'Again the mysterious voices replied, "Gabriel Grub! Gabriel Grub!"

'"I am afraid my friends want you, Gabriel," said the goblin, thrusting his tongue farther into his cheek than ever—and a most astonishing tongue it was—"I'm afraid my friends want you, Gabriel," said the goblin.

'"Under favour, Sir," replied the horror-stricken sexton, "I don't think they can, Sir; they don't know me, Sir; I don't think the gentlemen have ever seen me, Sir."

'"Oh, yes, they have," replied the goblin; "we know the man with the sulky face and grim scowl, that came down the street to-night, throwing his evil looks at the children, and grasping his burying-spade the tighter. We know the man who struck the boy in the envious malice of his heart, because the boy could be merry, and he could not. We know him, we know him."

'Here, the goblin gave a loud, shrill laugh, which the echoes returned twentyfold; and throwing his legs up in the air, stood upon his head, or rather upon the very point of his sugar-loaf hat, on the narrow edge of the tombstone, whence he threw a Somerset with extraordinary agility, right to the sexton's feet, at which he planted himself in the attitude in which tailors generally sit upon the shop-board.

'"I—I—am afraid I must leave you, Sir," said the sexton, making an effort to move.

'"Leave us!" said the goblin, "Gabriel Grub going to leave us. Ho! ho! ho!"

'As the goblin laughed, the sexton observed, for one instant, a brilliant illumination within the windows of the church, as if the whole building were lighted up; it disappeared, the organ pealed forth a lively air, and whole troops of goblins, the very counterpart of the first one, poured into the churchyard, and began playing at leap-frog with the tombstones, never stopping for an instant to take breath, but "overing" the highest among them, one after the other, with the most marvellous dexterity. The first goblin was a most astonishing leaper, and none of the others could come near him; even in the extremity of his terror the sexton could not help observing, that while his friends were content to leap over the common-sized gravestones, the first one took the family vaults, iron railings and all, with as much ease as if they had been so many street-posts.

'At last the game reached to a most exciting pitch; the organ played quicker and quicker, and the goblins leaped faster and faster, coiling themselves up, rolling head over heels upon the ground, and bounding over the tombstones like footballs. The sexton's brain whirled round with the rapidity of the motion he beheld, and his legs reeled beneath him, as the spirits flew before his eyes; when the goblin king, suddenly darting towards him, laid his hand upon his collar, and sank with him through the earth.

'When Gabriel Grub had had time to fetch his breath, which the rapidity of his descent had for the moment taken away, he found himself in what appeared to be a large cavern, surrounded on all sides by crowds of goblins, ugly and grim; in the centre of the room, on an elevated seat, was stationed his friend of the churchyard; and close behind him stood Gabriel Grub himself, without power of motion. '"Cold to-night," said the king of the goblins, "very cold. A glass of something warm here!"

'At this command, half a dozen officious goblins, with a perpetual smile upon their faces, whom Gabriel Grub imagined to be courtiers, on that account, hastily disappeared, and presently returned with a goblet of liquid fire, which they presented to the king.

'"Ah!" cried the goblin, whose cheeks and throat were transparent, as he tossed down the flame, "this warms one, indeed! Bring a bumper of the same, for Mr. Grub."

'It was in vain for the unfortunate sexton to protest that he was not in the habit of taking anything warm at night; one of the goblins held him while another poured the blazing liquid down his throat; the whole assembly screeched with laughter, as he coughed and choked, and wiped away the tears which gushed plentifully from his eyes, after swallowing the burning draught.

'"And now," said the king, fantastically poking the taper corner of his sugar-loaf hat into the sexton's eye, and thereby occasioning him the most exquisite pain; "and now, show the man of misery and gloom, a few of the pictures from our own great storehouse!"

'As the goblin said this, a thick cloud which obscured the remoter end of the cavern rolled gradually away, and disclosed, apparently at a great distance, a small and scantily furnished, but neat and clean apartment. A crowd of little children were gathered round a bright fire, clinging to their mother's gown, and gambolling around her chair. The mother occasionally rose, and drew aside the window-curtain, as if to look for some expected object; a frugal meal was ready spread upon the table; and an elbow chair was placed near the fire. A knock was heard at the door; the mother opened it, and the children crowded round her, and clapped their hands for joy, as their father entered. He was wet and weary, and shook the snow from his garments, as the children crowded round him, and seizing his cloak, hat, stick, and gloves, with busy zeal, ran with them from the room. Then, as he sat down to his meal before the fire, the children climbed about his knee, and the mother sat by his side, and all seemed happiness and comfort.

'But a change came upon the view, almost imperceptibly. The scene was altered to a small bedroom, where the fairest and youngest child lay dying; the roses had fled from his cheek, and the light from his eye; and even as the sexton looked upon him with an interest he had never felt or known before, he died. His young brothers and sisters crowded round his little bed, and seized his tiny hand, so cold and heavy; but they shrank back from its touch, and looked with awe on his infant face; for calm and tranquil as it was, and sleeping in rest and peace as the beautiful child seemed to be, they saw that he was dead, and they knew that he was an angel looking down upon, and blessing them, from a bright and happy Heaven.

'Again the light cloud passed across the picture, and again the subject changed. The father and mother were old and helpless now, and the number of those about them was diminished more than half; but content and cheerfulness sat on every face, and beamed in every eye, as they crowded round the fireside, and told and listened to old stories of earlier and bygone days. Slowly and peacefully, the father sank into the grave, and, soon after, the sharer of all his cares and troubles followed him to a place of rest. The few who yet survived them, kneeled by their tomb, and watered the green turf which covered it with their tears; then rose, and turned away, sadly and mournfully, but not with bitter cries, or despairing lamentations, for they knew that they should one day meet again; and once more they mixed with the busy world, and their content and cheerfulness were restored. The cloud settled upon the picture, and concealed it from the sexton's view.

'"What do you think of THAT?" said the goblin, turning his large face towards Gabriel Grub.

'Gabriel murmured out something about its being very pretty, and looked somewhat ashamed, as the goblin bent his fiery eyes upon him.

'"You miserable man!" said the goblin, in a tone of excessive contempt. "You!" He appeared disposed to add more, but indignation choked his utterance, so he lifted up one of his very pliable legs, and, flourishing it above his head a little, to insure his aim, administered a good sound kick to Gabriel Grub; immediately after which, all the goblins in waiting crowded round the wretched sexton, and kicked him without mercy, according to the established and invariable custom of courtiers upon earth, who kick whom royalty kicks, and hug whom royalty hugs.

'"Show him some more!" said the king of the goblins.

'At these words, the cloud was dispelled, and a rich and beautiful landscape was disclosed to view—there is just such another, to this day, within half a mile of the old abbey town. The sun shone from out the clear blue sky, the water sparkled beneath his rays, and the trees looked greener, and the flowers more gay, beneath its cheering influence. The water rippled on with a pleasant sound, the trees rustled in the light wind that murmured among their leaves, the birds sang upon the boughs, and the lark carolled on high her welcome to the morning. Yes, it was morning; the bright, balmy morning of summer; the minutest leaf, the smallest blade of grass, was instinct with life. The ant crept forth to her daily toil, the butterfly fluttered and basked in the warm rays of the sun; myriads of insects spread their transparent wings, and revelled in their brief but happy existence. Man walked forth, elated with the scene; and all was brightness and splendour.

'"YOU a miserable man!" said the king of the goblins, in a more contemptuous tone than before. And again the king of the goblins gave his leg a flourish; again it descended on the shoulders of the sexton; and again the attendant goblins imitated the example of their chief.

'Many a time the cloud went and came, and many a lesson it taught to Gabriel Grub, who, although his shoulders smarted with pain from the frequent applications of the goblins' feet thereunto, looked on with an interest that nothing could diminish. He saw that men who worked hard, and earned their scanty bread with lives of labour, were cheerful and happy; and that to the most ignorant, the sweet face of Nature was a never-failing source of cheerfulness and joy. He saw

{58}

those who had been delicately nurtured, and tenderly brought up, cheerful under privations, and superior to suffering, that would have crushed many of a rougher grain, because they bore within their own bosoms the materials of happiness, contentment, and peace. He saw that women, the tenderest and most fragile of all God's creatures, were the oftenest superior to sorrow, adversity, and distress; and he saw that it was because they bore, in their own hearts, an inexhaustible well-spring of affection and devotion. Above all, he saw that men like himself, who snarled at the mirth and cheerfulness of others, were the foulest weeds on the fair surface of the earth; and setting all the good of the world against the evil, he came to the conclusion that it was a very decent and respectable sort of world after all. No sooner had he formed it, than the cloud which had closed over the last picture, seemed to settle on his senses, and lull him to repose. One by one, the goblins faded from his sight; and, as the last one disappeared, he sank to sleep.

'The day had broken when Gabriel Grub awoke, and found himself lying at full length on the flat gravestone in the churchyard, with the wicker bottle lying empty by his side, and his coat, spade, and lantern, all well whitened by the last night's frost, scattered on the ground. The stone on which he had first seen the goblin seated, stood bolt upright before him, and the grave at which he had worked, the night before, was not far off. At first, he began to doubt the reality of his adventures, but the acute pain in his shoulders when he attempted to rise, assured him that the kicking of the goblins was certainly not ideal. He was staggered again, by observing no traces of footsteps in the snow on which the goblins had played at leap-frog with the gravestones, but he speedily accounted for this circumstance when he remembered that, being spirits, they would leave no visible impression behind them. So, Gabriel Grub got on his feet as well as he could, for the pain in his back; and, brushing the frost off his coat, put it on, and turned his face towards the town.

'But he was an altered man, and he could not bear the thought of returning to a place where his repentance would be scoffed at, and his reformation disbelieved. He hesitated for a few moments; and then turned away to wander where he might, and seek his bread elsewhere.

'The lantern, the spade, and the wicker bottle were found, that day, in the churchyard. There were a great many speculations about the sexton's fate, at first, but it was speedily determined that he had been carried away by the goblins; and there were not wanting some very credible witnesses who had distinctly seen him whisked through the air on the back of a chestnut horse blind of one eye, with the hind-quarters of a lion, and the tail of a bear. At length all this was devoutly believed; and the new sexton used to exhibit to the curious, for a trifling emolument, a good-sized piece of the church weathercock which had been accidentally kicked off by the aforesaid horse in his aerial flight, and picked up by himself in the churchyard, a year or two afterwards.

'Unfortunately, these stories were somewhat disturbed by the unlooked-for reappearance of Gabriel Grub himself, some ten years afterwards, a ragged, contented, rheumatic old man. He told his story to the clergyman, and also to the mayor; and in course of time it began to be received as a matter of history, in which form it has continued down to this very day. The believers in the weathercock tale, having misplaced their confidence once, were not easily prevailed upon to part with it again, so they looked as wise as they could, shrugged their shoulders, touched their foreheads, and murmured something about Gabriel Grub having drunk all the Hollands, and then fallen asleep on the flat tombstone; and they affected to explain what he supposed he had witnessed in the goblin's cavern, by saying that he had seen the world, and grown wiser. But this opinion, which was by no means a popular one at any time, gradually died off; and be the matter how it may, as Gabriel Grub was afflicted with rheumatism to the end of his days, this story has at least one moral, if it teach no better one—and that is, that if a man turn sulky and drink by himself at Christmas time, he may make up his mind to be not a bit the better for it: let the spirits be never so good, or let them be even as many degrees beyond proof, as those which Gabriel Grub saw in the goblin's cavern.'

BETWEEN THE LIGHTS
E. F. Benson

THE day had been one unceasing fall of snow from sunrise until the gradual withdrawal of the vague white light outside indicated that the sun had set again. But as usual at this hospitable and delightful house of Everard Chandler where I often spent Christmas, and was spending it now, there had been no lack of entertainment, and the hours had passed with a rapidity that had surprised us. A short billiard tournament had filled up the time between breakfast and lunch, with Badminton and the morning papers for those who were temporarily not engaged, while afterwards, the interval till tea-time had been occupied by the majority of the party in a huge game of hide-and-seek all over the house, barring the billiard-room, which was sanctuary for any who desired peace. But few had done that; the enchantment of Christmas, I must suppose, had, like some spell, made children of us again, and it was with palsied terror and trembling misgivings that we had tip-toed up and down the dim passages, from any corner of which some wild screaming form might dart out on us. Then, wearied with exercise and emotion, we had assembled again for tea in the hall, a room of shadows and panels on which the light from the wide open fireplace, where there burned a divine mixture of peat and logs, flickered and grew bright again on the walls. Then, as was proper, ghost-stories, for the narration of which the electric light was put out, so that the listeners might conjecture anything they pleased to be lurking in the corners, succeeded, and we vied with each other in blood, bones, skeletons, armour and shrieks. I had, just given my contribution, and was reflecting with some complacency that probably the worst was now known, when Everard, who had not yet administered to the horror of his guests, spoke. He was sitting opposite me in the full blaze of the fire, looking, after the illness he had gone through during the autumn, still rather pale and delicate. All the same he had been among the boldest and best in the exploration of dark places that afternoon, and the look on his face now rather startled me.

"No, I don't mind that sort of thing," he said. "The paraphernalia of ghosts has become somehow rather hackneyed, and when I hear of screams and skeletons I feel I am on familiar ground, and can at least hide my head under the bed-clothes."

"Ah, but the bed-clothes were twitched away by my skeleton," said I, in self-defence.

"I know, but I don't even mind that. Why, there are seven, eight skeletons in this room now, covered with blood and skin and other horrors. No, the nightmares of one's childhood were the really frightening things, because they were vague. There was the true atmosphere of horror about them because one didn't know what one feared. Now if one could recapture that--"

Mrs. Chandler got quickly out of her seat.

"Oh, Everard," she said, "surely you don't wish to recapture it again. I should have thought once was enough."

This was enchanting. A chorus of invitation asked him to proceed: the real true ghost-story first-hand, which was what seemed to be indicated, was too precious a thing to lose.

Everard laughed. "No, dear, I don't want to recapture it again at all," he said to his wife.

Then to us: "But really the--well, the nightmare perhaps, to which I was referring, is of the vaguest and most unsatisfactory kind. It has no apparatus about it at all. You will probably all say that it was nothing, and wonder why I was frightened. But I was; it frightened me out of my wits. And I only just saw something, without being able to swear what it was, and heard something which might have been a falling stone."

"Anyhow, tell us about the falling stone," said I.

There was a stir of movement about the circle round the fire, and the movement was not of purely physical order. It was as if--this is only what I personally felt--it was as if the childish gaiety of the hours we had passed that day was suddenly withdrawn; we had jested on certain subjects, we had played hide-and-seek with all the power of earnestness that was in us. But now--so it seemed to me--there was going to be real hide-and-seek, real terrors were going to lurk in dark corners, or if not real terrors, terrors so convincing as to assume the garb of reality, were going to pounce on us. And Mrs. Chandler's exclamation as she sat down again, "Oh, Everard, won't it excite you?" tended in any case to excite us. The room still remained in dubious darkness except for the sudden lights disclosed on the walls by the leaping flames on the hearth, and there was wide field for conjecture as to what might lurk in the dim corners. Everard, moreover, who had been sitting in bright light before, was banished by the extinction of some flaming log into the shadows. A voice alone spoke to us, as he sat back in his low chair, a voice rather slow but very distinct.

"Last year," he said, "on the twenty-fourth of December, we were down here, as usual, Amy and I, for Christmas. Several of you who are here now were here then. Three or four of you at least."

I was one of these, but like the others kept silence, for the identification, so it seemed to me, was not asked for. And he went on again without a pause.

"Those of you who were here then," he said, "and are here now, will remember how very warm it was this day year. You will remember, too, that we played croquet that day on the lawn. It was perhaps a little cold for croquet, and we played it rather in order to be able to say--with sound evidence to back the statement--that we had done so."

Then he turned and addressed the whole little circle.

"We played ties of half-games," he said, "just as we have played billiards to-day, and it was certainly as warm on the lawn then as it was in the billiard-room this morning directly after breakfast, while to-day I should not wonder if there was three feet of snow outside. More, probably; listen."

A sudden draught fluted in the chimney, and the fire flared up as the current of air caught it.

The wind also drove the snow against the windows, and as he said, "Listen," we heard a soft scurry of the falling flakes against the panes, like the soft tread of many little people who stepped lightly, but with the persistence of multitudes who were flocking to some rendezvous. Hundreds of little feet seemed to be gathering outside; only the glass kept them out. And of the eight skeletons present four or five, anyhow, turned and looked at the windows. These were small-paned, with leaden bars. On the leaden bars little heaps of snow had accumulated, but there was nothing else to be seen.

"Yes, last Christmas Eve was very warm and sunny," went on Everard. "We had had no frost that autumn, and a temerarious dahlia was still in flower. I have always thought that it must have been mad."

He paused a moment.

"And I wonder if I were not mad too," he added.

No one interrupted him; there was something arresting, I must suppose, in what he was saying; it chimed in anyhow with the hide-and-seek, with the suggestions of the lonely snow.

Mrs. Chandler had sat down again, but I heard her stir in her chair. But never was there a gay party so reduced as we had been in the last five minutes. Instead of laughing at ourselves for playing silly games, we were all taking a serious game seriously.

"Anyhow, I was sitting out," he said to me, "while you and my wife played your half-game of croquet. Then it struck me that it was not so warm as I had supposed, because quite suddenly I shivered. And shivering I looked up. But I did not see you and her playing croquet at all. I saw something which had no relation to you and her--at least I hope not."

Now the angler lands his fish, the stalker kills his stag, and the speaker holds his audience.

And as the fish is gaffed, and as the stag is shot, so were we held. There was no getting away till he had finished with us.

"You all know the croquet lawn," he said, "and how it is bounded all round by a flower border with a brick wall behind it, through which, you will remember, there is only one gate.

"Well, I looked up and saw that the lawn--I could for one moment see it was still a lawn--was shrinking, and the walls closing in upon it. As they closed in too, they grew higher, and simultaneously the light began to fade and be sucked from the sky, till it grew quite dark overhead and only a glimmer of light came in through the gate.

"There was, as I told you, a dahlia in flower that day, and as this dreadful darkness and bewilderment came over me, I remember that my eyes sought it in a kind of despair, holding on, as it were, to any familiar object. But it was no longer a dahlia, and for the red of its petals I saw only the red of some feeble firelight. And at that moment the hallucination was complete. I was no longer sitting on the lawn watching croquet, but I was in a low-roofed room, something like a cattle-shed, but round. Close above my head, though I was sitting down, ran rafters from

{63}

wall to wall. It was nearly dark, but a little light came in from the door opposite to me, which seemed to lead into a passage that communicated with the exterior of the place. Little, however, of the wholesome air came into this dreadful den; the atmosphere was oppressive and foul beyond all telling, it was as if for years it had been the place of some human menagerie, and for those years had been uncleaned and unsweetened by the winds of heaven. Yet that oppressiveness was nothing to the awful horror of the place from the view of the spirit. Some dreadful atmosphere of crime and abomination dwelt heavy in it, its denizens, whoever they were, were scarce human, so it seemed to me, and though men and women, were akin more to the beasts of the field. And in addition there was present to me some sense of the weight of years; I had been taken and thrust down into some epoch of dim antiquity."

He paused a moment, and the fire on the hearth leaped up for a second and then died down again. But in that gleam I saw that all faces were turned to Everard, and that all wore some look of dreadful expectancy. Certainly I felt it myself, and waited in a sort of shrinking horror for what was coming.

"As I told you," he continued, "where there had been that unseasonable dahlia, there now burned a dim firelight, and my eyes were drawn there. Shapes were gathered round it; what they were I could not at first see. Then perhaps my eyes got more accustomed to the dusk, or the fire burned better, for I perceived that they were of human form, but very small, for when one rose with a horrible chattering, to his feet, his head was still some inches off the low roof. He was dressed in a sort of shirt that came to his knees, but his arms were bare and covered with hair.

"Then the gesticulation and chattering increased, and I knew that they were talking about me, for they kept pointing in my direction. At that my horror suddenly deepened, for I became aware that I was powerless and could not move hand or foot; a helpless, nightmare impotence had possession of me. I could not lift a finger or turn my head. And in the paralysis of that fear I tried to scream, but not a sound could I utter.

"All this I suppose took place with the instantaneousness of a dream, for at once, and without transition, the whole thing had vanished, and I was back on the lawn again, while the stroke for which my wife was aiming was still unplayed. But my face was dripping with perspiration, and I was trembling all over.

"Now you may all say that I had fallen asleep, and had a sudden nightmare. That may be so; but I was conscious of no sense of sleepiness before, and I was conscious of none afterwards. It was as if someone had held a book before me, whisked the pages open for a second and closed them again."

Somebody, I don't know who, got up from his chair with a sudden movement that made me start, and turned on the electric light. I do not mind confessing that I was rather glad of this.

Everard laughed.

"Really I feel like Hamlet in the play-scene," he said, "and as if there was a guilty uncle present. Shall I go on?"

I don't think anyone replied, and he went on.

"Well, let us say for the moment that it was not a dream exactly, but a hallucination.

"Whichever it was, in any case it haunted me; for months, I think, it was never quite out of my mind, but lingered somewhere in the dusk of consciousness, sometimes sleeping quietly, so to speak, but sometimes stirring in its sleep. It was no good my telling myself that I was disquieting myself in vain, for it was as if something had actually entered into my very soul, as if some seed of horror had been planted there. And as the weeks went on the seed began to sprout, so that I could no longer even tell myself that that vision had been a moment's disorderment only. I can't say that it actually affected my health. I did not, as far as I know, sleep or eat insufficiently, but morning after morning I used to wake, not gradually and through pleasant dozings into full consciousness, but with absolute suddenness, and find myself plunged in an abyss of despair.

"Often too, eating or drinking, I used to pause and wonder if it was worth while.

"Eventually, I told two people about my trouble, hoping that perhaps the mere communication would help matters, hoping also, but very distantly, that though I could not believe at present that digestion or the obscurities of the nervous system were at fault, a doctor by some simple dose might convince me of it. In other words I told my wife, who laughed at me, and my doctor, who laughed also, and assured me that my health was quite unnecessarily robust.

"At the same time he suggested that change of air and scene does wonders for the delusions that exist merely in the imagination. He also told me, in answer to a direct question, that he would stake his reputation on the certainty that I was not going mad.

"Well, we went up to London as usual for the season, and though nothing whatever occurred to remind me in any way of that single moment on Christmas Eve, the reminding was seen to all right, the moment itself took care of that, for instead of fading as is the way of sleeping or waking dreams, it grew every day more vivid, and ate, so to speak, like some corrosive acid into my mind, etching itself there. And to London succeeded Scotland.

"I took last year for the first time a small forest up in Sutherland, called Glen Callan, very remote and wild, but affording excellent stalking. It was not far from the sea, and the gillies used always to warn me to carry a compass on the hill, because sea-mists were liable to come up with frightful rapidity, and there was always a danger of being caught by one, and of having perhaps to wait hours till it cleared again. This at first I always used to do, but, as everyone knows, any precaution that one takes which continues to be unjustified gets gradually relaxed, and at the end of a few weeks, since the weather had been uniformly clear, it was natural that, as often as not, my compass remained at home.

"One day the stalk took me on to a part of my ground that I had seldom been on before, a very high table-land on the limit of my forest, which went down very steeply on one side to a loch that lay below it, and on the other, by gentler gradations, to the river that came from the loch, six miles below which stood the lodge. The wind had necessitated our climbing up--or so my stalker had insisted--not by the easier way, but up the crags from the loch. I had argued the point with him for it seemed to me that it was impossible that the deer could get our scent if we went by the more natural path, but he still held to his opinion; and therefore, since after all this was his part of the job, I yielded. A dreadful climb we had of it, over big boulders with deep holes in between, masked by clumps of heather, so that a wary eye and a prodding stick were necessary for each step if one wished to avoid broken bones. Adders also literally swarmed in the heather; we must have seen a dozen at least on our way up, and adders are a beast for which I have no manner of use. But a couple of hours saw us to the top, only to find that the stalker had been utterly at fault, and that the deer must quite infallibly have got wind of us, if they had remained in the place where we last saw them. That, when we could spy the ground again, we saw had happened; in any case they had gone. The man insisted the wind had changed, a palpably stupid excuse, and I wondered at that moment what other reason he had--for reason I felt sure there must be--for not wishing to take what would clearly now have been a better route. But this piece of bad management did not spoil our luck, for within an hour we had spied more deer, and about two o'clock I got a shot, killing a heavy stag. Then sitting on the heather I ate lunch, and enjoyed a well-earned bask and smoke in the sun. The pony meantime had been saddled with the stag, and was plodding homewards.

"The morning had been extraordinarily warm, with a little wind blowing off the sea, which lay a few miles off sparkling beneath a blue haze, and all morning in spite of our abominable climb I had had an extreme sense of peace, so much so that several times I had probed my mind, so to speak, to find if the horror still lingered there. But I could scarcely get any response from it.

"Never since Christmas had I been so free of fear, and it was with a great sense of repose, both physical and spiritual, that I lay looking up into the blue sky, watching my smoke-whorls curl slowly away into nothingness. But I was not allowed to take my ease long, for Sandy came and begged that I would move. The weather had changed, he said, the wind had shifted again, and he wanted me to be off this high ground and on the path again as soon as possible, because it looked to him as if a sea-mist would presently come up."

"'And yon's a bad place to get down in the mist,' he added, nodding towards the crags we had come up.

"I looked at the man in amazement, for to our right lay a gentle slope down on to the river, and there was now no possible reason for again tackling those hideous rocks up which we had climbed this morning. More than ever I was sure he had some secret reason for not wishing to go the obvious way. But about one thing he was certainly right, the mist was coming up from the sea, and I felt in my pocket for the compass, and found I had forgotten to bring it.

"Then there followed a curious scene which lost us time that we could really ill afford to waste, I insisting on going down by the way that common sense directed, he imploring me to take his word for it that the crags were the better

{66}

way. Eventually, I marched off to the easier descent, and told him not to argue any more but follow. What annoyed me about him was that he would only give the most senseless reasons for preferring the crags. There were mossy places, he said, on the way I wished to go, a thing patently false, since the summer had been one spell of unbroken weather; or it was longer, also obviously untrue; or there were so many vipers about.

"But seeing that none of these arguments produced any effect, at last he desisted, and came after me in silence.

"We were not yet half down when the mist was upon us, shooting up from the valley like the broken water of a wave, and in three minutes we were enveloped in a cloud of fog so thick that we could barely see a dozen yards in front of us. It was therefore another cause for self-congratulation that we were not now, as we should otherwise have been, precariously clambering on the face of those crags up which we had come with such difficulty in the morning, and as I rather prided myself on my powers of generalship in the matter of direction, I continued leading, feeling sure that before long we should strike the track by the river. More than all, the absolute freedom from fear elated me; since Christmas I had not known the instinctive joy of that; I felt like a schoolboy home for the holidays. But the mist grew thicker and thicker, and whether it was that real rain-clouds had formed above it, or that it was of an extraordinary density itself, I got wetter in the next hour than I have ever been before or since. The wet seemed to penetrate the skin, and chill the very bones. And still there was no sign of the track for which I was making.

"Behind me, muttering to himself, followed the stalker, but his arguments and protestations were dumb, and it seemed as if he kept close to me, as if afraid.

"Now there are many unpleasant companions in this world; I would not, for instance, care to be on the hill with a drunkard or a maniac, but worse than either, I think, is a frightened man, because his trouble is infectious, and, insensibly. I began to be afraid of being frightened too.

"From that it is but a short step to fear. Other perplexities too beset us. At one time we seemed to be walking on flat ground, at another I felt sure we were climbing again, whereas all the time we ought to have been descending, unless we had missed the way very badly indeed. Also, for the month was October, it was beginning to get dark, and it was with a sense of relief that I remembered that the full moon would rise soon after sunset. But it had grown very much colder, and soon, instead of rain, we found we were walking through a steady fall of snow.

"Things were pretty bad, but then for the moment they seemed to mend, for, far away to the left, I suddenly heard the brawling of the river. It should, it is true, have been straight in front of me and we were perhaps a mile out of our way, but this was better than the blind wandering of the last hour, and turning to the left, I walked towards it. But before I had gone a hundred yards, I heard a sudden choked cry behind me, and just saw Sandy's form flying as if in terror of pursuit, into the mists. I called to him, but got no reply, and heard only the spurned stones of his running.

"What had frightened him I had no idea, but certainly with his disappearance, the infection of his fear disappeared also, and I went on, I may almost say, with gaiety. On the moment, however, I saw a sudden well-defined blackness in front of me, and before I knew what I was doing I was half stumbling, half walking up a very steep grass slope.

"During the last few minutes the wind had got up, and the driving snow was peculiarly uncomfortable, but there had been a certain consolation in thinking that the wind would soon disperse these mists, and I had nothing more than a moonlight walk home. But as I paused on this slope, I became aware of two things, one, that the blackness in front of me was very close, the other that, whatever it was, it sheltered me from the snow. So I climbed on a dozen yards into its friendly shelter, for it seemed to me to be friendly.

"A wall some twelve feet high crowned the slope, and exactly where I struck it there was a hole in it, or door rather, through which a little light appeared. Wondering at this I pushed on, bending down, for the passage was very low, and in a dozen yards came out on the other side.

"Just as I did this the sky suddenly grew lighter, the wind, I suppose, having dispersed the mists, and the moon, though not yet visible through the flying skirts of cloud, made sufficient illumination.

"I was in a circular enclosure, and above me there projected from the walls some four feet from the ground, broken stones which must have been intended to support a floor. Then simultaneously two things occurred.

"The whole of my nine months' terror came back to me, for I saw that the vision in the garden was fulfilled, and at the same moment I saw stealing towards me a little figure as of a man, but only about three foot six in height. That my eyes told me; my ears told me that he stumbled on a stone; my nostrils told me that the air I breathed was of an overpowering foulness, and my soul told me that it was sick unto death. I think I tried to scream, but could not; I know I tried to move and could not. And it crept closer.

"Then I suppose the terror which held me spellbound so spurred me that I must move, for next moment I heard a cry break from my lips, and was stumbling through the passage. I made one leap of it down the grass slope, and ran as I hope never to have to run again. What direction I took I did not pause to consider, so long as I put distance between me and that place. Luck, however, favoured me, and before long I struck the track by the river, and an hour afterwards reached the lodge.

"Next day I developed a chill, and as you know pneumonia laid me on my back for six weeks.

"Well, that is my story, and there are many explanations. You may say that I fell asleep on the lawn, and was reminded of that by finding myself, under discouraging circumstances, in an old Picts' castle, where a sheep or a goat that, like myself, had taken shelter from the storm, was moving about. Yes, there are hundreds of ways in which you may explain it. But the coincidence was an odd one, and those who believe in second sight might find an instance of their hobby in it."

"And that is all?" I asked.

"Yes, it was nearly too much for me. I think the dressing-bell has sounded."

THE DEAD SEXTON
J. Sheridan Le Fanu

THE sunsets were red, the nights were long, and the weather pleasantly frosty; and Christmas, the glorious herald of the New Year, was at hand, when an event--still recounted by winter firesides, with a horror made delightful by the mellowing influence of years--occurred in the beautiful little town of Golden Friars, and signalized, as the scene of its catastrophe, the old inn known throughout a wide region of the Northumbrian counties as the George and Dragon.

Toby Crooke, the sexton, was lying dead in the old coach-house in the inn yard. The body had been discovered, only half an hour before this story begins, under strange circumstances, and in a place where it might have lain the better part of a week undisturbed; and a dreadful suspicion astounded the village of Golden Friars.

A wintry sunset was glaring through a gorge of the western mountains, turning into fire the twigs of the leafless elms, and all the tiny blades of grass on the green by which the quaint little town is surrounded. It is built of light, grey stone, with steep gables and slender chimneys rising with airy lightness from the level sward by the margin of the beautiful lake, and backed by the grand amphitheatre of the fells at the other side, whose snowy peaks show faintly against the sky, tinged with the vaporous red of the western light. As you descend towards the margin of the lake, and see Golden Friars, its taper chimneys and slender gables, its curious old inn and gorgeous sign, and over all the graceful tower and spire of the ancient church, at this hour or by moonlight, in the solemn grandeur and stillness of the natural scenery that surrounds it, it stands before you like a fairy town.

Toby Crooke, the lank sexton, now fifty or upwards, had passed an hour or two with some village cronies, over a solemn pot of purl, in the kitchen of that cosy hostelry, the night before. He generally turned in there at about seven o'clock, and heard the news. This contented him: for he talked little, and looked always surly.

Many things are now raked up and talked over about him.

In early youth, he had been a bit of a scamp. He broke his indentures, and ran away from his master, the tanner of Bryemere; he had got into fifty bad scrapes and out again; and, just as the little world of Golden Friars had come to the conclusion that it would be well for all parties--except, perhaps, himself--and a happy riddance for his afflicted mother, if he were sunk, with a gross of quart pots about his neck, in the bottom of the lake in which the grey gables, the elms, and the towering fells of Golden Friars are mirrored, he suddenly returned, a reformed man at the ripe age of forty.

For twelve years he had disappeared, and no one knew what had become of him. Then, suddenly, as I say, he reappeared at Golden Friars--a very black and silent man, sedate and orderly. His mother was dead and buried; but the "prodigal son" was received good-naturedly. The good vicar, Doctor Jenner, reported to his wife:

"His hard heart has been softened, dear Dolly. I saw him dry his eyes, poor fellow, at the sermon yesterday."

"I don't wonder, Hugh darling. I know the part--'There is joy in Heaven.' I am sure it was--wasn't it? It was quite beautiful. I almost cried myself."

The Vicar laughed gently, and stooped over her chair and kissed her, and patted her cheek fondly.

"You think too well of your old man's sermons," he said. "I preach, you see, Dolly, very much to the *poor*. If *they* understand me, I am pretty sure everyone else must; and I think that my simple style goes more home to both feelings and conscience--"

"You ought to have told me of his crying before. You *are* so eloquent," exclaimed Dolly Jenner. "No one preaches like my man. I have never heard such sermons."

Not many, we may be sure; for the good lady had not heard more than six from any other divine for the last twenty years.

The personages of Golden Friars talked Toby Crooke over on his return. Doctor Lincote said:

"He must have led a hard life; he had *dried in* so, and got a good deal of hard muscle; and he rather fancied he had been soldiering--he stood like a soldier; and the mark over his right eye looked like a gunshot."

People might wonder how he could have survived a gunshot over the eye; but was not Lincote a doctor--and an army doctor to boot--when he was young; and who, in Golden Friars, could dispute with him on points of surgery? And I believe the truth is, that this mark had been really made by a pistol bullet.

Mr. Jarlcot, the attorney, would "go bail" he had picked up some sense in his travels; and honest Turnbull, the host of the George and Dragon, said heartily:

"We must look out something for him to put his hand to. *Now's* the time to make a man of him."

The end of it was that he became, among other things, the sexton of Golden Friars.

He was a punctual sexton. He meddled with no other person's business; but he was a silent man, and by no means popular. He was reserved in company; and he used to walk alone by the shore of the lake, while other fellows played at fives or skittles; and when he visited the kitchen of the George, he had his liquor to himself, and in the midst of the general talk was a saturnine listener. There was something sinister in this man's face; and when things went wrong with him, he could look dangerous enough.

There were whispered stories in Golden Friars about Toby Crooke. Nobody could say how they got there. Nothing is more mysterious than the spread of rumour. It is like a vial poured on the air. It travels, like an epidemic, on the sightless currents of the atmosphere, or by the laws of a telluric influence equally intangible. These stories treated, though darkly, of the long period of his absence from his native village; but they took no well-defined shape, and no one could refer them to any authentic source.

The Vicar's charity was of the kind that thinketh no evil; and in such cases he always insisted on proof. Crooke was, of course, undisturbed in his office.

On the evening before the tragedy came to light--trifles are always remembered after the catastrophe--a boy, returning along the margin of the mere, passed him by seated on a prostrate trunk of a tree, under the "bield" of a rock, counting silver money. His lean body and limbs were bent together, his knees were up to his chin, and his long fingers were telling the coins over hurriedly in the hollow of his other hand. He glanced at the boy, as the old English saying is, like "the devil looking over Lincoln." But a black and sour look from Mr. Crooke, who never had a smile for a child nor a greeting for a wayfarer, was nothing strange.

Toby Crooke lived in the grey stone house, cold and narrow, that stands near the church porch, with the window of its staircase looking out into the churchyard, where so much of his labour, for many a day, had been expended. The greater part of this house was untenanted.

The old woman who was in charge of it slept in a settle-bed, among broken stools, old sacks, rotten chests and other rattle-traps, in the small room at the rear of the house, floored with tiles.

At what time of the night she could not tell, she awoke, and saw a man, with his hat on, in her room. He had a candle in his hand, which he shaded with his coat from her eye; his back was towards her, and he was rummaging in the drawer in which she usually kept her money.

Having got her quarter's pension of two pounds that day, however, she had placed it, folded in a rag, in the corner of her tea caddy, and locked it up in the "eat-malison" or cupboard.

She was frightened when she saw the figure in her room, and she could not tell whether her visitor might not have made his entrance from the contiguous churchyard. So, sitting bolt upright in her bed, her grey hair almost lifting her kerchief off her head, and all over in "a fit o' t' creepins," as she expressed it, she demanded:

"In God's name, what want ye thar?"

"Whar's the peppermint ye used to hev by ye, woman? I'm bad wi' an inward pain."

"It's all gane a month sin'," she answered; and offered to make him a "het" drink if he'd get to his room.

But he said:

"Never mind, I'll try a mouthful o' gin."

And, turning on his heel, he left her.

In the morning the sexton was gone. Not only in his lodging was there no account of him, but, when inquiry began to be extended, nowhere in the village of Golden Friars could he be found.

Still he might have gone off, on business of his own, to some distant village, before the town was stirring; and the sexton had no near kindred to trouble their

{71}

heads about him. People, therefore, were willing to wait, and take his return ultimately for granted.

At three o'clock the good Vicar, standing at his hall door, looking across the lake towards the noble fells that rise, steep and furrowed, from that beautiful mere, saw two men approaching across the green, in a straight line, from a boat that was moored at the water's edge. They were carrying between them something which, though not very large, seemed ponderous.

"Ye'll ken this, sir," said one of the boatmen as they set down, almost at his feet, a small church bell, such as in old-fashioned chimes yields the treble notes.

"This won't be less nor five stean. I ween it's fra' the church steeple yon."

"What! one of our church bells?" ejaculated the Vicar--for a moment lost in horrible amazement. "Oh, no!--no, that can't possibly be! Where did you find it?"

He had found the boat, in the morning, moored about fifty yards from her moorings where he had left it the night before, and could not think how that came to pass; and now, as he and his partner were about to take their oars, they discovered this bell in the bottom of the boat, under a bit of canvas, also the sexton's pick and spade--"tom-spey'ad," they termed that peculiar, broad-bladed implement.

"Very extraordinary! We must try whether there is a bell missing from the tower," said the Vicar, getting into a fuss. "Has Crooke come back yet? Does anyone know where he is?"

The sexton had not yet turned up.

"That's odd--that's provoking," said the Vicar. "However, my key will let us in. Place the bell in the hall while I get it; and then we can see what all this means."

To the church, accordingly, they went, the Vicar leading the way, with his own key in his hand. He turned it in the lock, and stood in the shadow of the ground porch, and shut the door.

A sack, half full, lay on the ground, with open mouth, a piece of cord lying beside it. Something clanked within it as one of the men shoved it aside with his clumsy shoe.

The Vicar opened the church door and peeped in. The dusky glow from the western sky, entering through a narrow window, illuminated the shafts and arches, the old oak carvings, and the discoloured monuments, with the melancholy glare of a dying fire.

The Vicar withdrew his head and closed the door. The gloom of the porch was deeper than ever as, stooping, he entered the narrow door that opened at the foot of the winding stair that leads to the first loft; from which a rude ladder-stair of wood, some five and twenty feet in height, mounts through a trap to the ringers' loft.

Up the narrow stairs the Vicar climbed, followed by his attendants, to the first loft. It was very dark: a narrow bow-slit in the thick wall admitted the only light they had to guide them. The ivy leaves, seen from the deep shadow, flashed and flickered redly, and the sparrows twittered among them.

"Will one of you be so good as to go up and count the bells, and see if they are all right?" said the Vicar. "There should be--"

"Agoy! what's that?" exclaimed one of the men, recoiling from the foot of the ladder.

"By Jen!" ejaculated the other, in equal surprise.

"Good gracious!" gasped the Vicar, who, seeing indistinctly a dark mass lying on the floor, had stooped to examine it, and placed his hand upon a cold, dead face.

The men drew the body into the streak of light that traversed the floor.

It was the corpse of Toby Crooke! There was a frightful scar across his forehead.

The alarm was given. Doctor Lincote, and Mr. Jarlcot, and Turnbull, of the George and Dragon, were on the spot immediately; and many curious and horrified spectators of minor importance.

The first thing ascertained was that the man must have been many hours dead. The next was that his skull was fractured, across the forehead, by an awful blow. The next was that his neck was broken.

His hat was found on the floor, where he had probably laid it, with his handkerchief in it.

The mystery now began to clear a little; for a bell--one of the chime hung in the tower--was found where it had rolled to, against the wall, with blood and hair on the rim of it, which corresponded with the grizzly fracture across the front of his head.

The sack that lay in the vestibule was examined, and found to contain all the church plate; a silver salver that had disappeared, about a month before, from Dr. Lincote's store of valuables; the Vicar's gold pencil-case, which he thought he had forgot in the vestry book; silver spoons, and various other contributions, levied from time to time off a dozen different households, the mysterious disappearance of which spoils had, of late years, begun to make the honest little community uncomfortable. Two bells had been taken down from the chime; and now the shrewd part of the assemblage, putting things together, began to comprehend the nefarious plans of the sexton, who lay mangled and dead on the floor of the tower, where only two days ago he had tolled the holy bell to call the good Christians of Golden Friars to worship.

The body was carried into the yard of the George and Dragon and laid in the old coach-house; and the townsfolk came grouping in to have a peep at the corpse, and stood round, looking darkly, and talking as low as if they were in a church.

The Vicar, in gaiters and slightly shovel hat, stood erect, as one in a little circle of notables--the doctor, the attorney, Sir Geoffrey Mardykes, who happened to be in the town, and Turnbull, the host--in the centre of the paved yard, they having made an inspection of the body, at which troops of the village stragglers, to-ing and fro-ing, were gaping and frowning as they whispered their horrible conjectures.

{73}

"What d'ye think o' that?" said Tom Scales, the old hostler of the George, looking pale, with a stern, faint smile on his lips, as he and Dick Linklin sauntered out of the coach-house together.

"The deaul will hev his ain noo," answered Dick, in his friend's ear. "T' sexton's got a craigthraw like he gav' the lass over the clints of Scarsdale; ye mind what the ald soger telt us when he hid his face in the kitchen of the George here? By Jen! I'll ne'er forget that story."

"I ween 'twas all true enough," replied the hostler; "and the sizzup he gav' the sleepin' man wi' t' poker across the forehead. See whar the edge o' t' bell took him, and smashed his ain, the self-same lids. By ma sang, I wonder the deaul did na carry awa' his corpse i' the night, as he did wi' Tam Lunder's at Mooltern Mill."

"Hout, man, who ever sid t' deaul inside o' a church?"

"The corpse is ill-faur'd enew to scare Satan himsel', for that matter; though it's true what you say. Ay, ye're reet tul a trippet, thar; for Beelzebub dar'n't show his snout inside the church, not the length o' the black o' my nail."

While this discussion was going on, the gentlefolk who were talking the matter over in the centre of the yard had dispatched a message for the coroner all the way to the town of Hextan.

The last tint of sunset was fading from the sky by this time; so, of course, there was no thought of an inquest earlier than next day.

In the meantime it was horribly clear that the sexton had intended to rob the church of its plate, and had lost his life in the attempt to carry the second bell, as we have seen, down the worn ladder of the tower. He had tumbled backwards and broken his neck upon the floor of the loft; and the heavy bell, in its fall, descended with its edge across his forehead.

Never was a man more completely killed by a double catastrophe, in a moment.

The bells and the contents of the sack, it was surmised, he meant to have conveyed across the lake that night, and with the help of his spade and pick to have buried them in Clousted Forest, and returned, after an absence of but a few hours--as he easily might--before morning, unmissed and unobserved. He would no doubt, having secured his booty, have made such arrangements as would have made it appear that the church had been broken into. He would, of course, have taken all measures to divert suspicion from himself, and have watched a suitable opportunity to repossess himself of the buried treasure and dispose of it in safety.

And now came out, into sharp relief, all the stories that had, one way or other, stolen after him into the town. Old Mrs. Pullen fainted when she saw him, and told Doctor Lincote, after, that she thought he was the highwayman who fired the shot that killed the coachman the night they were robbed on Hounslow Heath. There were the stories also told by the wayfaring old soldier with the wooden leg, and fifty others, up to this more than half disregarded, but which now seized on the popular belief with a startling grasp.

The fleeting light soon expired, and twilight was succeeded by the early night

The inn yard gradually became quiet; and the dead sexton lay alone, in the dark, on his back, locked up in the old coach-house, the key of which was safe in the pocket of Tom Scales, the trusty old hostler of the George.

It was about eight o'clock, and the hostler, standing alone on the road in the front of the open door of the George and Dragon, had just smoked his pipe out. A bright moon hung in the frosty sky. The fells rose from the opposite edge of the lake like phantom mountains. The air was stirless. Through the boughs and sprays of the leafless elms no sigh or motion, however hushed, was audible. Not a ripple glimmered on the lake, which at one point only reflected the brilliant moon from its dark blue expanse like burnished steel. The road that runs by the inn door, along the margin of the lake, shone dazzlingly white.

White as ghosts, among the dark holly and juniper, stood the tall piers of the Vicar's gate, and their great stone balls, like heads, overlooking the same road, a few hundred yards up the lake, to the left. The early little town of Golden Friars was quiet by this time. Except for the townsfolk who were now collected in the kitchen of the inn itself, no inhabitant was now outside his own threshold.

Tom Scales was thinking of turning in. He was beginning to fell a little queer. He was thinking of the sexton, and could not get the fixed features of the dead man out of his head, when he heard the sharp though distant ring of a horse's hoof upon the frozen road. Tom's instinct apprized him of the approach of a guest to the George and Dragon. His experienced ear told him that the horseman was approaching by the Dardale road, which, after crossing that wide and dismal moss, passes the southern fells by Dunner Cleugh and finally enters the town of Golden Friars by joining the Mardykes road, at the edge of the lake, close to the gate of the Vicar's house.

A clump of tall trees stood at this point; but the moon shone full upon the road and cast their shadow backward.

The hoofs were plainly coming at a gallop, with a hollow rattle. The horseman was a long time in appearing. Tom wondered how he had heard the sound--so sharply frosty as the air was--so very far away.

He was right in his guess. The visitor was coming over the mountainous road from Dardale Moss; and he now saw a horseman, who must have turned the corner of the Vicar's house at the moment when his eye was wearied; for when he saw him for the first time he was advancing, in the hazy moonlight, like the shadow of a cavalier, at a gallop, upon the level strip of road that skirts the margin of the mere, between the George and the Vicar's piers.

The hostler had not long to wonder why the rider pushed his beast at so furious a pace, and how he came to have heard him, as he now calculated, at least three miles away. A very few moments sufficed to bring horse and rider to the inn door.

It was a powerful black horse, something like the great Irish hunter that figured a hundred years ago, and would carry sixteen stone with ease across country. It would have made a grand charger. Not a hair turned. It snorted, it pawed, it arched its neck; then threw back its ears and down its head, and looked ready to lash, and then to rear; and seemed impatient to be off again, and incapable of standing quiet for a moment.

The rider got down

As light as shadow falls.

But he was a tall, sinewy figure. He wore a cape or short mantle, a cocked hat, and a pair of jack-boots, such as held their ground in some primitive corners of England almost to the close of the last century.

"Take him, lad," said he to old Scales. "You need not walk or wisp him--he never sweats or tires. Give him his oats, and let him take his own time to eat them. House!" cried the stranger--in the old-fashioned form of summons which still lingered, at that time, in out-of-the-way places--in a deep and piercing voice.

As Tom Scales led the horse away to the stables it turned its head towards its master with a short, shill neigh.

"About *your* business, old gentleman--we must not go too fast," the stranger cried back again to his horse, with a laugh as harsh and piercing; and he strode into the house.

The hostler led this horse into the inn yard. In passing, it sidled up to the coach-house gate, within which lay the dead sexton--snorted, pawed and lowered its head suddenly, with ear close to the plank, as if listening for a sound from within; then uttered again the same short, piercing neigh.

The hostler was chilled at this mysterious coquetry with the dead. He liked the brute less and less every minute.

In the meantime, its master had proceeded.

"I'll go to the inn kitchen," he said, in his startling bass, to the drawer who met him in the passage.

And on he went, as if he had known the place all his days: not seeming to hurry himself--stepping leisurely, the servant thought--but gliding on at such a rate, nevertheless, that he had passed his guide and was in the kitchen of the George before the drawer had got much more than half-way to it.

A roaring fire of dry wood, peat and coal lighted up this snug but spacious apartment--flashing on pots and pans, and dressers high-piled with pewter plates and dishes; and making the uncertain shadows of the long "hanks" of onions and many a flitch and ham, depending from the ceiling, dance on its glowing surface.

The doctor and the attorney, even Sir Geoffrey Mardykes, did not disdain on this occasion to take chairs and smoke their pipes by the kitchen fire, where they were in the thick of the gossip and discussion excited by the terrible event.

The tall stranger entered uninvited.

He looked like a gaunt, athletic Spaniard of forty, burned half black in the sun, with a bony, flattened nose. A pair of fierce black eyes were just visible under the edge of his hat; and his mouth seemed divided, beneath the moustache, by the deep scar of a hare-lip.

Sir Geoffrey Mardykes and the host of the George, aided by the doctor and the attorney, were discussing and arranging, for the third or fourth time, their theories about the death and the probable plans of Toby Crooke, when the stranger entered.

The new-comer lifted his hat, with a sort of smile, for a moment from his black head.

"What do you call this place, gentlemen?" asked the stranger.

"The town of Golden Friars, sir," answered the doctor politely.

"The George and Dragon, sir: Anthony Turnbull, at your service," answered mine host, with a solemn bow, at the same moment--so that the two voices went together, as if the doctor and the innkeeper were singing a catch.

"The George and the Dragon," repeated the horseman, expanding his long hands over the fire which he had approached. "Saint George, King George, the Dragon, the Devil: it is a very grand idol, that outside your door, sir. You catch all sorts of worshippers--courtiers, fanatics, scamps: all's fish, eh? Everybody welcome, provided he drinks like one. Suppose you brew a bowl or two of punch. I'll stand it. How many are we? *Here*--count, and let us have enough. Gentlemen, I mean to spend the night here, and my horse is in the stable. What holiday, fun, or fair has got so many pleasant faces together? When I last called here--for, now I bethink me, I have seen the place before--you all looked sad. It was on a Sunday, that dismalest of holidays; and it would have been positively melancholy only that your sexton--that saint upon earth--Mr. Crooke, was here." He was looking round, over his shoulder, and added: "Ha! don't I see him there?"

Frightened a good deal were some of the company. All gaped in the direction in which, with a nod, he turned his eyes.

"He's *not* thar--he *can't* be thar--we *see* he's not thar," said Turnbull, as dogmatically as old Joe Willet might have delivered himself--for he did not care that the George should earn the reputation of a haunted house. "He's met an accident, sir: he's dead--he's elsewhere--and therefore can't be here."

Upon this the company entertained the stranger with the narrative--which they made easy by a division of labour, two or three generally speaking at a time, and no one being permitted to finish a second sentence without finding himself corrected and supplanted.

"The man's in Heaven, so sure as you're not," said the traveller so soon as the story was ended. "What! he was fiddling with the church bell, was he, and d----d for that--eh? Landlord, get us some drink. A sexton d----d for pulling down a church bell he has been pulling at for ten years!"

"You came, sir, by the Dardale-road, I believe?" said the doctor (village folk are curious). "A dismal moss is Dardale Moss, sir; and a bleak clim' up the fells on t' other side."

"I say 'Yes' to all--from Dardale Moss, as black as pitch and as rotten as the grave, up that zigzag wall you call a road, that looks like chalk in the moonlight, through Dunner Cleugh, as dark as a coal-pit, and down here to the George and the Dragon, where you have a roaring fire, wise men, good punch--here it is--and a corpse in your coach-house. Where the carcase is, there will the eagles be gathered together. Come, landlord, ladle out the nectar. Drink, gentlemen--drink, all. Brew another bowl at the bar. How divinely it stinks of alcohol! I hope you like it, gentlemen: it smells all over of spices, like a mummy. Drink, friends. Ladle, landlord. Drink, all. Serve it out."

The guest fumbled in his pocket, and produced three guineas, which he slipped into Turnbull's fat palm.

"Let punch flow till that's out. I'm an old friend of the house. I call here, back and forward. I know you well, Turnbull, though you don't recognize me."

"You have the advantage of me, sir," said Mr. Turnbull, looking hard on that dark and sinister countenance--which, or the like of which, he could have sworn he had never seen before in his life. But he liked the weight and colour of his guineas, as he dropped them into his pocket. "I hope you will find yourself comfortable while you stay."

"You have given me a bedroom?"

"Yes, sir--the cedar chamber."

"I know it--the very thing. No--no punch for me. By and by, perhaps."

The talk went on, but the stranger had grown silent. He had seated himself on an oak bench by the fire, towards which he extended his feet and hands with seeming enjoyment; his cocked hat being, however, a little over his face.

Gradually the company began to thin. Sir Geoffrey Mardykes was the first to go; then some of the humbler townsfolk. The last bowl of punch was on its last legs. The stranger walked into the passage and said to the drawer:

"Fetch me a lantern. I must see my nag. Light it--hey! That will do. No--you need not come."

The gaunt traveller took it from the man's hand and strode along the passage to the door of the stableyard, which he opened and passed out.

Tom Scales, standing on the pavement, was looking through the stable window at the horses when the stranger plucked his shirtsleeve. With an inward shock the hostler found himself alone in presence of the very person he had been thinking of.

"I say--they tell me you have something to look at in there"--he pointed with his thumb at the old coach-house door. "Let us have a peep."

Tom Scales happened to be at that moment in a state of mind highly favourable to anyone in search of a submissive instrument. He was in great perplexity, and even perturbation. He suffered the stranger to lead him to the coach-house gate.

"You must come in and hold the lantern," said he. "I'll pay you handsomely."

The old hostler applied his key and removed the padlock.

"What are you afraid of? Step in and throw the light on his face," said the stranger grimly. "Throw open the lantern: stand *there*. Stoop over him a little--he won't bite you. Steady, or you may pass the night with him!"

    *   *   *   *   *

In the meantime the company at the George had dispersed; and, shortly after, Anthony Turnbull--who, like a good landlord, was always last in bed, and first up, in his house--was taking, alone, his last look round the kitchen before making his final visit to the stable-yard, when Tom Scales tottered into the kitchen, looking like death, his hair standing upright; and he sat down on an oak chair, all in a tremble, wiped his forehead with his hand, and, instead of speaking, heaved a great sigh or two.

It was not till after he had swallowed a dram of brandy that he found his voice, and said:

"We've the deaul himsel' in t' house! By Jen! ye'd best send fo t' sir" (the clergyman). "Happen he'll tak him in hand wi' holy writ, and send him elsewhidder deftly. Lord atween us and harm! I'm a sinfu' man. I tell ye, Mr. Turnbull, I dar' n't stop in t' George to-night under the same roof wi' him."

"Ye mean the ra-beyoned, black-feyaced lad, wi' the brocken neb? Why, that's a gentleman wi' a pocket ful o' guineas, man, and a horse worth fifty pounds!"

"That horse is no better nor his rider. The nags that were in the stable wi' him, they all tuk the creepins, and sweated like rain down a thack. I tuk them all out o' that, away from him, into the hack-stable, and I thocht I cud never get them past him. But that's not all. When I was keekin inta t' winda at the nags, he comes behint me and claps his claw on ma shouther, and he gars me gang wi' him, and open the aad coach-house door, and haad the cannle for him, till he pearked into the deed man't feyace; and, as God's my judge, I sid the corpse open its eyes and wark its mouth, like a man smoorin' and strivin' to talk. I cudna move or say a word, though I felt my hair rising on my heed; but at lang-last I gev a yelloch, and say I, 'La! what is that?' And he himsel' looked round on me, like the devil he is; and, wi' a skirl o' a laugh, he strikes the lantern out o' my hand. When I cum to myself we were outside the coach-house door. The moon was shinin' in, ad I cud see the corpse stretched on the table whar we left it; and he kicked the door to wi' a purr o' his foot. 'Lock it,' says he; and so I did. And here's the key for ye--tak it yoursel', sir. He offer'd me money: he said he'd mak me a rich man if I'd sell him the corpse, and help him awa' wi' it."

"Hout, man! What cud he want o' t' corpse? He's not doctor, to do a' that lids. He was takin' a rise out o' ye, lad," said Turnbull.

"Na, na--he wants the corpse. There's summat you a' me can't tell he wants to do wi' 't; and he'd liefer get it wi' sin and thievin', and the damage of my soul. He's one of them freytens a boo or a dobbies off Dardale Moss, that's always astir wi' the like after nightfall; unless--Lord save us!--he be the deaul himsel.'"

"Whar is he noo?" asked the landlord, who was growing uncomfortable.

"He spang'd up the back stair to his room. I wonder you didn't hear him trampin' like a wild horse; and he clapt his door that the house shook again--but Lord knows whar he is noo. Let us gang awa's up to the Vicar's, and gan *him* come down, and talk wi' him."

"Hoity toity, man--you're too easy scared," said the landlord, pale enough by this time. "'Twould be a fine thing, truly, to send abroad that the house was haunted by the deaul himsel'! Why, 'twould be the ruin o' the George. You're sure ye locked the door on the corpse?"

"Aye, sir--sartain."

"Come wi' me, Tom--we'll gi' a last look round the yard."

So, side by side, with many a jealous look right and left, and over their shoulders, they went in silence. On entering the old-fashioned quadrangle, surrounded by stables and other offices--built in the antique cagework fashion-- they stopped for a while under the shadow of the inn gable, and looked round the yard, and listened. All was silent--nothing stirring.

The stable lantern was lighted; and with it in his hand Tony Turnbull, holding Tom Scales by the shoulder, advanced. He hauled Tom after him for a step or two; then stood still and shoved him before him for a step or two more; and thus cautiously--as a pair of skirmishers under fire--they approached the coach-house door.

"There, ye see--all safe," whispered Tom, pointing to the lock, which hung-- distinct in the moonlight--in its place. "Cum back, I say!"

"Cum on, say I!" retorted the landlord valorously. "It would never do to allow any tricks to be played with the chap in there"--he pointed to the coachhouse door.

"The coroner here in the morning, and never a corpse to sit on!" He unlocked the padlock with these words, having handed the lantern to Tom. "Here, keck in, Tom," he continued; "ye hev the lantern--and see if all's as ye left it."

"Not me--na, not for the George and a' that's in it!" said Tom, with a shudder, sternly, as he took a step backward.

"What the--what are ye afraid on? Gi' me the lantern--it is all one: *I* will."

And cautiously, little by little, he opened the door; and, holding the lantern over his head in the narrow slit, he peeped in--frowning and pale--with one eye, as if he expected something to fly in his face. He closed the door without speaking, and locked it again.

"As safe as a thief in a mill," he whispered with a nod to his companion. And at that moment a harsh laugh overhead broke the silence startlingly, and set all the poultry in the yard gabbling.

"Thar he be!" said Tom, clutching the landlord's arm--"in the winda--see!"

The window of the cedar-room, up two pair of stairs, was open; and in the shadow a darker outline was visible of a man, with his elbows on the window-stone, looking down upon them.

"Look at his eyes--like two live coals!" gasped Tom.

The landlord could not see all this so sharply, being confused, and not so long-sighted as Tom.

"Time, sir," called Tony Turnbull, turning cold as he thought he saw a pair of eyes shining down redly at him--"time for honest folk to be in their beds, and asleep!"

"As sound as your sexton!" said the jeering voice from above.

"Come out of this," whispered the landlord fiercely to his hostler, plucking him hard by the sleeve.

They got into the house, and shut the door.

{80}

"I wish we were shot of him," said the landlord, with something like a groan, as he leaned against the wall of the passage. "I'll sit up, anyhow--and, Tom, you'll sit wi' me. Cum into the gun-room. No one shall steal the dead man out of my yard while I can draw a trigger."

The gun-room in the George is about twelve feet square. It projects into the stable-yard and commands a full view of the old coach-house; and, through a narrow side window, a flanking view of the back door of the inn, through which the yard is reached.

Tony Turnbull took down the blunderbuss--which was the great ordnance of the house--and loaded it with a stiff charge of pistol bullets.

He put on a great-coat which hung there, and was his covering when he went out at night, to shoot wild ducks. Tom made himself comfortable likewise. They then sat down at the window, which was open, looking into the yard, the opposite side of which was white in the brilliant moonlight.

The landlord laid the blunderbuss across his knees, and stared into the yard. His comrade stared also. The door of the gun-room was locked; so they felt tolerably secure.

An hour passed; nothing had occurred. Another. The clock struck one. The shadows had shifted a little; but still the moon shone full on the old coach-house, and the stable where the guest's horse stood.

Turnbull thought he heard a step on the back-stair. Tom was watching the back-door through the side window, with eyes glazing with the intensity of his stare. Anthony Turnbull, holding his breath, listened at the room door. It was a false alarm.

When he came back to the window looking into the yard:

"Hish! Look thar!" said he in a vehement whisper.

From the shadow at the left they saw the figure of the gaunt horseman, in short cloak and jack-boots, emerge. He pushed open the stable door, and led out his powerful black horse. He walked it across the front of the building till he reached the old coach-house door; and there, with its bridle on its neck, he left it standing, while he stalked to the yard gate; and, dealing it a kick with his heel, it sprang back with the rebound, shaking from top to bottom, and stood open. The stranger returned to the side of his horse; and the door which secured the corpse of the dead sexton seemed to swing slowly open of itself as he entered, and returned with the corpse in his arms, and swung it across the shoulders of the horse, and instantly sprang into the saddle.

"Fire!" shouted Tom, and bang went the blunderbuss with a stunning crack. A thousand sparrows' wings winnowed through the air from the thick ivy. The watch-dog yelled a furious bark. There was a strange ring and whistle in the air. The blunderbuss had burst to shivers right down to the very breech. The recoil rolled the inn-keeper upon his back on the floor, and Tom Scales was flung against the side of the recess of the window, which had saved him from a tumble as violent. In this position they heard the searing laugh of the departing horseman, and saw him ride out of the gate with his ghastly burden.

Perhaps some of my readers, like myself, have heard this story told by Roger Turnbull, now host of the George and Dragon, the grandson of the very Tony who then swayed the spigot and keys of that inn, in the identical kitchen of which the fiend treated so many of the neighbours to punch.

What infernal object was subserved by the possession of the dead villain's body, I have not learned. But a very curious story, in which a vampire resuscitation of Crooke the sexton figures, may throw a light upon this part of the tale.

The result of Turnbull's shot at the disappearing fiend certainly justifies old Andrew Moreton's dictum, which is thus expressed in his curious "History of Apparitions": "I warn rash brands who, pretending not to fear the devil, are for using the ordinary violences with him, which affect one man from another--or with an apparition, in which they may be sure to receive some mischief. I knew one fired a gun at an apparition and the gun burst in a hundred pieces in his hand; another struck at an apparition with a sword, and broke his sword in pieces and wounded his hand grievously; and 'tis next to madness for anyone to go that way to work with any spirit, be it angel or be it devil."

THE TAPESTRIED CHAMBER
Sir Walter Scott

EDITOR'S NOTE: The following story is not set during Christmas or even wintertime, but has found a special place in British culture as being one of the quintessential English ghost stories. A fan favorite, to this day it is still traditionally told or read in December.

ABOUT the end of the American war, when the officers of Lord Cornwallis's army which surrendered at Yorktown, and others, who had been made prisoners during the impolitic and ill-fated controversy, were returning to their own country, to relate their adventures and repose themselves after their fatigues, there was amongst them a general officer, to whom Miss S. gave the name of Browne, but merely, as I understood, to save the inconvenience of introducing a nameless agent in the narrative. He was an officer of merit, as well as a gentleman of high consideration for family and attainments.

Some business had carried General Browne upon a tour through the western counties, when, in the conclusion of a morning stage, he found himself in the vicinity of a small country town, which presented a scene of uncommon beauty and of a character peculiarly English.

The little town, with its stately old church whose tower bore testimony to the devotion of ages long past, lay amidst pasture and corn-fields of small extent, but bounded and divided with hedgerow timber of great age and size. There were few marks of modern improvement. The environs of the place intimated neither the solitude of decay, nor the bustle of novelty; the houses were old, but in good repair; and the beautiful little river murmured freely on its way to the left of the town, neither restrained by a dam, nor bordered by a towing-path.

Upon a gentle eminence, nearly a mile to the southward of the town, were seen amongst many venerable oaks and tangled thickets the turrets of a castle, as old as the wars of York and Lancaster, but which seemed to have received important alterations during the age of Elizabeth and her successors. It had not been a place of great size; but whatever accommodation it formerly afforded, was, it must be supposed, still to be obtained within its walls; at least, such was the inference which General Browne drew from observing the smoke arise merrily from several of the ancient wreathed and carved chimney-stalks.

The wall of the park ran alongside of the highway for two or three hundred yards, and, through the different points by which the eye found glimpses into the woodland scenery, it seemed to be well stocked. Other points of view opened in succession; now a full one, of the front of the old castle, and now a side glimpse at its particular towers; the former rich in all the bizarrerie of the Elizabethan school, while the simple and solid strength of other parts of the building seemed to show that they had been raised more for defence than ostentation.

Delighted with the partial glimpses which he obtained of the castle through the woods and glades by which this ancient feudal fortress was surrounded, our military traveller was determined to inquire whether it might not deserve a nearer view, and whether it contained family pictures or other objects of curiosity worthy of a stranger's visit, when, leaving the vicinity of the park, he rolled through a clean and well-paved street, and stopped at the door of a well-frequented inn.

Before ordering horses to proceed on his journey, General Browne made inquiries concerning the proprietor of the château which had so attracted his admiration, and was equally surprised and pleased at hearing in reply a nobleman named whom we shall call Lord Woodville. How fortunate! Much of Browne's early recollections, both at school and at college, had been connected with young Woodville, whom, by a few questions, he now ascertained to be the same with the owner of this fair domain. He had been raised to the peerage by the decease of his father a few months before, and, as the General learned from the landlord, the term of mourning being ended, was now taking possession of his paternal estate in the jovial season of merry autumn, accompanied by a select party of friends to enjoy the sports of a country famous for game.

This was delightful news to our traveller. Frank Woodville had been Richard Browne's fag at Eton, and his chosen intimate at Christ Church; their pleasures and their tasks had been the same; and the honest soldier's heart warmed to find his early friend in possession of so delightful a residence, and of an estate, as the landlord assured him with a nod and a wink, fully adequate to maintain and add to his dignity. Nothing was more natural than that the traveller should suspend a journey, which there was nothing to render hurried, to pay a visit to an old friend under such agreeable circumstances.

The fresh horses, therefore, had only the brief task of conveying the General's travelling-carriage to Woodville Castle. A porter admitted them at a modern Gothic lodge, built in that style to correspond with the castle itself, and at the same time rang a bell to give warning of the approach of visitors. Apparently the sound of the bell had suspended the separation of the company, bent on the various amusements of the morning; for, on entering the court of the château, several young men were lounging about in their sporting-dresses, looking at, and criticizing, the dogs which the keepers held in readiness to attend their pastime.

As General Browne alighted, the young lord came to the gate of the hall, and for an instant gazed, as at a stranger, upon the countenance of his friend, on which war, with its fatigues and its wounds, had made a great alteration. But the uncertainty lasted no longer than till the visitor had spoken, and the hearty greeting which followed was such as can only be exchanged betwixt those who have passed together merry days of careless boyhood or early youth.

"If I could have formed a wish, my dear Browne," said Lord Woodville, "it would have been to have you here, of all men, upon this occasion, which my friends are good enough to hold as a sort of holiday. Do not think you have been unwatched during the years you have been absent from us. I have traced you through your dangers, your triumphs, your misfortunes, and was delighted to see that, whether in victory or defeat, the name of my old friend was always distinguished with applause."

The General made a suitable reply, and congratulated his friend on his new dignities, and the possession of a place and domain so beautiful.

"Nay, you have seen nothing of it as yet," said Lord Woodville, "and I trust you do not mean to leave us till you are better acquainted with it. It is true, I confess, that my present party is pretty large, and the old house, like other places of the kind, does not possess so much accommodation as the extent of the outward walls appears to promise. But we can give you a comfortable old-fashioned room, and I venture to suppose that your campaigns have taught you to be glad of worse quarters."

The General shrugged his shoulders, and laughed. "I presume," he said, "the worst apartment in your château is considerably superior to the old tobacco-cask, in which I was fain to take up my night's lodging when I was in the Bush, as the Virginians call it, with the light corps. There I lay, like Diogenes himself, so delighted with my covering from the elements, that I made a vain attempt to have it rolled on to my next quarters; but my commander for the time would give way to no such luxurious provision, and I took farewell of my beloved cask with tears in my eyes."

"Well, then, since you do not fear your quarters," said Lord Woodville "you will stay with me a week at least. Of guns, dogs, fishing-rods, flies, and means of sport by sea and land, we have enough and to spare: you cannot pitch on an amusement, but we will pitch on the means of pursuing it. But if you prefer the gun and pointers, I will go with you myself, and see whether you have mended your shooting since you have been amongst the Indians of the back settlements."

The General gladly accepted his friendly host's proposal in all its points. After a morning of manly exercise, the company met at dinner, where it was the delight of Lord Woodville to conduce to the display of the high properties of his recovered friend, so as to recommend him to his guests, most of whom were persons of distinction. He led General Browne to speak of the scenes he had witnessed; and as every word marked alike the brave officer and the sensible man, who retained possession of his cool judgement under the most imminent dangers, the company looked upon the soldier with general respect, as on one who had proved himself possessed of an uncommon portion of personal courage--that attribute, of all others, of which everybody desires to be thought possessed.

The day at Woodville Castle ended as usual in such mansions. The hospitality stopped within the limits of good order; music, in which the young lord was a proficient, succeeded to the circulation of the bottle; cards and billiards, for those who preferred such amusements, were in readiness; but the exercise of the morning required early hours, and not long after eleven o'clock the guests began to retire to their several apartments.

The young lord himself conducted his friend, General Browne, to the chamber destined for him, which answered the description he had given of it, being comfortable, but old-fashioned. The bed was of the massive form used in the end of the seventeenth century, and the curtains of faded silk, heavily trimmed with tarnished gold. But then the sheets, pillows, and blankets looked delightful to the campaigner, when he thought of his "mansion, the cask."

There was an air of gloom in the tapestry hangings which, with their worn-out graces, curtained the walls of the little chamber, and gently undulated as the autumnal breeze found its way through the ancient lattice-window, which pattered and whistled as the air gained entrance. The toilet too, with its mirror, turbaned, after the manner of the beginning of the century, with a coiffure of murrey-coloured silk, and its hundred strange-shaped boxes, providing for arrangements which had been obsolete for more than fifty years, had an antique, and in so far a melancholy, aspect. But nothing could blaze more brightly and cheerfully than the two large wax candles; or if aught could rival them, it was the flaming bickering fagots in the chimney, that sent at once their gleam and their warmth through the snug apartment; which, notwithstanding the general antiquity of its appearance, was not wanting in the least convenience that modern habits rendered either necessary or desirable.

"This is an old-fashioned sleeping apartment, General," said the young lord; "but I hope you will find nothing that makes you envy your old tobacco-cask."

"I am not particular respecting my lodgings," replied the General; "yet were I to make any choice, I would prefer this chamber by many degrees, to the gayer and more modern rooms of your family mansion. Believe me that when I unite its modern air of comfort with its venerable antiquity, and recollect that it is your lordship's property, I shall feel in better quarters here, than if I were in the best hotel London could afford."

"I trust--I have no doubt--that you will find yourself as comfortable as I wish you, my dear General," said the young nobleman; and once more bidding his guest good night, he shook him by the hand and withdrew.

The General once more looked round him, and internally congratulating himself on his return to peaceful life, the comforts of which were endeared by the recollection of the hardships and dangers he had lately sustained, undressed himself, and prepared himself for a luxurious night's rest.

Here, contrary to the custom of this species of tale, we leave the General in possession of his apartment until the next morning.

The company assembled for breakfast at an early hour, but without the appearance of General Browne, who seemed the guest that Lord Woodville was desirous of honouring above all whom his hospitality had assembled around him. He more than once expressed surprise at the General's absence, and at length sent a servant to make inquiry after him. The man brought back information that General Browne had been walking abroad since an early hour of the morning, in defiance of the weather, which was misty and ungenial.

"The custom of a soldier," said the young nobleman to his friends: "many of them acquire habitual vigilance, and cannot sleep after the early hour at which their duty usually commands them to be alert."

Yet the explanation which Lord Woodville thus offered to the company seemed hardly satisfactory to his own mind, and it was in a fit of silence and abstraction that he awaited the return of the General. It took place near an hour after the breakfast-bell had rung. He looked fatigued and feverish. His hair, the powdering and arrangement of which was at this time one of the most important occupations of a man's whole day, and marked his fashion as much as, in the present time, the tying of a cravat or the want of one, was dishevelled, uncurled, void of powder, and dank with dew. His clothes were huddled on with a careless negligence, remarkable in a military man, whose real or supposed duties are usually held to include some attention to the toilet; and his looks were haggard and ghastly in a peculiar degree.

"So you have stolen a march upon us this morning, my dear General," said Lord Woodville; "or you have not found your bed so much to your mind as I had hoped and you seemed to expect. How did you rest last night?"

"Oh, excellently well--remarkably well--never better in my life!" said General Browne rapidly, and yet with an air of embarrassment which was obvious to his friend. He then hastily swallowed a cup of tea, and, neglecting or refusing whatever else was offered, seemed to fall into a fit of abstraction.

"You will take the gun to-day, General?" said his friend and host, but had to repeat the question twice ere he received the abrupt answer, "No, my Lord; I am sorry I cannot have the honour of spending another day with your lordship; my post horses are ordered, and will be here directly."

All who were present showed surprise, and Lord Woodville immediately replied, "Post horses, my good friend! What can you possibly want with them, when you promised to stay with me quietly for at least a week?"

"I believe," said the General, obviously much embarrassed, "that I might, in the pleasure of my first meeting with your lordship, have said something about stopping here a few days; but I have since found it altogether impossible."

"That is very extraordinary," answered the young nobleman. "You seemed quite disengaged yesterday, and you cannot have had a summons to-day; for our post has not come up from the town, and therefore you cannot have received any letters."

General Browne, without giving any further explanation, muttered something of indispensable business, and insisted on the absolute necessity of his departure in a manner which silenced all opposition on the part of his host, who saw that his resolution was taken, and forbore further importunity.

"At least, however," he said, "permit me, my dear Browne, since go you will or must, to show you the view from the terrace, which the mist that is now rising, will soon display."

He threw open a sash-window, and stepped down upon the terrace as he spoke. The General followed him mechanically, but seemed little to attend to what his host was saying, as, looking across an extended and rich prospect, he pointed out the different objects worthy of observation. Thus they moved on till Lord Woodville had attained his purpose of drawing his guest entirely apart from the rest of the company, when, turning round upon him with an air of great solemnity, he addressed him thus:

"Richard Browne, my old and very dear friend, we are now alone. Let me conjure you to answer me upon the word of a friend, and the honour of a soldier. How did you in reality rest during last night?"

"Most wretchedly indeed, my lord," answered the General, in the same tone of solemnity; "so miserably, that I would not run the risk of such a second night, not only for all the lands belonging to this castle, but for all the country which I see from this elevated point of view."

"This is most extraordinary," said the young lord, as if speaking to himself; "then there must be something in the reports concerning that apartment." Again turning to the General, he said, "For God's sake, my dear friend, be candid with me, and let me know the disagreeable particulars which have befallen you under a roof where, with consent of the owner, you should have met nothing save comfort."

The General seemed distressed by this appeal, and paused a moment before he replied. "My dear lord," he at length said, "what happened to me last night is of nature so peculiar and so unpleasant, that I could hardly bring myself to detail it even to your lordship, were it not that, independent of my wish to gratify any request of yours, I think that sincerity on my part may lead to some explanation about a circumstance equally painful and mysterious. To others, the communications I am about to make, might place me in the light of a weak-minded, superstitious fool who suffered his own imagination to delude and bewilder him; but you have known me in childhood and youth, and will not suspect me of having adopted in manhood the feelings and frailties from which my early years were free." Here he paused, and his friend replied:

"Do not doubt my perfect confidence in the truth of your communication, however strange it may be," replied Lord Woodville. "I know your firmness of disposition too well, to suspect you could be made the object of imposition, and am aware that your honour and your friendship will equally deter you from exaggerating whatever you may have witnessed."

"Well then," said the General, "I will proceed with my story as well as I can, relying upon your candour; and yet distinctly feeling that I would rather face a battery than recall to my mind the odious recollections of last night."

He paused a second time, and then perceiving that Lord Woodville remained silent and in an attitude of attention, he commenced, though not without obvious reluctance, the history of his night's adventures in the Tapestried Chamber.

"I undressed and went to bed, so soon as your lordship left me yesterday evening; but the wood in the chimney, which nearly fronted my bed, blazed brightly and cheerfully, and, aided by a hundred exciting recollections of my childhood and youth, which had been recalled by the unexpected pleasure of meeting your lordship, prevented me from falling immediately asleep. I ought, however, to say that these reflections were all of a pleasant and agreeable kind, grounded on a sense of having for a time exchanged the labour, fatigues, and dangers of my profession, for the enjoyments of a peaceful life, and the reunion of those friendly and affectionate ties which I had torn asunder at the rude summons of war.

"While such pleasing reflections were stealing over my mind, and gradually lulling me to slumber, I was suddenly aroused by a sound like that of the rustling of a silken gown, and the tapping of a pair of high-heeled shoes, as if a woman were walking in the apartment. Ere I could draw the curtain to see what the matter

{88}

was, the figure of a little woman passed between the bed and the fire. The back of this form was turned to me, and I could observe, from the shoulders and neck, it was that of an old woman, whose dress was an old-fashioned gown, which, I think, ladies call a sacque--that is, a sort of robe, completely loose in the body, but gathered into broad plaits upon the neck and shoulders, which fall down to the ground, and terminate in a species of train.

"I thought the intrusion singular enough, but never harboured for a moment the idea that what I saw was anything more than the mortal form of some old woman about the establishment, who had a fancy to dress like her grandmother, and who, having perhaps (as your lordship mentioned that you were rather straitened for room) been dislodged from her chamber for my accommodation, had forgotten the circumstance, and returned by twelve to her old haunt. Under this persuasion I moved myself in bed and coughed a little, to make the intruder sensible of my being in possession of the premises. She turned slowly round, but gracious Heaven! My lord, what a countenance did she display to me!

"There was no longer any question what she was, or any thought of her being a living being. Upon a face which wore the fixed features of a corpse, were imprinted the traces of the vilest and most hideous passions which had animated her while she lived. The body of some atrocious criminal seemed to have been given up from the grave, and the soul restored from the penal fire, in order to form, for a space, a union with the ancient accomplice of its guilt. I started up in bed, and sat upright, supporting myself on my palms, as I gazed on this horrible spectre. The hag made, as it seemed, a single and swift stride to the bed where I lay, and squatted herself down upon it, in precisely the same attitude which I had assumed in the extremity of horror, advancing her diabolical countenance within half a yard of mine, with a grin which seemed to intimate the malice and the derision of an incarnate fiend."

Here General Browne stopped, and wiped from his brow the cold perspiration with which the recollection of his horrible vision had covered it.

"My lord," he said, "I am no coward. I have been in all the mortal dangers incidental to my profession, and I may truly boast that no man ever knew Richard Browne dishonour the sword he wears; but in these horrible circumstances, under the eyes, and as it seemed, almost in the grasp of an incarnation of an evil spirit, all firmness forsook me, all manhood melted from me like wax in the furnace, and I felt my hair individually bristle. The current of my life-blood ceased to flow, and I sank back in a swoon, as very a victim to panic terror as ever was a village girl or a child of ten years old. How long I lay in this condition I cannot pretend to guess.

"But I was roused by the castle clock striking one, so loud that it seemed as if it were in the very room. It was some time before I dared open my eyes, lest they should again encounter the horrible spectacle. When, however, I summoned courage to look up, she was no longer visible. My first idea was to pull my bell, wake the servants, and remove to a garret or a hay-loft, to be ensured against a second visitation. Nay, I will confess the truth, that my resolution was altered, not by the shame of exposing myself, but by the very fear that, as the bell-cord hung by the chimney, I might, in making my way to it, be again crossed by the fiendish hag, who, I figured to myself, might be still lurking about some corner of the apartment.

"I will not pretend to describe what hot and cold fever-fits tormented me for the rest of the night, through broken sleep, weary vigils, and that dubious state which forms the neutral ground between them. An hundred terrible objects appeared to haunt me; but there was the great difference betwixt the vision which I have described, and those which followed, that I knew the last to be deceptions of my own fancy and overexcited nerves.

"Day at last appeared, and I rose from my bed ill in health, and humiliated in mind. I was ashamed of myself as a man and a soldier, and still more so, at feeling my own extreme desire to escape from the haunted apartment, which, however, conquered all other considerations; so that, huddling on my clothes with the most careless haste, I made my escape from your lordship's mansion, to seek in the open air some relief to my nervous system, shaken as it was by this horrible rencountre with a visitant, for such I must believe her, from the other world. Your lordship has now heard the cause of my discomposure, and of my sudden desire to leave your hospitable castle. In other places I trust we may often meet; but God protect me from ever spending a second night under that roof!"

Strange as the General's tale was, he spoke with such a deep air of conviction, that it cut short all the usual commentaries which are made on such stories. Lord Woodville never once asked him if he was sure he did not dream of the apparition, or suggested any of the possibilities by which it is fashionable to explain supernatural appearances, as wild vagaries of the fancy or deceptions of the optic nerves. On the contrary, he seemed deeply impressed with the truth and reality of what he had heard; and, after a considerable pause, regretted, with much appearance of sincerity, that his early friend should in his house have suffered so severely.

"I am the more sorry for your pain, my dear Browne," he continued, "that it is the unhappy, though most unexpected, result of an experiment of my own. You must know that, for my father and grandfather's time, at least, the apartment which was assigned to you last night had been shut on account of reports that it was disturbed by supernatural sights and noises. When I came, a few weeks since, into possession of the estate, I thought the accommodation which the castle afforded for my friends was not extensive enough to permit the inhabitants of the invisible world to retain possession of a comfortable sleeping-apartment. I therefore caused the Tapestried Chamber, as we call it, to be opened; and without destroying its air of antiquity, I had such new articles of furniture placed in it as became the modern times.

"Yet, as the opinion that the room was haunted very strongly prevailed among the domestics, and was also known in the neighbourhood and to many of my friends, I feared some prejudice might be entertained by the first occupant of the Tapestried Chamber, which might tend to revive the evil report which it had laboured under, and so disappoint my purpose of rendering it a useful part of the house. I must confess, my dear Browne, that your arrival yesterday, agreeable to me for a thousand reasons besides, seemed the most favourable opportunity of removing the unpleasant rumours which attached to the room, since your courage was indubitable, and your mind free of any preoccupation on the subject. I could not, therefore, have chosen a more fitting subject for my experiment."

"Upon my life," said General Browne, somewhat hastily, "I am infinitely obliged to your lordship--very particularly indebted indeed. I am likely to remember for some time the consequences of the experiment, as your lordship is pleased to call it."

"Nay, now you are unjust, my dear friend," said Lord Woodville. "You have only to reflect for a single moment, in order to be convinced that I could not augur the possibility of the pain to which you have been so unhappily exposed. I was yesterday morning a complete sceptic on the subject of supernatural appearances. Nay, I am sure that, had I told you what was said about that room, those very reports would have induced you, by your own choice, to select it for your accommodation. It was my misfortune, perhaps my error, but really cannot be termed my fault, that you have been afflicted so strangely."

"Strangely indeed!" said the General, resuming his good temper; "and I acknowledge that I have no right to be offended with your lordship for treating me like what I used to think myself, a man of some firmness and courage. But I see my post-horses are arrived, and I must not detain your lordship from your amusement."

"Nay, my old friend," said Lord Woodville, "since you cannot stay with us another day, which, indeed, I can no longer urge, give me at least half an hour more. You used to love pictures, and I have a gallery of portraits, some of them by Vandyke, representing ancestry to whom this property and castle formerly belonged. I think that several of them will strike you as possessing merit."

General Browne accepted the invitation, though somewhat unwillingly. It was evident he was not to breathe freely or at ease until he left Woodville Castle far behind him. He could not refuse his friend's invitation, however; and the less so, that he was a little ashamed of the peevishness which he had displayed towards his well-meaning entertainer.

The general, therefore, followed Lord Woodville through several rooms, into a long gallery hung with pictures, which the latter pointed out to his guest, telling the names, and giving some account, of the personages whose portraits presented themselves in progression. General Browne was but little interested in the details which these accounts conveyed to him. They were, indeed, of the kind which are usually found in an old family gallery. Here was a cavalier who had ruined the estate in the royal cause; there, a fine lady who had reinstated it by contracting a match with a wealthy Roundhead. There hung a gallant who had been in danger for corresponding with the exiled court at St. Germain's; here, one who had taken arms for William at the Revolution; and there, a third that had thrown his weight alternately into the scale of Whig and Tory.

{91}

While Lord Woodville was cramming these words into his guest's ear, "against the stomach of his sense," they gained the middle of the gallery, when he beheld General Browne suddenly start, and assume an attitude of the utmost surprise, not unmixed with fear, as his eyes were caught and suddenly riveted by a portrait of an old lady in a sacque, the fashionable dress of the end of the 17th century.

"There she is!" he exclaimed--"there she is, in form and features, though inferior in demoniac expression to the accursed hag who visited me last night!"

"If that be the case," said the young nobleman, "there can remain no longer any doubt of the horrible reality of your apparition. That is the picture of a wretched ancestress of mine, of whose crimes a black and fearful catalogue is recorded in a family history in my charter-chest. The recital of them would be too horrible; it is enough to say, that in yon fatal apartment incest and unnatural murder were committed. I will restore it to the solitude to which the better judgement of those who preceded me had consigned it; and never shall any one, so long as I can prevent it, be exposed to a repetition of the supernatural horrors which could shake such courage as yours."

Thus the friends, who had met with such glee, parted in a very different mood--Lord Woodville to command the Tapestried Chamber to be unmantled and the door built up; and General Browne to seek in some less beautiful country, and with some less dignified friend, forgetfulness of the painful night which he had passed in Woodville Castle.

THE STEP
E. F. Benson

JOHN Cresswell was returning home one night from the Britannia Club at Alexandria, where, as was his custom three or four times in the week, he had dined very solidly and fluidly, and played bridge afterwards as long as a table could be formed. It had been rather an expensive evening, for all his skill at cards had been unable to cope with such a continuous series of ill-favoured hands as had been his. But he had consoled himself with reasonable doses of whisky, and now he stepped homewards in very cheerful spirits, for his business affairs were going most prosperously and a loss of twenty-five or thirty pounds to-night would be amply compensated for in the morning. Besides, his bridge-account for the year showed a credit which proved that cards were a very profitable pleasure.

It was a hot night of October, and, being a big plethoric man, he strolled at a very leisurely pace across the square and up the long street at the far end of which was his house. There were no taxis on the rank, or he would have taken one and saved himself this walk of nearly a mile; but he had no quarrel with that, for the night air with a breeze from the sea was refreshing after so long a session in a smoke-laden atmosphere. Above, a moon near to its full cast a very clear white light on his road. There was a narrow strip of sharp-cut shadow beneath the houses on his right, but the rest of the street and the pavement on the left of it, where he walked, were in bright illumination.

At first his way lay between rows of shops, European for the most part, with here and there a café where a few customers still lingered. Pleasant thoughts beguiled his progress; the Egyptian sugar-crop, in which he was much interested, had turned out very well and he saw a big profit on his options. Not less satisfactory were other businesses in which he did not figure so openly. He lent money, for instance, on a large scale, to the native population, and these operations extended far up the Nile. Only last week he had been at Luxor, where he had concluded a transaction of a very remunerative sort. He had made a loan some months ago to a small merchant there and now the appropriate interest on this was in default: in consequence the harvest of a very fruitful acreage of sugar-cane was his. A similar and even richer windfall had just come his way in Alexandria, for he had advanced money a year ago to a Levantine tobacco merchant on the security of his freehold store. This had brought him in very handsome interest, but a day or two ago the unfortunate fellow had failed, and Cresswell owned a most desirable freehold. The whole affair had been very creditable to his enterprise and sagacity, for he had privately heard that the municipality was intending to lay out the neighbourhood, a slum at present, where this store was situated, in houses of flats, and make it a residential quarter, and his newly acquired freehold would thus become a valuable property.

At present the tobacco merchant lived with his family in holes and corners of the store, and they must be evicted to-morrow morning. John Cresswell had already arranged for this, and had told the man that he would have to quit: he would go round there in the forenoon and see that they and their sticks of furniture were duly bundled out into the street. He would see personally that this was done, and looked forward to doing so. The old couple were beastly creatures, the woman a perfect witch who eyed him and muttered, but there was a daughter who was not ill-looking, and someone of the beggared family would be obliged to earn bread. He did not dwell on this, but the thought just flitted through his brain.... Then doors would be locked and windows barred in the store that was now his, and he would lunch at the club afterwards. He was popular there; he had a jovial geniality about him, and a habit of offering drinks before they could be offered to him. That, too, was good for business.

Ten minutes' strolling brought him to the end of the shops and cafés that formed the street, and now the road ran between residential houses, each detached and with a space of garden surrounding it, where dry-leaved palms rattled in this wind from the sea. He was approaching the flamboyant Roman Catholic church, to which was attached a monastic establishment, a big white barrack-looking house where the Brothers of Poverty or some such order lived. Something to do with St. Mark, he vaguely remembered, who by tradition had brought Christianity to Egypt nearly nineteen hundred years ago. Often he met one of these odd sandal-footed creatures with his brown habit, his rosary and his cowled head going in or out of their gate, or toiling in their garden. He did not like them: lousy fellows he would have called them. Sometimes in their mendicant errands they came to his door asking alms for the indigent Copts. Not long ago he had found one actually ringing the bell of his front door, instead of going humbly round to the back, as befitted his quality, and Cresswell told him that he would loose his bulldog on the next of their breed who ventured within his garden gate. How the fellow had skipped off when he heard talk of the dog! He dropped one of his sandals in his haste to be gone, and not sparing the time to adjust it again, had hopped and hobbled over the sharp gravel to gain the street. Cresswell had laughed aloud to see his precipitancy, and the best of the joke was that he had not got any sort of dog on his premises at all. At the remembrance of that humorous incident he grinned to himself as he passed the porch of the church.

He paused a moment to mop his forehead and to light a cigarette, looking about him in great good humour. Before him and behind the road was quite empty: lights gleamed behind venetian shutters from a few upper windows of the houses, but all the world was in bed or on its way there. There were still three or four hundred yards to go before he came to his house, and as he turned his face homewards again and walked a little more briskly, he heard a step behind him, sharp and distinct, not far in his rear. He paid no heed: someone, late like himself, was going home, walking in the same direction, for the step followed him.

His cigarette was ill-lit; a little core of burning stuff fell from it on to the pavement and he stopped to rekindle it. Possibly some subconscious region of his mind was occupied with the step which had sprung up so oddly behind him in the empty street, for while he was getting his cigarette to burn again he noticed that

{94}

the step had ceased. It was hardly worth while to turn round (so little the matter interested him), but a casual glance showed him that the wayfarer must have turned into one of the houses he had just passed, for the whole street, brightly moonlit, was as empty as when he surveyed it a few minutes before. Soon he came to his own gate and clanged it behind him.

The eviction of the Levantine merchant took place in the morning, and Cresswell watched his porters carrying out the tawdry furniture—a few tables, a few chairs, a sofa covered in tattered crimson plush, a couple of iron bedsteads, a bundle of dirty sheets and blankets. He was not certain in his own mind whether these paltry articles did not by rights belong to him, but they were fit for nothing except the dust-heap, and he had no use for them. There they stood in the clean bright sunshine, rubbish and no more, blocking the pavement, and a policeman told their owner that he had best clear them away at once unless he wanted trouble. There was the usual scene to which he was quite accustomed: the man's wife snivelling and slovenly, witch-like and early old, knelt and kissed his hand, and wheezingly besought his compassion. She called him "Excellency," she promised him her prayers, which he desired as little as her pots and pans. She invoked blessings on his head, for she knew that out of his pity he would give them a little more time. They had nowhere to go nor any roof to shelter them: her husband had money owing to him, and he would collect these debts and pay his default as sure as there was a God in heaven. This was a changed note from her mutterings of yesterday, but of course Cresswell had a deaf ear for this oily rigmarole, and presently he went into the store to see that everything had been removed.

It was in a filthy, dirty state; floors were rotten and the paint peeling, but the whole place would soon be broken up and he was not going to spend a piastre on it, so long as the ground on which it stood was his. Then he saw to the barring of the windows and the doors, and he gave the policeman quite a handsome tip to keep an eye on the place and take care that these folk did not get ingress again. When he came out, he found that the old man had procured a handcart, and he and his son were loading it up, so of course they had somewhere to go: it was all a pack of lies about their being homeless. The old hag was squatting against the house wall, but now there were no more prayers and blessings for him, and she had taken to her mutterings again. As for the daughter, seen in the broad daylight, she had a handsome face, but she was sullen and dirty and forbidding, and he gave no further thought to her. He hailed a taxi and went off to the club for lunch.

Though Cresswell, in common parlance, "did himself well," taking his fill of food and drink and tobacco, he was also careful of that great strong body of his, and the occasions were few when he omitted, at the end of the day's work, to walk out in the direction of Ramleh for a brisk hour or two, or, during the hotter months, to have a good swim in the sea and a bask in the sun. On the day following this eviction he took a tramp along the firm sands of the coast, and then, turning inland, struck the road that would bring him back to his own house. This stood quite at the end of the rows of detached houses past which he had walked two evenings before: beyond, the road ran between tumbled sand-dunes and scrub-covered flats. Here and there in sheltered hollows a few Arab goatherds and such had made themselves nomadic tentlike habitations of a primitive sort: half a dozen posts set in the sand supported a roof of rugs and blankets stitched together. If they encroached too near the outskirts of the town the authorities periodically made a clearance of them, for they were apt to be light-fingered, pilfering folk, whose close vicinity was not desirable.

To-day as he returned from his walk, Cresswell saw that a tent of this kind had newly been set up within twenty yards of his own garden wall. That would not do at all, that must be seen to, and he determined as soon as he had had his bath and his change of clothes to ring up his very good friend the chief inspector of police and request its removal. As he got nearer to it he saw that it was not quite of the usual type. The roof was clearly an outworn European carpet, and standing outside it on the sand were chairs and a sofa. Somehow these seemed familiar to him, though he could not localize the association. Then out of the tent came that old Levantine hag who had kissed his hand and knelt to him yesterday, invoking on him all sorts of blessings and prosperities, if only he would have compassion. She saw him, for now not more than a few dozen yards separated them, and then, suddenly pointing at him, she broke out into a gabble and yell of curses. That made him smile.

"So you've changed your tune again, have you?" he thought, "for that doesn't sound much like good wishes. Curse away, old woman, if it relieves your mind, for it doesn't hurt me. But you'll have to be shifting once more, for I'm not going to have you and your like squatting there."

Cresswell rang up his friend the chief inspector of police, and was most politely told that matter should be seen to in the morning. Sure enough when he set out to go to his office next day, he saw that it was being attended to, for the European carpet which had served for a roof was already down, and the handcart was being laden with the stuff. He noticed, quite casually, that the two women and the boy were employed in lading it; the Levantine was lying on the sand and taking no part in the work. Two days later he had occasion to pass the pauper cemetery of Alexandria, where the poorest kind of funeral was going on. The coffin was being pushed to the side of the shallow grave on a handcart: a boy and two women followed it. He could see who they were.

He dined that night at the club in rare good-humour with the affairs of life. Already the municipality had offered him for his newly acquired freehold a sum that was double the debt for which it had been security, and though possibly he might get more if he stuck out for a higher price he had accepted it, and the money had been paid into his bank that day. To get a hundred per cent in a week was very satisfactory business, and who knew but that some new scheme of improvement might cause them to change their plans, leaving him with a ramshackle building on his hands for which he had no manner of use? He enjoyed his dinner and his wine, and particularly did he enjoy the rubber of bridge that followed. All went well with his finesses; he doubled his adversaries two or three times with the happiest results, they doubled him and were sorry for having spoken, and there would be a very pleasant item to enter in his card-account that evening.

It was later than usual when he quitted the club. Just outside there was a beggar-woman squatting at the edge of the pavement, who held her palm towards him and whined out blessings. Good-naturedly he fumbled in his pocket for a couple of piastres, and the blessings poured out in greater shrillness and copiousness as she pushed back the black veil that half shrouded her face to thank him for his beneficence to the needy widow. Next moment she threw his alms on the pavement, she spat at him, and like a moth she flitted away into the shadows.

Cresswell recognized her even as she had recognized him and picked up his piastres. It was amusing to think that the old hag so hated him that even his alms were abhorrent to her. "I'll drop them into that collecting-box outside the church," he thought to himself.

To-night, late though it was, there were many folk about in the square, natives for the most part, padding softly along, and there were still a few taxis on the rank. But he preferred to walk home, for he had been so busy all day that he had given his firm fat body no sort of exercise. So crossing the square he went up the street which led to his house. Here the cafés were already closed, and soon the pavements grew empty. The waning moon had risen, and though the lights of the street grew more sparse as he emerged into the residential quarter, his way lay bright before him. In his hand he still held the two piastres which had been flung back at him ready for the collection-box. He walked briskly, for the night was cool, and it was no exercise to saunter. Not a breath of wind stirred the air, and the clatter of the dry palm-leaves was dumb.

He was now approaching the Roman Catholic church, when a step suddenly sounded out crisp and distinct behind him. He remembered then for the first time what had happened some nights ago and halted and listened: not a sound broke the stillness. He whisked round, but the street seemed empty. On he went again, now more slowly, and there was the following step again, neither gaining on him nor falling behind; to judge by the loudness of it, it could not be more than a dozen paces in his rear. Then a very obvious explanation occurred to him: no doubt this was some echo of his own footsteps. He went more quickly, and the steps behind him quickened; he stopped and they stopped. The whole thing was clear enough, and not a shadow of uneasiness, or anything approaching it, was in his mind. He slipped his ironical alms into the collecting-box outside the church, and was amused to hear that they evoked no tinkle from within. "Quite a little windfall for those brown-gowned fellows; they'll buy another rosary," he said to himself, and soon, with the echo of his own steps following, he turned in at his gate. Once inside, he slipped behind a myrtle bush that stood at the edge of the gravel walk, to see if by chance anyone passed on the road outside. But nothing happened, and his theory of the echo, though it was odd that he should never have noticed it till so lately, seemed quite confirmed.

{97}

From that night onwards he made it a practice, if he dined at the club, to walk home. Sometimes the step followed him, but not always, and this was an objection to that sensible echo theory. But the matter was no sort of worry to him except sometimes when he woke in the night, and found that his brain, still drowsy and not in complete control, was brooding over it with an ever-increasing preoccupation. Often that misgiving faded away and he dropped off to dreamless sleep again; sometimes it was sufficiently disquieting to bring him broad awake, and then with all his senses about him, it vanished. But there was this condition, half-way between waking and sleeping, when in the twilight chamber of his brain something listened, something feared. When fully awake he no more thought of it than he thought of that frowsy Levantine tobacco merchant whom he had evicted and whose funeral he chanced to have seen.

Early in December his cousin and partner in the sugar-business came down from Cairo to spend a week with him. Bill Cresswell may be succinctly described as "a hot lot," and often after dinner at the club he left his cousin to his cronies and the sedater pleasures of bridge, and went out with a duplicate latchkey in his pocket on livelier private affairs. One night, the last of Bill's sojourn here, there was "nothing doing" and the two set forth together homewards from the club.

"Nice night, let's walk," said John. "Nothing like a walk when there's liquid on board. Clears the brain for you and I must have a final powwow to-night, if you're off to-morrow. There are some bits of things still to go through."

Bill acquiesced. The cafés were all closed, there was nothing very promising.

"Night life here ain't a patch on Cairo," he observed. "Everyone seems to go to bed here just about when we begin to get going. Not but what I haven't enjoyed my stay with you. Capital good fellows at your club and brandy to match."

He stopped and ruefully scanned the quiet and emptiness of the street.

"Not a soul anywhere," he said. "Shutters up, all gone to bed. Nothing for it but a powwow, I guess."

They walked on in silence for a while. Then behind them, firm and distinct to John's ears, there sprang up the sound of the footsteps, for which now he knew that he waited and listened. He wheeled round.

"What's up?" asked Bill.

"Curious thing," said John. "Night after night now, though not every night, when I walk home, I hear a step following me. I heard it then."

Bill gave a vinous giggle.

"No such luck for me," he said. "I like to hear a step following me about one of a morning. Something agreeable may come of it. Wish I could hear it."

They walked on, and again, clearer than before, John heard what was inaudible to the other. He told himself, as he often did now, that it was an echo. But it was odd that the echo only repeated the footfalls of one of them. As he recognized this, he felt for the first time, when he was fully awake, some sudden chill of fear. It was as if a cold hand closed for a moment on his heart, just pressing it softly, almost tenderly. But they were now close to his own gate, and presently it clanged behind them.

{98}

Bill returned next day to the gladder life of Cairo. John Cresswell saw him off at the station and was passing out into the street again through the crowd of loungers and porters and passengers when there defined itself to his ear the sound of that footstep which he now knew so well. How he recognized it and isolated it from the tread of so many other feet he had no idea: simply his brain told him that it was following him again. He took a taxi to his office, and as he mounted the white stone stairs once more it was on his track. Once more the gentle pressure of cold fingers seemed to assure him of the presence that, though invisible, was very close to him, and now it was as if those fingers were pressed on some bell-push in his brain, and there sounded out a shrill tingle of fear. So hard-headed and sensible a man, of course, had nothing but scorn for all the clap-trap bogy tales of spirits and ghosts and hauntings, and he would have welcomed any sort of apparition in which the step manifested itself, in order to have the pleasure of laughing in its face. He would have liked to see a skeleton or some shrouded figure stand close to him; he would have slashed at it with his stick and convinced himself that there was nothing there. Whatever his own eyes appeared to see could not be so unnerving as these tokens of the invisible.

A stiff drink pulled him together again, and for the rest of the day there occurred no repetition of that tapping step which had begun to sprout with terror for him. In any case he was determined to fight it, for he realized that it was chiefly his own fear that troubled him. No doubt he was suffering from some small nervous derangement; he had been working very hard, and after Christmas, if the thing continued to worry him, probably he would see a doctor, who would prescribe him some tonic or some sedative which would send the step into the limbo from which it had come. But it was more probable that his cure was in his own hands: his own resistance was all the medicine he needed.

It was in pursuance of this very sane policy that he set out that night after an evening at the club to walk home: he faced it just because he knew that some black well was digging itself into his soul. To yield, to take a taxi, was to retreat, and if he did that, if he gave way an inch, he guessed that he might be soon flying in panic before an invading and imaginary host of phantoms. He had no use for phantoms; the solid satisfactions of life were enough occupation. Once more, as he drew near the church, the step sprang up, and now he sought no longer to tell himself it was an echo. Instead he fixed his mind on it, saying to himself, "There it is and it can't hurt me. Let it walk all day and night behind me if it chooses. It's got a fancy for me." Then his garden gate shut behind him, and with a sigh of relief he knew that he had passed out of its beat, for when once he was within, it never came farther.

He stood for a moment on his threshold, after he had opened his door, pleased with himself for having faced it. The bright light shone full on to the straight gravel walk he had just traversed. It was quite empty, and nothing was looking in through his gate. Then he heard from close at hand the crunch of the gravel underneath the heel of some invisible wayfarer. Now was the time to assert himself again, to look his fear in the eyes and mock at it.

"Come along, whoever you are," he called, "and have a drink before you get back to hell. Something cooling. Drop of cold water, isn't it?"

Thick sweat had broken out on his forehead, and his hand on the door-knob shook as with ague as he stood there looking out on to the bright empty path. But he did not flinch from the lesson he was teaching himself. The seconds ticked away: he could count them from the pulse that hammered in his throat. "I'll give it a hundred beats," he said to himself, "and then I'll say good night to Mr. Nothing-at-all."

He counted his hundred, he gave ten beats more for good luck. "Good night, you old fraud," he said, and went in and secured the door.

It seemed indeed for the week that followed that he had rightly gauged the nature of the hallucination which had threatened to establish its awful dominion over him. Never once, whether by day or night, did there come to his ears that footfall which he feared and listened for, nor, if in the dead hours of the darkness he lay for a while between sleep and waking, did he quake with a sense that something unseen and aware was watching him. A little courage, a flat denial of his fears had been sufficient not only to scotch them, but to snuff out the manifestation which had caused them. He kept his thoughts well in hand, he would not even conjecture what had been the cause of that visitation. Occasionally, while it still vexed him, he had cast about for the origin of it, he had wondered whether that shrill Levantine hag calling curses on him could somehow have found root in his mind. But now it was past and done with: he would have a few days' remission from work, if it was overwork that had been at the bottom of it, at Christmas, and perhaps it would be prudent not to be quite so free with the club brandy.

On Christmas Eve he and his friends sat at their bridge till close on midnight, then lingered over a drink, wished each other seasonable greetings and dispersed. Cresswell hesitated as to whether he should not take a taxi home, for the object with which he had trudged back there so often seemed to be gained, and he no longer feared the recurrence of the step. But he thought he would just set the seal on his victory and went on foot.

He had come to the point in his walk where he had first heard the step. To-night, as usual, there was none, and he stopped a moment looking round him securely and serenely. It was a bright night, luminous with a moon a little after the full, and it amazed him to think that he had ever fashioned a terror to himself in this quiet, orderly street. From not far ahead there came the sound of the bells of the church saluting Christmas morning. They would have been holding their midnight Mass there. He breathed the night air with content, and throwing the butt of his spent cigar into the roadway, he walked on again.

With a sudden sinking of his heart, he heard behind him the step which he thought he had silenced for ever. It was faint at first, but to-night, instead of keeping at a uniform distance behind him, it was approaching. Louder and more crisp it sounded, until it was close to him. On and on it came, still gaining on him, and now there brushed by him, though not quite touching him, the figure of a man in European dress, with his head wrapped in a shawl.

{100}

"Hullo, you there," called Cresswell. "You're the skunk who's been following me, are you, and slipping out of sight again? No more of your damned conjuring tricks. Let's have a look at you."

The figure, now some two or three yards ahead of him, stopped at the sound of his voice and turned round. The shawl covered its face, but for a narrow chink between the edges.

"So you understand English," said Cresswell. "Now I'll thank you to take that shawl off your face, and let me see who it is that's been dogging me."

The man raised his hands and threw back the shawl. The moonlight shone on his face, and that face was just a slab of smooth yellowish flesh extending from ear to ear, empty as the oval of an egg without eyes or nose or mouth. From the upper edge of the shawl where it crossed the forehead there depended a few wisps of grey hair.

Cresswell looked, and a wave of panic fear submerged his very soul. He gave a little thin squeal and started to run, listening the while in an agony of terror to hear if the steps of that nameless, faceless, creature were following. He must run, he must run, to get away from that thing out of hell which had manifested itself.

Then close at hand he saw the lights of the church, and there perhaps he could find sanctuary from it. The door was open, and he sprang up the steps. Close by there were lights burning on the altar of a side chapel, and he flung himself on his knees. Not for years had he attempted to pray, and now in the agony of his soul he could but say in a gabbling whisper, "O my God: O my God." Over and over he said it.

By degrees some sort of self-control came back to him. There were holy images, there was a sacred picture above the altar, a smell of hallowing incense was in the air. Surely there was protection here, a power that would intervene between him and the terror of that face. A sort of tranquillity overscored his panic, and he began to look round.

The church was darker than it had been when he entered, and he saw that some of those cowled brown-habited men of the order were moving quietly about, quenching the lights. Those at the altar in front of which he knelt were still bright, and now he saw one of these cowled figures move up close to him, as if waiting for him to finish his devotions. He was calm now, his panic had quite passed, and he rose from his knees.

"I've had a terrible fright, Father," he said to the monk. "I saw something just now out in the street which must have come out of hell."

The figure turned a little towards him: the cowl concealed its face altogether, and the voice came muffled.

"Indeed, my son," he said. "Tell me what it is that frightened you."

Cresswell felt some backwash of his panic returning.

"A man passed me as I was going back to my house," he said, "and I told him to stop and let me have a look at him. He wore a shawl over his head and he threw it back. Oh, my God, that face!"

The monk quietly raised his hands and grasped the edges of his cowl. Then with a quick movement he threw it back.

"That sort of face?" he said.

THE KIT-BAG
Algernon Blackwood

WHEN the words 'Not Guilty' sounded through the crowded courtroom that dark December afternoon, Arthur Wilbraham, the great criminal KC, and leader for the triumphant defence, was represented by his junior; but
Johnson, his private secretary, carried the verdict across to his chambers like lightning.

'It's what we expected, I think,' said the barrister, without emotion; 'and, personally, I am glad the case is over.' There was no particular sign of pleasure that his defence of John Turk, the murderer, on a plea of insanity, had been successful, for no doubt he felt, as everybody who had watched the case felt, that no man had ever better deserved the gallows.

'I'm glad too,' said Johnson. He had sat in the court for ten days watching the face of the man who had carried out with callous detail one of the most brutal and cold-blooded murders of recent years.

The counsel glanced up at his secretary. They were more than employer and employed; for family and other reasons, they were friends. 'Ah, I remember; yes,' he said with a kind smile, 'and you want to get away for Christmas? You're going to skate and ski in the Alps, aren't you? If I was your age I'd come with you.'

Johnson laughed shortly. He was a young man of twenty-six, with a delicate face like a girl's. 'I can catch the morning boat now,' he said; 'but that's not the reason I'm glad the trial is over. I'm glad it's over because I've seen the last of that man's dreadful face. It positively haunted me. Bat white skin, with the black hair brushed low over the forehead, is a thing I shall never forget, and the description of the way the dismembered body was crammed and packed with lime into that—'

'Don't dwell on it, my dear fellow,' interrupted the other, looking at him curiously out of his keen eyes, 'don't think about it. Such pictures have a trick of coming back when one least wants them.' He paused a moment. 'Now go,' he added presently, 'and enjoy your holiday. I shall want all your energy for my Parliamentary work when you get back. And don't break your neck skiing.'

Johnson shook hands and took his leave. At the door he turned suddenly.

'I knew there was something I wanted to ask you,' he said. 'Would you mind lending me one of your kit-bags? It's too late to get one tonight, and I leave in the morning before the shops are open.'

'Of course; I'll send Henry over with it to your rooms. You shall have it the moment I get home.'

'I promise to take great care of it,' said Johnson gratefully, delighted to think that within thirty hours he would be nearing the brilliant sunshine of the high Alps in winter. Be thought of that criminal court was like an evil dream in his mind.

He dined at his club and went on to Bloomsbury, where he occupied the top floor in one of those old, gaunt houses in which the rooms are large and lofty. The

floor below his own was vacant and unfurnished, and below that were other lodgers whom he did not know. It was cheerless, and he looked forward heartily to a change. The night was even more cheerless: it was miserable, and few people were about. A cold, sleety rain was driving down the streets before the keenest east wind he had ever felt. It howled dismally among the big, gloomy houses of the great squares, and when he reached his rooms he heard it whistling and shouting over the world of black roofs beyond his windows.

In the hall he met his landlady, shading a candle from the draughts with her thin hand. 'This come by a man from Mr Wilbr'im's, sir.'

She pointed to what was evidently the kit-bag, and Johnson thanked her and took it upstairs with him. 'I shall be going abroad in the morning for ten days, Mrs Monks,' he said. 'I'll leave an address for letters.'

'And I hope you'll 'ave a merry Christmas, sir,' she said, in a raucous, wheezy voice that suggested spirits, 'and better weather than this.'

'I hope so too,' replied her lodger, shuddering a little as the wind went roaring down the street outside.

When he got upstairs he heard the sleet volleying against the window panes. He put his kettle on to make a cup of hot coffee, and then set about putting a few things in order for his absence. 'And now I must pack—such as my packing is,' he laughed to himself, and set to work at once.

He liked the packing, for it brought the snowy mountains so vividly before him, and made him forget the unpleasant scenes of the past ten days. Besides, it was not elaborate in nature. His friend had lent him the very thing—a stout canvas kit-bag, sack-shaped, with holes round the neck for the brass bar and padlock. It was a bit shapeless, true, and not much to look at, but its capacity was unlimited, and there was no need to pack carefully. He shoved in his waterproof coat, his fur cap and gloves, his skates and climbing boots, his sweaters, snow-boots, and ear-caps; and then on the top of these he piled his woolen shirts and underwear, his thick socks, puttees, and knickerbockers. The dress suit came next, in case the hotel people dressed for dinner, and then, thinking of the best way to pack his white shirts, he paused a moment to reflect. 'That's the worst of these kit-bags,' he mused vaguely, standing in the centre of the sitting-room, where he had come to fetch some string.

It was after ten o'clock. A furious gust of wind rattled the windows as though to hurry him up, and he thought with pity of the poor Londoners whose Christmas would be spent in such a climate, whilst he was skimming over snowy slopes in bright sunshine, and dancing in the evening with rosy-checked girls—Ah! that reminded him; he must put in his dancing-pumps and evening socks. He crossed over from his sitting-room to the cupboard on the landing where he kept his linen.

And as he did so he heard someone coming softly up the stairs.

He stood still a moment on the landing to listen. It was Mrs Monks's step, he thought; she must he coming up with the last post. But then the steps ceased suddenly, and he heard no more. They were at least two flights down, and he came to the conclusion they were too heavy to be those of his bibulous landlady. No

{104}

doubt they belonged to a late lodger who had mistaken his floor. He went into his bedroom and packed his pumps and dress-shirts as best he could.

The kit-bag by this time was two-thirds full, and stood upright on its own base like a sack of flour. For the first time he noticed that it was old and dirty, the canvas faded and worn, and that it had obviously been subjected to rather rough treatment. It was not a very nice bag to have sent him—certainly not a new one, or one that his chief valued. He gave the matter a passing thought, and went on with his packing. Once or twice, however, he caught himself wondering who it could have been wandering down below, for Mrs Monks had not come up with letters, and the floor was empty and unfurnished. From time to time, moreover, he was almost certain he heard a soft tread of someone padding about over the bare boards—cautiously, stealthily, as silently as possible—and, further, that the sounds had been lately coming distinctly nearer.

For the first time in his life he began to feel a little creepy. Then, as though to emphasize this feeling, an odd thing happened: as he left the bedroom, having, just packed his recalcitrant white shirts, he noticed that the top of the kit-bag lopped over towards him with an extraordinary resemblance to a human face. The camas fell into a fold like a nose and forehead, and the brass rings for the padlock just filled the position of the eyes. A shadow—or was it a travel stain? for he could not tell exactly—looked like hair. It gave him rather a turn, for it was so absurdly, so outrageously, like the face of John Turk the murderer. He laughed, and went into the front room, where the light was stronger.

'That horrid case has got on my mind,' he thought; 'I shall be glad of a change of scene and air.' In the sitting-room, however, he was not pleased to hear again that stealthy tread upon the stairs, and to realize that it was much closer than before, as well as unmistakably real. And this time he got up and went out to see who it could be creeping about on the upper staircase at so late an hour.

But the sound ceased; there was no one visible on the stairs. He went to the floor below, not without trepidation, and turned on the electric light to make sure that no one was hiding in the empty rooms of the unoccupied suite. There was not a stick of furniture large enough to hide a dog. Then he called over the banisters to Mrs Monks, but there was no answer, and his voice echoed down into the dark vault of the house, and was lost in the roar of the gale that howled outside. Everyone was in bed and asleep—everyone except himself and the owner of this soft and stealthy tread.

'My absurd imagination, I suppose,' he thought. 'It must have been the wind after all, although—it seemed so *very* real and close, I thought.' He went back to his packing. It was by this time getting on towards midnight. He drank his coffee up and lit another pipe—the last before turning in.

It is difficult to say exactly at what point fear begins, when the causes of that fear are not plainly before the eyes. Impressions gather on the surface of the mind, film by film, as ice gathers upon the surface of still water, but often so lightly that they claim no definite recognition from the consciousness. Then a point is reached where the accumulated impressions become a definite emotion, and the mind

{105}

realizes that something has happened. With something of a start, Johnson suddenly recognized that he felt nervous—oddly nervous; also, that for some time past the causes of this feeling had been gathering slowly in his mind, but that he had only just reached the point where he was forced to acknowledge them.

It was a singular and curious malaise that had come over him, and he hardly knew what to make of it. He felt as though he were doing something that was strongly objected to by another person, another person, moreover, who had some right to object. It was a most disturbing and disagreeable feeling, not unlike the persistent promptings of conscience: almost, in fact, as if he were doing something he knew to be wrong. Yet, though he searched vigorously and honestly in his mind, he could nowhere lay his finger upon the secret of this growing uneasiness, and it perplexed him. More, it distressed and frightened him.

'Pure nerves, I suppose,' he said aloud with a forced laugh. 'Mountain air will cure all that! Ah,' he added, still speaking to himself, 'and that reminds me—my snow-glasses.'

He was standing by the door of the bedroom during this brief soliloquy, and as he passed quickly towards the sitting-room to fetch them from the cupboard he saw out of the corner of his eye the indistinct outline of a figure standing on the stairs, a few feet from the top. It was someone in a stooping position, with one hand on the banisters, and the face peering up towards the landing. And at the same moment he heard a shuffling footstep. The person who had been creeping about below all this time had at last come up to his own floor. Who in the world could it be? And what in the name of Heaven did he want?

Johnson caught his breath sharply and stood stock still. Then, after a few seconds' hesitation, he found his courage, and turned to investigate. The stairs, he saw to his utter amazement, were empty; there was no one. He felt a series of cold shivers run over him, and something about the muscles of his legs gave a little and grew weak. For the space of several minutes he peered steadily into the shadows that congregated about the top of the staircase where he had seen the figure, and then he walked fast—almost ran, in fact—into the light of the front room; but hardly had he passed inside the doorway when he heard someone come up the stairs behind him with a quick bound and go swiftly into his bedroom. It was a heavy, but at the same time a stealthy footstep—the tread of somebody who did not wish to be seen. And it was at this precise moment that the nervousness he had hitherto experienced leaped the boundary line, and entered the state of fear, almost of acute, unreasoning fear. Before it turned into terror there was a further boundary to cross, and beyond that again lay the region of pure horror. Johnson's position was an unenviable one.

'By Jove! That was someone on the stairs, then,' he muttered, his flesh crawling all over; 'and whoever it was has now gone into my bedroom.' His delicate, pale face turned absolutely white, and for some minutes he hardly knew what to think or do. Then he realized intuitively that delay only set a premium upon fear; and he crossed the landing boldly and went straight into the other room, where, a few seconds before, the steps had disappeared.

'Who's there? Is that you, Mrs Monks?' he called aloud, as he went, and heard the first half of his words echo down the empty stairs, while the second half fell dead against the curtains in a room that apparently held no other human figure than his own.

'Who's there?' he called again, in a voice unnecessarily loud and that only just held firm. 'What do you want here?'

The curtains swayed very slightly, and, as he saw it, his heart felt as if it almost missed a beat; yet he dashed forward and drew them aside with a rush. A window, streaming with rain, was all that met his gaze. He continued his search, but in vain; the cupboards held nothing but rows of clothes, hanging motionless; and under the bed there was no sign of anyone hiding. He stepped backwards into the middle of the room, and, as he did so, something all but tripped him up. Turning with a sudden spring of alarm he saw—the kit-bag.

'Odd!' he thought. 'That's not where I left it!' A few moments before it had surely been on his right, between the bed and the bath; he did not remember having moved it. It was very curious. What in the world was the matter with everything? Had all of his senses gone queer? A terrific gust of wind tore at the windows, dashing the sleet against the glass with the force of small gunshot, and then fled away howling dismally over the waste of Bloomsbury roofs. A sudden vision of the Channel next day rose in his mind and recalled him sharply to realities.

'There's no one here at any rate; that's quite clear!' he exclaimed aloud.

Yet at the time he uttered them he knew perfectly well that his words were not true and that he did not believe them himself. He felt exactly as though someone was hiding close about him, watching all his movements, trying to hinder his packing in some way. 'And two of my senses,' he added, keeping up the pretence, 'have played me the most absurd tricks: the steps I heard and the figure I saw were both entirely imaginary.'

He went back to the front room, poked the fire into a blaze, and sat down before it to think. What impressed him more than anything else was the fact that the kit-bag was no longer where he had left at. It had been dragged nearer to the door.

What happened afterwards that night happened, of course, to a man already excited by fear, and was perceived by a mind that had not the full and proper control, therefore, of the senses. Outwardly, Johnson remained calm and master of himself to the end, pretending to the very last that everything he witnessed had a natural explanation, or was merely delusions of his tired nerves. But inwardly, in his very heart, he knew all along that someone had been hiding downstairs in the empty suite when he came in, that this person had watched his opportunity and then stealthily made his way up to the bedroom, and that all he saw and heard afterwards, from the moving of the kit-bag to—well, to the other things this story has to tell—were caused directly by the presence of this invisible person.

And it was here, just when he most desired to keep his mind and thoughts controlled, that the vivid pictures received day after day upon the mental plates exposed in the courtroom of the Old Bailey, came strongly to light and developed themselves in the dark room of his inner vision. Unpleasant, haunting memories

{107}

have a way of coming to life again just when the mind least desires them—in the silent watches of the night, on sleepless pillows, during the lonely hours spent by sick and dying beds. And so now, in the same way, Johnson saw nothing but the dreadful face of John Turk, the murderer, lowering at him from every corner of his mental field of vision; the white skin, the evil eyes, and the fringe of black hair low over the forehead. All the pictures of those ten days in court crowded back into his mind unbidden, and very vivid.

'This is all rubbish and nerves,' he exclaimed at length, springing with sudden energy from his chair. 'I shall finish my packing and go to bed.
I'm overwrought, overtired. No doubt, at this rate I shall hear steps and things all night!'

But his face was deadly white all the same. He snatched up his field-glasses and walked across to the bedroom, humming a music-hall song as he went—a trifle too loud to be natural; and the instant he crossed the threshold and stood within the room something turned cold about his heart, and he felt that every hair on his head stood up.

The kit-bag lay close in front of him, several feet nearer to the door than he had left it, and just over its crumpled top he saw a head and face slowly sinking down out of sight as though someone were crouching behind it to hide, and at the same moment a sound like a long-drawn sigh was distinctly audible in the still air about him between the gusts of the storm outside.

Johnson had more courage and will-power than the girlish indecision of his face indicated; but at first such a wave of terror came over him that for some seconds he could do nothing but stand and stare. A violent trembling ran down his back and legs, and he was conscious of a foolish, almost a hysterical, impulse to scream aloud. That sigh seemed in his very ear, and the air still quivered with it. It was unmistakably a human sigh.

'Who's there?' he said at length, finding his voice; but thought he meant to speak with loud decision, the tones came out instead in a faint whisper, for he had partly lost the control of his tongue and lips.

He stepped forward, so that he could see all round and over the kit-bag. Of course there was nothing there, nothing but the faded carpet and the bulging canvas sides. He put out his hands and threw open the mouth of the sack where it had fallen over, being only three parts full, and then he saw for the first time that round the inside, some six inches from the top, there ran a broad smear of dull crimson. It was an old and faded blood stain. He uttered a scream, and drew hack his hands as if they had been burnt. At the same moment the kit-bag gave a faint, but unmistakable, lurch forward towards the door.

Johnson collapsed backwards, searching with his hands for the support of something solid, and the door, being further behind him than he realized, received his weight just in time to prevent his falling, and shut to with a resounding bang. At the same moment the swinging of his left arm accidentally touched the electric switch, and the light in the room went out.

It was an awkward and disagreeable predicament, and if Johnson had not been possessed of real pluck he might have done all manner of foolish things. As it was, however, he pulled himself together, and groped furiously for the little brass knob to turn the light on again. But the rapid closing of the door had set the coats hanging on it a-swinging, and his fingers became entangled in a confusion of sleeves and pockets, so that it was some moments before he found the switch. And in those few moments of bewilderment and terror two things happened that sent him beyond recall over the boundary into the region of genuine horror—he distinctly heard the kit-bag shuffling heavily across the floor in jerks, and close in front of his face sounded once again the sigh of a human being.

In his anguished efforts to find the brass button on the wall he nearly scraped the nails from his fingers, but even then, in those frenzied moments of alarm—so swift and alert are the impressions of a mind keyed-up by a vivid emotion—he had time to realize that he dreaded the return of the light, and that it might be better for him to stay hidden in the merciful screen of darkness. It was but the impulse of a moment, however, and before he had time to act upon it he had yielded automatically to the original desire, and the room was flooded again with light.

But the second instinct had been right. It would have been better for him to have stayed in the shelter of the kind darkness. For there, close before him, bending over the half-packed kit-bag, clear as life in the merciless glare of the electric light, stood the figure of John Turk, the murderer. Not three feet from him the man stood, the fringe of black hair marked plainly against the pallor of the forehead, the whole horrible presentment of the scoundrel, as vivid as he had seen him day after day in the Old Bailey, when he stood there in the dock, cynical and callous, under the very shadow of the gallows.

In a flash Johnson realized what it all meant: the dirty and much-used bag; the smear of crimson within the top; the dreadful stretched condition of the bulging sides. He remembered how the victim's body had been stuffed into a canvas bag for burial, the ghastly, dismembered fragments forced with lime into this very bag; and the bag itself produced as evidence—it all came back to him as clear as day...

Very softly and stealthily his hand groped behind him for the handle of the door, but before he could actually turn it the very thing that he most of all dreaded came about, and John Turk lifted his devil's face and looked at him. At the same moment that heavy sigh passed through the air of the room, formulated somehow into words: 'It's my bag. And I want it.'

Johnson just remembered clawing the door open, and then falling in a heap upon the floor of the landing, as he tried frantically to make his way into the front room.

He remained unconscious for a long time, and it was still dark when he opened his eyes and realized that he was lying, stiff and bruised, on the cold boards. Then the memory of what he had seen rushed back into his mind, and he promptly fainted again. When he woke the second time the wintry dawn was just beginning to peep in at the windows, painting the stairs a cheerless, dismal grey, and he managed to crawl into the front room, and cover himself with an overcoat in the armchair, where at length he fell asleep.

A great clamour woke him. He recognized Mrs Monks's voice, loud and voluble.

'What! You ain't been to bed, sir! Are you ill, or has anything 'appened? And there's an urgent gentleman to see you, though it ain't seven o'clock yet, and—'

'Who is it?' he stammered. 'I'm all right, thanks. Fell asleep in my chair, I suppose.'

'Someone from Mr Wilb'rim's, and he says he ought to see you quick before you go abroad, and I told him—'

'Show him up, please, at once,' said Johnson, whose head was whirling, and his mind was still full of dreadful visions.

Mr Wilbraham's man came in with many apologies, and explained briefly and quickly that an absurd mistake had been made, and that the wrong kit-bag had been sent over the night before.

'Henry somehow got hold of the one that came over from the courtroom, and Mr Wilbraham only discovered it when he saw his own lying in his room, and asked why it had not gone to you,' the man said.

'Oh!' said Johnson stupidly.

'And he must have brought you the one from the murder case instead, sir, I'm afraid,' the man continued, without the ghost of an expression on his face. "The one John Turk packed the dead body in. Mr Wilbraham's awful upset about it, sir, and told me to come over first thing this morning with the right one, as you were leaving by the boat.'

He pointed to a clean-looking kit-bag on the floor, which he had just brought. 'And I was to bring the other one back, sir,' he added casually.

For some minutes Johnson could not find his voice. At last he pointed in the direction of his bedroom. 'Perhaps you would kindly unpack it for me. Just empty the things out on the floor.'

The man disappeared into the other room, and was gone for five minutes. Johnson heard the shifting to and fro of the bag, and the rattle of the skates and boots being unpacked.

' Thank you, sir,' the man said, returning with the bag folded over his arm. 'And can I do anything more to help you, sir?'

'What is it?' asked Johnson, seeing that he still had something he wished to say.

The man shuffled and looked mysterious. 'Beg pardon, sir, but knowing your interest in the Turk case, I thought you'd maybe like to know what's happened—'

'Yes.'

'John Turk killed hisself last night with poison immediately on getting his release, and he left a note for Mr Wilbraham saying as he'd be much obliged if they'd have him put away, same as the woman he murdered, in the old kit-hag.'

'What time—did he do it?' asked Johnson.

'Ten o'clock last night, sir, the warder says.'

{110}

THE OLD NURSE'S STORY
Elizabeth Gaskell

YOU know my dears, that your mother was an orphan, and an only child; and I dare say you have heard that your grandfather was a clergyman up in Westmoreland, where I come from. I was just a girl in the village school, when, one day, your grandmother came in to ask the mistress if there was any scholar there who would do for a nurse-maid; and mighty proud I was, I can tell ye, when the mistress called me up, and spoke to my being a good girl at my needle, and a steady, honest girl, and one whose parents were very respectable, though they might be poor. I thought I should like nothing better than to serve the pretty young lady, who was blushing as deep as I was, as she spoke of the coming baby, and what I should have to do with it. However, I see you don't care so much for this part of my story, as for what you think is to come, so I'll tell you at once. I was engaged and settled at the parsonage before Miss Rosamond (that was the baby, who is now your mother) was born. To be sure, I had little enough to do with her when she came, for she was never out of her mother's arms, and slept by her all night long; and proud enough was I sometimes when missis trusted her to me. There never was such a baby before or since, though you've all of you been fine enough in your turns; but for sweet, winning ways, you've none of you come up to your mother. She took after her mother, who was a real lady born; a Miss Furnivall, a grand-daughter of Lord Furnivall's, in Northumberland. I believe she had neither brother nor sister, and had been brought up in my lord's family till she had married your grandfather, who was just a curate, son to a shopkeeper in Carlisle—but a clever, fine gentleman as ever was—and one who was a right-down hard worker in his parish, which was very wide, and scattered all abroad over the Westmoreland Fells. When your mother, little Miss Rosamond, was about four or five years old, both her parents died in a fortnight— one after the other. Ah! that was a sad time. My pretty young mistress and me was looking for another baby, when my master came home from one of his long rides, wet and tired, and took the fever he died of; and then she never held up her head again, but just lived to see her dead baby, and have it laid on her breast, before she sighed away her life. My mistress had asked me, on her death-bed, never to leave Miss Rosamond; but if she had never spoken a word, I would have gone with the little child to the end of the world.

The next thing, and before we had well stilled our sobs, the executors and guardians came to settle the affairs. They were my poor young mistress's own cousin, Lord Furnivall, and Mr. Esthwaite, my master's brother, a shopkeeper in Manchester; not so well-to-do then as he was afterwards, and with a large family rising about him. Well! I don't know if it were their settling, or because of a letter my mistress wrote on her death-bed to her cousin, my lord; but somehow it was settled that Miss Rosamond and me were to go to Furnivall Manor House, in Northumberland; and my lord spoke as if it had been her mother's wish that she should live with his family, and as if he had no objections, for that one or two more

or less could make no difference in so grand a household. So, though that was not the way in which I should have wished the coming of my bright and pretty pet to have been looked at—who was like a sunbeam in any family, be it never so grand— I was well pleased that all the folks in the Dale should stare and admire, when they heard I was going to be young lady's maid at my Lord Furnivall's at Furnivall Manor.

But I made a mistake in thinking we were to go and live where my lord did. It turned out that the family had left Furnivall Manor House fifty years or more. I could not bear that my poor young mistress had ever been there, though she had been brought up in the family; and I was sorry for that, for I should have liked Miss Rosamond's youth to have passed where her mother's had been.

My lord's gentleman, from whom I asked as many questions as I durst, said that the Manor House was at the foot of the Cumberland Fells, and a very grand place; that an old Miss Furnivall, a great-aunt of my lord's, lived there, with only a few servants; but that it was a very healthy place, and my lord had thought that it would suit Miss Rosamond very well for a few years, and that her being there might perhaps amuse his old aunt.

I was bidden by my lord to have Miss Rosamond's things ready by a certain day. He was a stern, proud man, as they say all the Lords Furnivall were; and he never spoke a word more than was necessary. Folk did say he had loved my young mistress; but that, because she knew that his father would object, she would never listen to him, and married Mr. Esthwaite; but I don't know. He never married, at any rate. But he never took much notice of Miss Rosamond; which I thought he might have done if he had cared for her dead mother. He sent his gentleman with us to the Manor House, telling him to join him at Newcastle that same evening; so there was no great length of time for him to make us known to all the strangers before he, too, shook us off; and we were left, two lonely young things (I was not eighteen) in the great old Manor House. It seems like yesterday that we drove there. We had left our own dear parsonage very early, and we had both cried as if our hearts would break, though we were travelling in my lord's carriage, which I thought so much of once. And now it was long past noon on a September day, and we stopped to change horses for the last time at a little smoky town, all full of colliers and miners. Miss Rosamond had fallen asleep, but Mr. Henry told me to waken her, that she might see the park and the Manor House as we drove up. I thought it rather a pity; but I did what he bade me, for fear he should complain of me to my lord. We had left all signs of a town, or even a village, and were then inside the gates of a large wild park—not like the parks here in the south, but with rocks, and the noise of running water, and gnarled thorn-trees, and old oaks, all white and peeled with age.

The road went up about two miles, and then we saw a great and stately house, with many trees close around it, so close that in some places their branches dragged against the walls when the wind blew, and some hung broken down; for no one seemed to take much charge of the place—to lop the wood, or to keep the moss-covered carriage-way in order. Only in front of the house all was clear. The great oval drive was without a weed; and neither tree nor creeper was allowed to grow over the long, many-windowed front; at both sides of which a wing projected, which were each the ends of other side fronts; for the house, although it was so desolate, was even grander than I expected. Behind it rose the Fells, which seemed unenclosed and bare enough; and on the left hand of the house, as you stood facing it, was a little, old-fashioned flower-garden, as I found out afterwards. A door opened out upon it from the west front; it had been scooped out of the thick, dark wood for some old Lady Furnivall; but the branches of the great forest-trees had grown and overshadowed it again, and there were very few flowers that would live there at that time.

When we drove up to the great front entrance, and went into the hall, I thought we should be lost—it was so large, and vast, and grand. There was a chandelier all of bronze, hung down from the middle of the ceiling; and I had never seen one before, and looked at it all in amaze. Then, at one end of the hall, was a great fireplace, as large as the sides of the houses in my country, with massy andirons and dogs to hold the wood; and by it were heavy, old-fashioned sofas. At the opposite end of the hall, to the left as you went in—on the western side—was an organ built into the wall, and so large that it filled up the best part of that end. Beyond it, on the same side, was a door; and opposite, on each side of the fireplace, were also doors leading to the east front; but those I never went through as long as I stayed in the house, so I can't tell you what lay beyond.

∞

The afternoon was closing in, and the hall, which had no fire lighted in it, looked dark and gloomy; but we did not stay there a moment. The old servant, who had opened the door for us, bowed to Mr. Henry, and took us in through the door at the further side of the great organ, and led us through several smaller halls and passages into the west drawing-room, where he said that Miss Furnivall was sitting. Poor little Miss Rosamond held very tight to me, as if she were scared and lost in that great place; and as for myself, I was not much better. The west drawing-room was very cheerful-looking, with a warm fire in it, and plenty of good, comfortable furniture about. Miss Furnivall was an old lady not far from eighty, I should think, but I do not know. She was thin and tall, and had a face as full of fine wrinkles as if they had been drawn all over it with a needle's point. Her eyes were very watchful, to make up, I suppose, for her being so deaf as to be obliged to use a trumpet. Sitting with her, working at the same great piece of tapestry, was Mrs. Stark, her maid and companion, and almost as old as she was. She had lived with Miss Furnivall ever since they both were young, and now she seemed more like a friend than a servant; she looked so cold, and grey, and stony, as if she had never loved or cared for any one; and I don't suppose she did care for any one, except her mistress; and, owing to the great deafness of the latter, Mrs. Stark treated her very much as if she were a child. Mr. Henry gave some message from my lord, and then he bowed good-bye to us all—taking no notice of my sweet little Miss Rosamond's outstretched hand—and left us standing there, being looked at by the two old ladies through their spectacles.

I was right glad when they rung for the old footman who had shown us in at first, and told him to take us to our rooms. So we went out of that great drawing-room, and into another sitting-room, and out of that, and then up a great flight of stairs, and along a broad gallery—which was something like a library, having books all down one side, and windows and writing-tables all down the other—till we came to our rooms, which I was not sorry to hear were just over the kitchens; for I began to think I should be lost in that wilderness of a house. There was an old nursery, that had been used for all the little lords and ladies long ago, with a pleasant fire burning in the grate, and the kettle boiling on the hob, and tea-things spread out on the table; and out of that room was the night-nursery, with a little crib for Miss Rosamond close to my bed. And old James called up Dorothy, his wife, to bid us welcome; and both he and she were so hospitable and kind, that by-and-by Miss Rosamond and me felt quite at home; and by the time tea was over, she was sitting on Dorothy's knee, and chattering away as fast as her little tongue could go. I soon found out that Dorothy was from Westmoreland, and that bound her and me together, as it were; and I would never wish to meet with kinder people than were old James and his wife. James had lived pretty nearly all his life in my lord's family, and thought there was no one so grand as they. He even looked down a little on his wife; because, till he had married her, she had never lived in any but a farmer's household. But he was very fond of her, as well he might be. They had one servant under them, to do all the rough work. Agnes they called her; and she and me, and James and Dorothy, with Miss Furnivall and Mrs. Stark, made up the family; always remembering my sweet little Miss Rosamond! I used to wonder what they had done before she came, they thought so much of her now. Kitchen and drawing-room, it was all the same. The hard, sad Miss Furnivall, and the cold Mrs. Stark, looked pleased when she came fluttering in like a bird, playing and pranking hither and thither, with a continual murmur, and pretty prattle of gladness. I am sure, they were sorry many a time when she flitted away into the kitchen, though they were too proud to ask her to stay with them, and were a little surprised at her taste; though to be sure, as Mrs. Stark said, it was not to be wondered at, remembering what stock her father had come of. The great, old rambling house was a famous place for little Miss Rosamond. She made expeditions all over it, with me at her heels: all, except the east wing, which was never opened, and whither we never thought of going. But in the western and northern part was many a pleasant room; full of things that were curiosities to us, though they might not have been to people who had seen more. The windows were darkened by the sweeping boughs of the trees, and the ivy which had overgrown them; but, in the green gloom, we could manage to see old china jars and carved ivory boxes, and great heavy books, and, above all, the old pictures!

Once, I remember, my darling would have Dorothy go with us to tell us who they all were; for they were all portraits of some of my lord's family, though Dorothy could not tell us the names of every one. We had gone through most of the rooms, when we came to the old state drawing-room over the hall, and there was a picture of Miss Furnivall; or, as she was called in those days, Miss Grace, for she was the younger sister. Such a beauty she must have been! but with such a set, proud look, and such scorn looking out of her handsome eyes, with her eyebrows just a little raised, as if she wondered how anyone could have the impertinence to look at her, and her lip curled at us, as we stood there gazing. She had a dress on, the like of which I had never seen before, but it was all the fashion when she was young: a hat of some soft white stuff like beaver, pulled a little over her brows, and a beautiful plume of feathers sweeping round it on one side; and her gown of blue satin was open in front to a quilted white stomacher. "Well, to be sure!" said I, when I had gazed my fill. "Flesh is grass, they do say; but who would have thought that Miss Furnivall had been such an out-and-out beauty, to see her now?"

"Yes," said Dorothy. "Folks change sadly. But if what my master's father used to say was true, Miss Furnivall, the elder sister, was handsomer than Miss Grace. Her picture is here somewhere; but, if I show it you, you must never let on, even to James, that you have seen it Can the little lady hold her tongue, think you?" asked she.

I was not so sure, for she was such a little sweet, bold, open-spoken child, so I set her to hide herself; and then I helped Dorothy to turn a great picture, that leaned with its face towards the wall, and was not hung up as the others were. To be sure, it beat Miss Grace for beauty; and I think, for scornful pride, too, though in that matter it might be hard to choose. I could have looked at it an hour but Dorothy seemed half frightened at having shown it to me, and hurried it back again, and bade me run and find Miss Rosamond, for that there were some ugly places about the house, where she should like ill for the child to go. I was a brave, high-spirited girl, and thought little of what the old woman said, for I liked hide-and-seek as well as any child in the parish; so off I ran to find my little one.

As winter drew on, and the days grew shorter, I was sometimes almost certain that I heard a noise as if some one was playing on the great organ in the hall. I did not hear it every evening; but, certainly, I did very often, usually when I was sitting with Miss Rosamond, after I had put her to bed, and keeping quite still and silent in the bedroom. Then I used to hear it booming and swelling away in the distance. The first night, when I went down to my supper, I asked Dorothy who had been playing music, and James said very shortly that I was a gowk to take the wind soughing among the trees for music; but I saw Dorothy look at him very fearfully, and Bessy, the kitchen-maid, said something beneath her breath, and went quite white. I saw they did not like my question, so I held my peace till I was with Dorothy alone, when I knew I could get a good deal out of her. So, the next day, I watched my time, and I coaxed and asked her who it was that played the organ; for I knew that it was the organ and not the wind well enough, for all I had kept silence before James. But Dorothy had had her lesson, I'll warrant, and never a word could I get from her. So then I tried Bessy, though I had always held my head rather above her, as I was evened to James and Dorothy, and she was little better than their servant so she said I must never, never tell; and if ever told, I was never to say she had told me; but it was a very strange noise, and she had heard it many a time, but most of all on winter nights, and before storms; and folks did say it was the old lord playing on the great organ in the hall, just as he used to do when he was alive; but who the old lord was, or why he played, and why he played on stormy winter evenings in particular, she either could not or would not tell me. Well! I told you I had a brave heart; and I thought it was rather pleasant to have that grand music rolling about the house, let who would be the player; for now it rose above the great gusts of wind, and wailed and triumphed just like a living creature, and then it fell to a softness most complete, only it was always music, and tunes, so it was nonsense to call it the wind. I thought at first, that it might be Miss Furnivall who played, unknown to Bessy; but one day, when I was in the hall by myself, I opened the organ and peeped all about it and around it, as I had done to the organ in Crosthwaite Church once before, and I saw it was all broken and destroyed inside, though it looked so brave and fine; and then, though it was noon-day, my flesh began to creep a little, and I shut it up, and run away pretty quickly to my own bright nursery; and I did not like hearing the music for some time after that, any more than James and Dorothy did. All this time Miss Rosamond was making herself more and more beloved. The old ladies liked her to dine with them at their early dinner James stood behind Miss Furnivall's chair, and I behind Miss Rosamond's all in state; and, after dinner, she would play about in a corner of the great drawing-room as still as any mouse, while Miss Furnivall slept, and I had my dinner in the kitchen. But she was glad enough to come to me in the nursery afterwards; for, as she said Miss Furnivall was so sad, and Mrs. Stark so dull; but she and were merry enough; and, by-and-by, I got not to care for that weird rolling music, which did one no harm, if we did not know where it came from.

℘

That winter was very cold. In the middle of October the frosts began, and lasted many, many weeks. I remember one day, at dinner, Miss Furnivall lifted up her sad, heavy eyes, and said to Mrs. Stark, "I am afraid we shall have a terrible winter," in a strange kind of meaning way. But Mrs. Stark pretended not to hear, and talked very loud of something else. My little lady and I did not care for the frost; not we! As long as it was dry, we climbed up the steep brows behind the house, and went up on the Fells which were bleak and bare enough, and there we ran races in the fresh, sharp air; and once we came down by a new path, that took us past the two old gnarled holly-trees, which grew about half-way down by the east side of the house.

But the days grew shorter and shorter, and the old lord, if it was he, played away, more and more stormily and sadly, on the great organ. One Sunday afternoon—it must have been towards the end of November—I asked Dorothy to take charge of little missy when she came out of the drawing-room, after Miss Furnivall had had her nap; for it was too cold to take her with me to church, and yet I wanted to go, and Dorothy was glad enough to promise and was so fond of the child, that all seemed well; and Bessy and I set off very briskly, though the sky hung heavy and black over the white earth, as if the night had never fully gone away, and the air, though still, was very biting.

"We shall have a fall of snow," said Bessy to me. And sure enough, even while we were in church, it came down thick, in great large flakes—so thick, it almost darkened the windows. It had stopped snowing before we came out, but it lay soft, thick, and deep beneath our feet, as we tramped home. Before we got to the hall, the moon rose, and I think it was lighter then—what with the moon, and what with the white dazzling snow—than it had been when we went to church, between two and

{117}

three o'clock. I have not told you that Miss Furnivall and Mrs. Stark never went to church; they used to read the prayers together, in their quiet, gloomy way; they seemed to feel the Sunday very long without their tapestry-work to be busy at. So when I went to Dorothy in the kitchen, to fetch Miss Rosamond and take her upstairs with me, I did not much wonder when the old woman told me that the ladies had kept the child with them, and that she had never come to the kitchen, as I had bidden her, when she was tired of behaving pretty in the drawing-room. So I took off my things and went to find her, and bring her to her supper in the nursery. But when I went into the best drawing-room, there sat the two old ladies, very still and quiet, dropping out a word now and then, but looking as if nothing so bright and merry as Miss Rosamond had ever been near them. Still I thought she might be hiding from me; it was one of her pretty ways—and that she had persuaded them to look as if they knew nothing about her; so I went softly peeping under this sofa and behind that chair, making believe I was sadly frightened at not finding her.

"What's the matter, Hester?" said Mrs. Stark sharply. I don't know if Miss Furnivall had seen me for, as I told you, she was very deaf, and she sat quite still, idly staring into the fire, with her hopeless face. "I'm only looking for my little Rosy Posy," replied I, still thinking that the child was there, and near me, though I could not see her.

"Miss Rosamond is not here," said Mrs. Stark. "She went away, more than an hour ago, to find Dorothy." And she, too, turned and went on looking into the fire.

My heart sank at this, and I began to wish I had never left my darling. I went back to Dorothy and told her. James was gone out for the day, but she, and me, and Bessy took lights, and went up into the nursery first; and then we roamed over the great, large house, calling and entreating Miss Rosamond to come out of her hiding-place, and not frighten us to death in that way. But there was no answer; no sound.

"Oh!" said I, at last, "can she have got into the east wing and hidden there?" But Dorothy said it was not possible, for that she herself had never been in there; that the doors were always locked, and my lord's steward had the keys, she believed; at any rate, neither she nor James had ever seen them: so I said I would go back, and see if, after all, she was not hidden in the drawing-room, unknown to the old ladies; and if I found her there, I said, I would whip her well for the fright she had given me; but I never meant to do it. Well, I went back to the west drawing-room, and I told Mrs. Stark we could not find her anywhere, and asked for leave to look all about the furniture there, for I thought now that she might have fallen asleep in some warm, hidden corner; but no! we looked—Miss Furnivall got up and looked, trembling all over—and she was nowhere there; then we set off again, every one in the house, and looked in all the places we had searched before, but we could not find her. Miss Furnivall shivered and shook so much that Mrs. Stark took her back into the warm drawing-room; but not before they had made me promise to bring her to them when she was found. Well-a-day! I began to think she never would be found, when I bethought me to look into the great front court, all covered with snow. I was upstairs when I looked out; but, it was such clear moonlight, I could see, quite plain, two little footprints, which might be traced from the hall-door and round the corner of the east wing. I don't know how I got down, but I tugged open the great stiff hall-door, and, throwing the skirt of my gown over my head for a cloak, I ran out. I turned the east corner, and there a black shadow fell on the snow but when I came again into the moonlight, there were the little footmarks going up— up to the Fells. It was bitter cold; so cold, that the air almost took the skin off my face as I ran; but I ran on, crying to think how my poor little darling must be perished and frightened. I was within sight of the holly-trees, when I saw a shepherd coming down the hill, bearing something in his arms wrapped in his maud. He shouted to me, and asked me if I had lost a bairn; and, when I could not speak for crying, he bore towards me, and I saw my wee bairnie, lying still, and white, and stiff in his arms, as if she had been dead. He told me he had been up the Fells to gather in his sheep, before the deep cold of night came on, and that under the holly-trees (black marks on the hill-side, where no other bush was for miles around) he had found my little lady— my lamb—my queen—my darling—stiff and cold in the terrible sleep which is frost-begotten. Oh! the joy and the tears of having her in my arms once again I for I would not let him carry her; but took her, maud and all, into my own arms, and held her near my own warm neck and heart, and felt the life stealing slowly back again into her little gentle limbs. But she was still insensible when we reached the hall, and I had no breath for speech. We went in by the kitchen-door.

"Bring the warming-pan," said I; and I carried her upstairs, and began undressing her by the nursery fire, which Bessy had kept up. I called my little lammie all the sweet and playful names I could think of—even while my eyes were blinded by my tears; and at last, oh! at length she opened her large blue eyes. Then I put her into her warm bed, and sent Dorothy down to tell Miss Furnivall that all was well; and I made up my mind to sit by my darling's bedside the live-long night. She fell away into a soft sleep as soon as her pretty head had touched the pillow, and I watched by her till morning light; when she wakened up bright and clear—or so I thought at first—and, my dears, so I think now.

℘

She said, that she had fancied that she should like to go to Dorothy, for that both the old ladies were asleep, and it was very dull in the drawing-room; and that, as she was going through the west lobby, she saw the snow through the high window falling—falling—soft and steady; but she wanted to see it lying pretty and white on the ground; so she made her way into the great hall: and then, going to the window, she saw it bright and soft upon the drive; but while she stood there, she saw a little girl, not so old as she was, "but so pretty," said my darling; "and this little girl beckoned to me to come out; and oh, she was so pretty and so sweet, I could not choose but go." And then this other little girl had taken her by the hand, and side by side the two had gone round the east corner.

"Now you are a naughty little girl, and telling stories," said I. "What would your good mamma, that is in heaven, and never told a story in her life, say to her little Rosamond, if she heard her—and I dare say she does— telling stories!"

"Indeed, Hester," sobbed out my child, "I'm telling you true. Indeed I am."

"Don't tell me!" said I, very stern. "I tracked you by your foot-marks through the snow; there were only yours to be seen: and if you had had a little girl to go hand-in-hand with you up the hill, don't you think the footprints would have gone along with yours?"

"I can't help it, dear, dear Hester," said she, crying, "if they did not; I never looked at her feet, but she held my hand fast and tight in her little one, and it was very, very cold. She took me up the Fell-path, up to the holly-trees; and there I saw a lady weeping and crying; but when she saw me, she hushed her weeping, and smiled very proud and grand, and took me on her knee, and began to lull me to sleep, and that's all, Hester—but that is true; and my dear mamma knows it is," said she, crying. So I thought the child was in a fever, and pretended to believe her, as she went over her story—over and over again, and always the same. At last Dorothy knocked at the door with Miss Rosamond's breakfast; and she told me the old ladies were down in the eating parlour, and that they wanted to speak to me. They had both been into the night-nursery the evening before, but it was after Miss Rosamond was asleep; so they had only looked at her—not asked me any questions.

"I shall catch it," thought I to myself, as I went along the north gallery. "And yet," I thought, taking courage, "it was in their charge I left her; and it's they that's to blame for letting her steal away unknown and unwatched." So I went in boldly, and told my story. I told it all to Miss Furnivall, shouting it close to her ear; but when I came to the mention of the other little girl out in the snow, coaxing and tempting her out, and wiling her up to the grand and beautiful lady by the holly-tree, she threw her arms up—her old and withered arms—and cried aloud, "Oh! Heaven forgive! Have mercy!"

Mrs. Stark took hold of her; roughly enough, I thought; but she was past Mrs. Stark's management, and spoke to me, in a kind of wild warning and authority.

"Hester! keep her from that child! It will lure her to her death! That evil child! Tell her it is a wicked, naughty child." Then, Mrs. Stark hurried me out of the room, where, indeed, I was glad enough to go; but Miss Furnivall kept shrieking out, "Oh, have mercy! Wilt Thou never forgive! It is many a long year ago"—

I was very uneasy in my mind after that. I durst never leave Miss Rosamond, night or day, for fear lest she might slip off again, after some fancy or other; and all the more, because I thought I could make out that Miss Furnivall was crazy, from their odd ways about her; and I was afraid lest something of the same kind (which might be in the family, you know) hung over my darling. And the great frost never ceased all this time; and, whenever it was a more stormy night than usual, between the gusts, and through the wind we heard the old lord playing on the great organ. But, old lord, or not, wherever Miss Rosamond went, there I followed; for my love for her, pretty, helpless orphan, was stronger than my fear for the grand and terrible sound. Besides, it rested with me to keep her cheerful and merry, as beseemed her age. So we played together, and wandered together, here and there, and everywhere; for I never dared to lose sight of her again in that large and rambling house. And so it happened, that one afternoon, not long before Christmas-day, we were playing together on the billiard-table in the great hall (no that we knew the right way of playing, but she liked to roll the smooth ivory balls with her pretty hands, and I liked to do whatever she did); and, by-and-by, without our noticing it, it grew dusk indoors, though it was still light in the open air, and I was thinking of taking her back into the nursery, when, all of a sudden, she cried out—

"Look, Hester! look! there is my poor little girl out in the snow!"

I turned towards the long narrow windows, and there, sure enough, I saw a little girl, less than my Miss Rosamond—dressed all unfit to be out-of-doors such a bitter night—crying, and beating against the window panes, as if she wanted to be let in. She seemed to sob and wail, till Miss Rosamond could bear it no longer, and was flying to the door to open it, when, all of a sudden, and close upon us, the great organ pealed out so loud and thundering, it fairly made me tremble; and all the more, when I remembered me that, even in the stillness of that dead-cold weather, I had heard no sound of little battering hands upon the window-glass, although the phantom child had seemed to put forth all its force; and, although I had seen it wail and cry, no faintest touch of sound had fallen upon my ears. Whether I remembered all this at the very moment, I do not know; the great organ sound had so stunned me into terror; but this I know, I caught up Miss Rosamond before she got the hall-door opened, and clutched her, and carried her away, kicking and screaming, into the large, bright kitchen, where Dorothy and Agnes were busy with their mince-pies.

"What is the matter with my sweet one?" cried Dorothy, as I bore in Miss Rosamond, who was sobbing as if her heart would break.

"She won't let me open the door for my little girl to come in; and she'll die if she is out on the Fells all night. Cruel, naughty Hester," she said, slapping me; but she might have struck harder, for I had seen a look of ghastly terror on Dorothy's face, which made my very blood run cold.

"Shut the back-kitchen door fast, and bolt it well," said she to Agues. She said no more; she gave me raisins and almonds to quiet Miss Rosamond; but she sobbed about the little girl in the snow, and would not touch any of the good things. I was thankful when she cried herself to sleep in bed. Then I stole down to the kitchen, and told Dorothy I had made up my mind. I would carry my darling back to my father's house in Applethwaite; where, if we lived humbly, we lived at peace. I said I had been frightened enough with the old lord's organ-playing; but now that I had seen for myself this little moaning child, all decked out as no child in the neighbourhood could be, beating and battering to get in, yet always without any sound or noise— with the dark wound on its right shoulder; and that Miss Rosamond had known it again for the phantom that had nearly lured her to death (which Dorothy knew was true); I would stand it no longer.

I saw Dorothy change colour once or twice. When I had done, she told me she did not think I could take Miss Rosamond with me, for that she was my lord's ward, and I had no right over her; and she asked me would I leave the child that I was so fond of just for sounds and sights that could do me no harm; and that they had all had to get used to in their turns? I was all in a hot, trembling passion; and I said it was very well for her to talk, that knew what these sights and noises betokened, and that had, perhaps, had something to do with the spectre child while it was alive. And I taunted her so, that she told me all she knew at last; and then I wished I had never been told, for it only made me more afraid than ever.

She said she had heard the tale from old neighbours that were alive when she was first married; when folks used to come to the hall sometimes, before it had got such a bad name on the country side: it might not be true, or it might, what she had been told.

℘

The old lord was Miss Furnivall's father—Miss Grace, as Dorothy called her, for Miss Maude was the elder, and Miss Furnivall by lights. The old lord was eaten up with pride. Such a proud man was never seen or heard of; and his daughters were like him. No one was good enough to wed them, although they had choice enough; for they were the great beauties of their day, as I had seen by their portraits, where they hung in the state drawing-room. But, as the old saying is, "Pride will have a fall;" and these two haughty beauties fell in love with the same man, and he no better than a foreign musician, whom their father had down from London to play music with him at the Manor House. For, above all things, next to his pride, the old lord loved music. He could play on nearly every instrument that ever was heard of; and it was a strange thing it did not soften him; but he was a fierce, dour old man, and had broken his poor wife's heart with his cruelty, they said. He was mad after music, and would pay any money for it. So he got this foreigner to come; who made such beautiful music, that they said the very birds on the trees stopped their singing to listen. And, by degrees, this foreign gentleman got such a hold over the old lord, that nothing would serve him but that he must come every year; and it was he that had the great organ brought from Holland, and built up in the hall, where it stood now. He taught the old lord to play on it; but many and many a time, when Lord Furnivall was thinking of nothing but his fine organ, and his finer music, the dark foreigner was walking abroad in the woods, with one of the young ladies: now Miss Maude, and then Miss Grace.

Miss Maude won the day and carried off the prize, such as it was; and he and she were married, all unknown to any one; and, before he made his next yearly visit, she had been confined of a little girl at a farm-house on the Moors, while her father and Miss Grace thought she was away at Doncaster Races. But though she was a wife and a mother, she was not a bit softened, but as haughty and as passionate as ever; and perhaps more so, for she was jealous of Miss Grace, to whom her foreign husband paid a deal of court—by way of blinding her—as he told his wife. But Miss Grace triumphed over Miss Maude, and Miss Maude grew fiercer and fiercer, both with her husband and with her sister; and the former—who could easily shake off what was disagreeable, and hide himself in foreign countries—went away a month before his usual time that summer, and half-threatened that he would never come back again. Meanwhile, the little girl was left at the farm-house, and her mother used to have her horse saddled and gallop wildly over the hills to see her once every week, at the very least; for where she loved she loved, and where she hated she hated. And the old lord went on playing—playing on his organ; and the servants thought the sweet music he made had soothed down his awful temper, of which (Dorothy said) some terrible tales could be told. He grew infirm too, and had to walk with a crutch; and his son—that was the present Lord Furnivall's father—was with the army in America, and the other son at sea; so Miss Maude had it pretty much her own way, and she and Miss Grace grew colder and bitterer to each other every day; till at last they hardly ever spoke, except when the old lord was by. The foreign musician came again the next summer, but it was for the last time; for they led him such a life with their jealousy and their passions, that he grew weary, and went away, and never was heard of again. And Miss Maude, who had always meant to have her marriage acknowledged when her father should be dead, was left now a deserted wife, whom nobody knew to have been married, with a child that she dared not own, although she loved it to distraction; living with a father whom she feared, and a sister whom she hated. When the next summer passed over, and the dark foreigner never came, both Miss Maude and Miss Grace grew gloomy and sad; they had a haggard look about them, though they looked handsome as ever. But, by-and-by, Miss Maude brightened; for her father grew more and more infirm, and more than ever carried away by his music, and she and Miss Grace lived almost entirely apart, having separate rooms, the one on the west side, Miss Maude on the east—those very rooms which were now shut up. So she thought she might have her little girl with her, and no one need ever know except those who dared not speak about it, and were bound to believe that it was, as she said, a cottager's child she had taken a fancy to. All this, Dorothy said, was pretty well known; but what came afterwards no one knew, except Miss Grace and Mrs. Stark, who was even then her maid, and much more of a friend to her than ever her sister had been. But the servants supposed, from words that were dropped, that Miss Maude had triumphed over Miss Grace, and told her that all the time the dark foreigner had been mocking her with pretended love—he was her own husband. The colour left Miss Grace's cheek and lips that very day for ever, and she was heard to say many a time that sooner or later she would have her revenge; and Mrs. Stark was for ever spying about the east rooms.

One fearful night, just after the New Year had come in, when the snow was lying thick and deep; and the flakes were still falling—fast enough to blind any one who might be out and abroad—there was a great and violent noise heard, and the old lord's voice above all, cursing and swearing awfully, and the cries of a little child, and the proud defiance of a fierce woman, and the sound of a blow, and a dead stillness, and moans and wailings, dying away on the hill-side! Then the old lord summoned all his servants, and told them, with terrible oaths, and words more terrible, that his daughter had disgraced herself, and that he had turned her out of doors—her, and her child—and that if ever they gave her help, or food, or shelter, he prayed that they might never enter heaven. And, all the while, Miss Grace stood by him, white and still as any stone; and, when he had ended, she heaved a great sigh, as much as to say her work was done, and her end was accomplished. But the old lord never touched his organ again, and died within the year; and no wonder I for, on the morrow of that wild and fearful night, the shepherds, coming down the Fell side, found Miss Maude sitting, all crazy and smiling, under the holly-trees, nursing a dead child, with a terrible mark on its right shoulder. "But that was not what killed it," said Dorothy: "it was the frost and the cold. Every wild creature was in its hole, and every beast in its fold, while the child and its mother were turned out to wander on the Fells! And now you know all! And I wonder if you are less frightened now?"

I was more frightened than ever; but I said I was not. I wished Miss Rosamond and myself well out of that dreadful house for ever; but I would not leave her, and I dared not take her away. But oh, how I watched her, and guarded her! We bolted the doors, and shut the window-shutters fast, an hour or more before dark, rather than leave them open five minutes too late. But my little lady still heard the weird child crying and mourning; and not all we could do or say could keep her from wanting to go to her, and let her in from the cruel wind and snow. All this time I kept away from Miss Furnivall and Mrs. Stark, as much as ever I could; for I feared them—I knew no good could be about them, with their grey, hard faces, and their dreamy eyes, looking back into the ghastly years that were gone. But, even in my fear, I had a kind of pity for Miss Furnivall, at least. Those gone down to the pit can hardly have a more hopeless look than that which was ever on her face. At last I even got so sorry for her—who never said a word but what was quite forced from her—that I prayed for her; and I taught Miss Rosamond to pray for one who had done a deadly sin; but often, when she came to those words, she would listen, and start up from her knees, and say, "I hear my little girl plaining and crying, very sad—oh, let her in, or she will die!"

ℰ℧

One night—just after New Year's Day had come at last, and the long winter had taken a turn, as I hoped—I heard the west drawing-room bell ring three times, which was the signal for me. I would not leave Miss Rosamond alone, for all she was asleep—for the old lord had been playing wilder than ever—and I feared lest my darling should waken to hear the spectre child; see her I knew she could not. I had fastened the windows too well for that. So I took her out of her bed, and wrapped her up in such outer clothes as were most handy, and carried her down to the drawing-room, where the old ladies sat at their tapestry-work as usual. They looked up when I came in, and Mrs. Stark asked, quite astounded, "Why did I bring Miss Rosamond there, out of her warm bed?" I had begun to whisper, "Because I was afraid of her being tempted out while I was away, by the wild child in the snow," when she stopped me short (with a glance at Miss Furnivall), and said Miss Furnivall wanted me to undo some work she had done wrong, and which neither of them could see to unpick. So I laid my pretty dear on the sofa, and sat down on a stool by them, and hardened my heart against them, as I heard the wind rising and howling.

Miss Rosamond slept on sound, for all the wind blew so; and Miss Furnivall said never a word, nor looked round when the gusts shook the windows. All at once she started up to her full height, and put up one hand, as if to bid us listen.

"I hear voices!" said she. "I hear terrible screams—I hear my father's voice!"
Just at that moment my darling wakened with a sudden start: "My little girl is crying, oh, how she is crying!" and she tried to get up and go to her, but she got her feet

{124}

entangled in the blanket, and I caught her up; for my flesh had begun to creep at these noises, which they heard while we could catch no sound. In a minute or two the noises came, and gathered fast, and filled our ears; we, too, heard voices and screams, and no longer heard the winter's wind that raged abroad. Mrs. Stark looked at me, and I at her, but we dared not speak. Suddenly Miss Furnivall, went towards the door, out into the ante-room, through the west lobby, and opened the door into the great hall. Mrs. Stark followed, and I durst not be left, though my heart almost stopped beating for fear. I wrapped my darling tight in my arms, and went out with them. In the hall the screams were louder than ever; they seemed to come from the east wing—nearer and nearer—close on the other side of the locked-up doors— close behind them. Then I noticed that the great bronze chandelier seemed all alight, though the hall was dim, and that a fire was blazing in the vast hearth-place, though it gave no heat; and I shuddered up with terror, and folded my darling closer to me. But as I did so the east door shook, and she, suddenly struggling to get free from me, cried, "Hester! I must go. My little girl is there I hear her; she is coming! Hester, I must go!"

I held her tight with all my strength; with a set will, I held her. If I had died, my hands would have grasped her still, I was so resolved in my mind. Miss Furnivall stood listening, and paid no regard to my darling, who had got down to the ground, and whom I, upon my knees now, was holding with both my arms clasped round her neck; she still striving and crying to get free.

All at once, the east door gave way with a thundering crash, as if torn open in a violent passion, and there came into that broad and mysterious light, the figure of a tall old man, with grey hair and gleaming eyes. He drove before him, with many a relentless gesture of abhorrence, a stern and beautiful woman, with a little child clinging to her dress.

"O Hester! Hester!" cried Miss Rosamond; "it's the lady! The lady below the holly-trees; and my little girl is with her. Hester! Hester! let me go to her; they are drawing me to them. I feel them—I feel them. I must go!"

Again she was almost convulsed by her efforts to get away; but I held her tighter and tighter, till I feared I should do her a hurt; but rather that than let her go towards those terrible phantoms. They passed along towards the great hall-door, where the winds howled and ravened for their prey; but before they reached that, the lady turned; and I could see that she defied the old man with a fierce and proud defiance; but then she quailed—and then she threw up her arms wildly and piteously to save her child—her little child—from a blow from his uplifted crutch.

And Miss Rosamond was torn as by a power stronger than mine, and writhed in my arms, and sobbed (for by this time the poor darling was growing faint).

"They want me to go with them on to the Fells—they are drawing me to them. Oh, my little girl! I would come, but cruel, wicked Hester holds me very tight." But when she saw the uplifted crutch, she swooned away, and I thanked God for it. Just at this moment—when the tall old man, his hair streaming as in the blast of a furnace, was going to strike the little shrinking child—Miss Furnivall, the old woman by my side, cried out, "O father! father! Spare the little innocent child!" But just then I saw—we all saw— another phantom shape itself, and grow clear out of the blue and misty

{125}

light that filled the hall; we had not seen her till now, for it was another lady who stood by the old man, with a look of relentless hate and triumphant scorn. That figure was very beautiful to look upon, with a soft, white hat drawn down over the proud brows, and a red and curling lip. It was dressed in an open robe of blue satin. I had seen that figure before. It was the likeness of Miss Furnivall in her youth; and the terrible phantoms moved on, regardless of old Miss Furnivall's wild entreaty— and the uplifted crutch fell on the right shoulder of the little child, and the younger sister looked on, stony, and deadly serene. But at that moment, the dim lights, and the fire that gave no heat, went out of themselves, and Miss Furnivall lay at our feet stricken down by the palsy—death-stricken.

Yes! She was carried to her bed that night never to rise again. She lay with her face to the wall, muttering low, but muttering always: "Alas! alas! what is done in youth can never be undone in age! What is done in youth can never be undone in age!"

THE MAGIC SHOP
H. G. Wells

I had seen the Magic Shop from afar several times; I had passed it once or twice, a shop window of alluring little objects, magic balls, magic hens, wonderful cones, ventriloquist dolls, the material of the basket trick, packs of cards that looked all right, and all that sort of thing, but never had I thought of going in until one day, almost without warning, Gip hauled me by my finger right up to the window, and so conducted himself that there was nothing for it but to take him in. I had not thought the place was there, to tell the truth--a modest-sized frontage in Regent Street, between the picture shop and the place where the chicks run about just out of patent incubators--but there it was sure enough. I had fancied it was down nearer the Circus, or round the corner in Oxford Street, or even in Holborn; always over the way and a little inaccessible it had been, with something of the mirage in its position; but here it was now quite indisputably, and the fat end of Gip's pointing finger made a noise upon the glass.

"If I was rich," said Gip, dabbing a finger at the Disappearing Egg, "I'd buy myself that. And that"--which was The Crying Baby, Very Human--"and that," which was a mystery, and called, so a neat card asserted, "Buy One and Astonish Your Friends.

"Anything," said Gip, "will disappear under one of those cones. I have read about it in a book. And there, dadda, is the Vanishing Halfpenny--, only they've put it this way up so's we can't see how it's done."

Gip, dear boy, inherits his mother's breeding, and he did not propose to enter the shop or worry in any way; only you know, quite unconsciously he lugged my finger doorward, and he made his interest clear.

"That," he said, and pointed to the Magic Bottle.

"If you had that?" I said; at which promising inquiry he looked up with a sudden radiance.

"I could show it to Jessie," he said, thoughtful as ever of others.

"It's less than a hundred days to your birthday, Gibbles," I said, and laid my hand on the door-handle.

Gip made no answer, but his grip tightened on my finger, and so we came into the shop.

It was no common shop this; it was a magic shop, and all the prancing precedence Gip would have taken in the matter of mere toys was wanting. He left the burthen of the conversation to me.

It was a little, narrow shop, not very well lit, and the door-bell pinged again with a plaintive note as we closed it behind us. For a moment or so we were alone and could glance about us. There was a tiger in papier-mache on the glass case that covered the low counter--a grave, kind-eyed tiger that waggled his head in a methodical manner; there were several crystal spheres, a china hand holding magic cards, a stock of magic fish-bowls in various sizes, and an immodest magic

hat that shamelessly displayed its springs. On the floor were magic mirrors; one to draw you out long and thin, one to swell your head and vanish your legs, and one to make you short and fat like a draught; and while we were laughing at these the shopman, as I suppose, came in.

At any rate, there he was behind the counter--a curious, sallow, dark man, with one ear larger than the other and a chin like the toe-cap of a boot.

"What can we have the pleasure?" he said, spreading his long, magic fingers on the glass case; and so with a start we were aware of him.

"I want," I said, "to buy my little boy a few simple tricks."

"Legerdemain?" he asked. "Mechanical? Domestic?"

"Anything amusing?" said I.

"Um!" said the shopman, and scratched his head for a moment as if thinking. Then, quite distinctly, he drew from his head a glass ball. "Something in this way?" he said, and held it out.

The action was unexpected. I had seen the trick done at entertainments endless times before--it's part of the common stock of conjurers--but I had not expected it here.

"That's good," I said, with a laugh.

"Isn't it?" said the shopman.

Gip stretched out his disengaged hand to take this object and found merely a blank palm.

"It's in your pocket," said the shopman, and there it was!

"How much will that be?" I asked.

"We make no charge for glass balls," said the shopman politely. "We get them"-- he picked one out of his elbow as he spoke--"free." He produced another from the back of his neck, and laid it beside its predecessor on the counter. Gip regarded his glass ball sagely, then directed a look of inquiry at the two on the counter, and finally brought his round-eyed scrutiny to the shopman, who smiled.

"You may have those too," said the shopman, "and, if you don't mind, one from my mouth. So!"

Gip counselled me mutely for a moment, and then in a profound silence put away the four balls, resumed my reassuring finger, and nerved himself for the next event.

"We get all our smaller tricks in that way," the shopman remarked.

I laughed in the manner of one who subscribes to a jest. "Instead of going to the wholesale shop," I said. "Of course, it's cheaper."

"In a way," the shopman said. "Though we pay in the end. But not so heavily--as people suppose...Our larger tricks, and our daily provisions and all the other things we want, we get out of that hat... And you know sir, if you'll excuse my saying it, there isn't a wholesale shop, not for Genuine Magic goods, sir. I don't know if you noticed our inscription--the Genuine Magic shop." He drew a business-card from his cheek and handed it to me. "Genuine," he said, with his finger on the word, and added, "There is absolutely no deception, sir."

He seemed to be carrying out the joke pretty thoroughly, I thought.

He turned to Gip with a smile of remarkable affability. "You, you know, are the Right Sort of Boy."

I was surprised at his knowing that, because, in the interests of discipline, we keep it rather a secret even at home; but Gip received it in unflinching silence, keeping a steadfast eye on him.

"It's only the Right Sort of Boy gets through that doorway."

And, as if by way of illustration, there came a rattling at the door, and a squeaking little voice could be faintly heard. "Nyar! I warn a' go in there, dadda, I warn a' go in there. Ny-a-a-ah!" And then the accents of a down-trodden parent, urging consolations and propitiations. "It's locked, Edward," he said.

"But it isn't," said I.

"It is, sir," said the shopman, "always--for that sort of child," and as he spoke we had a glimpse of the other youngster, a little, white face, pallid from sweet-eating and over-sapid food, and distorted by evil passions, a ruthless little egotist, pawing at the enchanted pane. "It's no good sir," said the shopman, as I moved, with my natural helpfulness, doorward, and presently the spoilt child was carried off howling.

"How do you manage that?" I said, breathing a little more freely.

"Magic!" said the shopman, with a careless wave of the hand, and behold! Sparks of coloured fire flew out of his fingers and vanished into the shadows of the shop.

"You were saying," he said, addressing himself to Gip, "before you came in, that you would like one of our 'Buy One and Astonish your Friends' boxes?"

Gip, after a gallant effort, said "Yes."

"It's in your pocket."

And leaning over the counter--he really had an extraordinarily long body--this amazing person produced the article in the customary conjurer's manner. "Paper," he said, and took a sheet out of the empty hat with the springs; "string," and behold his mouth was a string-box, from which he drew an unending thread, which when he had tied his parcel he bit off--and, it seemed to me, swallowed the ball of string. And then he lit a candle at the nose of one of the ventriloquist's dummies, stuck one of his fingers (which had become sealing-wax red) into the flame, and so sealed the parcel. "Then there was the Disappearing Egg," he remarked, and produced one from within my coat-breast and packed it, and also The Crying Baby, Very Human. I handed each parcel to Gip as it was ready, and he clasped them to his chest.

He said very little, but his eyes were eloquent; the clutch of his arms was eloquent. He was the play-ground of unspeakable emotions. These you know, were real magics. Then, with a start, I discovered something moving about in my hat--something soft and jumpy. I whipped it off, and a ruffled pigeon--no doubt a confederate--dropped out and ran on the counter, and went, I fancy, into a cardboard box behind the papier-mache tiger.

"Tut, tut!" said the shopman, dexterously relieving me of my headdress; "careless bird, and--as I live--nesting!"

{130}

He shook my hat, and shook out into his extended hand two or three eggs, a large marble, a watch, about half-a-dozen of the inevitable glass balls, and then crumpled, crinkled paper, more and more and more, talking all the time of the way in which people neglect to brush their hats inside as well as out, politely of course, but with a certain personal application. "All sorts of things accumulate, sir...Not you, of course, in particular...Nearly every customer...Astonishing what they carry about with them..." The crumpled paper rose and billowed on the counter more and more and more, until he was nearly hidden from us, until he was altogether hidden, and still his voice went on and on. "We none of us know what the fair semblance of a human being may conceal, sir. Are we all then no better than brushed exteriors, whited sepulchres--"

His voice stopped--exactly like when you hit a neighbour's gramophone with a well-aimed brick, the same instant silence, and the rustle of the paper stopped, and everything was still...

"Have you done with my hat?" I said, after an interval.

There was no answer.

I stared at Gip, and Gip stared at me, and there were our distortions in the magic mirrors, looking very rum, and grave, and quiet...

"I think we'll go now," I said. "Will you tell me how much all this comes to...?

"I say," I said, on a rather louder note, "I want the bill; and my hat, please."

It might have been a sniff from behind the paper pile...

"Let's look behind the counter, Gip," I said. "He's making fun of us."

I led Gip round the head-wagging tiger, and what do you think there was behind the counter? No one at all! Only my hat on the floor, and a common conjurer's lop-eared white rabbit lost in meditation, and looking as stupid and crumpled as only a conjurer's rabbit can do. I resumed my hat, and the rabbit lolloped a lollop or so out of my way.

"Dadda!" said Gip, in a guilty whisper.

"What is it, Gip?" said I.

"I do like this shop, dadda."

"So should I," I said to myself, "if the counter wouldn't suddenly extend itself to shut one off from the door." But I didn't call Gip's attention to that. "Pussy!" he said, with a hand out to the rabbit as it came lolloping past us; "Pussy, do Gip a magic!" And his eyes followed it as it squeezed through a door I had certainly not remarked a moment before. Then this door opened wider, and the man with one ear larger than the other appeared again. He was smiling still, but his eye met mine with something between amusement and defiance. "You'd like to see our show-room, sir," he said, with an innocent suavity. Gip tugged my finger forward. I glanced at the counter and met the shopman's eye again. I was beginning to think the magic just a little too genuine. "We haven't very much time," I said. But somehow we were inside the show-room before I could finish that.

"All goods of the same quality," said the shopman, rubbing his flexible hands together, "and that is the Best. Nothing in the place that isn't genuine Magic, and warranted thoroughly rum. Excuse me, sir!"

{131}

I felt him pull at something that clung to my coat-sleeve, and then I saw he held a little, wriggling red demon by the tail--the little creature bit and fought and tried to get at his hand--and in a moment he tossed it carelessly behind a counter. No doubt the thing was only an image of twisted indiarubber, but for the moment--! And his gesture was exactly that of a man who handles some petty biting bit of vermin. I glanced at Gip, but Gip was looking at a magic rocking-horse. I was glad he hadn't seen the thing. "I say," I said, in an undertone, and indicating Gip and the red demon with my eyes, "you haven't many things like that about, have you?"

"None of ours! Probably brought it with you," said the shopman--also in an undertone, and with a more dazzling smile than ever. "Astonishing what people will carry about with them unawares!" And then to Gip, "Do you see anything you fancy here?"

There were many things that Gip fancied there.

He turned to this astonishing tradesman with mingled confidence and respect. "Is that a Magic Sword?" he said.

"A Magic Toy Sword. It neither bends, breaks, nor cuts the fingers. It renders the bearer invincible in battle against any one under eighteen. Half-a-crown to seven and sixpence, according to size. These panoplies on cards are for juvenile knights-errant and very useful--shield of safety, sandals of swiftness, helmet of invisibility."

"Oh, daddy!" gasped Gip.

I tried to find out what they cost, but the shopman did not heed me. He had got Gip now; he had got him away from my finger; he had embarked upon the exposition of all his confounded stock, and nothing was going to stop him. Presently I saw with a qualm of distrust and something very like jealousy that Gip had hold of this person's finger, as usually he has hold of mine. No doubt the fellow was interesting, I thought, and had an interestingly faked lot of stuff, really good faked stuff, still--

I wandered after them, saying very little, but keeping an eye on this prestidigital fellow. After all, Gip was enjoying it. And no doubt when the time came to go we should be able to go quite easily.

It was a long, rambling place, that show-room, a gallery broken up by stands and stalls and pillars, with archways leading off to other departments, in which the queerest-looking assistants loafed and stared at one, and with perplexing mirrors and curtains. So perplexing, indeed, were these that I was presently unable to make out the door by which we had come.

The shopman showed Gip magic trains that ran without steam or clockwork, just as you set the signals, and then some very, very valuable boxes of soldiers that all came alive directly you took off the lid and said--I myself haven't a very quick ear and it was a tongue-twisting sound, but Gip--he has his mother's ear--got it in no time. "Bravo!" said the shopman, putting the men back into the box unceremoniously and handing it to Gip. "Now," said the shopman, and in a moment Gip had made them all alive again.

"You'll take that box?" asked the shopman.

{132}

"We'll take that box," said I, "unless you charge its full value. In which case it would need a Trust Magnate--"

"Dear heart! No!" And the shopman swept the little men back again, shut the lid, waved the box in the air, and there it was, in brown paper, tied up and--with Gip's full name and address on the paper!

The shopman laughed at my amazement.

"This is the genuine magic," he said. "The real thing."

"It's a little too genuine for my taste," I said again.

After that he fell to showing Gip tricks, odd tricks, and still odder the way they were done. He explained them, he turned them inside out, and there was the dear little chap nodding his busy bit of a head in the sagest manner.

I did not attend as well as I might. "Hey, presto!" Said the Magic Shopman, and then would come the clear, small "Hey, presto!" Of the boy. But I was distracted by other things. It was being borne in upon me just how tremendously rum this place was; it was, so to speak, inundated by a sense of rumness. There was something a little rum about the fixtures even, about the ceiling, about the floor, about the casually distributed chairs. I had a queer feeling that whenever I wasn't looking at them straight they went askew, and moved about, and played a noiseless puss-in-the-corner behind my back. And the cornice had a serpentine design with masks-- masks altogether too expressive for proper plaster.

Then abruptly my attention was caught by one of the odd-looking assistants. He was some way off and evidently unaware of my presence--I saw a sort of three-quarter length of him over a pile of toys and through an arch--and you know, he was leaning against a pillar in an idle sort of way doing the most horrid things with his features! The particular horrid thing he did was with his nose. He did it just as though he was idle and wanted to amuse himself. First of all it was a short, blobby nose, and then suddenly he shot it out like a telescope, and then out it flew and became thinner and thinner until it was like a long, red, flexible whip. Like a thing in a nightmare it was! He flourished it about and flung it forth as a fly-fisher flings his line.

My instant thought was that Gip mustn't see him. I turned about, and there was Gip quite preoccupied with the shopman, and thinking no evil. They were whispering together and looking at me. Gip was standing on a little stool, and the shopman was holding a sort of big drum in his hand.

"Hide and seek, dadda!" cried Gip. "You're He!"

And before I could do anything to prevent it, the shopman had clapped the big drum over him. I saw what was up directly. "Take that off," I cried, "this instant! You'll frighten the boy. Take it off!"

The shopman with the unequal ears did so without a word, and held the big cylinder towards me to show its emptiness. And the little stool was vacant! In that instant my boy had utterly disappeared...?

You know, perhaps, that sinister something that comes like a hand out of the unseen and grips your heart about. You know it takes your common self away and leaves you tense and deliberate, neither slow nor hasty, neither angry nor afraid. So it was with me.

I came up to this grinning shopman and kicked his stool aside.

"Stop this folly!" I said. "Where is my boy?"

"You see," he said, still displaying the drum's interior, "there is no deception--"

I put out my hand to grip him, and he eluded me by a dexterous movement. I snatched again, and he turned from me and pushed open a door to escape. "Stop!" I said, and he laughed, receding. I leapt after him--into utter darkness.

Thud!

"Lor' bless my 'eart! I didn't see you coming, sir!"

I was in Regent Street, and I had collided with a decent-looking working man; and a yard away, perhaps, and looking a little perplexed with himself, was Gip. There was some sort of apology, and then Gip had turned and come to me with a bright little smile, as though for a moment he had missed me.

And he was carrying four parcels in his arm!

He secured immediate possession of my finger.

For the second I was rather at a loss. I stared round to see the door of the magic shop, and behold, it was not there! There was no door, no shop, nothing, only the common pilaster between the shop where they sell pictures and the window with the chicks...!

I did the only thing possible in that mental tumult; I walked straight to the kerbstone and held up my umbrella for a cab.

"'Ansoms," said Gip, in a note of culminating exultation.

I helped him in, recalled my address with an effort, and got in also. Something unusual proclaimed itself in my tail-coat pocket, and I felt and discovered a glass ball. With a petulant expression I flung it into the street.

Gip said nothing.

For a space neither of us spoke.

"Dada!" said Gip, at last. "That was a proper shop!"

I came round with that to the problem of just how the whole thing had seemed to him. He looked completely undamaged--so far, good; he was neither scared nor unhinged, he was simply tremendously satisfied with the afternoon's entertainment, and there in his arms were the four parcels.

Confound it! What could be in them?

"Um!" I said. "Little boys can't go to shops like that every day."

He received this with his usual stoicism, and for a moment I was sorry I was his father and not his mother, and so couldn't suddenly there, coram publico, in our hansom, kiss him. After all, I thought, the thing wasn't so very bad.

But it was only when we opened the parcels that I really began to be reassured. Three of them contained boxes of soldiers, quite ordinary lead soldiers, but of so good a quality as to make Gip altogether forget that originally these parcels had been Magic Tricks of the only genuine sort, and the fourth contained a kitten, a little living white kitten, in excellent health and appetite and temper.

I saw this unpacking with a sort of provisional relief. I hung about in the nursery for quite an unconscionable time...

That happened six months ago. And now I am beginning to believe it is all right. The kitten had only the magic natural to all kittens, and the soldiers seem as steady a company as any colonel could desire. And Gip--?

The intelligent parent will understand that I have to go cautiously with Gip.

But I went so far as this one day. I said, "How would you like your soldiers to come alive, Gip, and march about by themselves?"

"Mine do," said Gip. "I just have to say a word I know before I open the lid."

"Then they march about alone?"

"Oh, quite, dadda. I shouldn't like them if they didn't do that."

I displayed no unbecoming surprise, and since then I have taken occasion to drop in upon him once or twice, unannounced, when the soldiers were about, but so far I have never discovered them performing in anything like a magical manner.

It's so difficult to tell.

There's also a question of finance. I have an incurable habit of paying bills. I have been up and down Regent Street several times, looking for that shop. I am inclined to think, indeed that in that matter honour is satisfied, and that since Gip's name and address are known to them, I may very well leave it to these people, whoever they may be, to send in their bill in their own time.

THE DOLL'S GHOST

F. Marion Crawford

IT was a terrible accident, and for one moment the splendid machinery of Cranston House got out of gear and stood still. The butler emerged from the retirement in which he spent his elegant leisure, two grooms of the chambers appeared simultaneously from opposite directions, there were actually housemaids on the grand staircase, and those who remember the facts most exactly assert that Mrs. Pringle herself positively stood upon the landing. Mrs. Pringle was the housekeeper. As for the head nurse, the under nurse, and the nursery maid, their feelings cannot be described. The head nurse laid one hand upon the polished marble balustrade and stared stupidly before her, the under nurse stood rigid and pale, leaning against the polished marble wall, and the nursery-maid collapsed and sat down upon the polished marble step, just beyond the limits of the velvet carpet, and frankly burst into tears.

The Lady Gwendolen Lancaster-Douglas-Scroop, youngest daughter of the ninth Duke of Cranston, and aged six years and three months, picked herself up quite alone, and sat down on the third step from the foot of the grand staircase in Cranston House.

"Oh!" ejaculated the butler, and he disappeared again.

"Ah!" responded the grooms of the chambers, as they also went away.

"It's only that doll," Mrs. Pringle was distinctly heard to say, in a tone of contempt.

The under nurse heard her say it. Then the three nurses gathered round Lady Gwendolen and patted her, and gave her unhealthy things out of their pockets, and hurried her out of Cranston House as fast as they could, lest it should be found out upstairs that they had allowed the Lady Gwendolen Lancaster-Douglas-Scroop to tumble down the grand staircase with her doll in her arms. And as the doll was badly broken, the nursery-maid carried it, with the pieces, wrapped up in Lady Gwendolen's little cloak. It was not far to Hyde Park, and when they had reached a quiet place they took means to find out that Lady Gwendolen had no bruises. For the carpet was very thick and soft, and there was thick stuff under it to make it softer.

Lady Gwendolen Douglas-Scroop sometimes yelled, but she never cried. It was because she had yelled that the nurse had allowed her to go downstairs alone with Nina, the doll, under one arm, while she steadied herself with her other hand on the balustrade, and trod upon the polished marble steps beyond the edge of the carpet. So she had fallen, and Nina had come to grief.

When the nurses were quite sure that she was not hurt, they unwrapped the doll and looked at her in her turn. She had been a very beautiful doll, very large, and fair, and healthy, with real yellow hair, and eyelids that would open and shut over very grown-up dark eyes. Moreover, when you moved her right arm up and down she said "Pa-pa," and when you moved the left she said "Ma-ma," very distinctly.

"I heard her say 'Pa' when she fell," said the under nurse, who heard everything. "But she ought to have said 'Pa-pa.'"

"That's because her arm went up when she hit the step," said the head nurse. "She'll say the other 'Pa' when I put it down again."

"Pa," said Nina, as her right arm was pushed down, and speaking through her broken face. It was cracked right across, from the upper corner of the forehead, with a hideous gash, through the nose and down to the little frilled collar of the pale green silk Mother Hubbard frock, and two little three-cornered pieces of porcelain had fallen out.

"I'm sure it's a wonder she can speak at all, being all smashed," said the under nurse.

"You'll have to take her to Mr. Puckler," said her superior. "It's not far, and you'd better go at once."

Lady Gwendolen was occupied in digging a hole in the ground with a little spade, and paid no attention to the nurses.

"What are you doing?" enquired the nursery-maid, looking on.

"Nina's dead, and I'm diggin' her a grave," replied her ladyship thoughtfully.

"Oh, she'll come to life again all right," said the nursery-maid.

The under nurse wrapped Nina up again and departed. Fortunately a kind soldier, with very long legs and a very small cap, happened to be there; and as he had nothing to do, he offered to see the under nurse safely to Mr. Puckler's and back.

Mr. Bernard Puckler and his little daughter lived in a little house in a little alley, which led out off a quiet little street not very far from Belgrave Square. He was the great doll doctor, and his extensive practice lay in the most aristocratic quarter. He mended dolls of all sizes and ages, boy dolls and girl dolls, baby dolls in long clothes, and grown-up dolls in fashionable gowns, talking dolls and dumb dolls, those that shut their eyes when they lay down, and those whose eyes had to be shut for them by means of a mysterious wire. His daughter Else was only just over twelve years old, but she was already very clever at mending dolls' clothes, and at doing their hair, which is harder than you might think, though the dolls sit quite still while it is being done.

Mr. Puckler had originally been a German, but he had dissolved his nationality in the ocean of London many years ago, like a great many foreigners. He still had one or two German friends, however, who came on Saturday evenings, and smoked with him and played picquet or "skat" with him for farthing points, and called him "Herr Doctor," which seemed to please Mr. Puckler very much.

He looked older than he was, for his beard was rather long and ragged, his hair was grizzled and thin, and he wore horn-rimmed spectacles. As for Else, she was a thin, pale child, very quiet and neat, with dark eyes and brown hair that was plaited down her back and tied with a bit of black ribbon. She mended the dolls' clothes and took the dolls back to their homes when they were quite strong again.

The house was a little one, but too big for the two people who lived in it. There was a small sitting-room on the street, and the workshop was at the back, and there were three rooms upstairs. But the father and daughter lived most of their time in the workshop, because they were generally at work, even in the evenings.

Mr. Puckler laid Nina on the table and looked at her a long time, till the tears began to fill his eyes behind the horn-rimmed spectacles. He was a very susceptible man, and he often fell in love with the dolls he mended, and found it hard to part with them when they had smiled at him for a few days. They were real little people to him, with characters and thoughts and feelings of their own, and he was very tender with them all. But some attracted him especially from the first, and when they were brought to him maimed and injured, their state seemed so pitiful to him that the tears came easily. You must remember that he had lived among dolls during a great part of his life, and understood them.

"How do you know that they feel nothing?" he went on to say to Else. "You must be gentle with them. It costs nothing to be kind to the little beings, and perhaps it makes a difference to them."

And Else understood him, because she was a child, and she knew that she was more to him than all the dolls.

He fell in love with Nina at first sight, perhaps because her beautiful brown glass eyes were something like Else's own, and he loved Else first and best, with all his heart. And, besides, it was a very sorrowful case. Nina had evidently not been long in the world, for her complexion was perfect, her hair was smooth where it should be smooth, and curly where it should be curly, and her silk clothes were perfectly new. But across her face was that frightful gash, like a sabre-cut, deep and shadowy within, but clean and sharp at the edges. When he tenderly pressed her head to close the gaping wound, the edges made a fine grating sound, that was painful to hear, and the lids of the dark eyes quivered and trembled as though Nina were suffering dreadfully.

"Poor Nina!" he exclaimed sorrowfully. "But I shall not hurt you much, though you will take a long time to get strong."

He always asked the names of the broken dolls when they were brought to him, and sometimes the people knew what the children called them, and told him. He liked "Nina" for a name. Altogether and in every way she pleased him more than any doll he had seen for many years, and he felt drawn to her, and made up his mind to make her perfectly strong and sound, no matter how much labour it might cost him.

Mr. Puckler worked patiently a little at a time, and Else watched him. She could do nothing for poor Nina, whose clothes needed no mending. The longer the doll doctor worked, the more fond he became of the yellow hair and the beautiful brown glass eyes. He sometimes forgot all the other dolls that were waiting to be mended, lying side by side on a shelf, and sat for an hour gazing at Nina's face, while he racked his ingenuity for some new invention by which to hide even the smallest trace of the terrible accident.

She was wonderfully mended. Even he was obliged to admit that; but the scar was still visible to his keen eyes, a very fine line right across the face, downwards from right to left. Yet all the conditions had been most favourable for a cure, since the cement had set quite hard at the first attempt and the weather had been fine and dry, which makes a great difference in a dolls' hospital.

At last he knew that he could do no more, and the under nurse had already come twice to see whether the job was finished, as she coarsely expressed it.

"Nina is not quite strong yet," Mr. Puckler had answered each time, for he could not make up his mind to face the parting.

And now he sat before the square deal table at which he worked, and Nina lay before him for the last time with a big brown paper box beside her. It stood there like her coffin, waiting for her, he thought. He must put her into it, and lay tissue paper over her dear face, and then put on the lid, and at the thought of tying the string his sight was dim with tears again. He was never to look into the glassy depths of the beautiful brown eyes any more, nor to hear the little wooden voice say "Pa-pa" and "Ma-ma." It was a very painful moment.

In the vain hope of gaining time before the separation, he took up the little sticky bottles of cement and glue and gum and colour, looking at each one in turn, and then at Nina's face. And all his small tools lay there, neatly arranged in a row, but he knew that he could not use them again for Nina. She was quite strong at last, and in a country where there should be no cruel children to hurt her she might live a hundred years, with only that almost imperceptible line across her face to tell of the fearful thing that had befallen her on the marble steps of Cranston House.

Suddenly Mr. Puckler's heart was quite full, and he rose abruptly from his seat and turned away.

"Else," he said unsteadily, "you must do it for me. I cannot bear to see her go into the box."

So he went and stood at the window with his back turned, while Else did what he had not the heart to do.

"Is it done?" he asked, not turning round. "Then take her away, my dear. Put on your hat, and take her to Cranston House quickly, and when you are gone I will turn round."

Else was used to her father's queer ways with the dolls, and though she had never seen him so much moved by a parting, she was not much surprised.

"Come back quickly," he said, when he heard her hand on the latch. "It is growing late, and I should not send you at this hour. But I cannot bear to look forward to it any more."

When Else was gone, he left the window and sat down in his place before the table again, to wait for the child to come back. He touched the place where Nina had lain, very gently, and he recalled the softly tinted pink face, and the glass eyes, and the ringlets of yellow hair, till he could almost see them.

The evenings were long, for it was late in the spring. But it began to grow dark soon, and Mr. Puckler wondered why Else did not come back. She had been gone an hour and a half, and that was much longer than he had expected, for it was barely half a mile from Belgrave Square to Cranston House. He reflected that the child might have been kept waiting, but as the twilight deepened he grew anxious, and walked up and down in the dim workshop, no longer thinking of Nina, but of Else, his own living child, whom he loved.

An undefinable, disquieting sensation came upon him by fine degrees, a chilliness and a faint stirring of his thin hair, joined with a wish to be in any company rather than to be alone much longer. It was the beginning of fear.

He told himself in strong German-English that he was a foolish old man, and he began to feel about for the matches in the dusk. He knew just where they should be, for he always kept them in the same place, close to the little tin box that held bits of sealing-wax of various colours, for some kinds of mending. But somehow he could not find the matches in the gloom.

Something had happened to Else, he was sure, and as his fear increased, he felt as though it might be allayed if he could get a light and see what time it was. Then he called himself a foolish old man again, and the sound of his own voice startled him in the dark. He could not find the matches.

The window was grey still; he might see what time it was if he went close to it, and he could go and get matches out of the cupboard afterwards. He stood back from the table, to get out of the way of the chair, and began to cross the board floor.

Something was following him in the dark. There was a small pattering, as of tiny feet upon the boards. He stopped and listened, and the roots of his hair tingled. It was nothing, and he was a foolish old man. He made two steps more, and he was sure that he heard the little pattering again. He turned his back to the window, leaning against the sash so that the panes began to crack, and he faced the dark. Everything was quite still, and it smelt of paste and cement and wood-filings as usual.

"Is that you, Else?" he asked, and he was surprised by the fear in his voice.

There was no answer in the room, and he held up his watch and tried to make out what time it was by the grey dusk that was just not darkness. So far as he could see, it was within two or three minutes of ten o'clock. He had been a long time alone. He was shocked, and frightened for Else, out in London, so late, and he almost ran across the room to the door. As he fumbled for the latch, he distinctly heard the running of the little feet after him.

"Mice!" he exclaimed feebly, just as he got the door open.

He shut it quickly behind him, and felt as though some cold thing had settled on his back and were writhing upon him. The passage was quite dark, but he found his hat and was out in the alley in a moment, breathing more freely, and surprised to find how much light there still was in the open air. He could see the pavement clearly under his feet, and far off in the street to which the alley led he could hear the laughter and calls of children, playing some game out of doors. He wondered how he could have been so nervous, and for an instant he thought of going back into the house to wait quietly for Else. But instantly he felt that nervous fright of something stealing over him again. In any case it was better to walk up to

Cranston House and ask the servants about the child. One of the women had perhaps taken a fancy to her, and was even now giving her tea and cake.

He walked quickly to Belgrave Square, and then up the broad streets, listening as he went, whenever there was no other sound, for the tiny footsteps. But he heard nothing, and was laughing at himself when he rang the servants' bell at the big house. Of course, the child must be there.

The person who opened the door was quite an inferior person, for it was a back door, but affected the manners of the front, and stared at Mr. Puckler superciliously under the strong light.

No little girl had been seen, and he knew "nothing about no dolls."

"She is my little girl," said Mr. Puckler tremulously, for all his anxiety was returning tenfold, "and I am afraid something has happened."

The inferior person said rudely that "nothing could have happened to her in that house, because she had not been there, which was a jolly good reason why;" and Mr. Puckler was obliged to admit that the man ought to know, as it was his business to keep the door and let people in. He wished to be allowed to speak to the under nurse, who knew him; but the man was ruder than ever, and finally shut the door in his face.

When the doll doctor was alone in the street, he steadied himself by the railing, for he felt as though he were breaking in two, just as some dolls break, in the middle of the backbone.

Presently he knew that he must be doing something to find Else, and that gave him strength. He began to walk as quickly as he could through the streets, following every highway and byway which his little girl might have taken on her errand. He also asked several policemen in vain if they had seen her, and most of them answered him kindly, for they saw that he was a sober man and in his right senses, and some of them had little girls of their own.

It was one o'clock in the morning when he went up to his own door again, worn out and hopeless and broken-hearted. As he turned the key in the lock, his heart stood still, for he knew that he was awake and not dreaming, and that he really heard those tiny footsteps pattering to meet him inside the house along the passage.

But he was too unhappy to be much frightened any more, and his heart went on again with a dull regular pain, that found its way all through him with every pulse. So he went in, and hung up his hat in the dark, and found the matches in the cupboard and the candlestick in its place in the corner.

Mr. Puckler was so much overcome and so completely worn out that he sat down in his chair before the work-table and almost fainted, as his face dropped forward upon his folded hands. Beside him the solitary candle burned steadily with a low flame in the still warm air.

"Else! Else!" he moaned against his yellow knuckles. And that was all he could say, and it was no relief to him. On the contrary, the very sound of the name was a new and sharp pain that pierced his ears and his head and his very soul. For every time he repeated the name it meant that little Else was dead, somewhere out in the streets of London in the dark.

He was so terribly hurt that he did not even feel something pulling gently at the skirt of his old coat, so gently that it was like the nibbling of a tiny mouse. He might have thought that it was really a mouse if he had noticed it.

"Else! Else!" he groaned right against his hands.

Then a cool breath stirred his thin hair, and the low flame of the one candle dropped down almost to a mere spark, not flickering as though a draught were going to blow it out, but just dropping down as if it were tired out. Mr. Puckler felt his hands stiffening with fright under his face; and there was a faint rustling sound, like some small silk thing blown in a gentle breeze. He sat up straight, stark and scared, and a small wooden voice spoke in the stillness.

"Pa-pa," it said, with a break between the syllables.

Mr. Puckler stood up in a single jump, and his chair fell over backwards with a smashing noise upon the wooden floor. The candle had almost gone out.

It was Nina's doll voice that had spoken, and he should have known it among the voices of a hundred other dolls. And yet there was something more in it, a little human ring, with a pitiful cry and a call for help, and the wail of a hurt child. Mr. Puckler stood up, stark and stiff, and tried to look round, but at first he could not, for he seemed to be frozen from head to foot.

Then he made a great effort, and he raised one hand to each of his temples, and pressed his own head round as he would have turned a doll's. The candle was burning so low that it might as well have been out altogether, for any light it gave, and the room seemed quite dark at first. Then he saw something. He would not have believed that he could be more frightened than he had been just before that. But he was, and his knees shook, for he saw the doll standing in the middle of the floor, shining with a faint and ghostly radiance, her beautiful glassy brown eyes fixed on his. And across her face the very thin line of the break he had mended shone as though it were drawn in light with a fine point of white flame.

Yet there was something more in the eyes, too; there was something human, like Else's own, but as if only the doll saw him through them, and not Else. And there was enough of Else to bring back all his pain and to make him forget his fear.

"Else! my little Else!" he cried aloud.

The small ghost moved, and its doll-arm slowly rose and fell with a stiff, mechanical motion.

"Pa-pa," it said.

It seemed this time that there was even more of Else's tone echoing somewhere between the wooden notes that reached his ears so distinctly, and yet so far away. Else was calling him, he was sure.

His face was perfectly white in the gloom, but his knees did not shake any more, and he felt that he was less frightened.

"Yes, child! But where? Where?" he asked. "Where are you, Else?"

"Pa-pa!"

{143}

The syllables died away in the quiet room. There was a low rustling of silk, the glassy brown eyes turned slowly away, and Mr. Puckler heard the pitter-patter of the small feet in the bronze kid slippers as the figure ran straight to the door. Then the candle burned high again, the room was full of light, and he was alone.

Mr. Puckler passed his hand over his eyes and looked about him. He could see everything quite clearly, and he felt that he must have been dreaming, though he was standing instead of sitting down, as he should have been if he had just waked up. The candle burned brightly now. There were the dolls to be mended, lying in a row with their toes up. The third one had lost her right shoe, and Else was making one. He knew that, and he was certainly not dreaming now. He had not been dreaming when he had come in from his fruitless search and had heard the doll's footsteps running to the door. He had not fallen asleep in his chair. How could he possibly have fallen asleep when his heart was breaking? He had been awake all the time.

He steadied himself, set the fallen chair upon its legs, and said to himself again very emphatically that he was a foolish old man. He ought to be out in the streets looking for his child, asking questions, and enquiring at the police stations, where all accidents were reported as soon as they were known, or at the hospitals.

"Pa-pa!"

The longing, wailing, pitiful little wooden cry rang from the passage, outside the door, and Mr. Puckler stood for an instant with white face, transfixed and rooted to the spot. A moment later his hand was on the latch. Then he was in the passage, with the light streaming from the open door behind him.

Quite at the other end he saw the little phantom shining clearly in the shadow, and the right hand seemed to beckon to him as the arm rose and fell once more. He knew all at once that it had not come to frighten him but to lead him, and when it disappeared, and he walked boldly towards the door, he knew that it was in the street outside, waiting for him. He forgot that he was tired and had eaten no supper, and had walked many miles, for a sudden hope ran through and through him, like a golden stream of life.

And sure enough, at the corner of the alley, and at the corner of the street, and out in Belgrave Square, he saw the small ghost flitting before him. Sometimes it was only a shadow, where there was other light, but then the glare of the lamps made a pale green sheen on its little Mother Hubbard frock of silk; and sometimes, where the streets were dark and silent, the whole figure shone out brightly, with its yellow curls and rosy neck. It seemed to trot along like a tiny child, and Mr. Puckler could almost hear the pattering of the bronze kid slippers on the pavement as it ran. But it went very fast, and he could only just keep up with it, tearing along with his hat on the back of his head and his thin hair blown by the night breeze, and his horn-rimmed spectacles firmly set upon his broad nose.

On and on he went, and he had no idea where he was. He did not even care, for he knew certainly that he was going the right way.

Then at last, in a wide, quiet street, he was standing before a big, sober-looking door that had two lamps on each side of it, and a polished brass bell-handle, which he pulled.

And just inside, when the door was opened, in the bright light, there was the little shadow, and the pale green sheen of the little silk dress, and once more the small cry came to his ears, less pitiful, more longing.

"Pa-pa!"

The shadow turned suddenly bright, and out of the brightness the beautiful brown glass eyes were turned up happily to his, while the rosy mouth smiled so divinely that the phantom doll looked almost like a little angel just then.

"A little girl was brought in soon after ten o'clock," said the quiet voice of the hospital doorkeeper. "I think they thought she was only stunned. She was holding a big brown-paper box against her, and they could not get it out of her arms. She had a long plait of brown hair that hung down as they carried her."

"She is my little girl," said Mr. Puckler, but he hardly heard his own voice.

He leaned over Else's face in the gentle light of the children's ward, and when he had stood there a minute the beautiful brown eyes opened and looked up to his.

"Pa-pa!" cried Else, softly, "I knew you would come!"

Then Mr. Puckler did not know what he did or said for a moment, and what he felt was worth all the fear and terror and despair that had almost killed him that night. But by and by Else was telling her story, and the nurse let her speak, for there were only two other children in the room, who were getting well and were sound asleep.

"They were big boys with bad faces," said Else, "and they tried to get Nina away from me, but I held on and fought as well as I could till one of them hit me with something, and I don't remember any more, for I tumbled down, and I suppose the boys ran away, and somebody found me there. But I'm afraid Nina is all smashed."

"Here is the box," said the nurse. "We could not take it out of her arms till she came to herself. Should you like to see if the doll is broken?"

And she undid the string cleverly, but Nina was all smashed to pieces. Only the gentle light of the children's ward made a pale green sheen in the folds of the little Mother Hubbard frock.

THE OPEN DOOR
Mrs Oliphant

I took the house in Brentwood on my return from India in 18--, for the temporary accommodation of my family, until I could find a permanent home for them. It had many advantages which made it peculiarly appropriate. It was within reach of Edinburgh; and my boy Roland, whose education had been considerably neglected, could go in and out to school; which was thought to be better for him than either leaving home altogether or staying there always with a tutor. The first of these expedients would have seemed preferable to me; the second commended itself to his mother. The doctor, like a judicious man, took the midway between. "Put him on his pony, and let him ride into the High School every morning; it will do him all the good in the world," Dr. Simson said; "and when it is bad weather, there is the train." His mother accepted this solution of the difficulty more easily than I could have hoped; and our pale-faced boy, who had never known anything more invigorating than Simla, began to encounter the brisk breezes of the North in the subdued severity of the month of May. Before the time of the vacation in July we had the satisfaction of seeing him begin to acquire something of the brown and ruddy complexion of his schoolfellows. The English system did not commend itself to Scotland in these days. There was no little Eton at Fettes; nor do I think, if there had been, that a genteel exotic of that class would have tempted either my wife or me. The lad was doubly precious to us, being the only one left us of many; and he was fragile in body, we believed, and deeply sensitive in mind. To keep him at home, and yet to send him to school, — to combine the advantages of the two systems, — seemed to be everything that could be desired. The two girls also found at Brentwood everything they wanted. They were near enough to Edinburgh to have masters and lessons as many as they required for completing that never-ending education which the young people seem to require nowadays. Their mother married me when she was younger than Agatha; and I should like to see them improve upon their mother! I myself was then no more than twenty-five, — an age at which I see the young fellows now groping about them, with no notion what they are going to do with their lives. However, I suppose every generation has a conceit of itself which elevates it, in its own opinion above that which comes after it.

Brentwood stands on that fine and wealthy slope of country — one of the richest in Scotland — which lies between the Pentland Hills and the Firth. In clear weather you could see the blue gleam — like a bent bow, embracing the wealthy fields and scattered houses — of the great estuary on one side of you; and on the other the blue heights, not gigantic like those we had been used to, but just high enough for all the glories of the atmosphere, the play of clouds, and sweet reflections, which give to a hilly country an interest and a charm which nothing else can emulate. Edinburgh — with its two lesser heights, the Castle and the Calton Hill, its spires and towers piercing through the smoke, and Arthur's Seat lying crouched behind,

like a guardian no longer very needful, taking his repose beside the well-beloved charge, which is now, so to speak, able to take care of itself without him — lay at our right hand. From the lawn and drawing-room windows we could see all these varieties of landscape. The color was sometimes a little chilly, but sometimes, also, as animated and full of vicissitude as a drama. I was never tired of it. Its color and freshness revived the eyes which had grown weary of arid plains and blazing skies. It was always cheery, and fresh, and full of repose.

The village of Brentwood lay almost under the house, on the other side of the deep little ravine, down which a stream — which ought to have been a lovely, wild, and frolicsome little river — flowed between its rocks and trees. The river, like so many in that district, had, however, in its earlier life been sacrificed to trade, and was grimy with paper-making. But this did not affect our pleasure in it so much as I have known it to affect other streams. Perhaps our water was more rapid; perhaps less clogged with dirt and refuse. Our side of the dell was charmingly *accidenté*, and clothed with fine trees, through which various paths wound down to the river-side and to the village bridge which crossed the stream. The village lay in the hollow, and climbed, with very prosaic houses, the other side. Village architecture does not flourish in Scotland. The blue slates and the gray stone are sworn foes to the picturesque; and though I do not, for my own part, dislike the interior of an old-fashioned pewed and galleried church, with its little family settlements on all sides, the square box outside, with its bit of a spire like a handle to lift it by, is not an improvement to the landscape. Still a cluster of houses on differing elevations, with scraps of garden coming in between, a hedgerow with clothes laid out to dry, the opening of a street with its rural sociability, the women at their doors, the slow wagon lumbering along, gives a centre to the landscape. It was cheerful to look at, and convenient in a hundred ways. Within ourselves we had walks in plenty, the glen being always beautiful in all its phases, whether the woods were green in the spring or ruddy in the autumn. In the park which surrounded the house were the ruins of the former mansion of Brentwood, — a much smaller and less important house than the solid Georgian edifice which we inhabited. The ruins were picturesque, however, and gave importance to the place. Even we, who were but temporary tenants, felt a vague pride in them, as if they somehow reflected a certain consequence upon ourselves. The old building had the remains of a tower, — an indistinguishable mass of mason-work, overgrown with ivy; and the shells of walls attached to this were half filled up with soil. I had never examined it closely, I am ashamed to say. There was a large room, or what had been a large room, with the lower part of the windows still existing, on the principal floor, and underneath other windows, which were perfect, though half filled up with fallen soil, and waving with a wild growth of brambles and chance growths of all kinds. This was the oldest part of all. At a little distance were some very commonplace and disjointed fragments of building, one of them suggesting a certain pathos by its very commonness and the complete wreck which it showed. This was the end of a low gable, a bit of gray wall, all incrusted with lichens, in which was a common door-way. Probably it had been a servants' entrance, a back-door, or opening into what

{148}

are called "the offices" in Scotland. No offices remained to be entered, — pantry and kitchen had all been swept out of being; but there stood the doorway open and vacant, free to all the winds, to the rabbits, and every wild creature. It struck my eye, the first time I went to Brentwood, like a melancholy comment upon a life that was over. A door that led to nothing, — closed once, perhaps, with anxious care, bolted and guarded, now void of any meaning. It impressed me, I remember, from the first; so perhaps it may be said that my mind was prepared to attach to it an importance which nothing justified.

The summer was a very happy period of repose for us all. The warmth of Indian suns was still in our veins. It seemed to us that we could never have enough of the greenness, the dewiness, the freshness of the northern landscape. Even its mists were pleasant to us, taking all the fever out of us, and pouring in vigor and refreshment. In autumn we followed the fashion of the time, and went away for change which we did not in the least require. It was when the family had settled down for the winter, when the days were short and dark, and the rigorous reign of frost upon us, that the incidents occurred which alone could justify me in intruding upon the world my private affairs. These incidents were, however, of so curious a character, that I hope my inevitable references to my own family and pressing personal interests will meet with a general pardon.

I was absent in London when these events began. In London an old Indian plunges back into the interests with which all his previous life has been associated, and meets old friends at every step. I had been circulating among some half-dozen of these, — enjoying the return to my former life in shadow, though I had been so thankful in substance to throw it aside, — and had missed some of my home letters, what with going down from Friday to Monday to old Benbow's place in the country, and stopping on the way back to dine and sleep at Sellar's and to take a look into Cross's stables, which occupied another day. It is never safe to miss one's letters. In this transitory life, as the Prayer-book says, how can one ever be certain what is going to happen? All was well at home. I knew exactly (I thought) what they would have to say to me: "The weather has been so fine, that Roland has not once gone by train, and he enjoys the ride beyond anything." "Dear papa, be sure that you don't forget anything, but bring us so-and-so, and so-and-so," — a list as long as my arm. Dear girls and dearer mother! I would not for the world have forgotten their commissions, or lost their little letters, for all the Benbows and Crosses in the world.

But I was confident in my home-comfort and peacefulness. When I got back to my club, however, three or four letters were lying for me, upon some of which I noticed the "immediate," "urgent," which old-fashioned people and anxious people still believe will influence the post-office and quicken the speed of the mails. I was about to open one of these, when the club porter brought me two telegrams, one of which, he said, had arrived the night before. I opened, as was to be expected, the last first, and this was what I read: "Why don't you come or answer? For God's sake, come. He is much worse." This was a thunderbolt to fall upon a man's head who had one only son, and he the light of his eyes! The other telegram, which I opened with hands trembling so much that I lost time by my haste, was to much the same purport: "No better; doctor afraid of brain-fever. Calls for you day and night. Let nothing detain you." The first thing I did was to look up the time-tables to see if there was any way of getting off sooner than by the night-train, though I knew well enough there was not; and then I read the letters, which furnished, alas! too clearly, all the details. They told me that the boy had been pale for some time, with a scared look. His mother had noticed it before I left home, but would not say anything to alarm me. This look had increased day by day; and soon it was observed that Roland came home at a wild gallop through the park, his pony panting and in foam, himself "as white as a sheet," but with the perspiration streaming from his forehead. For a long time he had resisted all questioning, but at length had developed such strange changes of mood, showing a reluctance to go to school, a desire to be fetched in the carriage at night, — which was a ridiculous piece of luxury, — an unwillingness to go out into the grounds, and nervous start at every sound, that his mother had insisted upon an explanation. When the boy — our boy Roland, who had never known what fear was — began to talk to her of voices he had heard in the park, and shadows that had appeared to him among the ruins, my wife promptly put him to bed and sent for Dr. Simson, which, of course, was the only thing to do.

I hurried off that evening, as may be supposed, with an anxious heart. How I got through the hours before the starting of the train, I cannot tell. We must all be thankful for the quickness of the railway when in anxiety; but to have thrown myself into a post-chaise as soon as horses could be put to, would have been a relief. I got to Edinburgh very early in the blackness of the winter morning, and scarcely dared look the man in the face, at whom I gasped, "What news?" My wife had sent the brougham for me, which I concluded, before the man spoke, was a bad sign. His answer was that stereotyped answer which leaves the imagination so wildly free, — "Just the same." Just the same! What might that mean? The horses seemed to me to creep along the long dark country road. As we dashed through the park, I thought I heard some one moaning among the trees, and clenched my fist at him (whoever he might be) with fury. Why had the fool of a woman at the gate allowed any one to come in to disturb the quiet of the place? If I had not been in such hot haste to get home, I think I should have stopped the carriage and got out to see what tramp it was that had made an entrance, and chosen my grounds, of all places in the world, — when my boy was ill! — to grumble and groan in. But I had no reason to complain of our slow pace here. The horses flew like lightning along the intervening path, and drew up at the door all panting, as if they had run a race. My wife stood waiting to receive me, with a pale face, and a candle in her hand, which made her look paler still as the wind blew the flame about. "He is sleeping," she said in a whisper, as if her voice might wake him. And I replied, when I could find my voice, also in a whisper, as though the jingling of the horses' furniture and the sound of their hoofs must not have been more dangerous. I stood on the steps with her a moment, almost afraid to go in, now that I was here; and it seemed to me that I saw without observing, if I may say so, that the horses were unwilling to turn round, though their stables lay that way, or that the men were unwilling. These things occurred to me afterwards, though at the moment I was not capable of anything but to ask questions and to hear of the condition of the boy.

I looked at him from the door of his room, for we were afraid to go near, lest we should disturb that blessed sleep. It looked like actual sleep, not the lethargy into which my wife told me he would sometimes fall. She told me everything in the next room, which communicated with his, rising now and then and going to the door of communication; and in this there was much that was very startling and confusing to the mind. It appeared that ever since the winter began — since it was early dark, and night had fallen before his return from school — he had been hearing voices among the ruins: at first only a groaning, he said, at which his pony was as much alarmed as he was, but by degrees a voice.

The tears ran down my wife's cheeks as she described to me how he would start up in the night and cry out, "Oh, mother, let me in! oh, mother, let me in!" with a pathos which rent her heart. And she sitting there all the time, only longing to do everything his heart could desire! But though she would try to soothe him, crying, "You are at home, my darling. I am here. Don't you know me? Your mother is here!" he would only stare at her, and after a while spring up again with the same cry. At other times he would be quite reasonable, she said, asking eagerly when I was coming, but declaring that he must go with me as soon as I did so, "to let them in." "The doctor thinks his nervous system must have received a shock," my wife said. "Oh, Henry, can it be that we have pushed him on too much with his work — a delicate boy like Roland? And what is his work in comparison with his health? Even you would think little of honors or prizes if it hurt the boy's health." Even I! — as if I were an inhuman father sacrificing my child to my ambition. But I would not increase her trouble by taking any notice. After a while they persuaded me to lie down, to rest, and to eat, none of which things had been possible since I received their letters. The mere fact of being on the spot, of course, in itself was a great thing; and when I knew that I could be called in a moment, as soon as he was awake and wanted me, I felt capable, even in the dark, chill morning twilight, to snatch an hour or two's sleep. As it happened, I was so worn out with the strain of anxiety, and he so quieted and consoled by knowing I had come, that I was not disturbed till the afternoon, when the twilight had again settled down. There was just daylight enough to see his face when I went to him; and what a change in a fortnight! He was paler and more worn, I thought, than even in those dreadful days in the plains before we left India. His hair seemed to me to have grown long and lank; his eyes were like blazing lights projecting out of his white face. He got hold of my hand in a cold and tremulous clutch, and waved to everybody to go away. "Go away — even mother," he said; "go away." This went to her heart; for she did not like that even I should have more of the boy's confidence than herself; but my wife has never been a woman to think of herself, and she left us alone. "Are they all gone?" he said eagerly. "They would not let me speak. The doctor treated me as if I were a fool. You know I am not a fool, papa." "Yes, yes, my boy, I know. But you are ill, and quiet is so necessary. You are not only *not* a fool, Roland, but you are reasonable and understand. When you are ill you must deny yourself; you must not do everything that you might do being well."

{151}

He waved his thin hand with a sort of indignation. "Then, father, I am not ill," he cried. "Oh, I thought when you came you would not stop me, — you would see the sense of it! What do you think is the matter with me, all of you? Simson is well enough; but he is only a doctor. What do you think is the matter with me? I am no more ill than you are. A doctor, of course, he thinks you are ill the moment he looks at you — that 's what he's there for — and claps you into bed."

"Which is the best place for you at present, my dear boy."

"I made up my mind," cried the little fellow, "that I would stand it till you came home. I said to myself, I won't frighten mother and the girls. But now, father," he cried, half jumping out of bed, "it's not illness: it's a secret."

His eyes shone so wildly, his face was so swept with strong feeling, that my heart sank within me. It could be nothing but fever that did it, and fever had been so fatal. I got him into my arms to put him back into bed. "Roland," I said, humoring the poor child, which I knew was the only way, "if you are going to tell me this secret to do any good, you know you must be quite quiet, and not excite yourself. If you excite yourself, I must not let you speak."

"Yes, father," said the boy. He was quiet directly, like a man, as if he quite understood. When I had laid him back on his pillow, he looked up at me with that grateful, sweet look with which children, when they are ill, break one's heart, the water coming into his eyes in his weakness. "I was sure as soon as you were here you would know what to do," he said.

"To be sure, my boy. Now keep quiet, and tell it all out like a man." To think I was telling lies to my own child! for I did it only to humor him, thinking, poor little fellow, his brain was wrong.

"Yes, father. Father, there is some one in the park, — some one that has been badly used."

"Hush, my dear; you remember there is to be no excitement. Well, who is this somebody, and who has been ill-using him? We will soon put a stop to that."

"Ah," cried Roland, "but it is not so easy as you think. I don't know who it is. It is just a cry. Oh, if you could hear it! It gets into my head in my sleep. I heard it as clear — as clear; and they think that I am dreaming, or raving perhaps," the boy said, with a sort of disdainful smile.

This look of his perplexed me; it was less like fever than I thought. "Are you quite sure you have not dreamed it, Roland?" I said.

"Dreamed? — that!" He was springing up again when he suddenly bethought himself, and lay down flat, with the same sort of smile on his face. "The pony heard it, too," he said. "She jumped as if she had been shot. If I had not grasped at the reins — for I was frightened, father —"

"No shame to you, my boy," said I, though I scarcely knew why.

"If I hadn't held to her like a leech, she'd have pitched me over her head, and never drew breath till we were at the door. Did the pony dream it?" he said, with a soft disdain, yet indulgence for my foolishness. Then he added slowly, "It was only a cry the first time, and all the time before you went away. I wouldn't tell you, for it was so wretched to be frightened. I thought it might be a hare or a rabbit snared, and I

{152}

went in the morning and looked; but there was nothing. It was after you went I heard it really first; and this is what he says." He raised himself on his elbow close to me, and looked me in the face: "'Oh, mother, let me in! oh, mother, let me in!'" As he said the words a mist came over his face, the mouth quivered, the soft features all melted and changed, and when he had ended these pitiful words, dissolved in a shower of heavy tears.

Was it a hallucination? Was it the fever of the brain? Was it the disordered fancy caused by great bodily weakness? How could I tell? I thought it wisest to accept it as if it were all true.

"This is very touching, Roland," I said.

"Oh, if you had just heard it, father! I said to myself, if father heard it he would do something; but mamma, you know, she 's given over to Simson, and that fellow 's a doctor, and never thinks of anything but clapping you into bed."

"We must not blame Simson for being a doctor, Roland."

"No, no," said my boy, with delightful toleration and indulgence; "oh, no; that 's the good of him; that 's what he's for; I know that. But you — you are different; you are just father; and you'll do something — directly, papa, directly; this very night."

"Surely," I said. "No doubt it is some little lost child."

He gave me a sudden, swift look, investigating my face as though to see whether, after all, this was everything my eminence as "father" came to, — no more than that. Then he got hold of my shoulder, clutching it with his thin hand: "Look here," he said, with a quiver in his voice; "suppose it wasn't — living at all!"

"My dear boy, how then could you have heard it?" I said.

He turned away from me with a pettish exclamation, — "As if you didn't know better than that!"

"Do you want to tell me it is a ghost?" I said.

Roland withdrew his hand; his countenance assumed an aspect of great dignity and gravity; a slight quiver remained about his lips. "Whatever it was — you always said we were not to call names. It was something — in trouble. Oh, father, in terrible trouble!"

"But, my boy," I said (I was at my wits' end), "if it was a child that was lost, or any poor human creature — but, Roland, what do you want me to do?"

"I should know if I was you," said the child eagerly. "That is what I always said to myself, — Father will know. Oh, papa, papa, to have to face it night after night, in such terrible, terrible trouble, and never to be able to do it any good! I don't want to cry; it's like a baby, I know; but what can I do else? Out there all by itself in the ruin, and nobody to help it! I can't bear it! I can't bear it!" cried my generous boy. And in his weakness he burst out, after many attempts to restrain it, into a great childish fit of sobbing and tears.

I do not know that I ever was in a greater perplexity in my life; and afterwards, when I thought of it, there was something comic in it too. It is bad enough to find your child's mind possessed with the conviction that he has seen, or heard, a ghost; but that he should require you to go instantly and help that ghost was the most bewildering experience that had ever come my way. I am a sober man myself, and not superstitious — at least any more than everybody is superstitious. Of course I do not believe in ghosts; but I don't deny, any more than other people, that there are stories which I cannot pretend to understand. My blood got a sort of chill in my veins at the idea that Roland should be a ghost-seer; for that generally means a hysterical temperament and weak health, and all that men most hate and fear for their children. But that I should take up his ghost and right its wrongs, and save it from its trouble, was such a mission as was enough to confuse any man. I did my best to console my boy without giving any promise of this astonishing kind; but he was too sharp for me: he would have none of my caresses. With sobs breaking in at intervals upon his voice, and the rain-drops hanging on his eyelids, he yet returned to the charge.

"It will be there now! — it will be there all the night! Oh, think, papa, — think if it was me! I can't rest for thinking of it. Don't!" he cried, putting away my hand, — "don't! You go and help it, and mother can take care of me."

"But, Roland, what can I do?"

My boy opened his eyes, which were large with weakness and fever, and gave me a smile such, I think, as sick children only know the secret of. "I was sure you would know as soon as you came. I always said, Father will know. And mother," he cried, with a softening of repose upon his face, his limbs relaxing, his form sinking with a luxurious ease in his bed, — "mother can come and take care of me."

I called her, and saw him turn to her with the complete dependence of a child; and then I went away and left them, as perplexed a man as any in Scotland. I must say, however, I had this consolation, that my mind was greatly eased about Roland. He might be under a hallucination; but his head was clear enough, and I did not think him so ill as everybody else did. The girls were astonished even at the ease with which I took it. "How do you think he is?" they said in a breath, coming round me, laying hold of me. "Not half so ill as I expected," I said; "not very bad at all." "Oh, papa, you are a darling!" cried Agatha, kissing me, and crying upon my shoulder; while little Jeanie, who was as pale as Roland, clasped both her arms round mine, and could not speak at all. I knew nothing about it, not half so much as Simson; but they believed in me: they had a feeling that all would go right now. God is very good to you when your children look to you like that. It makes one humble, not proud. I was not worthy of it; and then I recollected that I had to act the part of a father to Roland's ghost, — which made me almost laugh, though I might just as well have cried. It was the strangest mission that ever was intrusted to mortal man.

It was then I remembered suddenly the looks of the men when they turned to take the brougham to the stables in the dark that morning. They had not liked it, and the horses had not liked it. I remembered that even in my anxiety about Roland I had heard them tearing along the avenue back to the stables, and had made a memorandum mentally that I must speak of it. It seemed to me that the best thing I could do was to go to the stables now and make a few inquiries. It is impossible to fathom the minds of rustics; there might be some devilry of practical joking, for anything I knew; or they might have some interest in getting up a bad reputation for the Brentwood avenue. It was getting dark by the time I went out, and nobody who knows the country will need to be told how black is the darkness of a November night under high laurel-bushes and yew-trees. I walked into the heart of the shrubberies two or three times, not seeing a step before me, till I came out upon the broader carriage-road, where the trees opened a little, and there was a faint gray glimmer of sky visible, under which the great limes and elms stood darkling like ghosts; but it grew black again as I approached the corner where the ruins lay. Both eyes and ears were on the alert, as may be supposed; but I could see nothing in the absolute gloom, and, so far as I can recollect, I heard nothing. Nevertheless there came a strong impression upon me that somebody was there. It is a sensation which most people have felt. I have seen when it has been strong enough to awake me out of sleep, the sense of some one looking at me. I suppose my imagination had been affected by Roland's story; and the mystery of the darkness is always full of suggestions. I stamped my feet violently on the gravel to rouse myself, and called out sharply, "Who's there?" Nobody answered, nor did I expect any one to answer, but the impression had been made. I was so foolish that I did not like to look back, but went sideways, keeping an eye on the gloom behind. It was with great relief that I spied the light in the stables, making a sort of oasis in the darkness. I walked very quickly into the midst of that lighted and cheerful place, and thought the clank of the groom's pail one of the pleasantest sounds I had ever heard. The coachman was the head of this little colony, and it was to his house I went to pursue my investigations. He was a native of the district, and had taken care of the place in the absence of the family for years; it was impossible but that he must know everything that was going on, and all the traditions of the place. The men, I could see, eyed me anxiously when I thus appeared at such an hour among them, and followed me with their eyes to Jarvis's house, where he lived alone with his old wife, their children being all married and out in the world. Mrs. Jarvis met me with anxious questions. How was the poor young gentleman? But the others knew, I could see by their faces, that not even this was the foremost thing in my mind.

ଛ

"Noises? — ou ay, there 'll be noises, — the wind in the trees, and the water soughing down the glen. As for tramps, Cornel, no, there 's little o' that kind o' cattle about here; and Merran at the gate's a careful body." Jarvis moved about with some embarrassment from one leg to another as he spoke. He kept in the shade, and did not look at me more than he could help. Evidently his mind was perturbed, and he had reasons for keeping his own counsel. His wife sat by, giving him a quick look now and then, but saying nothing. The kitchen was very snug and warm and bright, — as different as could be from the chill and mystery of the night outside. "I think you are trifling with me, Jarvis," I said.

"Triflin', Cornel? No me. What would I trifle for? If the deevil himsel was in the auld hoose, I have no interest in 't one way or another ——"

"Sandy, hold your peace!" cried his wife imperatively.

"And what am I to hold my peace for, wi' the Cornel standing there asking a' thae questions? I 'm saying, if the deevil himsel ——"

{155}

"And I 'm telling ye hold your peace!" cried the woman, in great excitement. "Dark November weather and lang nichts, and us that ken a' we ken. How daur ye name — a name that shouldna be spoken?" She threw down her stocking and got up, also in great agitation. "I tellt ye you never could keep it. It 's no a thing that will hide; and the haill toun kens as weel as you or me. Tell the Cornel straight out — or see, I 'll do it. I dinna hold wi' your secrets, and a secret that the haill toun kens!" She snapped her fingers with an air of large disdain. As for Jarvis, ruddy and big as he was, he shrank to nothing before this decided woman. He repeated to her two or three times her own adjuration, "Hold your peace!" then, suddenly changing his tone, cried out, "Tell him then, confound ye! I 'll wash my hands o 't. If a' the ghosts in Scotland were in the auld hoose, is that ony concern o' mine?"

After this I elicited without much difficulty the whole story. In the opinion of the Jarvises, and of everybody about, the certainty that the place was haunted was beyond all doubt. As Sandy and his wife warmed to the tale, one tripping up another in their eagerness to tell everything, it gradually developed as distinct a superstition as I ever heard, and not without poetry and pathos. How long it was since the voice had been heard first, nobody could tell with certainty. Jarvis's opinion was that his father, who had been coachman at Brentwood before him, had never heard anything about it, and that the whole thing had arisen within the last ten years, since the complete dismantling of the old house; which was a wonderfully modern date for a tale so well authenticated. According to these witnesses, and to several whom I questioned afterwards, and who were all in perfect agreement, it was only in the months of November and December that "the visitation" occurred. During these months, the darkest of the year, scarcely a night passed without the recurrence of these inexplicable cries. Nothing, it was said, had ever been seen, — at least, nothing that could be identified. Some people, bolder or more imaginative than the others, had seen the darkness moving, Mrs. Jarvis said, with unconscious poetry. It began when night fell, and continued, at intervals, till day broke. Very often it was only an inarticulate cry and moaning, but sometimes the words which had taken possession of my poor boy's fancy had been distinctly audible, — "Oh, mother, let me in!" The Jarvises were not aware that there had ever been any investigation into it. The estate of Brentwood had lapsed into the hands of a distant branch of the family, who had lived but little there; and of the many people who had taken it, as I had done, few had remained through two Decembers. And nobody had taken the trouble to make a very close examination into the facts. "No, no," Jarvis said, shaking his head, "No, no, Cornel. Wha wad set themsels up for a laughin'-stock to a' the country-side, making a wark about a ghost? Naebody believes in ghosts. It bid to be the wind in the trees, the last gentleman said, or some effec' o' the water wrastlin' among the rocks. He said it was a' quite easy explained; but he gave up the hoose. And when you cam, Cornel, we were awfu' anxious you should never hear. What for should I have spoiled the bargain and hairmed the property for no-thing?"

"Do you call my child's life nothing?" I said in the trouble of the moment, unable to restrain myself. "And instead of telling this all to me, you have told it to him, —

to a delicate boy, a child unable to sift evidence or judge for himself, a tender-hearted young creature —"

I was walking about the room with an anger all the hotter that I felt it to be most likely quite unjust. My heart was full of bitterness against the stolid retainers of a family who were content to risk other people's children and comfort rather than let a house lie empty. If I had been warned I might have taken precautions, or left the place, or sent Roland away, a hundred things which now I could not do; and here I was with my boy in a brain-fever, and his life, the most precious life on earth, hanging in the balance, dependent on whether or not I could get to the reason of a commonplace ghost-story! I paced about in high wrath, not seeing what I was to do; for to take Roland away, even if he were able to travel, would not settle his agitated mind; and I feared even that a scientific explanation of refracted sound or reverberation, or any other of the easy certainties with which we elder men are silenced, would have very little effect upon the boy.

"Cornel," said Jarvis solemnly, "and *she 'll* bear me witness, — the young gentleman never heard a word from me — no, nor from either groom or gardener; I 'll gie ye my word for that. In the first place, he's no a lad that invites ye to talk. There are some that are, and some that arena. Some will draw ye on, till ye 've tellt them a' the clatter of the toun, and a' ye ken, and whiles mair. But Maister Roland, his mind 's fu' of his books. He 's aye civil and kind, and a fine lad; but no that sort. And ye see it's for a' our interest, Cornel, that you should stay at Brentwood. I took it upon me mysel to pass the word, — 'No a syllable to Maister Roland, nor to the young leddies — no a syllable.' The women-servants, that have little reason to be out at night, ken little or nothing about it. And some think it grand to have a ghost so long as they 're no in the way of coming across it. If you had been tellt the story to begin with, maybe ye would have thought so yourself."

This was true enough, though it did not throw any light upon my perplexity. If we had heard of it to start with, it is possible that all the family would have considered the possession of a ghost a distinct advantage. It is the fashion of the times. We never think what a risk it is to play with young imaginations, but cry out, in the fashionable jargon, "A ghost! — nothing else was wanted to make it perfect." I should not have been above this myself. I should have smiled, of course, at the idea of the ghost at all, but then to feel that it was mine would have pleased my vanity. Oh, yes, I claim no exemption. The girls would have been delighted. I could fancy their eagerness, their interest, and excitement. No; if we had been told, it would have done no good, — we should have made the bargain all the more eagerly, the fools that we are. "And there has been no attempt to investigate it," I said, "to see what it really is?"

"Eh, Cornel," said the coachman's wife, "wha would investigate, as ye call it, a thing that no-body believes in? Ye would be the laughin'-stock of a' the country-side, as my man says."

"But you believe in it," I said, turning upon her hastily. The woman was taken by surprise. She made a step backward out of my way.

"Lord, Cornel, how ye frichten a body! Me! — there's awfu' strange things in this world. An unlearned person doesna ken what to think. But the minister and the gentry they just laugh in your face. Inquire into the thing that is not! Na, na, we just let it be."

"Come with me, Jarvis," I said hastily, "and we'll make an attempt at least. Say nothing to the men or to anybody. I'll come back after dinner, and we'll make a serious attempt to see what it is, if it is anything. If I hear it, — which I doubt, — you may be sure I shall never rest till I make it out. Be ready for me about ten o'clock."

"Me, Cornel!" Jarvis said, in a faint voice. I had not been looking at him in my own preoccupation, but when I did so, I found that the greatest change had come over the fat and ruddy coachman. "Me, Cornel!" he repeated, wiping the perspiration from his brow. His ruddy face hung in flabby folds, his knees knocked together, his voice seemed half extinguished in his throat. Then he began to rub his hands and smile upon me in a deprecating, imbecile way. "There's nothing I wouldna do to pleasure ye, Cornel," taking a step further back. "I'm sure *she* kens I've aye said I never had to do with a mair fair, weel-spoken gentleman —" Here Jarvis came to a pause, again looking at me, rubbing his hands.

"Well?" I said.

"But eh, sir!" he went on, with the same imbecile yet insinuating smile, "if ye'll reflect that I am no used to my feet. With a horse atween my legs, or the reins in my hand, I'm maybe nae worse than other men; but on fit, Cornel — It's no the — bogles; — but I've been cavalry, ye see," with a little hoarse laugh, "a' my life. To face a thing ye didna understan' — on your feet, Cornel."

"Well, sir, if *I* do it," said I tartly, "why shouldn't you?"

"Eh, Cornel, there's an awfu' difference. In the first place, ye tramp about the haill countryside, and think naething of it; but a walk tires me mair than a hunard miles' drive; and then ye're a gentleman, and do your ain pleasure; and you're no so auld as me; and it's for your ain bairn, ye see, Cornel; and then ——"

"He believes in it, Cornel, and you dinna believe in it," the woman said.

"Will you come with me?" I said, turning to her.

She jumped back, upsetting her chair in her bewilderment. "Me!" with a scream, and then fell into a sort of hysterical laugh. "I wouldna say but what I would go; but what would the folk say to hear of Cornel Mortimer with an auld silly woman at his heels?"

The suggestion made me laugh too, though I had little inclination for it. "I'm sorry you have so little spirit, Jarvis," I said. "I must find some one else, I suppose."

Jarvis, touched by this, began to remonstrate, but I cut him short. My butler was a soldier who had been with me in India, and was not supposed to fear anything, — man or devil, — certainly not the former; and I felt that I was losing time. The Jarvises were too thankful to get rid of me. They attended me to the door with the most anxious courtesies. Outside, the two grooms stood close by, a little confused by my sudden exit. I don't know if perhaps they had been listening, — as least standing as near as possible, to catch any scrap of the conversation. I waved my hand to them as I went past, in answer to their salutations, and it was very apparent to me that they also were glad to see me go.

And it will be thought very strange, but it would be weak not to add, that I myself, though bent on the investigation I have spoken of, pledged to Roland to carry it out, and feeling that my boy's health, perhaps his life, depended on the result of my inquiry, — I felt the most unaccountable reluctance to pass these ruins on my way home. My curiosity was intense; and yet it was all my mind could do to pull my body along. I daresay the scientific people would describe it the other way, and attribute my cowardice to the state of my stomach. I went on; but if I had followed my impulse, I should have turned and bolted. Everything in me seemed to cry out against it: my heart thumped, my pulses all began, like sledge-hammers, beating against my ears and every sensitive part. It was very dark, as I have said; the old house, with its shapeless tower, loomed a heavy mass through the darkness, which was only not entirely so solid as itself. On the other hand, the great dark cedars of which we were so proud seemed to fill up the night. My foot strayed out of the path in my confusion and the gloom together, and I brought myself up with a cry as I felt myself knock against something solid. What was it? The contact with hard stone and lime and prickly bramble-bushes restored me a little to myself. "Oh, it's only the old gable," I said aloud, with a little laugh to reassure myself. The rough feeling of the stones reconciled me. As I groped about thus, I shook off my visionary folly. What so easily explained as that I should have strayed from the path in the darkness? This brought me back to common existence, as if I had been shaken by a wise hand out of all the silliness of superstition. How silly it was, after all! What did it matter which path I took? I laughed again, this time with better heart, when suddenly, in a moment, the blood was chilled in my veins, a shiver stole along my spine, my faculties seemed to forsake me. Close by me, at my side, at my feet, there was a sigh. No, not a groan, not a moaning, not anything so tangible, — a perfectly soft, faint, inarticulate sigh. I sprang back, and my heart stopped beating. Mistaken! no, mistake was impossible. I heard it as clearly as I hear myself speak; a long, soft, weary sigh, as if drawn to the utmost, and emptying out a load of sadness that filled the breast. To hear this in the solitude, in the dark, in the night (though it was still early), had an effect which I cannot describe. I feel it now, — something cold creeping over me, up into my hair, and down to my feet, which refused to move. I cried out, with a trembling voice, "Who is there?" as I had done before; but there was no reply. I got home I don't quite know how; but in my mind there was no longer any indifference as to the thing, whatever it was, that haunted these ruins. My scepticism disappeared like a mist. I was as firmly determined that there was something as Roland was. I did not for a moment pretend to myself that it was possible I could be deceived; there were movements and noises which I understood all about, — cracklings of small branches in the frost, and little rolls of gravel on the path, such as have a very eerie sound sometimes, and perplex you with wonder as to who has done it, *when there is no real mystery;* but I assure you all these little movements of nature don't affect you one bit *when there is something.* I understood *them.* I did not understand the sigh. That was not simple nature; there was meaning in it, feeling, the soul of a creature invisible. This is the thing that human nature trembles at, — a creature invisible, yet with sensations, feelings, a power somehow of expressing itself. I had not the same sense of unwillingness to turn my back upon the scene of the mystery which I had experienced in going to the stables; but I almost ran home, impelled by eagerness to get everything done that had to be done, in order to apply myself to finding it out. Bagley was in the hall as usual when I went in. He was always there in the afternoon, always with the appearance of perfect occupation, yet, so far as I know, never doing anything. The door was open, so that I hurried in without any pause, breathless; but the sight of his calm regard, as he came to help me off with my overcoat, subdued me in a moment. Anything out of the way, anything incomprehensible, faded to nothing in the presence of Bagley. You saw and wondered how *he* was made: the parting of his hair, the tie of his white neckcloth, the fit of his trousers, all perfect as works of art; but you could see how they were done, which makes all the difference. I flung myself upon him, so to speak, without waiting to note the extreme unlikeness of the man to anything of the kind I meant. "Bagley," I said, "I want you to come out with me to-night to watch for ——"

"Poachers, Colonel?" he said, a gleam of pleasure running all over him.

"No, Bagley; a great deal worse," I cried.

"Yes, Colonel; at what hour, sir?" the man said; but then I had not told him what it was.

It was ten o'clock when we set out. All was perfectly quiet indoors. My wife was with Roland, who had been quite calm, she said, and who (though, no doubt, the fever must run its course) had been better ever since I came. I told Bagley to put on a thick greatcoat over his evening coat, and did the same myself, with strong boots; for the soil was like a sponge, or worse. Talking to him, I almost forgot what we were going to do. It was darker even than it had been before, and Bagley kept very close to me as we went along. I had a small lantern in my hand, which gave us a partial guidance. We had come to the corner where the path turns. On one side was the bowling-green, which the girls had taken possession of for their croquet-ground, — a wonderful enclosure surrounded by high hedges of holly three hundred years old and more; on the other, the ruins. Both were black as night; but before we got so far, there was a little opening in which we could just discern the trees and the lighter line of the road. I thought it best to pause there and take breath. "Bagley," I said, "there is something about these ruins I don't understand. It is there I am going. Keep your eyes open and your wits about you. Be ready to pounce upon any stranger you see, — anything man or woman. Don't hurt, but seize — anything you see." "Colonel," said Bagley, with a little tremor in his breath, "they do say there's things there — as is neither man nor woman." There was no time for words. "Are you game to follow me, my man? that's the question," I said. Bagley fell in without a word, and saluted. I knew then I had nothing to fear.

We went, so far as I could guess, exactly as I had come, when I heard that sigh. The darkness, however, was so complete that all marks, as of trees or paths, disappeared. One moment we felt our feet on the gravel, another sinking noiselessly into the slippery grass, that was all. I had shut up my lantern, not wishing to scare any one,

{160}

whoever it might be. Bagley followed, it seemed to me, exactly in my footsteps as I made my way, as I supposed, towards the mass of the ruined house. We seemed to take a long time groping along seeking this; the squash of the wet soil under our feet was the only thing that marked our progress. After a while I stood still to see, or rather feel, where we were. The darkness was very still, but no stiller than is usual in a winter's night. The sounds I have mentioned — the crackling of twigs, the roll of a pebble, the sound of some rustle in the dead leaves, or creeping creature on the grass — were audible when you listened, all mysterious enough when your mind is disengaged, but to me cheering now as signs of the livingness of nature, even in the death of the frost. As we stood still there came up from the trees in the glen the prolonged hoot of an owl. Bagley started with alarm, being in a state of general nervousness, and not knowing what he was afraid of. But to me the sound was encouraging and pleasant, being so comprehensible. "An owl," I said, under my breath. "Y—es, Colonel," said Bagley, his teeth chattering. We stood still about five minutes, while it broke into the still brooding of the air, the sound widening out in circles, dying upon the darkness. This sound, which is not a cheerful one, made me almost gay. It was natural, and relieved the tension of the mind. I moved on with new courage, my nervous excitement calming down.

When all at once, quite suddenly, close to us, at our feet, there broke out a cry. I made a spring backwards in the first moment of surprise and horror, and in doing so came sharply against the same rough masonry and brambles that had struck me before. This new sound came upwards from the ground, — a low, moaning, wailing voice, full of suffering and pain. The contrast between it and the hoot of the owl was indescribable, — the one with a wholesome wildness and naturalness that hurt nobody; the other, a sound that made one's blood curdle, full of human misery. With a great deal of fumbling, — for in spite of everything I could do to keep up my courage my hands shook, — I managed to remove the slide of my lantern. The light leaped out like something living, and made the place visible in a moment. We were what would have been inside the ruined building had anything remained but the gable-wall which I have described. It was close to us, the vacant door-way in it going out straight into the blackness outside. The light showed the bit of wall, the ivy glistening upon it in clouds of dark green, the bramble-branches waving, and below, the open door, — a door that led to nothing. It was from this the voice came which died out just as the light flashed upon this strange scene. There was a moment's silence, and then it broke forth again. The sound was so near, so penetrating, so pitiful, that, in the nervous start I gave, the light fell out of my hand. As I groped for it in the dark my hand was clutched by Bagley, who, I think, must have dropped upon his knees; but I was too much perturbed myself to think much of this. He clutched at me in the confusion of his terror, forgetting all his usual decorum. "For God's sake, what is it, sir?" he gasped. If I yielded, there was evidently an end of both of us. "I can't tell," I said, "any more than you; that's what we 've got to find out. Up, man, up!" I pulled him to his feet. "Will you go round and examine the other side, or will you stay here with the lantern?" Bagley gasped at me with a face of horror. "Can't we stay together, Colonel?" he said; his knees were trembling under him. I pushed him against the corner of the wall, and put the light into his hands. "Stand fast till I come back; shake yourself together, man; let nothing pass you," I said. The voice was within two or three feet of us; of that there could be no doubt.

I went myself to the other side of the wall, keeping close to it. The light shook in Bagley's hand, but, tremulous though it was, shone out through the vacant door, one oblong block of light marking all the crumbling corners and hanging masses of foliage. Was that something dark huddled in a heap by the side of it? I pushed forward across the light in the door-way, and fell upon it with my hands; but it was only a juniper-bush growing close against the wall. Meanwhile, the sight of my figure crossing the doorway had brought Bagley's nervous excitement to a height: he flew at me, gripping my shoulder.

"I've got him, Colonel! I've got him!" he cried, with a voice of sudden exultation. He thought it was a man, and was at once relieved. But at that moment the voice burst forth again between us, at our feet, — more close to us than any separate being could be. He dropped off from me, and fell against the wall, his jaw dropping as if he were dying. I suppose, at the same moment, he saw that it was me whom he had clutched. I, for my part, had scarcely more command of myself. I snatched the light out of his hand, and flashed it all about me wildly. Nothing, — the juniper-bush which I thought I had never seen before, the heavy growth of the glistening ivy, the brambles waving. It was close to my ears now, crying, crying, pleading as if for life. Either I heard the same words Roland had heard, or else, in my excitement, his imagination got possession of mine. The voice went on, growing into distinct articulation, but wavering about, now from one point, now from another, as if the owner of it were moving slowly back and forward. "Mother! mother!" and then an outburst of wailing. As my mind steadied, getting accustomed (as one's mind gets accustomed to anything), it seemed to me as if some uneasy, miserable creature was pacing up and down before a closed door. Sometimes — but that must have been excitement — I thought I heard a sound like knocking, and then another burst, "Oh, mother! mother!" All this close, close to the space where I was standing with my lantern, now before me, now behind me: a creature restless, unhappy, moaning, crying, before the vacant door-way, which no one could either shut or open more.

"Do you hear it, Bagley? do you hear what it is saying?" I cried, stepping in through the door-way. He was lying against the wall, his eyes glazed, half dead with terror. He made a motion of his lips as if to answer me, but no sounds came; then lifted his hand with a curious imperative movement as if ordering me to be silent and listen. And how long I did so I cannot tell. It began to have an interest, an exciting hold upon me, which I could not describe. It seemed to call up visibly a scene any one could understand, — a something shut out, restlessly wandering to and fro; sometimes the voice dropped, as if throwing itself down, sometimes wandered off a few paces, growing sharp and clear. "Oh, mother, let me in! oh, mother, mother, let me in! oh, let me in!" Every word was clear to me. No wonder the boy had gone wild with pity. I tried to steady my mind upon Roland, upon his conviction that I could do something, but my head swam with the excitement, even when I partially overcame the terror. At last the words died away, and there was a sound of sobs and moaning. I cried out, "In the name of God, who are you?" with a kind of feeling in my mind that to use the name of God was profane, seeing that I did not believe in ghosts or anything supernatural; but I did it all the same, and waited, my heart giving a leap of terror lest there should be a reply. Why this should have been I cannot tell, but I had a feeling that if there was an answer it would be more than I could bear. But there was no answer; the moaning went on, and then, as if it had been real, the voice rose a little higher again, the words recommenced, "Oh, mother, let me in! oh, mother, let me in!" with an expression that was heart-breaking to hear.

As if it had been real! What do I mean by that? I suppose I got less alarmed as the thing went on. I began to recover the use of my senses, — I seemed to explain it all to myself by saying that this had once happened, that it was a recollection of a real scene. Why there should have seemed something quite satisfactory and composing in this explanation I cannot tell, but so it was. I began to listen almost as if it had been a play, forgetting Bagley, who, I almost think, had fainted, leaning against the wall. I was startled out of this strange spectatorship that had fallen upon me by the sudden rush of something which made my heart jump once more, a large black figure in the door-way waving its arms. "Come in! come in! come in!" it shouted out hoarsely at the top of a deep bass voice, and then poor Bagley fell down senseless across the threshold. He was less sophisticated than I, — he had not been able to bear it any longer. I took him for something supernatural, as he took me, and it was some time before I awoke to the necessities of the moment. I remembered only after, that from the time I began to give my attention to the man, I heard the other voice no more. It was some time before I brought him to. It must have been a strange scene: the lantern making a luminous spot in the darkness, the man's white face lying on the black earth, I over him, doing what I could for him. Probably I should have been thought to be murdering him had any one seen us. When at last I succeeded in pouring a little brandy down his throat, he sat up and looked about him wildly. "What's up?" he said; then recognizing me, tried to struggle to his feet with a faint "Beg your pardon, Colonel." I got him home as best I could, making him lean upon my arm. The great fellow was as weak as a child. Fortunately he did not for some time remember what had happened. From the time Bagley fell the voice had stopped, and all was still.

ॐ

"You've got an epidemic in your house, Colonel," Simson said to me next morning. 'What's the meaning of it all? Here's your butler raving about a voice. This will never do, you know; and so far as I can make out, you are in it too."

"Yes, I am in it, Doctor. I thought I had better speak to you. Of course you are treating Roland all right, but the boy is not raving, he is as sane as you or me. It's all true."

"As sane as — I — or you. I never thought the boy insane. He's got cerebral excitement, fever. I don't know what you've got. There's something very queer about

{163}

the look of your eyes."

"Come," said I, "you can't put us all to bed, you know. You had better listen and hear the symptoms in full."

The Doctor shrugged his shoulders, but he listened to me patiently. He did not believe a word of the story, that was clear; but he heard it all from beginning to end. "My dear fellow," he said, "the boy told me just the same. It's an epidemic. When one person falls a victim to this sort of thing, it's as safe as can be, — there's always two or three."

"Then how do you account for it?" I said.

"Oh, account for it! — that's a different matter; there's no accounting for the freaks our brains are subject to. If it's delusion, if it's some trick of the echoes or the winds, — some phonetic disturbance or other —"

"Come with me to-night, and judge for yourself," I said.

Upon this he laughed aloud, then said, "That's not such a bad idea; but it would ruin me forever if it were known that John Simson was ghost-hunting."

"There it is," said I; "you dart down on us who are unlearned with your phonetic disturbances, but you daren't examine what the thing really is for fear of being laughed at. That's science!"

"It's not science, — it's common-sense," said the Doctor. "The thing has delusion on the front of it. It is encouraging an unwholesome tendency even to examine. What good could come of it? Even if I am convinced, I shouldn't believe."

"I should have said so yesterday; and I don't want you to be convinced or to believe," said I. "If you prove it to be a delusion, I shall be very much obliged to you for one. Come; somebody must go with me."

"You are cool," said the Doctor. "You've disabled this poor fellow of yours, and made him — on that point — a lunatic for life; and now you want to disable me. But, for once, I'll do it. To save appearance, if you'll give me a bed, I'll come over after my last rounds."

It was agreed that I should meet him at the gate, and that we should visit the scene of last night's occurrences before we came to the house, so that nobody might be the wiser. It was scarcely possible to hope that the cause of Bagley's sudden illness should not somehow steal into the knowledge of the servants at least, and it was better that all should be done as quietly as possible. The day seemed to me a very long one. I had to spend a certain part of it with Roland, which was a terrible ordeal for me, for what could I say to the boy? The improvement continued, but he was still in a very precarious state, and the trembling vehemence with which he turned to me when his mother left the room filled me with alarm. "Father?" he said quietly. "Yes, my boy, I am giving my best attention to it; all is being done that I can do. I have not come to any conclusion — yet. I am neglecting nothing you said," I cried. What I could not do was to give his active mind any encouragement to dwell upon the mystery. It was a hard predicament, for some satisfaction had to be given him. He looked at me very wistfully, with the great blue eyes which shone so large and brilliant out of his white and worn face. "You must trust me," I said. "Yes, father. Father understands," he said to himself, as if to soothe some inward doubt. I left him as soon as I could. He was about the most precious thing I had on earth, and his health my first thought; but yet somehow, in the excitement of this other subject, I put that aside, and preferred not to dwell upon Roland, which was the most curious part of it all.

That night at eleven I met Simson at the gate. He had come by train, and I let him in gently myself. I had been so much absorbed in the coming experiment that I passed the ruins in going to meet him, almost without thought, if you can understand that. I had my lantern; and he showed me a coil of taper which he had ready for use. "There is nothing like light," he said, in his scoffing tone. It was a very still night, scarcely a sound, but not so dark. We could keep the path without difficulty as we went along. As we approached the spot we could hear a low moaning, broken occasionally by a bitter cry. "Perhaps that is your voice," said the Doctor; "I thought it must be something of the kind. That's a poor brute caught in some of these infernal traps of yours; you'll find it among the bushes somewhere." I said nothing. I felt no particular fear, but a triumphant satisfaction in what was to follow. I led him to the spot where Bagley and I had stood on the previous night. All was silent as a winter night could be, — so silent that we heard far off the sound of the horses in the stables, the shutting of a window at the house. Simson lighted his taper and went peering about, poking into all the corners. We looked like two conspirators lying in wait for some unfortunate traveller; but not a sound broke the quiet. The moaning had stopped before we came up; a star or two shone over us in the sky, looking down as if surprised at our strange proceedings. Dr. Simson did nothing but utter subdued laughs under his breath. "I thought as much," he said. "It is just the same with tables and all other kinds of ghostly apparatus; a sceptic's presence stops everything. When I am present nothing ever comes off. How long do you think it will be necessary to stay here? Oh, I don't complain; only when *you* are satisfied, *I* am — quite."

I will not deny that I was disappointed beyond measure by this result. It made me look like a credulous fool. It gave the Doctor such a pull over me as nothing else could. I should point all his morals for years to come; and his materialism, his scepticism, would be increased beyond endurance. "It seems, indeed," I said, "that there is to be no — " "Manifestation," he said, laughing; "that is what all the mediums say. No manifestations, in consequence of the presence of an unbeliever." His laugh sounded very uncomfortable to me in the silence; and it was now near midnight. But that laugh seemed the signal; before it died away the moaning we had heard before was resumed. It started from some distance off, and came towards us, nearer and nearer, like some one walking along and moaning to himself. There could be no idea now that it was a hare caught in a trap. The approach was slow, like that of a weak person, with little halts and pauses. We heard it coming along the grass straight towards the vacant door-way. Simson had been a little startled by the first sound. He said hastily, "That child has no business to be out so late." But he felt, as well as I, that this was no child's voice. As it came nearer, he grew silent, and, going to the door-way with his taper, stood looking out towards the sound. The taper being unprotected blew about in the night air, though there was scarcely any

{165}

wind. I threw the light of my lantern steady and white across the same space. It was in a blaze of light in the midst of the blackness. A little icy thrill had gone over me at the first sound, but as it came close, I confess that my only feeling was satisfaction. The scoffer could scoff no more. The light touched his own face, and showed a very perplexed countenance. If he was afraid, he concealed it with great success, but he was perplexed. And then all that had happened on the previous night was enacted once more. It fell strangely upon me with a sense of repetition. Every cry, every sob seemed the same as before. I listened almost without any emotion at all in my own person, thinking of its effect upon Simson. He maintained a very bold front, on the whole. All that coming and going of the voice was, if our ears could be trusted, exactly in front of the vacant, blank door-way, blazing full of light, which caught and shone in the glistening leaves of the great hollies at a little distance. Not a rabbit could have crossed the turf without being seen; but there was nothing. After a time, Simson, with a certain caution and bodily reluctance, as it seemed to me, went out with his roll of taper into this space. His figure showed against the holly in full outline. Just at this moment the voice sank, as was its custom, and seemed to fling itself down at the door. Simson recoiled violently, as if some one had come up against him, then turned, and held his taper low, as if examining something. "Do you see anybody?" I cried in a whisper, feeling the chill of nervous panic steal over me at this action. "It 's nothing but a — confounded juniper-bush," he said. This I knew very well to be nonsense, for the juniper-bush was on the other side. He went about after this round and round, poking his taper everywhere, then returned to me on the inner side of the wall. He scoffed no longer; his face was contracted and pale. "How long does this go on?" he whispered to me, like a man who does not wish to interrupt some one who is speaking. I had become too much perturbed myself to remark whether the successions and changes of the voice were the same as last night. It suddenly went out in the air almost as he was speaking, with a soft reiterated sob dying away. If there had been anything to be seen, I should have said that the person was at that moment crouching on the ground close to the door.

We walked home very silent afterwards. It was only when we were in sight of the house that I said, "What do you think of it?" "I can't tell what to think of it," he said quickly. He took — though he was a very temperate man — not the claret I was going to offer him, but some brandy from the tray, and swallowed it almost undiluted. "Mind you, I don't believe a word of it," he said, when he had lighted his candle; "but I can't tell what to think," he turned round to add, when he was half-way upstairs.

All of this, however, did me no good with the solution of my problem. I was to help this weeping, sobbing thing, which was already to me as distinct a personality as anything I knew; or what should I say to Roland? It was on my heart that my boy would die if I could not find some way of helping this creature. You may be surprised that I should speak of it in this way I did not know if it was man or woman; but I no more doubted that it was a soul in pain than I doubted my own being; and it was my business to soothe this pain, — to deliver it, if that was possible. Was ever such a task given to an anxious father trembling for his only boy? I felt in my heart, fantastic as it may appear, that I must fulfil this somehow, or part with my child; and you may conceive that rather than do that I was ready to die. But even my dying would not have advanced me, unless by bringing me into the same world with that seeker at the door.

&

Next morning Simson was out before breakfast, and came in with evident signs of the damp grass on his boots, and a look of worry and weariness, which did not say much for the night he had passed. He improved a little after breakfast, and visited his two patients, — for Bagley was still an invalid. I went out with him on his way to the train, to hear what he had to say about the boy. "He is going on very well," he said; "there are no complications as yet. But mind you, that's not a boy to be trifled with, Mortimer. Not a word to him about last night." I had to tell him then of my last interview with Roland, and of the impossible demand he had made upon me, by which, though he tried to laugh, he was much discomposed, as I could see. "We must just perjure ourselves all round," he said, "and swear you exorcised it;" but the man was too kind-hearted to be satisfied with that. "It's frightfully serious for you, Mortimer. I can't laugh as I should like to. I wish I saw a way out of it, for your sake. By the way," he added shortly, "didn't you notice that juniper-bush on the left-hand side?" "There was one on the right hand of the door. I noticed you made that mistake last night." "Mistake!" he cried, with a curious low laugh, pulling up the collar of his coat as though he felt the cold, — "there's no juniper there this morning, left or right. Just go and see." As he stepped into the train a few minutes after, he looked back upon me and beckoned me for a parting word. "I'm coming back to-night," he said.

I don't think I had any feeling about this as I turned away from that common bustle of the railway which made my private preoccupations feel so strangely out of date. There had been a distinct satisfaction in my mind before, that his scepticism had been so entirely defeated. But the more serious part of the matter pressed upon me now. I went straight from the railway to the manse, which stood on a little plateau on the side of the river opposite to the woods or Brentwood. The minister was one of a class which is not so common in Scotland as it used to be. He was a man of good family, well educated in the Scotch way, strong in philosophy, not so strong in Greek, strongest of all in experience, — a man who had "come across," in the course of his life, most people of note that had ever been in Scotland, and who was said to be very sound in doctrine, without infringing the toleration with which old men, who are good men, are generally endowed. He was old-fashioned; perhaps he did not think so much about the troublous problems of theology as many of the young men, nor ask himself any hard questions about the Confession of Faith; but he understood human nature, which is perhaps better. He received me with a cordial welcome. "Come away, Colonel Mortimer," he said; "I 'm all the more glad to see you, that I feel it's a good sign for the boy. He's doing well? — God be praised, — and the Lord bless him and keep him. He has many a poor body's prayers, and that

{167}

can do nobody harm."

"He will need them all, Dr. Moncrieff," I said, "and your counsel too." And I told him the story, — more than I had told Simson. The old clergyman listened to me with many suppressed exclamations, and at the end the water stood in his eyes.

"That's just beautiful," he said. "I do not mind to have heard anything like it; it's as fine as Burns when he wished deliverance to one — that is prayed for in no kirk. Ay, ay! so he would have you console the poor lost spirit? God bless the boy! There's something more than common in that, Colonel Mortimer. And also the faith of him in his father! — I would like to put that into a sermon." Then the old gentleman gave me an alarmed look, and said, "No, no; I was not meaning a sermon; but I must write it down for the 'Children's Record.'" I saw the thought that passed through his mind. Either he thought, or he feared I would think, of a funeral sermon. You may believe this did not make me more cheerful.

I can scarcely say that Dr. Moncrieff gave me any advice. How could any one advise on such a subject? But he said, "I think I'll come too. I 'm an old man; I 'm less liable to be frightened than those that are further off the world unseen. It behooves me to think of my own journey there. I've no cut-and-dry beliefs on the subject. I'll come too; and maybe at the moment the Lord will put into our heads what to do."

This gave me a little comfort, — more than Simson had given me. To be clear about the cause of it was not my grand desire. It was another thing that was in my mind, — my boy. As for the poor soul at the open door, I had no more doubt, as I have said, of its existence than I had of my own. It was no ghost to me. I knew the creature, and it was in trouble. That was my feeling about it, as it was Roland's. To hear it first was a great shock to my nerves, but not now; a man will get accustomed to anything. But to do something for it was the great problem; how was I to be serviceable to a being that was invisible, that was mortal no longer? "Maybe at the moment the Lord will put it into our heads." This is very old-fashioned phraseology, and a week before, most likely, I should have smiled (though always with kindness) at Dr. Moncrieff's credulity; but there was a great comfort, whether rational or otherwise I cannot say, in the mere sound of the words.

The road to the station and the village lay through the glen, not by the ruins; but though the sunshine and the fresh air, and the beauty of the trees, and the sound of the water were all very soothing to the spirits, my mind was so full of my own subject that I could not refrain from turning to the right hand as I got to the top of the glen, and going straight to the place which I may call the scene of all my thoughts. It was lying full in the sunshine, like all the rest of the world. The ruined gable looked due east, and in the present aspect of the sun the light streamed down through the door-way as our lantern had done, throwing a flood of light upon the damp grass beyond. There was a strange suggestion in the open door, — so futile, a kind of emblem of vanity: all free around, so that you could go where you pleased, and yet that semblance of an enclosure, — that way of entrance, unnecessary, leading to nothing. And why any creature should pray and weep to get in — to nothing, or be kept out — by nothing! You could not dwell upon it, or it made your brain go round. I remembered, however, what Simson said about the juniper, with a little smile on my own mind as to the inaccuracy of recollection which even a scientific man will be guilty of. I could see now the light of my lantern gleaming upon the wet glistening surface of the spiky leaves at the right hand, — and he ready to go to the stake for it that it was the left! I went round to make sure. And then I saw what he had said. Right or left there was no juniper at all! I was confounded by this, though it was entirely a matter of detail: nothing at all, — a bush of brambles waving, the grass growing up to the very walls. But after all, though it gave me a shock for a moment, what did that matter? There were marks as if a number of footsteps had been up and down in front of the door, but these might have been our steps; and all was bright and peaceful and still. I poked about the other ruin — the larger ruins of the old house — for some time, as I had done before. There were marks upon the grass here and there — I could not call them footsteps — all about; but that told for nothing one way or another. I had examined the ruined rooms closely the first day. They were half filled up with soil and debris, withered brackens and bramble, — no refuge for any one there. It vexed me that Jarvis should see me coming from that spot when he came up to me for his orders. I don't know whether my nocturnal expeditions had got wind among the servants. But there was a significant look in his face. Something in it I felt was like my own sensation when Simson in the midst of his scepticism was struck dumb. Jarvis felt satisfied that his veracity had been put beyond question. I never spoke to a servant of mine in such a peremptory tone before. I sent him away "with a flea in his lug," as the man described it afterwards. Interference of any kind was intolerable to me at such a moment.

But what was strangest of all was, that I could not face Roland. I did not go up to his room, as I would have naturally done, at once. This the girls could not understand. They saw there was some mystery in it. "Mother has gone to lie down." Agatha said: "he has had such a good night." "But he wants you so, papa!" cried little Jeanie, always with her two arms embracing mine in a pretty way she had. I was obliged to go at last, but what could I say? I could only kiss him, and tell him to keep still, — that I was doing all I could. There is something mystical about the patience of a child. "It will come all right, won't it, father?" he said. "God grant it may! I hope so, Roland." "Oh, yes, it will come all right." Perhaps he understood that in the midst of my anxiety I could not stay with him as I should have done otherwise. But the girls were more surprised than it is possible to describe. They looked at me with wondering eyes. "If I were ill, papa, and you only stayed with me a moment, I should break my heart," said Agatha. But the boy had a sympathetic feeling. He knew that of my own will I would not have done it. I shut myself up in the library, where I could not rest, but kept pacing up and down like a caged beast. What could I do? and if I could do nothing, what would become of my boy? These were the questions that, without ceasing, pursued each other through my mind. Simson came out to dinner, and when the house was all still, and most of the servants in bed, we went out and met Dr. Moncrieff, as we had appointed, at the head of the glen. Simson, for his part, was disposed to scoff at the Doctor. "If there are to be any spells you know, I'll cut the whole concern," he said. I did not make

{169}

him any reply. I had not invited him; he could go or come as he pleased. He was very talkative, far more so than suited my humor, as we went on. "One thing is certain, you know; there must be some human agency," he said. "It is all bosh about apparitions. I never have investigated the laws of sound to any great extent, and there's a great deal in ventriloquism that we don't know much about." "If it's the same to you," I said, "I wish you'd keep all that to yourself, Simson. It doesn't suit my state of mind." "Oh, I hope I know how to respect idiosyncrasy," he said. The very tone of his voice irritated me beyond measure. These scientific fellows, I wonder people put up with them as they do, when you have no mind for their cold-blooded confidence. Dr. Moncrieff met us about eleven o'clock, the same time as on the previous night. He was a large man, with a venerable countenance and white hair, — old, but in full vigor, and thinking less of a cold night walk than many a younger man. He had his lantern, as I had. We were fully provided with means of lighting the place, and we were all of us resolute men. We had a rapid consultation as we went up, and the result was that we divided to different posts. Dr. Moncrieff remained inside the wall — if you can call that inside where there was no wall but one. Simson placed himself on the side next the ruins, so as to intercept any communication with the old house, which was what his mind was fixed upon. I was posted on the other side. To say that nothing could come near without being seen was self-evident. It had been so also on the previous night. Now with our three lights in the midst of the darkness, the whole place seemed illuminated. Dr. Moncrieff's lantern, which was a large one, without any means of shutting up, — an old-fashioned lantern with a pierced and ornamental top, — shone steadily, the rays shooting out of it upward into the gloom. He placed it on the grass, where the middle of the room, if this had been a room, would have been. The usual effect of the light streaming out of the door-way was prevented by the illumination which Simson and I on either side supplied. With these differences, everything seemed as on the previous night. And what occurred was exactly the same, with the same air of repetition, point for point, as I had formerly remarked. I declare that it seemed to me as if I were pushed against, put aside, by the owner of the voice as he paced up and down in his trouble, — though these are perfectly futile words, seeing that the stream of light from my lantern, and that from Simson's taper, lay broad and clear, without a shadow, without the smallest break, across the entire breadth of the grass. I had ceased even to be alarmed, for my part. My heart was rent with pity and trouble, — pity for the poor suffering human creature that moaned and pleaded so, and trouble for myself and my boy. God! if I could not find any help, — and what help could I find? — Roland would die.

We were all perfectly still till the first outburst was exhausted, as I knew, by experience, it would be. Dr. Moncrieff, to whom it was new, was quite motionless on the other side of the wall, as we were in our places. My heart had remained almost at its usual beating during the voice. I was used to it; it did not rouse all my pulses as it did at first. But just as it threw itself sobbing at the door (I cannot use other words), there suddenly came something which sent the blood coursing through my veins, and my heart into my mouth. It was a voice inside the wall, — the minister's well-known voice. I would have been prepared for it in any kind of adjuration, but I was not prepared for what I heard. It came out with a sort of stammering, as if too much moved for utterance. "Willie, Willie! Oh, God preserve us! is it you?"

These simple words had an effect upon me that the voice of the invisible creature had ceased to have. I thought the old man, whom I had brought into this danger, had gone mad with terror. I made a dash round to the other side of the wall, half crazed myself with the thought. He was standing where I had left him, his shadow thrown vague and large upon the grass by the lantern which stood at his feet. I lifted my own light to see his face as I rushed forward. He was very pale, his eyes wet and glistening, his mouth quivering with parted lips. He neither saw nor heard me. We that had gone through this experience before, had crouched towards each other to get a little strength to bear it. But he was not even aware that I was there. His whole being seemed absorbed in anxiety and tenderness. He held out his hands, which trembled, but it seemed to me with eagerness, not fear. He went on speaking all the time. "Willie, if it is you, — and it's you, if it is not a delusion of Satan, — Willie, lad! why come ye here fright'ing them that know you not? Why came ye not to me?"

He seemed to wait for an answer. When his voice ceased, his countenance, every line moving, continued to speak. Simson gave me another terrible shock, stealing into the open door-way with his light, as much awe-stricken, as wildly curious, as I. But the minister resumed, without seeing Simson, speaking to some one else. His voice took a tone of expostulation:—

"Is this right to come here? Your mother's gone with your name on her lips. Do you think she would ever close her door on her own lad? Do ye think the Lord will close the door, ye faint-hearted creature? No! — I forbid ye! I forbid ye!" cried the old man. The sobbing voice had begun to resume its cries. He made a step forward, calling out the last words in a voice of command. "I forbid ye! Cry out no more to man. Go home, ye wandering spirit! go home! Do you hear me? — me that christened ye, that have struggled with ye, that have wrestled for ye with the Lord!" Here the loud tones of his voice sank into tenderness. "And her too, poor woman! poor woman! her you are calling upon. She's no here. You'll find her with the Lord. Go there and seek her, not here. Do you hear me, lad? go after her there. He'll let you in, though it's late. Man, take heart! if you will lie and sob and greet, let it be at heaven's gate, and no your poor mother's ruined door."

He stopped to get his breath; and the voice had stopped, not as it had done before, when its time was exhausted and all its repetitions said, but with a sobbing catch in the breath as if overruled. Then the minister spoke again, "Are you hearing me, Will? Oh, laddie, you've liked the beggarly elements all your days. Be done with them now. Go home to the Father — the Father! Are you hearing me?" Here the old man sank down upon his knees, his face raised upwards, his hands held up with a tremble in them, all white in the light in the midst of the darkness. I resisted as long as I could, though I cannot tell why; then I, too, dropped upon my knees. Simson all the time stood in the door-way, with an expression in his face such as words could not tell, his under lip dropped, his eyes wild, staring. It seemed to be to him, that image of blank ignorance and wonder, that we were praying. All the time the voice,

{171}

with a low arrested sobbing, lay just where he was standing, as I thought.

"Lord," the minister said, — "Lord, take him into Thy everlasting habitations. The mother he cries to is with Thee. Who can open to him but Thee? Lord, when is it too late for Thee, or what is too hard for Thee? Lord, let that woman there draw him inower! Let her draw him inower!"

I sprang forward to catch something in my arms that flung itself wildly within the door. The illusion was so strong, that I never paused till I felt my forehead graze against the wall and my hands clutch the ground, — for there was nobody there to save from falling, as in my foolishness I thought. Simson held out his hand to me to help me up. He was trembling and cold, his lower lip hanging, his speech almost inarticulate. "It's gone," he said, stammering, — "it's gone!" We leaned upon each other for a moment, trembling so much, both of us, that the whole scene trembled as if it were going to dissolve and disappear; and yet as long as I live I will never forget it, — the shining of the strange lights, the blackness all round, the kneeling figure with all the whiteness of the light concentrated on its white venerable head and uplifted hands. A strange solemn stillness seemed to close all round us. By intervals a single syllable, "Lord! Lord!" came from the old minister's lips. He saw none of us, nor thought of us. I never knew how long we stood, like sentinels guarding him at his prayers, holding our lights in a confused dazed way, not knowing what we did. But at last he rose from his knees, and standing up at his full height, raised his arms, as the Scotch manner is at the end of a religious service, and solemnly gave the apostolical benediction, — to what? to the silent earth, the dark woods, the wide breathing atmosphere; for we were but spectators gasping an Amen!

It seemed to me that it must be the middle of the night, as we all walked back. It was in reality very late. Dr. Moncrieff put his arm into mine. He walked slowly, with an air of exhaustion. It was as if we were coming from a death-bed. Something hushed and solemnized the very air. There was that sense of relief in it which there always is at the end of a death-struggle. And nature, persistent, never daunted, came back in all of us, as we returned into the ways of life. We said nothing to each other, indeed, for a time; but when we got clear of the trees and reached the opening near the house, where we could see the sky, Dr. Moncrieff himself was the first to speak. "I must be going," he said; "it's very late, I 'm afraid. I will go down the glen, as I came."

"But not alone. I am going with you, Doctor."

"Well, I will not oppose it. I am an old man, and agitation wearies more than work. Yes; I'll be thankful of your arm. To-night, Colonel, you've done me more good turns than one."

I pressed his hand on my arm, not feeling able to speak. But Simson, who turned with us, and who had gone along all this time with his taper flaring, in entire unconsciousness, came to himself, apparently at the sound of our voices, and put out that wild little torch with a quick movement, as if of shame. "Let me carry your lantern," he said; "it is heavy." He recovered with a spring; and in a moment, from the awe-stricken spectator he had been, became himself, sceptical and cynical. "I should like to ask you a question," he said. "Do you believe in Purgatory, Doctor? It 's not in the tenets of the Church, so far as I know."

"Sir," said Dr. Moncrieff, "an old man like me is sometimes not very sure what he believes. There is just one thing I am certain of — and that is the loving-kindness of God."

"But I thought that was in this life. I am no theologian —"

"Sir," said the old man again, with a tremor in him which I could feel going over all his frame, "if I saw a friend of mine within the gates of hell, I would not despair but his Father would take him by the hand still, if he cried like yon."

"I allow it is very strange, very strange. I cannot see through it. That there must be human agency, I feel sure. Doctor, what made you decide upon the person and the name?"

The minister put out his hand with the impatience which a man might show if he were asked how he recognized his brother. "Tuts!" he said, in familiar speech; then more solemnly, "How should I not recognize a person that I know better — far better — than I know you?"

"Then you saw the man?"

Dr. Moncrieff made no reply. He moved his hand again with a little impatient movement, and walked on, leaning heavily on my arm. And we went on for a long time without another word, threading the dark paths, which were steep and slippery with the damp of the winter. The air was very still, — not more than enough to make a faint sighing in the branches, which mingled with the sound of the water to which we were descending. When we spoke again, it was about indifferent matters, — about the height of the river, and the recent rains. We parted with the minister at his own door, where his old housekeeper appeared in great perturbation, waiting for him. "Eh, me, minister! the young gentleman will be worse?" she cried.

"Far from that — better. God bless him!" Dr. Moncrieff said.

I think if Simson had begun again to me with his questions, I should have pitched him over the rocks as we returned up the glen; but he was silent, by a good inspiration. And the sky was clearer than it had been for many nights, shining high over the trees, with here and there a star faintly gleaming through the wilderness of dark and bare branches. The air, as I have said, was very soft in them, with a subdued and peaceful cadence. It was real, like every natural sound, and came to us like a hush of peace and relief I thought there was a sound in it as of the breath of a sleeper, and it seemed clear to me that Roland must be sleeping, satisfied and calm. We went up to his room when we went in. There we found the complete hush of rest. My wife looked up out of a doze, and gave me a smile: "I think he is a great deal better; but you are very late," she said in a whisper, shading the light with her hand that the Doctor might see his patient. The boy had got back something like his own color. He woke as we stood all round his bed. His eyes had the happy, half-awakened look of childhood, glad to shut again, yet pleased with the interruption and glimmer of the light. I stooped over him and kissed his forehead, which was moist and cool. "All is well, Roland," I said. He looked up at me with a glance of pleasure, and took my hand and laid his cheek upon it, and so went to sleep.

{173}

For some nights after, I watched among the ruins, spending all the dark hours up to midnight patrolling about the bit of wall which was associated with so many emotions; but I heard nothing, and saw nothing beyond the quiet course of nature; nor, so far as I am aware, has anything been heard again. Dr. Moncrieff gave me the history of the youth, whom he never hesitated to name. I did not ask, as Simson did, how he recognized him. He had been a prodigal, — weak, foolish, easily imposed upon, and "led away," as people say. All that we had heard had passed actually in life, the Doctor said. The young man had come home thus a day or two after his mother died, — who was no more than the housekeeper in the old house, — and distracted with the news, had thrown himself down at the door and called upon her to let him in. The old man could scarcely speak of it for tears. To me it seemed as if — Heaven help us, how little do we know about anything! — a scene like that might impress itself somehow upon the hidden heart of nature. I do not pretend to know how, but the repetition had struck me at the time as, in its terrible strangeness and incomprehensibility, almost mechanical, — as if the unseen actor could not exceed or vary, but was bound to re-enact the whole. One thing that struck me, however, greatly, was the likeness between the old minister and my boy in the manner of regarding these strange phenomena. Dr. Moncrieff was not terrified, as I had been myself, and all the rest of us. It was no "ghost," as I fear we all vulgarly considered it, to him, — but a poor creature whom he knew under these conditions, just as he had known him in the flesh, having no doubt of his identity. And to Roland it was the same. This spirit in pain, — if it was a spirit, — this voice out of the unseen, — was a poor fellow-creature in misery, to be succored and helped out of his trouble, to my boy. He spoke to me quite frankly about it when he got better. "I knew father would find out some way," he said. And this was when he was strong and well, and an idea that he would turn hysterical or become a seer of visions had happily passed away.

I must add one curious fact, which does not seem to me to have any relation to the above, but which Simson made great use of, as the human agency which he was determined to find somehow. We had examined the ruins very closely at the time of these occurrences; but afterwards, when all was over, as we went casually about them one Sunday afternoon in the idleness of that unemployed day, Simson with his stick penetrated an old window which had been entirely blocked up with fallen soil. He jumped down into it in great excitement, and called me to follow. There we found a little hole, — for it was more a hole than a room, — entirely hidden under the ivy and ruins, in which there was a quantity of straw laid in a corner, as if some one had made a bed there, and some remains of crusts about the floor. Some one had lodged there, and not very long before, he made out; and that this unknown being was the author of all the mysterious sounds we heard he is convinced. "I told you it was human agency," he said triumphantly. He forgets, I suppose, how he and I stood with our lights, seeing nothing, while the space between us was audibly traversed by something that could speak, and sob, and suffer. There is no argument with men of this kind. He is ready to get up a laugh against me on this slender ground. "I was puzzled myself, — I could not make it out, — but I always felt convinced human agency was at the bottom of it. And here it is, — and a clever fellow he must have been," the Doctor says. Bagley left my service as soon as he got well. He assured me it was no want of respect, but he could not stand "them kind of things;" and the man was so shaken and ghastly that I was glad to give him a present and let him go. For my own part, I made a point of staying out the time — two years — for which I had taken Brentwood; but I did not renew my tenancy. By that time we had settled, and found for ourselves a pleasant home of our own.

I must add, that when the Doctor defies me, I can always bring back gravity to his countenance, and a pause in his railing, when I remind him of the juniper-bush. To me that was a matter of little importance. I could believe I was mistaken. I did not care about it one way or other; but on his mind the effect was different. The miserable voice, the spirit in pain, he could think of as the result of ventriloquism, or reverberation, or — anything you please: an elaborate prolonged hoax, executed somehow by the tramp that had found a lodging in the old tower; but the juniper-bush staggered him. Things have effects so different on the minds of different men.

THE WONDERSMITH
Fitz-James O'Brien

A small lane, the name of which I have forgotten, or do not choose to remember, slants suddenly off from Chatham Street, (before that headlong thoroughfare reaches into the Park,) and retreats suddenly down towards the East River, as if it were disgusted with the smell of old clothes, and had determined to wash itself clean. This excellent intention it has, however, evidently contributed towards the making of that imaginary pavement mentioned in the old adage; for it is still emphatically a dirty street. It has never been able to shake off the Hebraic taint of filth which it inherits from the ancestral thoroughfare. It is slushy and greasy, as if it were twin brother of the Roman Ghetto.

I like a dirty slum; not because I am naturally unclean,--I have not a drop of Neapolitan blood in my veins,--but because I generally find a certain sediment of philosophy precipitated in its gutters. A clean street is terribly prosaic. There is no food for thought in carefully swept pavements, barren kennels, and vulgarly spotless houses. But when I go down a street which has been left so long to itself that it has acquired a distinct outward character, I find plenty to think about. The scraps of sodden letters lying in the ash-barrel have their meaning: desperate appeals, perhaps, from Tom, the baker's assistant, to Amelia, the daughter of the dry-goods retailer, who is always selling at a sacrifice in consequence of the late fire. That may be Tom himself who is now passing me in a white apron, and I look up at the windows of the house (which does not, however, give any signs of a recent conflagration) and almost hope to see Amelia wave a white pocket-handkerchief. The bit of orange-peel lying on the sidewalk inspires thought. Who will fall over it? who but the industrious mother of six children, the eldest of which is only nine months old, all of whom are dependent on her exertions for support? I see her slip and tumble. I see the pale face convulsed with agony, and the vain struggle to get up; the pitying crowd closing her off from all air; the anxious young doctor who happened to be passing by; the manipulation of the broken limb, the shake of the head, the moan of the victim, the litter borne on men's shoulders, the gates of the New York Hospital unclosing, the subscription taken up on the spot. There is some food for speculation in that three-year-old, tattered child, masked with dirt, who is throwing a brick at another three-year-old, tattered child, masked with dirt. It is not difficult to perceive that he is destined to lurk, as it were, through life. His bad, flat face--or, at least, what can be seen of it--does not look as if it were made for the light of day. The mire in which he wallows now is but a type of the moral mire in which he will wallow hereafter. The feeble little hand lifted at this instant to smite his companion, half in earnest, half in jest, will be raised against his fellow-beings forevermore.

Golosh Street--as I will call this nameless lane before alluded to--is an interesting locality. All the oddities of trade seem to have found their way thither and made an eccentric mercantile settlement. There is a bird-shop at one corner, wainscoted with

little cages containing linnets, waxwings, canaries, blackbirds, Mino-birds, with a hundred other varieties, known only to naturalists. Immediately opposite is an establishment where they sell nothing but ornaments made out of the tinted leaves of autumn, varnished and gummed into various forms. Farther down is a second-hand book-stall, which looks like a sentry-box mangled out flat, and which is remarkable for not containing a complete set of any work. There is a small chink between two ordinary-sized houses, in which a little Frenchman makes and sells artificial eyes, specimens of which, ranged on a black velvet cushion, stare at you unwinkingly through the window as you pass, until you shudder and hurry on, thinking how awful the world would be, if every one went about without eyelids. There are junk-shops in Golosh Street that seem to have got hold of all the old nails in the Ark and all the old brass of Corinth. Madame Filomel, the fortune-teller, lives at No. 12 Golosh Street, second story front, pull the bell on the left-hand side. Next door to Madame is the shop of Herr Hippe, commonly called the Wondersmith.

Herr Hippe's shop is the largest in Golosh Street, and to all appearance is furnished with the smallest stock. Beyond a few packing-cases, a turner's lathe, and a shelf laden with dissected maps of Europe, the interior of the shop is entirely unfurnished. The window, which is lofty and wide, but much begrimed with dirt, contains the only pleasant object in the place. This is a beautiful little miniature theatre,--that is to say, the orchestra and stage. It is fitted with charmingly painted scenery and all the appliances for scenic changes. There are tiny traps, and delicately constructed "lifts," and real footlights fed with burning-fluid, and in the orchestra sits a diminutive conductor before his desk, surrounded by musical manikins, all provided with the smallest of violoncellos, flutes, oboes, drums, and such like. There are characters also on the stage. A Templar in a white cloak is dragging a fainting female form to the parapet of a ruined bridge, while behind a great black rock on the left one can see a man concealed, who, kneeling, levels an arquebuse at the knight's heart. But the orchestra is silent; the conductor never beats the time, the musicians never play a note. The Templar never drags his victim an inch nearer to the bridge, the masked avenger takes an eternal aim with his weapon. This repose appears unnatural; for so admirably are the figures executed, that they seem replete with life. One is almost led to believe, in looking on them, that they are resting beneath some spell which hinders their motion. One expects every moment to hear the loud explosion of the arquebuse,--to see the blue smoke curling, the Templar falling,--to hear the orchestra playing the requiem of the guilty.

Few people knew what Herr Hippe's business or trade really was. That he worked at something was evident; else why the shop? Some people inclined to the belief that he was an inventor, or mechanician. His workshop was in the rear of the store, and into that sanctuary no one but himself had admission. He arrived in Golosh Street eight or ten years ago, and one fine morning, the neighbors, taking down their shutters, observed that No. 13 had got a tenant. A tall, thin, sallow-faced man stood on a ladder outside the shop-entrance, nailing up a large board, on which "Herr Hippe, Wondersmith," was painted in black letters on a yellow ground. The little theatre stood in the window, where it stood ever after, and Herr Hippe was established.

But what was a Wondersmith? people asked each other. No one could reply. Madame Filomel was consulted, but she looked grave, and said that it was none of her business. Mr. Pippel, the bird-fancier, who was a German, and ought to know best, thought it was the English for some singular Teutonic profession; but his replies were so vague, that Golosh Street was as unsatisfied as ever. Solon, the little humpback, who kept the odd-volume book-stall at the lowest corner, could throw no light upon it. And at length people had to come to the conclusion, that Herr Hippe was either a coiner or a magician, and opinions were divided.

A BOTTLEFUL OF SOULS.

IT was a dull December evening. There was little trade doing in Golosh Street, and the shutters were up at most of the shops. Hippe's store had been closed at least an hour, and the Mino-birds and Bohemian waxwings at Mr. Pippel's had their heads tucked under their wings in their first sleep.

Herr Hippe sat in his parlor, which was lit by a pleasant wood-fire. There were no candles in the room, and the flickering blaze played fantastic tricks on the pale gray walls. It seemed the festival of shadows. Processions of shapes, obscure and indistinct, passed across the leaden-hued panels and vanished in the dusk corners. Every fresh blaze flung up by the wayward logs created new images. Now it was a funeral throng, with the bowed figures of mourners, the shrouded coffin, the plumes that waved like extinguished torches; now a knightly cavalcade with flags and lances, and weird horses, that rushed silently along until they met the angle of the room, when they pranced through the wall and vanished.

On a table close to where Herr Hippe sat was placed a large square box of some dark wood, while over it was spread a casing of steel, so elaborately wrought in an open arabesque pattern that it seemed like a shining blue lace which was lightly stretched over its surface.

Herr Hippe lay luxuriously in his arm-chair, looking meditatively into the fire. He was tall and thin, and his skin was of a dull saffron hue. Long, straight hair,--sharply cut, regular features,--a long, thin moustache, that curled like a dark asp around his mouth, the expression of which was so bitter and cruel that it seemed to distil the venom of the ideal serpent,--and a bony, muscular form, were the prominent characteristics of the Wondersmith.

The profound silence that reigned in the chamber was broken by a peculiar scratching at the panel of the door, like that which at the French court was formerly substituted for the ordinary knock, when it was necessary to demand admission to the royal apartments. Herr Hippe started, raised his head, which vibrated on his long neck like the head of a cobra when about to strike, and after a moment's silence uttered a strange guttural sound. The door unclosed, and a squat, broad-shouldered woman, with large, wild, Oriental eyes, entered softly.

{179}

"Ah! Filomel, you are come!" said the Wondersmith, sinking back in his chair. "Where are the rest of them?"

"They will be here presently," answered Madame Filomel, seating herself in an arm-chair much too narrow for a person of her proportions, and over the sides of which she bulged like a pudding.

"Have you brought the souls?" asked the Wondersmith.

"They are here," said the fortune-teller, drawing a large pot-bellied black bottle from under her cloak. "Ah! I have had such trouble with them!"

"Are they of the right brand,--wild, tearing, dark, devilish fellows? We want no essence of milk and honey, you know. None but souls bitter as hemlock or scorching as lightning will suit our purpose."

"You will see, you will see, Grand Duke of Egypt! They are ethereal demons, every one of them. They are the pick of a thousand births. Do you think that I, old midwife that I am, don't know the squall of the demon child from that of the angel child, the very moment they are delivered? Ask a musician, how he knows, even in the dark, a note struck by Thalberg from one struck by Listz!"

"I long to test them," cried the Wondersmith, rubbing his hands joyfully. "I long to see how the little devils will behave when I give them their shapes. Ah! it will be a proud day for us when we let them loose upon the cursed Christian children! Through the length and breadth of the land they will go; wherever our wandering people set foot, and wherever they are, the children of the Christians shall die. Then we, the despised Bohemians, the gypsies, as they call us, will be once more lords of the earth, as we were in the days when the accursed things called cities did not exist, and men lived in the free woods and hunted the game of the forest. Toys indeed! Ay, ay, we will give the little dears toys! toys that all day will sleep calmly in their boxes, seemingly stiff and wooden and without life,--but at night, when the souls enter them, will arise and surround the cots of the sleeping children, and pierce their hearts with their keen, envenomed blades! Toys indeed! oh, yes! I will sell them toys!"

And the Wondersmith laughed horribly, while the snaky moustache on his upper lip writhed as if it had truly a serpent's power and could sting.

"Have you got your first batch, Herr Hippe?" asked Madame Filomel. "Are they all ready?"

"Oh, ay! they are ready," answered the Wondersmith with gusto,--opening, as he spoke, the box covered with the blue steel lace-work; "they are here."

The box contained a quantity of exquisitely carved wooden manikins of both sexes, painted with great dexterity so as to present a miniature resemblance to Nature. They were, in fact, nothing more than admirable specimens of those toys which children delight in placing in various positions on the table,--in regiments, or sitting at meals, or grouped under the stiff green trees which always accompany them in the boxes in which they are sold at the toy-shops.

The peculiarity, however, about the manikins of Herr Hippe was not alone the artistic truth with which the limbs and the features were gifted; but on the countenance of each little puppet the carver's art had wrought an expression of wickedness that was appalling. Every tiny face had its special stamp of ferocity. The lips were thin and brimful of malice; the small black bead-like eyes glittered with the fire of a universal hate. There was not one of the manikins, male or female, that did not hold in his or her hand some miniature weapon. The little men, scowling like demons, clasped in their wooden fingers swords delicate as a housewife's needle. The women, whose countenances expressed treachery and cruelty, clutched infinitesimal daggers, with which they seemed about to take some terrible vengeance.

"Good!" said Madame Filomel, taking one of the manikins out of the box, and examining it attentively; "you work well, Duke Balthazar! These little ones are of the right stamp; they look as if they had mischief in them. Ah! here come our brothers."

At this moment the same scratching that preceded the entrance of Madame Filomel was heard at the door, and Herr Hippe replied with a hoarse, guttural cry. The next moment two men entered. The first was a small man with very brilliant eyes. He was wrapt in a long shabby cloak, and wore a strange nondescript species of cap on his head, such a cap as one sees only in the low billiard-rooms in Paris. His companion was tall, long-limbed, and slender; and his dress, although of the ordinary cut, either from the disposition of colors, or from the careless, graceful attitudes of the wearer, assumed a certain air of picturesqueness. Both the men possessed the same marked Oriental type of countenance which distinguished the Wondersmith and Madame Filomel. True gypsies they seemed, who would not have been out of place telling fortunes, or stealing chickens in the green lanes of England, or wandering with their wild music and their sleight-of-hand tricks through Bohemian villages.

"Welcome, brothers!" said the Wondersmith; "you are in time. Sister Filomel has brought the souls, and we are about to test them. Monsieur Kerplonne, take off your cloak. Brother Oaksmith, take a chair. I promise you some amusement this evening; so make yourselves comfortable. Here is something to aid you."

And while the Frenchman Kerplonne, and his tall companion, Oaksmith, were obeying Hippe's invitation, he reached over to a little closet let into the wall, and took thence a squat bottle and some glasses, which he placed on the table.

"Drink, brothers!" he said; "it is not Christian blood, but good stout wine of Oporto. It goes right to the heart, and warms one like the sunshine of the South."

"It is good," said Kerplonne, smacking his lips with enthusiasm.

"Why don't you keep brandy? Hang wine!" cried Oaksmith, after having swallowed two bumpers in rapid succession.

"Bah! Brandy has been the ruin of our race. It has made us sots and thieves. It shall never cross my threshold," cried the Wondersmith, with a sombre indignation.

"A little of it is not bad, though, Duke," said the fortune-teller. "It consoles us for our misfortunes; it gives us the crowns we once wore; it restores to us the power we once wielded; it carries us back, as if by magic, to that land of the sun from which fate has driven us; it darkens the memory of all the evils that we have for centuries suffered."

{181}

"It is a devil; may it be cursed!" cried Herr Hippe, passionately. "It is a demon that stole from me my son, the finest youth in all Courland. Yes! my son, the son of the Waywode Balthazar, Grand Duke of Lower Egypt, died raving in a gutter, with an empty brandy-bottle in his hands. Were it not that the plant is a sacred one to our race, I would curse the grape and the vine that bore it."

This outburst was delivered with such energy that the three gypsies kept silence. Oaksmith helped himself to another glass of Port, and the fortune-teller rocked to and fro in her chair, too much overawed by the Wondersmith's vehemence of manner to reply. The little Frenchman, Kerplonne, took no part in the discussion, but seemed lost in admiration of the manikins, which he took from the box in which they lay, handling them with the greatest care. After the silence had lasted for about a minute, Herr Hippe broke it with the sudden question,---

"How does your eye get on, Kerplonne?"

"Excellently, Duke. It is finished. I have it here." And the little Frenchman put his hand into his breeches-pocket and pulled out a large artificial human eye. Its great size was the only thing in this eye that would lead any one to suspect its artificiality. It was at least twice the size of life; but there was a fearful speculative light in its iris, which seemed to expand and contract like the eye of a living being, that rendered it a horrible staring paradox. It looked like the naked eye of the Cyclops, torn from his forehead, and still burning with wrath and the desire for vengeance.

The little Frenchman laughed pleasantly as he held the eye in his hand, and gazed down on that huge dark pupil, that stared back at him, it seemed, with an air of defiance and mistrust.

"It is a devil of an eye," said the little man, wiping the enamelled surface with an old silk pocket-handkerchief; "it reads like a demon. My niece--the unhappy one-- has a wretch of a lover, and I have a long time feared that she would run away with him. I could not read her correspondence, for she kept her writing-desk closely locked. But I asked her yesterday to keep this eye in some very safe place for me. She put it, as I knew she would, into her desk, and by its aid I read every one of her letters. She was to run away next Monday, the ungrateful! but she will find herself disappointed."

And the little man laughed heartily at the success of his stratagem, and polished and fondled the great eye until that optic seemed to grow sore with rubbing.

"And you have been at work, too, I see, Herr Hippe. Your manikins are excellent. But where are the souls?"

"In that bottle," answered the Wondersmith, pointing to the pot-bellied black bottle that Madame Filomel had brought with her. "Yes, Monsieur Kerplonne," he continued, "my manikins are well made. I invoked the aid of Abigor, the demon of soldiery, and he inspired me. The little fellows will be famous assassins when they are animated. We will try them to-night."

"Good!" cried Kerplonne, rubbing his hands joyously. "It is close upon New Year's Day. We will fabricate millions of the little murderers by New Year's Even, and sell them in large quantities; and when the households are all asleep, and the Christian children are waiting for Santa Claus to come, the small ones will troop from their boxes and the Christian children will die. It is famous! Health to Abigor!"

"Let us try them at once," said Oaksmith. "Is your daughter, Zonela, in bed, Herr Hippe? Are we secure from intrusion?"

"No one is stirring about the house," replied the Wondersmith, gloomily.

Filomel leaned over to Oaksmith, and said, in an undertone,---

"Why do you mention his daughter? You know he does not like to have her spoken about."

"I will take care that we are not disturbed," said Kerplonne, rising. "I will put my eye outside the door, to watch."

He went to the door and placed his great eye upon the floor with tender care. As he did so, a dark form, unseen by him or his second vision, glided along the passage noiselessly and was lost in the darkness.

"Now for it!" exclaimed Madam Filomel, taking up her fat black bottle. "Herr Hippe, prepare your manikins!"

The Wondersmith took the little dolls out, one by one, and set them upon the table. Such an array of villanous countenances was never seen. An army of Italian bravos, seen through the wrong end of a telescope, or a band of prisoners at the galleys in Lilliput, will give some faint idea of the appearance they presented. While Madame Filomel uncorked the black bottle, Herr Hippe covered the dolls over with a species of linen tent, which he took also from the box. This done, the fortune-teller held the mouth of the bottle to the door of the tent, gathering the loose cloth closely round the glass neck. Immediately, tiny noises were heard inside the tent. Madame Filomel removed the bottle, and the Wondersmith lifted the covering in which he had enveloped his little people.

A wonderful transformation had taken place. Wooden and inflexible no longer, the crowd of manikins were now in full motion. The beadlike eyes turned, glittering, on all sides; the thin, wicked lips quivered with bad passions; the tiny hands sheathed and unsheathed the little swords and daggers. Episodes, common to life, were taking place in every direction. Here two martial manikins paid court to a pretty sly-faced female, who smiled on each alternately, but gave her hand to be kissed to a third manikin, an ugly little scoundrel, who crouched behind her back. There a pair of friendly dolls walked arm in arm, apparently on the best terms, while, all the time, one was watching his opportunity to stab the other in the back.

"I think they'll do," said the Wondersmith, chuckling, as he watched these various incidents. "Treacherous, cruel, bloodthirsty. All goes marvellously well. But stay! I will put the grand test to them."

So saying, he drew a gold dollar from his pocket, and let it fall on the table in the very midst of the throng of manikins. It had hardly touched the table, when there was a pause on all sides. Every head was turned towards the dollar. Then about twenty of the little creatures rushed towards the glittering coin. One, fleeter than the rest, leaped upon it, and drew his sword. The entire crowd of little people had now gathered round this new centre of attraction. Men and women struggled and shoved to get nearer to the piece of gold. Hardly had the first Liliputian mounted

{183}

upon the treasure, when a hundred blades flashed back a defiant answer to his, and a dozen men, sword in hand, leaped upon the yellow platform and drove him off at the sword's point. Then commenced a general battle. The miniature faces were convulsed with rage and avarice. Each furious doll tried to plunge dagger or sword into his or her neighbor, and the women seemed possessed by a thousand devils.

"They will break themselves into atoms," cried Filomel, as she watched with eagerness this savage melee. "You had better gather them up, Herr Hippe. I will exhaust my bottle and suck all the souls back from them."

"Oh, they are perfect devils! they are magnificent little demons!" cried the Frenchman, with enthusiasm. "Hippe, you are a wonderful man. Brother Oaksmith, you have no such man as Hippe among your English gypsies."

"Not exactly," answered Oaksmith, rather sullenly, "not exactly. But we have men there who can make a twelve-year-old horse look like a four-year-old,--and who can take you and Herr Hippe up with one hand, and throw you over their shoulders."

"The good God forbid!" said the little Frenchman. "I do not love such play. It is incommodious."

While Oaksmith and Kerplonne were talking, the Wondersmith had placed the linen tent over the struggling dolls, and Madame Filomel, who had been performing some mysterious manipulations with her black bottle, put the mouth once more to the door of the tent. In an instant the confused murmur within ceased. Madame Filomel corked the bottle quickly. The Wondersmith withdrew the tent, and, lo! the furious dolls were once more wooden-jointed and inflexible; and the old sinister look was again frozen on their faces.

"They must have blood, though," said Herr Hippe, as he gathered them up and put them into their box. "Mr. Pippel, the bird-fancier, is asleep. I have a key that opens his door. We will let them loose among the birds; it will be rare fun."

"Magnificent!" cried Kerplonne. "Let us go on the instant. But first let me gather up my eye."

The Frenchman pocketed his eye, after having given it a polish with the silk handkerchief; Herr Hippe extinguished the lamp; Oaksmith took a last bumper of Port; and the four gypsies departed for Mr. Pippel's, carrying the box of manikins with them.

SOLON.

THE shadow that glided along the dark corridor, at the moment that Monsieur Kerplonne deposited his sentinel eye outside the door of the Wondersmith's apartment, sped swiftly through the passage and ascended the stairs to the attic. Here the shadow stopped at the entrance to one of the chambers and knocked at the door. There was no reply.

"Zonela, are you asleep?" said the shadow, softly.

"Oh, Solon, is it you?" replied a sweet low voice from within. "I thought it was Herr Hippe. Come in."

The shadow opened the door and entered. There were neither candles nor lamp in the room; but through the projecting window, which was open, there came the

{184}

faint gleams of the starlight, by which one could distinguish a female figure seated on a low stool in the middle of the floor.

"Has he left you without light again, Zonela?" asked the shadow, closing the door of the apartment. "I have brought my little lantern with me, though."

"Thank you, Solon," answered she called Zonela; "you are a good fellow. He never gives me any light of an evening, but bids me go to bed. I like to sit sometimes and look at the moon and the stars,--the stars more than all; for they seem all the time to look right back into my face, very sadly, as if they would say, 'We see you, and pity you, and would help you, if we could.' But it is so mournful to be always looking at such myriads of melancholy eyes! and I long so to read those nice books that you lend me, Solon!"

By this time the shadow had lit the lantern and was a shadow no longer. A large head, covered with a profusion of long blonde hair, which was cut after that fashion known as a l'enfants d'Edouard; a beautiful pale face, lit with wide, blue, dreamy eyes; long arms and slender hands, attenuated legs, and--an enormous hump;--such was Solon, the shadow. As soon as the humpback had lit the lamp, Zonela arose from the low stool on which she had been seated, and took Solon's hand affectionately in hers.

Zonela was surely not of gypsy blood. That rich auburn hair, that looked almost black in the lamp-light, that pale, transparent skin, tinged with an under-glow of warm rich blood, the hazel eyes, large and soft as those of a fawn, were never begotten of a Zingaro. Zonela was seemingly about sixteen; her figure, although somewhat thin and angular, was full of the unconscious grace of youth. She was dressed in an old cotton print, which had been once of an exceedingly boisterous pattern, but was now a mere suggestion of former splendor; while round her head was twisted, in fantastic fashion, a silk handkerchief of green ground spotted with bright crimson. This strange headdress gave her an elfish appearance.

"I have been out all day with the organ, and I am so tired, Solon!--not sleepy, but weary, I mean. Poor Furbelow was sleepy, though, and he's gone to bed."

"I'm weary, too, Zonela;--not weary as you are, though, for I sit in my little book-stall all day long, and do not drag round an organ and a monkey and play old tunes for pennies,--but weary of myself, of life, of the load that I carry on my shoulders;" and, as he said this, the poor humpback glanced sideways, as if to call attention to his deformed person.

"Well, but you ought not to be melancholy amidst your books, Solon. Gracious! If I could only sit in the sun and read as you do, how happy I should be! But it's very tiresome to trudge round all day with that nasty organ, and look up at the houses, and know that you are annoying the people inside; and then the boys play such bad tricks on poor Furbelow, throwing him hot pennies to pick up, and burning his poor little hands; and oh! sometimes, Solon, the men in the street make me so afraid,--they speak to me and look at me so oddly!--I'd a great deal rather sit in your book-stall and read."

"I have nothing but odd volumes in my stall," answered the humpback. "Perhaps that's right, though; for, after all, I'm nothing but an odd volume myself."

{185}

"Come, don't be melancholy, Solon. Sit down and tell me a story. I'll bring Furbelow to listen."

So saying, she went to a dusk corner of the cheerless attic-room, and returned with a little Brazilian monkey in her arms,--a poor, mild, drowsy thing, that looked as if it had cried itself to sleep. She sat down on her little stool, with Furbelow in her lap, and nodded her head to Solon, as much as to say, "Go on; we are attentive."

"You want a story, do you?" said the humpback, with a mournful smile. "Well, I'll tell you one. Only what will your father say, if he catches me here?"

"Herr Hippe is not my father," cried Zonela, indignantly. "He's a gypsy, and I know I'm stolen; and I'd run away from him, if I only knew where to run to. If I were his child, do you think that he would treat me as he does? make me trudge round the city, all day long, with a barrel-organ and a monkey,--though I love poor dear little Furbelow,--and keep me up in a garret, and give me ever so little to eat? I know I'm not his child, for he hates me."

"Listen to my story, Zonela, and we'll talk of that afterwards. Let me sit at your feet;"--and, having coiled himself up at the little maiden's feet, he commenced:---

"There once lived in a great city, just like this city of New York, a poor little hunchback. He kept a second-hand book-stall, where he made barely enough money to keep body and soul together. He was very sad at times, because he knew scarce any one, and those that he did know did not love him. He had passed a sickly, secluded youth. The children of his neighborhood would not play with him, for he was not made like them; and the people in the streets stared at him with pity, or scoffed at him when he went by. Ah! Zonela, how his poor heart was wrung with bitterness when he beheld the procession of shapely men and fine women that every day passed him by in the thoroughfares of the great city! How he repined and cursed his fate as the torrent of fleet-footed firemen dashed past him to the toll of the bells, magnificent in their overflowing vitality and strength! But there was one consolation left him,--one drop of honey in the jar of gall, so sweet that it ameliorated all the bitterness of life. God had given him a deformed body, but his mind was straight and healthy. So the poor hunchback shut himself into the world of books, and was, if not happy, at least contented. He kept company with courteous paladins, and romantic heroes, and beautiful women; and this society was of such excellent breeding that it never so much as once noticed his poor crooked back or his lame walk. The love of books grew upon him with his years. He was remarked for his studious habits; and when, one day, the obscure people that he called father and mother--parents only in name--died, a compassionate book-vendor gave him enough stock in trade to set up a little stall of his own. Here, in his book-stall, he sat in the sun all day, waiting for the customers that seldom came, and reading the fine deeds of the people of the ancient time, or the beautiful thoughts of the poets that had warmed millions of hearts before that hour, and still glowed for him with undiminished fire. One day, when he was reading some book, that, small as it was, was big enough to shut the whole world out from him, he heard some music in the street. Looking up from his book, he saw a little girl, with large eyes, playing an organ, while a monkey begged for alms from a crowd of idlers who had nothing in

{186}

their pockets but their hands. The girl was playing, but she was also weeping. The merry notes of the polka were ground out to a silent accompaniment of tears. She looked very sad, this organ-girl, and her monkey seemed to have caught the infection, for his large brown eyes were moist, as if he also wept. The poor hunchback was struck with pity, and called the little girl over to give her a penny,-- not, dear Zonela, because he wished to bestow alms, but because he wanted to speak with her. She came, and they talked together. She came the next day,--for it turned out that they were neighbors,--and the next, and, in short, every day. They became friends. They were both lonely and afflicted, with this difference, that she was beautiful, and he--was a hunchback."

"Why, Solon," cried Zonela, "that's the very way you and I met!"

"It was then," continued Solon, with a faint smile, "that life seemed to have its music. A great harmony seemed to the poor cripple to fill the world. The carts that took the flour-barrels from the wharves to the store-houses seemed to emit joyous melodies from their wheels. The hum of the great business-streets sounded like grand symphonies of triumph. As one who has been travelling through a barren country without much heed feels with singular force the sterility of the lands he has passed through when he reaches the fertile plains that lie at the end of his journey, so the humpback, after his vision had been freshened with this blooming flower, remembered for the first time the misery of the life that he had led. But he did not allow himself to dwell upon the past. The present was so delightful that it occupied all his thoughts. Zonela, he was in love with the organ-girl."

"Oh, that's so nice!" said Zonela, innocently,--pinching poor Furbelow, as she spoke, in order to dispel a very evident snooze that was creeping over him. "It's going to be a love-story."

"Ah! but, Zonela, he did not know whether she loved him in return. You forget that he was deformed."

"But," answered the girl, gravely, "he was good."

A light like the flash of an aurora illuminated Solon's face for an instant. He put out his hand suddenly, as if to take Zonela's and press it to his heart; but an unaccountable timidity seemed to arrest the impulse, and he only stroked Furbelow's head,--upon which that individual opened one large brown eye to the extent of the eighth of an inch, and, seeing that it was only Solon, instantly closed it again, and resumed his dream of a city where there were no organs and all the copper coin of the realm was iced.

"He hoped and feared," continued Solon, in a low, mournful voice; "but at times he was very miserable, because he did not think it possible that so much happiness was reserved for him as the love of this beautiful, innocent girl. At night, when he was in bed, and all the world was dreaming, he lay awake looking up at the old books that hung against the walls, thinking how he could bring about the charming of her heart. One night, when he was thinking of this, with his eyes fixed upon the mouldy backs of the odd volumes that lay on their shelves, and looked back at him wistfully, as if they would say,--'We also are like you, and wait to be completed,'--it seemed as if he heard a rustle of leaves. Then, one by one, the books came down from their

{187}

places to the floor, as if shifted by invisible hands, opened their worm-eaten covers, and from between the pages of each the hunchback saw issue forth a curious throng of little people that danced here and there through the apartment. Each one of these little creatures was shaped so as to bear resemblance to some one of the letters of the alphabet. One tall, long-legged fellow seemed like the letter A; a burly fellow, with a big head and a paunch, was the model of B; another leering little chap might have passed for a Q; and so on through the whole. These fairies--for fairies they were--climbed upon the hunchback's bed, and clustered thick as bees upon his pillow. 'Come!' they cried to him, 'we will lead you into fairy-land.' So saying, they seized his hand, and he suddenly found himself in a beautiful country, where the light did not come from sun or moon or stars, but floated round and over and in everything like the atmosphere. On all sides he heard mysterious melodies sung by strangely musical voices. None of the features of the landscape were definite; yet when he looked on the vague harmonies of color that melted one into another before his sight, he was filled with a sense of inexplicable beauty. On every side of him fluttered radiant bodies which darted to and fro through the illumined space. They were not birds, yet they flew like birds; and as each one crossed the path of his vision, he felt a strange delight flash through his brain, and straightway an interior voice seemed to sing beneath the vaulted dome of his temples a verse containing some beautiful thought. The little fairies were all this time dancing and fluttering around him, perching on his head, on his shoulders, or balancing themselves on his finger-tips. 'Where am I?' he asked, at last, of his friends, the fairies. 'Ah! Solon,' he heard them whisper, in tones that sounded like the distant tinkling of silver bells, 'this land is nameless; but those whom we lead hither, who tread its soil, and breathe its air, and gaze on its floating sparks of light, are poets forevermore!' Having said this, they vanished, and with them the beautiful indefinite land, and the flashing lights, and the illumined air; and the hunchback found himself again in bed, with the moonlight quivering on the floor, and the dusty books on their shelves, grim and mouldy as ever."

"You have betrayed yourself. You called yourself Solon," cried Zonela. "Was it a dream?"

"I do not know," answered Solon; "but since that night I have been a poet."

"A poet?" screamed the little organ-girl,--"a real poet, who makes verses which every one reads and every one talks of?"

"The people call me a poet," answered Solon, with a sad smile. "They do not know me by the name of Solon, for I write under an assumed title; but they praise me, and repeat my songs. But, Zonela, I can't sing this load off of my back, can I?"

"Oh, bother the hump!" said Zonela, jumping up suddenly. "You're a poet, and that's enough, isn't it? I'm so glad you're a poet, Solon! You must repeat all your best things to me, won't you?"

Solon nodded assent.

"You don't ask me," he said, "who was the little girl that the hunchback loved."

Zonela's face flushed crimson. She turned suddenly away, and ran into a dark corner of the room. In a moment she returned with an old hand-organ in her arms.

"Play, Solon, play!" she cried. "I am so glad that I want to dance. Furbelow, come and dance in honor of Solon the Poet."

It was her confession. Solon's eyes flamed, as if his brain had suddenly ignited. He said nothing; but a triumphant smile broke over his countenance. Zonela, the twilight of whose cheeks was still rosy with the setting blush, caught the lazy Furbelow by his little paws; Solon turned the crank of the organ, which wheezed out as merry a polka as its asthma would allow, and the girl and the monkey commenced their fantastic dance. They had taken but a few steps when the door suddenly opened, and the tall figure of the Wondersmith appeared on the threshold. His face was convulsed with rage, and the black snake that quivered on his upper lip seemed to rear itself as if about to spring upon the hunchback.

THE MANIKINS AND THE MINOS.

THE four gypsies left Herr Hippe's house cautiously, and directed their steps towards Mr. Pippel's bird-shop. Golosh Street was asleep. Nothing was stirring in that tenebrous slum, save a dog that savagely gnawed a bone which lay on a dust-heap, tantalizing him with the flavor of food without its substance. As the gypsies moved stealthily along in the darkness, they had a sinister and murderous air that would not have failed to attract the attention of the policeman of the quarter, if that worthy had not at the moment been comfortably ensconced in the neighboring "Rainbow" bar-room, listening to the improvisations of that talented vocalist, Mr. Harrison, who was making impromptu verses on every possible subject, to the accompaniment of a cithern which was played by a sad little Italian in a large cloak, to whom the host of the "Rainbow" gave so many toddies and a dollar for his nightly performance.

Mr. Pippel's shop was but a short distance from the Wondersmith's house. A few moments, therefore, brought the gypsy party to the door, when, by aid of a key which Herr Hippe produced, they silently slipped into the entry. Here the Wondersmith took a dark-lantern from under his cloak, removed the cap that shrouded the light, and led the way into the shop, which was separated from the entry only by a glass door, that yielded, like the outer one, to a key which Hippe took from his pocket. The four gypsies now entered the shop and closed the door behind them.

It was a little world of birds. On every side, whether in large or small cages, one beheld balls of various-colored feathers standing on one leg and breathing peacefully. Love-birds, nestling shoulder to shoulder, with their heads tucked under their wings and all their feathers puffed out, so that they looked like globes of malachite; English bullfinches, with ashen-colored backs, in which their black heads were buried, and corselets of a rosy down; Java sparrows, fat and sleek and cleanly; troupials, so glossy and splendid in plumage that they looked as if they were dressed in the celebrated armor of the Black Prince, which was jet, richly damascened with gold; a cock of the rock, gleaming, a ball of tawny fire, like a setting sun; the Campanero of Brazil, white as snow, with his dilatable tolling-tube hanging from his head, placid and silent;--these, with a humbler crowd of linnets, canaries, robins, mocking-birds, and phoebes, slumbered calmly in their little cages, that were hung so thickly on the wall as not to leave an inch of it visible.

"Splendid little morsels, all of them!" exclaimed Monsieur Kerplonne. "Ah we are going to have a rare beating!"

"So Pippel does not sleep in his shop," said the English gypsy, Oaksmith.

"No. The fellow lives somewhere up one of the avenues," answered Madame Filomel. "He came, the other evening, to consult me about his fortune. I did not tell him," she added, with a laugh, "that he was going to have so distinguished a sporting party on his premises."

"Come," said the Wondersmith, producing the box of manikins, "get ready with souls, Madame Filomel. I am impatient to see my little men letting out lives for the first time."

Just at the moment that the Wondersmith uttered this sentence, the four gypsies were startled by a hoarse voice issuing from a corner of the room, and propounding in the most guttural tones the intemperate query of "What'll you take?" This sottish invitation had scarce been given, when a second extremely thick voice replied from an opposite corner, in accents so rough that they seemed to issue from a throat torn and furrowed by the liquid lava of many barrooms, "Brandy and water."

"Hollo! who's here?" muttered Herr Hippe, flashing the light of his lantern round the shop.

Oaksmith turned up his coat-cuffs, as if to be ready for a fight; Madame Filomel glided, or rather rolled, towards the door; while Kerplonne put his hand into his pocket, as if to assure himself that his supernumerary optic was all right.

"What'll you take?" croaked the voice in the corner, once more.

"Brandy and water," rapidly replied the second voice in the other corner. And then, as if by a concerted movement, a series of bibular invitations and acceptances were rolled backwards and forwards with a volubility of utterance that threw Patter versus Clatter into the shade.

"What the Devil can it be?" muttered the Wondersmith, flashing his lantern here and there. "Ah! it is those Minos."

So saying, he stopped under one of the wicker cages that hung high up on the wall, and raised the lantern above his head, so as to throw the light upon that particular cage. The hospitable individual who had been extending all these hoarse invitations to partake of intoxicating beverages was an inhabitant of the cage. It was a large Mino-bird, who now stood perched on his cross-bar, with his yellowish orange bill sloped slightly over his shoulder, and his white eye cocked knowingly upon the Wondersmith. The respondent voice in the other corner came from another Mino-bird, who sat in the dusk in a similar cage, also attentively watching the Wondersmith. These Mino-birds, I may remark, in passing, have a singular aptitude for acquiring phrases.

"What'll you take?" repeated the Mino, cocking his other eye upon Herr Hippe.

"Mon Dieu! what a bird!" exclaimed the little Frenchman. "He is, in truth, polite."

"I don't know what I'll take," said Hippe, as if replying to the Mino-bird; "but I know what you'll get, old fellow! Filomel, open the cage-doors, and give me the bottle."

Filomel opened, one after another, the doors of the numberless little cages, thereby arousing from slumber their feathered occupants, who opened their beaks, and stretched their claws, and stared with great surprise at the lantern and the midnight visitors.

By this time the Wondersmith had performed the mysterious manipulations with the bottle, and the manikins were once more in full motion, swarming out of their box, sword and dagger in hand, with their little black eyes glittering fiercely, and their white teeth shining. The little creatures seemed to scent their prey. The gypsies stood in the centre of the shop, watching the proceedings eagerly, while the Liliputians made in a body towards the wall and commenced climbing from cage to cage. Then was heard a tremendous flittering of wings, and faint, despairing "quirks" echoed on all sides. In almost every cage there was a fierce manikin thrusting his sword or dagger vigorously into the body of some unhappy bird. It recalled the antique legend of the battles of the Pygmies and the Cranes. The poor love-birds lay with their emerald feathers dabbled in their hearts' blood, shoulder to shoulder in death as in life. Canaries gasped at the bottom of their cages, while the water in their little glass fountains ran red. The bullfinches wore an unnatural crimson on their breasts. The mocking-bird lay on his back, kicking spasmodically, in the last agonies, with a tiny sword-thrust cleaving his melodious throat in twain, so that from the instrument which used to gush with wondrous music only scarlet drops of blood now trickled. The manikins were ruthless. Their faces were ten times wickeder than ever, as they roamed from cage to cage, slaughtering with a fury that seemed entirely unappeasable. Presently the feathery rustlings became fewer and fainter, and the little pipings of despair died away; and in every cage lay a poor murdered minstrel, with the song that abode within him forever quenched;--in every cage but two, and those two were high up on the wall; and in each glared a pair of wild, white eyes; and an orange beak, touch as steel, pointed threateningly down. With the needles which they grasped as swords all wet and warm with blood, and their beadlike eyes flashing in the light of the lantern, the Liliputian assassins swarmed up the cages in two separate bodies, until they reached the wickets of the habitations in which the Minos abode. Mino saw them coming,--had listened attentively to the many death-struggles of his comrades, and had, in fact, smelt a rat. Accordingly he was ready for the manikins. There he stood at the barbican of his castle, with formidable beak couched like a lance. The manikins made a gallant charge. "What'll you take?" was rattled out by the Mino, in a deep bass, as with one plunge of his sharp bill he scattered the ranks of the enemy, and sent three of them flying to the floor, where they lay with broken limbs. But the manikins were brave automata, and again they closed and charged the gallant Mino. Again the wicked white eyes of the bird gleamed, and again the orange bill dealt destruction. Everything seemed to be going on swimmingly for Mino, when he found himself attacked in the rear by two treacherous manikins, who had stolen upon him from behind, through the latticework of the cage. Quick as lightning the Mino turned to repel this assault, but all too late; two slender quivering threads of steel crossed in his poor body, and he staggered into a corner of the cage. His white eyes closed, then opened; a shiver passed over his body, beginning at his shoulder-tips and dying off in the extreme tips of the wings; he gasped as if for air, and then, with a convulsive shudder, which ruffled all his feathers, croaked out feebly his little speech, "What'll you take?" Instantly from the opposite corner came the old response, still feebler than the question,--a mere gurgle, as it were, of "Brandy and water." Then all was silent. The Mino-birds were dead.

"They spill blood like Christians," said the Wondersmith, gazing fondly on the manikins. "They will be famous assassins."

TIED UP.

HERR HIPPE stood in the doorway, scowling. His eyes seemed to scorch the poor hunchback, whose form, physically inferior, crouched before that baneful, blazing glance, while his head, mentally brave, reared itself, as if to redeem the cowardice of the frame to which it belonged. So the attitude of the serpent: the body pliant, yielding, supple; but the crest thrown aloft, erect, and threatening. As for Zonela, she was frozen in the attitude of motion;--a dancing nymph in colored marble; agility stunned; elasticity petrified.

Furbelow, astonished at this sudden change, and catching, with all the mysterious rapidity of instinct peculiar to the lower animals, at the enigmatical character of the situation, turned his pleading, melancholy eyes from one to another of the motionless three, as if begging that his humble intellect (pardon me, naturalists, for the use of this word "intellect" in the matter of a monkey!) should be enlightened as speedily as possible. Not receiving the desired information, he, after the manner of trained animals, returned to his muttons; in other words, he conceived that this unusual entrance, and consequent dramatic tableau, meant "shop." He therefore dropped Zonela's hand and pattered on his velvety little feet over towards the grim figure of the Wondersmith, holding out his poor little paw for the customary copper. He had but one idea drilled into him,--soulless creature that he was,--and that was, alms. But I have seen creatures that professed to have souls, and that would have been indignant, if you had denied them immortality, who took to the soliciting of alms as naturally as if beggary had been the original sin, and was regularly born with them, and never baptized out of them. I will give these Bandits of the Order of Charity this credit, however, that they knew the best highways and the richest founts of benevolence,--unlike to Furbelow, who, unreasoning and undiscriminating, begged from the first person that was near. Furbelow, owing to this intellectual inferiority to the before-mentioned Alsatians, frequently got more kicks than coppers, and the present supplication which he indulged in towards the Wondersmith was a terrible confirmation of the rule. The reply to the extended pleading paw was what might be called a double-barrelled kick,--a kick to be represented by the power of two when the foot touched the object, multiplied by four when the entire leg formed an angle of 45 deg. with the

{192}

spinal column. The long, nervous leg of the Wondersmith caught the little creature in the centre of the body, doubled up his brown, hairy form, till he looked like a fur driving-glove, and sent him whizzing across the room into a far corner, where he dropped senseless and flaccid.

This vengeance which Herr Hippe executed upon Furbelow seemed to have operated as a sort of escape-valve, and he found voice. He hissed out the question, "Who are you?" to the hunchback; and in listening to that essence of sibilation, it really seemed as if it proceeded from the serpent that curled upon his upper lip.

"Who are you? Deformed dog, who are you? What do you here?"

"My name is Solon," answered the fearless head of the hunchback, while the frail, cowardly body shivered and trembled inch by inch into a corner.

"So you come to visit my daughter in the night-time, when I am away?" continued the Wondersmith, with a sneering tone that dropped from his snake-wreathed mouth like poison. "You are a brave and gallant lover, are you not? Where did you win that Order of the Curse of God that decorates your shoulders? The women turn their heads and look after you in the street, when you pass, do they not? lost in admiration of that symmetrical figure, those graceful limbs, that neck pliant as the stem that moors the lotus! Elegant, conquering Christian cripple, what do you here in my daughter's room?"

Can you imagine Jove, limitless in power and wrath, hurling from his vast grasp mountain after mountain upon the struggling Enceladus,--and picture the Titan sinking, sinking, deeper and deeper into the earth, crushed and dying, with nothing visible through the super-incumbent masses of Pelion and Ossa, but a gigantic head and two flaming eyes, that, despite the death which is creeping through each vein, still flash back defiance to the divine enemy? Well, Solon and Herr Hippe presented such a picture, seen through the wrong end of a telescope,--reduced in proportion, but alike in action. Solon's feeble body seemed to sink into utter annihilation beneath the horrible taunts that his enemy hurled at him, while the large, brave brow and unconquered eyes still sent forth a magnetic resistance.

Suddenly the poor hunchback felt his arm grasped. A thrill seemed to run through his entire body. A warm atmosphere, invigorating and full of delicious odor, surrounded him. It appeared as if invisible bandages were twisted all about his limbs, giving him a strange strength. His sinking legs straightened. His powerless arms were braced. Astonished, he glanced round for an instant, and beheld Zonela, with a world of love burning in her large lambent eyes, wreathing her round white arms about his humped shoulders. Then the poet knew the great sustaining power of love. Solon reared himself boldly.

"Sneer at my poor form," he cried, in strong vibrating tones, flinging out one long arm and one thin finger at the Wondersmith, as if he would have impaled him like a beetle. "Humiliate me, if you can. I care not. You are a wretch, and I am honest and pure. This girl is not your daughter. You are like one of those demons in the fairy tales that held beauty and purity locked in infernal spells. I do not fear you, Herr Hippe. There are stories abroad about you in the neighborhood, and when you pass, people say that they feel evil and blight hovering over their thresholds. You persecute this girl. You are her tyrant. You hate her. I am a cripple. Providence has cast this lump upon my shoulders. But that is nothing. The camel, that is the salvation of the children of the desert, has been given his hump in order that he might bear his human burden better. This girl, who is homeless as the Arab, is my appointed load in life, and, please God, I will carry her on this back, hunched though it may be. I have come to see her, because I love her,--because she loves me. You have no claim on her; so I will take her from you."

Quick as lightning, the Wondersmith had stridden a few paces, and grasped the poor cripple, who was yet quivering with the departing thunder of his passion. He seized him in his bony, muscular grasp, as he would have seized a puppet, and held him at arm's length gasping and powerless; while Zonela, pale, breathless, entreating, sank half-kneeling on the floor.

"Your skeleton will be interesting to science when you are dead, Mr. Solon," hissed the Wondersmith. "But before I have the pleasure of reducing you to an anatomy, which I will assuredly do, I wish to compliment you on your power of penetration, or sources of information; for I know not if you have derived your knowledge from your own mental research or the efforts of others. You are perfectly correct in your statement, that this charming young person, who day after day parades the streets with a barrel-organ and a monkey,--the last unhappily indisposed at present,--listening to the degrading jokes of ribald boys and depraved men,--you are quite correct, Sir, in stating that she is not my daughter. On the contrary, she is the daughter of an Hungarian nobleman who had the misfortune to incur my displeasure. I had a son, crooked spawn of a Christian!--a son, not like you, cankered, gnarled stump of life that you are,--but a youth tall and fair and noble in aspect, as became a child of one whose lineage makes Pharaoh modern,--a youth whose foot in the dance was as swift and beautiful to look at as the golden sandals of the sun when he dances upon the sea in summer. This youth was virtuous and good; and being of good race, and dwelling in a country where his rank, gypsy as he was, was recognized, he mixed with the proudest of the land. One day he fell in with this accursed Hungarian, a fierce drinker of that Devil's blood called brandy. My child until that hour had avoided this bane of our race. Generous wine he drank, because the soul of the sun our ancestor palpitated in its purple waves. But brandy, which is fallen and accursed wine, as devils are fallen and accursed angels, had never crossed his lips, until in an evil hour he was reduced by this Christian hog, and from that day forth his life was one fiery debauch, which set only in the black waves of death. I vowed vengeance on the destroyer of my child, and I kept my word. I have destroyed his child,--not compassed her death, but blighted her life, steeped her in misery and poverty, and now, thanks to the thousand devils, I have discovered a new torture for her heart. She thought to solace her life with a love-episode! Sweet little epicure that she was! She shall have her little crooked lover, shan't she? Oh, yes! She shall have him, cold and stark and livid, with that great, black, heavy hunch, which no back, however broad, can bear, Death, sitting between his shoulders!"

There was something so awful and demoniac in this entire speech and the manner in which it was delivered, that it petrified Zonela into a mere inanimate figure, whose eyes seemed unalterably fixed on the fierce, cruel face of the Wondersmith. As for Solon, he was paralyzed in the grasp of his foe. He heard, but could not reply. His large eyes, dilated with horror to far beyond their ordinary size, expressed unutterable agony.

The last sentence had hardly been hissed out by the gypsy when he took from his pocket a long, thin coil of whipcord, which he entangled in a complicated mesh around the cripple's body. It was not the ordinary binding of a prisoner. The slender lash passed and repassed in a thousand intricate folds over the powerless limbs of the poor humpback. When the operation was completed, he looked as if he had been sewed from head to foot in some singularly ingenious species of network.

"Now, my pretty lop-sided little lover," laughed Herr Hippe, flinging Solon over his shoulder, as a fisherman might fling a net-full of fish, "we will proceed to put you into your little cage until your little coffin is quite ready. Meanwhile we will lock up your darling beggar-girl to mourn over your untimely end."

So saying, he stepped from the room with his captive, and securely locked the door behind him.

When he had disappeared, the frozen Zonela thawed, and with a shriek of anguish flung herself on the inanimate body of Furbelow.

THE POISONING OF THE SWORDS.

IT was New Year's Eve, and eleven o'clock at night. All over this great land, and in every great city in the land, curly heads were lying on white pillows, dreaming of the coming of the generous Santa Claus. Innumerable stockings hung by countless bedsides. Visions of beautiful toys, passing in splendid pageantry through myriads of dimly lit dormitories, made millions of little hearts palpitate in sleep. Ah! what heavenly toys those were that the children of this soil beheld, that mystic night, in their dreams! Painted cars with orchestral wheels, making music more delicious than the roll of planets. Agile men of cylindrical figure, who sprang unexpectedly out of meek-looking boxes, with a supernatural fierceness in their crimson cheeks and fur-whiskers. Herds of marvellous sheep, with fleeces as impossible as the one that Jason sailed after; animals entirely indifferent to grass and water and "rot" and "ticks." Horses spotted with an astounding regularity, and furnished with the most ingenious methods of locomotion. Slender foreigners, attired in painfully short tunics, whose existence passed in continually turning heels over head down a steep flight of steps, at the bottom of which they lay in an exhausted condition with dislocated limbs, until they were restored to their former elevation, when they went at it again as if nothing had happened. Stately swans, that seemed to have a touch of the ostrich in them; for they swam continually after a piece of iron which was held before them, as if consumed with a ferruginous hunger. Whole farm-yards of roosters, whose tails curled the wrong way,--a slight defect, that was, however, amply atoned for by the size and brilliancy of their scarlet combs, which, it would appear, Providence had intended for pen-wipers. Pears, that, when applied to youthful lips, gave forth sweet and inspiring sounds. Regiments of soldiers, that performed neat, but limited evolutions on cross-jointed contractile battle-fields. All these things, idealized, transfigured, and illuminated by the powers and atmosphere and colored lamps of Dreamland, did the millions of dear sleeping children behold, the night of the New Year's Eve of which I speak.

It was on this night, when Time was preparing to shed his skin and come out young and golden and glossy as ever,--when, in the vast chambers of the universe, silent and infallible preparations were making for the wonderful birth of the coming year,--when mystic dews were secreted for his baptism, and mystic instruments were tuned in space to welcome him,--it was at this holy and solemn hour that the Wondersmith and his three gypsy companions sat in close conclave in the little parlor before mentioned.

There was a fire roaring in the grate. On a table, nearly in the centre of the room, stood a huge decanter of Port wine, that glowed in the blaze which lit the chamber like a flask of crimson fire. On every side, piled in heaps, inanimate, but scowling with the same old wondrous scowl, lay myriads of the manikins, all clutching in their wooden hands their tiny weapons. The Wondersmith held in one hand a small silver bowl filled with a green, glutinous substance, which he was delicately applying, with the aid of a camel's-hair brush, to the tips of tiny swords and daggers. A horrible smile wandered over his sallow face,--a smile as unwholesome in appearance as the sickly light that plays above reeking graveyards.

"Let us drink great draughts, brothers," he cried, leaving off his strange anointment for a while, to lift a great glass, filled with sparkling liquor, to his lips. "Let us drink to our approaching triumph. Let us drink to the great poison, Macousha. Subtle seed of Death,--swift hurricane that sweeps away Life,--vast hammer that crushes brain and heart and artery with its resistless weight,--I drink to it."

"It is a noble decoction, Duke Balthazar," said the old fortune-teller and mid-wife, Madame Filomel, nodding in her chair as she swallowed her wine in great gulps. "Where did you obtain it?"

"It is made," said the Wondersmith, swallowing another great goblet-full of wine ere he replied, "in the wild woods of Guiana, in silence and in mystery. But one tribe of Indians, the Macoushi Indians, know the secret. It is simmered over fires built of strange woods, and the maker of it dies in the making. The place, for a mile around the spot where it is fabricated, is shunned as accursed. Devils hover over the pot in which it stews; and the birds of the air, scenting the smallest breath of its vapor from far away, drop to earth with paralyzed wings, cold and dead."

"It kills, then, fast?" asked Kerplonne, the artificial eyemaker,--his own eyes gleaming, under the influence of the wine, with a sinister lustre, as if they had been fresh from the factory, and were yet untarnished by use.

"Kills?" echoed the Wondersmith, derisively; "it is swifter than thunderbolts, stronger than lightning. But you shall see it proved before we let forth our army on the city accursed. You shall see a wretch die, as if smitten by a falling fragment of the sun."

"What? Do you mean Solon?" asked Oaksmith and the fortune-teller together.

"Ah! you mean the young man who makes the commerce with books?" echoed Kerplonne. "It is well. His agonies will instruct us."

"Yes! Solon," answered Hippe, with a savage accent. "I hate him, and he shall die this horrid death. Ah! how the little fellows will leap upon him, when I bring him in, bound and helpless, and give their beautiful wicked souls to them! How they will pierce him in ten thousand spots with their poisoned weapons, until his skin turns blue and violet and crimson, and his form swells with the venom,--until his hump is lost in shapeless flesh! He hears what I say, every word of it. He is in the closet next door, and is listening. How comfortable he feels! How the sweat of terror rolls on his brow! How he tries to loosen his bonds, and curses all earth and heaven when he finds that he cannot! Ho! ho! Handsome lover of Zonela, will she kiss you when you are livid and swollen? Brothers, let us drink again,--drink always. Here, Oaksmith, take these brushes,--and you, Filomel,--and finish the anointing of these swords. This wine is grand. This poison is grand. It is fine to have good wine to drink, and good poison to kill with; is it not?" and, with flushed face and rolling eyes, the Wondersmith continued to drink and use his brush alternately.

The others hastened to follow his example. It was a horrible scene: those four wicked faces; those myriads of tiny faces, just as wicked; the certain unearthly air that pervaded the apartment; the red, unwholesome glare cast by the fire; the wild and reckless way in which the weird company drank the red-illumined wine.

The anointing of the swords went on rapidly, and the wine went as rapidly down the throats of the four poisoners. Their faces grew more and more inflamed each instant; their eyes shone like rolling fireballs; their hair was moist and dishevelled. The old fortune-teller rocked to and fro in her chair, like those legless plaster figures that sway upon convex loaded bottoms. All four began to mutter incoherent sentences, and babble unintelligible wickednesses. Still the anointing of the swords went on.

"I see the faces of millions of young corpses," babbled Herr Hippe, gazing, with swimming eyes, into the silver bowl that contained the Macousha poison,--"all young, all Christians,--and the little fellows dancing, dancing, and stabbing, stabbing. Filomel, Filomel, I say!"

"Well, Grand Duke," snored the old woman, giving a violent lurch.

"Where's the bottle of souls?"

"In my right-hand pocket, Herr Hippe"; and she felt, so as to assure herself that it was there. She half drew out the black bottle, before described in this narrative, and let it slide again into her pocket,--let it slide again, but it did not completely regain its former place. Caught by some accident, it hung half out, swaying over the edge of the pocket, as the fat midwife rolled backwards and forwards in her drunken efforts at equilibrium.

"All right," said Herr Hippe, "perfectly right! Let's drink."

He reached out his hand for his glass, and, with a dull sigh, dropped on the table, in the instantaneous slumber of intoxication. Oaksmith soon fell back in his chair, breathing heavily. Kerplonne followed. And the heavy, stertorous breathing of

Filomel told that she slumbered also; but still her chair retained its rocking motion, and still the bottle of souls balanced itself on the edge of her pocket.

LET LOOSE.

SURE enough, Solon heard every word of the fiendish talk of the Wondersmith. For how many days he had been shut up, bound in the terrible net, in that dark closet, he did not know; but now he felt that his last hour was come. His little strength was completely worn out in efforts to disentangle himself. Once a day a door opened, and Herr Hippe placed a crust of bread and a cup of water within his reach. On this meagre fare he had subsisted. It was a hard life; but, bad as it was, it was better than the horrible death that menaced him. His brain reeled with terror at the prospect of it. Then, where was Zonela? Why did she not come to his rescue? But she was, perhaps, dead. The darkness, too, appalled him. A faint light, when the moon was bright, came at night through a chink far up in the wall; and the only other hole in the chamber was an aperture through which, at some former time, a stove-pipe had been passed. Even if he were free, there would have been small hope of escape; but, laced as it were in a network of steel, what was to be done? He groaned and writhed upon the floor, and tore at the boards with his hands, which were free from the wrists down. All else was as solidly laced up as an Indian papoose. Nothing but pride kept him from shrieking aloud, when, on the night of New Year's Eve, he heard the fiendish Hippe recite the programme of his murder.

While he was thus wailing and gnashing his teeth in darkness and torture, he heard a faint noise above his head. Then something seemed to leap from the ceiling and alight softly on the floor. He shuddered with terror. Was it some new torture of the Wondersmith's invention? The next moment, he felt some small animal crawling over his body, and a soft, silky paw was pushed timidly across his face. His heart leaped with joy.

"It is Furbelow!" he cried. "Zonela has sent him. He came through the stove-pipe hole."

It was Furbelow, indeed, restored to life by Zonela's care, and who had come down a narrow tube, that no human being could have threaded, to console the poor captive. The monkey nestled closely into the hunchback's bosom, and, as he did so, Solon felt something cold and hard hanging from his neck. He touched it. It was sharp. By the dim light that struggled through the aperture high up in the wall, he discovered a knife, suspended by a bit of cord. Ah! how the blood came rushing through the veins that crossed over and through his heart, when life and liberty came to him in this bit of rusty steel! With his manacled hands he loosened the heaven-sent weapon; a few cuts were rapidly made in the cunning network of cord that enveloped his limbs, and in a few seconds he was free!--cramped and faint with hunger, but free!--

free to move, to use the limbs that God had given him for his preservation,--free to fight,--to die fighting, perhaps,--but still to die free. He ran to the door. The bolt was a weak one, for the Wondersmith had calculated more surely on his prison of cords than on any jail of stone,--and more; and with a few efforts the door opened.

He went cautiously out into the darkness, with Furbelow perched on his shoulder, pressing his cold muzzle against his cheek. He had made but a few steps when a trembling hand was put into his, and in another moment Zonela's palpitating heart was pressed against his own. One long kiss, an embrace, a few whispered words, and the hunchback and the girl stole softly towards the door of the chamber in which the four gypsies slept. All seemed still; nothing but the hard breathing of the sleepers, and the monotonous rocking of Madame Filomel's chair broke the silence. Solon stooped down and put his eye to the keyhole, through which a red bar of light streamed into the entry. As he did so, his foot crushed some brittle substance that lay just outside the door; at the same moment a howl of agony was heard to issue from the room within. Solon started; nor did he know that at that instant he had crushed into dust Monsieur Kerplonne's supernumerary eye, and the owner, though wrapt in a drunken sleep, felt the pang quiver through his brain.

While Solon peeped through the keyhole, all in the room was motionless. He had not gazed, however, for many seconds, when the chair of the fortune-teller gave a sudden lurch, and the black bottle, already hanging half out of her wide pocket, slipped entirely from its resting-place, and, falling heavily to the ground, shivered into fragments.

Then took place an astonishing spectacle. The myriads of armed dolls, that lay in piles about the room, became suddenly imbued with motion. They stood up straight, their tiny limbs moved, their black eyes flashed with wicked purposes, their thread-like swords gleamed as they waved them to and fro. The villanous souls imprisoned in the bottle began to work within them. Like the Liliputians, when they found the giant Gulliver asleep, they scaled in swarms the burly sides of the four sleeping gypsies. At every step they took, they drove their thin swords and quivering daggers into the flesh of the drunken authors of their being. To stab and kill was their mission, and they stabbed and killed with incredible fury. They clustered on the Wondersmith's sallow cheeks and sinewy throat, piercing every portion with their diminutive poisoned blades. Filomel's fat carcass was alive with them. They blackened the spare body of Monsieur Kerplonne. They covered Oaksmith's huge form like a cluster of insects.

Overcome completely with the fumes of wine, these tiny wounds did not for a few moments awaken the sleeping victims. But the swift and deadly poison Macousha, with which the weapons had been so fiendishly anointed, began to work. Herr Hippe, stung into sudden life, leaped to his feet, with a dwarf army clinging to his clothes and his hands,--always stabbing, stabbing, stabbing. For an instant, a look of stupid bewilderment clouded his face; then the horrible truth burst upon him. He gave a shriek like that which a horse utters when he finds himself fettered and surrounded by fire,--a shriek that curdled the air for miles and miles.

"Oaksmith! Kerplonne! Filomel! Awake! awake! We are lost! The souls have got loose! We are dead! poisoned! Oh, accursed ones! Oh, demons, ye are slaying me! Ah! fiends of Hell!"

Aroused by these frightful howls, the three gypsies sprang also to their feet, to find themselves stung to death by the manikins. They raved, they shrieked, they swore. They staggered round the chamber. Blinded in the eyes by the ever-stabbing weapons,--with the poison already burning in their veins like red-hot lead,--their forms swelling and discoloring visibly every moment,--their howls and attitudes and furious gestures made the scene look like a chamber in Hell.

Maddened beyond endurance, the Wondersmith, half-blind and choking with the venom that had congested all the blood-vessels of his body, seized dozens of the manikins and dashed them into the fire, trampling them down with his feet.

"Ye shall die too, if I die," he cried, with a roar like that of a tiger. "Ye shall burn, if I burn. I gave ye life,--I give ye death. Down!--down!--burn!--flame! Fiends that ye are, to slay us! Help me, brothers! Before we die, let us have our revenge!"

On this, the other gypsies, themselves maddened by approaching death, began hurling manikins, by handfuls, into the fire. The little creatures, being wooden of body, quickly caught the flames, and an awful struggle for life took place in miniature in the grate. Some of them escaped from between the bars and ran about the room, blazing, writhing in agony, and igniting the curtains and other draperies that hung around. Others fought and stabbed one another in the very core of the fire, like combating salamanders. Meantime, the motions of the gypsies grew more languid and slow, and their curses were uttered in choked guttural tones. The faces of all four were spotted with red and green and violet, like so many egg-plants. Their bodies were swollen to a frightful size, and at last they dropped on the floor, like over-ripe fruit shaken from the boughs by the winds of autumn.

The chamber was now a sheet of fire. The flames roared round and round, as if seeking for escape, licking every projecting cornice and sill with greedy tongues, as the serpent licks his prey before he swallows it. A hot, putrid breath came through the keyhole and smote Solon and Zonela like a wind of death. They clasped each other's hands with a moan of terror, and fled from the house.

The next morning, when the young Year was just unclosing its eyes, and the happy children all over the great city were peeping from their beds into the myriads of stockings hanging near by, the blue skies of heaven shone through a black network of stone and charred rafters. These were all that remained of the habitation of Herr Hippe, the Wondersmith.

THE SNOW-FIEND

Ann Radcliffe

HARK! To the Snow-Fiend's voice afar
That shrieks upon the troubled air!
Him by that shrilly call I know –
Though yet unseen, unfelt below –
And by the mist of livid grey,
That steals upon his onward way.
He from the ice-peaks of the North
In sounding majesty comes forth;
Dark amidst the wondrous light;
That streams o'er all the northern night.
A wan rime through the airy waste
Marks where unseen his car has past;
And veils the spectre-shapes, his train,
That wait upon his vengeful reign.
Disease and Want and shuddering Fear
Danger and Woe and Death are there.
Around his head for ever raves
A whirlwind cold of misty waves.
But oft, the parting surge between,
His visage, keen and white, is seen;
His savage eye and paly glare
Beneath a helm of ice appear;
A snowy plume was o'er the crest,
And wings of snow his form invest.
Aloft he bears a frozen wand;
The ice-bolt trembles in his hand;
And ever, when on sea he rides,
An iceberg for his throne provides.
As, fierce, he drives his distant way,
Agents remote his call obey,
From half-known Greenland's snow-piled shore
To Newfoundland and Labrador;
O'er solid seas, where nought is scanned
To mark a difference from land,
And sound itself does but explain
The desolation of his reign;
The moaning querulous and deep,
And the wild howl's infuriate sweep

{201}

Where'er he moves, some note of woe
Proclaims the presence of the foe;
While he, relentless, round him flings
The white shower from his flaky wings.
Hark! 'tis his voice: -- I shun his call,
And shuddering seek the blazing hall.
O! speak of mirth; O! raise the song!
Hear not the fiends, that round him throng!
Of curtained rooms and firesides tell,
Bid Fancy work her genial spell,
That wraps in marvel and delight
December's long tempestuous night;
Makes courtly groups in summer bowers
Dance through pale Winter's midnight hours;
And July's eve its rich glow shed
On the hoar wreath, that binds his head;
Or knights on strange adventure bent,
Or ladies into thralldom sent;
Whatever gaiety ideal
Can substitute for troubles real.
Then let the storms of Winter sing,
And his sad veil the Snow-Fiend fling,
Through wailing lays are in the wind,
They reach not then the 'tranced mind;
Nor murky form, nor dismal sound
May pass the high, enchanted bound!

THE FESTIVAL
H. P. Lovecraft

I was far from home, and the spell of the eastern sea was upon me. In the twilight I heard it pounding on the rocks, and I knew it lay just over the hill where the twisting willows writhed against the clearing sky and the first stars of evening. And because my fathers had called me to the old town beyond, I pushed on through the shallow, new-fallen snow along the road that soared lonely up to where Aldebaran twinkled among the trees; on toward the very ancient town I had never seen but often dreamed of.

It was the Yuletide, that men call Christmas though they know in their hearts it is older than Bethlehem and Babylon, older than Memphis and mankind. It was the Yuletide, and I had come at last to the ancient sea town where my people had dwelt and kept festival in the elder time when festival was forbidden; where also they had commanded their sons to keep festival once every century, that the memory of primal secrets might not be forgotten. Mine were an old people, and were old even when this land was settled three hundred years before. And they were strange, because they had come as dark furtive folk from opiate southern gardens of orchids, and spoken another tongue before they learnt the tongue of the blue-eyed fishers. And now they were scattered, and shared only the rituals of mysteries that none living could understand. I was the only one who came back that night to the old fishing town as legend bade, for only the poor and the lonely remember.

Then beyond the hill's crest I saw Kingsport outspread frostily in the gloaming; snowy Kingsport with its ancient vanes and steeples, ridgepoles and chimney-pots, wharves and small bridges, willow-trees and graveyards; endless labyrinths of steep, narrow, crooked streets, and dizzy church-crowned central peak that time durst not touch; ceaseless mazes of colonial houses piled and scattered at all angles and levels like a child's disordered blocks; antiquity hovering on grey wings over winter-whitened gables and gambrel roofs; fanlights and small-paned windows one by one gleaming out in the cold dusk to join Orion and the archaic stars. And against the rotting wharves the sea pounded; the secretive, immemorial sea out of which the people had come in the elder time.

Beside the road at its crest a still higher summit rose, bleak and windswept, and I saw that it was a burying-ground where black gravestones stuck ghoulishly through the snow like the decayed fingernails of a gigantic corpse. The printless road was very lonely, and sometimes I thought I heard a distant horrible creaking as of a gibbet in the wind. They had hanged four kinsmen of mine for witchcraft in 1692, but I did not know just where.

As the road wound down the seaward slope I listened for the merry sounds of a village at evening, but did not hear them. Then I thought of the season, and felt that these old Puritan folk might well have Christmas customs strange to me, and full of silent hearthside prayer. So after that I did not listen for merriment or look for wayfarers, but kept on down past the hushed lighted farmhouses and shadowy stone walls to where the signs of ancient shops and sea-taverns creaked in the salt breeze, and the grotesque knockers of pillared doorways glistened along deserted, unpaved lanes in the light of little, curtained windows.

I had seen maps of the town, and knew where to find the home of my people. It was told that I should be known and welcomed, for village legend lives long; so I hastened through Back Street to Circle Court, and across the fresh snow on the one full flagstone pavement in the town, to where Green Lane leads off behind the Market house. The old maps still held good, and I had no trouble; though at Arkham they must have lied when they said the trolleys ran to this place, since I saw not a wire overhead. Snow would have hid the rails in any case. I was glad I had chosen to walk, for the white village had seemed very beautiful from the hill; and now I was eager to knock at the door of my people, the seventh house on the left in Green Lane, with an ancient peaked roof and jutting second story, all built before 1650.

There were lights inside the house when I came upon it, and I saw from the diamond window-panes that it must have been kept very close to its antique state. The upper part overhung the narrow grass-grown street and nearly met the overhanging part of the house opposite, so that I was almost in a tunnel, with the low stone doorstep wholly free from snow. There was no sidewalk, but many houses had high doors reached by double flights of steps with iron railings. It was an odd scene, and because I was strange to New England I had never known its like before. Though it pleased me, I would have relished it better if there had been footprints in the snow, and people in the streets, and a few windows without drawn curtains.

When I sounded the archaic iron knocker I was half afraid. Some fear had been gathering in me, perhaps because of the strangeness of my heritage, and the bleakness of the evening, and the queerness of the silence in that aged town of curious customs. And when my knock was answered I was fully afraid, because I had not heard any footsteps before the door creaked open. But I was not afraid long, for the gowned, slippered old man in the doorway had a bland face that reassured me; and though he made signs that he was dumb, he wrote a quaint and ancient welcome with the stylus and wax tablet he carried.

He beckoned me into a low, candle-lit room with massive exposed rafters and dark, stiff, sparse furniture of the seventeenth century. The past was vivid there, for not an attribute was missing. There was a cavernous fireplace and a spinning-wheel at which a bent old woman in loose wrapper and deep poke-bonnet sat back toward me, silently spinning despite the festive season. An indefinite dampness seemed upon the place, and I marvelled that no fire should be blazing. The high-backed settle faced the row of curtained windows at the left, and seemed to be occupied, though I was not sure. I did not like everything about what I saw, and felt again the fear I had had. This fear grew stronger from what had before lessened it, for the more I looked at the old man's bland face the more its very blandness terrified me. The eyes never moved, and the skin was too like wax. Finally I was sure it was not a face at all, but a fiendishly cunning mask. But the flabby hands, curiously gloved, wrote genially on the tablet and told me I must wait a while before I could be led to the place of festival.

Pointing to a chair, table, and pile of books, the old man now left the room; and when I sat down to read I saw that the books were hoary and mouldy, and that they included old Morryster's wild *Marvells of Science*, the terrible *Saducismus Triumphatus* of Joseph Glanvill, published in 1681, the shocking *Daemonolatreia* of Remigius, printed in 1595 at Lyons, and worst of all, the unmentionable *Necronomicon* of the mad Arab Abdul Alhazred, in Olaus Wormius' forbidden Latin translation; a book which I had never seen, but of which I had heard monstrous things whispered. No one spoke to me, but I could hear the creaking of signs in the wind outside, and the whir of the wheel as the bonneted old woman continued her silent spinning, spinning. I thought the room and the books and the people very morbid and disquieting, but because an old tradition of my fathers had summoned me to strange feastings, I resolved to expect queer things. So I tried to read, and soon became tremblingly absorbed by something I found in that accursed *Necronomicon*; a thought and a legend too hideous for sanity or consciousness. But I disliked it when I fancied I heard the closing of one of the windows that the settle faced, as if it had been stealthily opened. It had seemed to follow a whirring that was not of the old woman's spinning-wheel. This was not much, though, for the old woman was spinning very hard, and the aged clock had been striking. After that I lost the feeling that there were persons on the settle, and was reading intently and shudderingly when the old man came back booted and dressed in a loose antique costume, and sat down on that very bench, so that I could not see him. It was certainly nervous waiting, and the blasphemous book in my hands made it doubly so. When eleven struck, however, the old man stood up, glided to a massive carved chest in a corner, and got two hooded cloaks; one of which he donned, and the other of which he draped round the old woman, who was ceasing her monotonous spinning. Then they both started for the outer door; the woman lamely creeping, and the old man, after picking up the very book I had been reading, beckoning me as he drew his hood over that unmoving face or mask.

We went out into the moonless and tortuous network of that incredibly ancient town; went out as the lights in the curtained windows disappeared one by one, and the Dog Star leered at the throng of cowled, cloaked figures that poured silently from every doorway and formed monstrous processions up this street and that, past the creaking signs and antediluvian gables, the thatched roofs and diamond-paned windows; threading precipitous lanes where decaying houses overlapped and crumbled together, gliding across open courts and churchyards where the bobbing lanthorns made eldritch drunken constellations.

Amid these hushed throngs I followed my voiceless guides; jostled by elbows that seemed preternaturally soft, and pressed by chests and stomachs that seemed abnormally pulpy; but seeing never a face and hearing never a word. Up, up, up the eerie columns slithered, and I saw that all the travellers were converging as they flowed near a sort of focus of crazy alleys at the top of a high hill in the centre of the town, where perched a great white church. I had seen it from the road's crest when I looked at Kingsport in the new dusk, and it had made me shiver because Aldebaran had seemed to balance itself a moment on the ghostly spire.

There was an open space around the church; partly a churchyard with spectral shafts, and partly a half-paved square swept nearly bare of snow by the wind, and lined with unwholesomely archaic houses having peaked roofs and overhanging gables. Death-fires danced over the tombs, revealing gruesome vistas, though queerly failing to cast any shadows. Past the churchyard, where there were no houses, I could see over the hill's summit and watch the glimmer of stars on the harbour, though the town was invisible in the dark. Only once in a while a lanthorn bobbed horribly through serpentine alleys on its way to overtake the throng that was now slipping speechlessly into the church. I waited till the crowd had oozed into the black doorway, and till all the stragglers had followed. The old man was pulling at my sleeve, but I was determined to be the last. Then I finally went, the sinister man and the old spinning woman before me. Crossing the threshold into that swarming temple of unknown darkness, I turned once to look at the outside world as the churchyard phosphorescence cast a sickly glow on the hill-top pavement. And as I did so I shuddered. For though the wind had not left much snow, a few patches did remain on the path near the door; and in that fleeting backward look it seemed to my troubled eyes that they bore no mark of passing feet, not even mine.

The church was scarce lighted by all the lanthorns that had entered it, for most of the throng had already vanished. They had streamed up the aisle between the high white pews to the trap-door of the vaults which yawned loathsomely open just before the pulpit, and were now squirming noiselessly in. I followed dumbly down the footworn steps and into the dank, suffocating crypt. The tail of that sinuous line of night-marchers seemed very horrible, and as I saw them wriggling into a venerable tomb they seemed more horrible still. Then I noticed that the tomb's floor had an aperture down which the throng was sliding, and in a moment we were all descending an ominous staircase of rough-hewn stone; a narrow spiral staircase damp and peculiarly odorous, that wound endlessly down into the bowels of the hill past monotonous walls of dripping stone blocks and crumbling mortar. It was a silent, shocking descent, and I observed after a horrible interval that the walls and steps were changing in nature, as if chiselled out of the solid rock. What mainly troubled me was that the myriad footfalls made no sound and set up no echoes. After more aeons of descent I saw some side passages or burrows leading from unknown recesses of blackness to this shaft of nighted mystery. Soon they became excessively numerous, like impious catacombs of nameless menace; and their pungent odour of decay grew quite unbearable. I knew we must have passed down through the mountain and beneath the earth of Kingsport itself, and I shivered that a town should be so aged and maggoty with subterraneous evil.

Then I saw the lurid shimmering of pale light, and heard the insidious lapping of sunless waters. Again I shivered, for I did not like the things that the night had brought, and wished bitterly that no forefather had summoned me to this primal rite. As the steps and the passage grew broader, I heard another sound, the thin, whining mockery of a feeble flute; and suddenly there spread out before me the boundless vista of an inner world—a vast fungous shore litten by a belching column of sick greenish flame and washed by a wide oily river that flowed from abysses frightful and unsuspected to join the blackest gulfs of immemorial ocean.

Fainting and gasping, I looked at that unhallowed Erebus of titan toadstools, leprous fire, and slimy water, and saw the cloaked throngs forming a semicircle around the blazing pillar. It was the Yule-rite, older than man and fated to survive him; the primal rite of the solstice and of spring's promise beyond the snows; the rite of fire and evergreen, light and music. And in the Stygian grotto I saw them do the rite, and adore the sick pillar of flame, and throw into the water handfuls gouged out of the viscous vegetation which glittered green in the chlorotic glare. I saw this, and I saw something amorphously squatted far away from the light, piping noisomely on a flute; and as the thing piped I thought I heard noxious muffled flutterings in the foetid darkness where I could not see. But what frightened me most was that flaming column; spouting volcanically from depths profound and inconceivable, casting no shadows as healthy flame should, and coating the nitrous stone above with a nasty, venomous verdigris. For in all that seething combustion no warmth lay, but only the clamminess of death and corruption.

The man who had brought me now squirmed to a point directly beside the hideous flame, and made stiff ceremonial motions to the semicircle he faced. At certain stages of the ritual they did grovelling obeisance, especially when he held above his head that abhorrent *Necronomicon* he had taken with him; and I shared all the obeisances because I had been summoned to this festival by the writings of my forefathers. Then the old man made a signal to the half-seen flute-player in the darkness, which player thereupon changed its feeble drone to a scarce louder drone in another key; precipitating as it did so a horror unthinkable and unexpected. At this horror I sank nearly to the lichened earth, transfixed with a dread not of this nor any world, but only of the mad spaces between the stars.

Out of the unimaginable blackness beyond the gangrenous glare of that cold flame, out of the Tartarean leagues through which that oily river rolled uncanny, unheard, and unsuspected, there flopped rhythmically a horde of tame, trained, hybrid winged things that no sound eye could ever wholly grasp, or sound brain ever wholly remember. They were not altogether crows, nor moles, nor buzzards, nor ants, nor vampire bats, nor decomposed human beings; but something I cannot and must not recall. They flopped limply along, half with their webbed feet and half with their membraneous wings; and as they reached the throng of celebrants the cowled figures seized and mounted them, and rode off one by one along the reaches of that unlighted river, into pits and galleries of panic where poison springs feed frightful and undiscoverable cataracts.

The old spinning woman had gone with the throng, and the old man remained only because I had refused when he motioned me to seize an animal and ride like the rest. I saw when I staggered to my feet that the amorphous flute-player had rolled out of sight, but that two of the beasts were patiently standing by. As I hung back, the old man produced his stylus and tablet and wrote that he was the true deputy of my fathers who had founded the Yule worship in this ancient place; that it had been decreed I should come back, and that the most secret mysteries were yet to be performed. He wrote this in a very ancient hand, and when I still hesitated he pulled from his loose robe a seal ring and a watch, both with my family arms, to prove that he was what he said. But it was a hideous proof, because I knew from old papers that that watch had been buried with my great-great-great-great-grandfather in 1698.

Presently the old man drew back his hood and pointed to the family resemblance in his face, but I only shuddered, because I was sure that the face was merely a devilish waxen mask. The flopping animals were now scratching restlessly at the lichens, and I saw that the old man was nearly as restless himself. When one of the things began to waddle and edge away, he turned quickly to stop it; so that the suddenness of his motion dislodged the waxen mask from what should have been his head. And then, because that nightmare's position barred me from the stone staircase down which we had come, I flung myself into the oily underground river that bubbled somewhere to the caves of the sea; flung myself into that putrescent juice of earth's inner horrors before the madness of my screams could bring down upon me all the charnel legions these pest-gulfs might conceal.

At the hospital they told me I had been found half frozen in Kingsport Harbour at dawn, clinging to the drifting spar that accident sent to save me. They told me I had taken the wrong fork of the hill road the night before, and fallen over the cliffs at Orange Point; a thing they deduced from prints found in the snow. There was nothing I could say, because everything was wrong. Everything was wrong, with the broad window shewing a sea of roofs in which only about one in five was ancient, and the sound of trolleys and motors in the streets below. They insisted that this was Kingsport, and I could not deny it. When I went delirious at hearing that the hospital stood near the old churchyard on Central Hill, they sent me to St. Mary's Hospital in Arkham, where I could have better care. I liked it there, for the doctors were broad-minded, and even lent me their influence in obtaining the carefully sheltered copy of Alhazred's objectionable *Necronomicon* from the library of Miskatonic University. They said something about a "psychosis", and agreed I had better get any harassing obsessions off my mind.

So I read again that hideous chapter, and shuddered doubly because it was indeed not new to me. I had seen it before, let footprints tell what they might; and where it was I had seen it were best forgotten. There was no one—in waking hours—who could remind me of it; but my dreams are filled with terror, because of phrases I dare not quote. I dare quote only one paragraph, put into such English as I can make from the awkward Low Latin.

"The nethermost caverns," wrote the mad Arab, "are not for the fathoming of eyes that see; for their marvels are strange and terrific. Cursed the ground where dead thoughts live new and oddly bodied, and evil the mind that is held by no head.

Wisely did Ibn Schacabao say, that happy is the tomb where no wizard hath lain, and happy the town at night whose wizards are all ashes. For it is of old rumour that the soul of the devil-bought hastes not from his charnel clay, but fats and instructs *the very worm that gnaws;* till out of corruption horrid life springs, and the dull scavengers of earth wax crafty to vex it and swell monstrous to plague it. Great holes secretly are digged where earth's pores ought to suffice, and things have learnt to walk that ought to crawl."

THE HORROR HORN
E. F. Benson

FOR the past ten days Alhubel had basked in the radiant midwinter weather proper to its eminence of over 6,000 feet. From rising to setting the sun (so surprising to those who have hitherto associated it with a pale, tepid plate indistinctly shining through the murky air of England) had blazed its way across the sparkling blue, and every night the serene and windless frost had made the stars sparkle like illuminated diamond dust. Sufficient snow had fallen before Christmas to content the skiers, and the big rink, sprinkled every evening, had given the skaters each morning a fresh surface on which to perform their slippery antics. Bridge and dancing served to while away the greater part of the night, and to me, now for the first time tasting the joys of a winter in the Engadine, it seemed that a new heaven and a new earth had been lighted, warmed, and refrigerated for the special benefit of those who like myself had been wise enough to save up their days of holiday for the winter.

But a break came in these ideal conditions: one afternoon the sun grew vapour-veiled and up the valley from the north-west a wind frozen with miles of travel over ice-bound hill-sides began scouting through the calm halls of the heavens. Soon it grew dusted with snow, first in small flakes driven almost horizontally before its congealing breath and then in larger tufts as of swansdown. And though all day for a fortnight before the fate of nations and life and death had seemed to me of far less importance than to get certain tracings of the skate-blades on the ice of proper shape and size, it now seemed that the one paramount consideration was to hurry back to the hotel for shelter: it was wiser to leave rocking-turns alone than to be frozen in their quest.

I had come out here with my cousin, Professor Ingram, the celebrated physiologist and Alpine climber. During the serenity of the last fortnight he had made a couple of notable winter ascents, but this morning his weather-wisdom had mistrusted the signs of the heavens, and instead of attempting the ascent of the Piz Passug he had waited to see whether his misgivings justified themselves. So there he sat now in the hall of the admirable hotel with his feet on the hot-water pipes and the latest delivery of the English post in his hands. This contained a pamphlet concerning the result of the Mount Everest expedition, of which he had just finished the perusal when I entered.

"A very interesting report," he said, passing it to me, "and they certainly deserve to succeed next year. But who can tell, what that final six thousand feet may entail? Six thousand feet more when you have already accomplished twenty-three thousand does not seem much, but at present no one knows whether the human frame can stand exertion at such a height. It may affect not the lungs and heart only, but possibly the brain. Delirious hallucinations may occur. In fact, if I did not know better, I should have said that one such hallucination had occurred to the climbers already."

"And what was that?" I asked.

"You will find that they thought they came across the tracks of some naked human foot at a great altitude. That looks at first sight like an hallucination. What more natural than that a brain excited and exhilarated by the extreme height should have interpreted certain marks in the snow as the footprints of a human being? Every bodily organ at these altitudes is exerting itself to the utmost to do its work, and the brain seizes on those marks in the snow and says 'Yes, I'm all right, I'm doing my job, and I perceive marks in the snow which I affirm are human footprints.' You know, even at this altitude, how restless and eager the brain is, how vividly, as you told me, you dream at night. Multiply that stimulus and that consequent eagerness and restlessness by three, and how natural that the brain should harbour illusions! What after all is the delirium which often accompanies high fever but the effort of the brain to do its work under the pressure of feverish conditions? It is so eager to continue perceiving that it perceives things which have no existence!"

"And yet you don't think that these naked human footprints were illusions," said I. "You told me you would have thought so, if you had not known better."

He shifted in his chair and looked out of the window a moment. The air was thick now with the density of the big snow-flakes that were driven along by the squealing north-west gale.

"Quite so," he said. "In all probability the human footprints were real human footprints. I expect that they were the footprints, anyhow, of a being more nearly a man than anything else.

"My reason for saying so is that I know such beings exist. I have even seen quite near at hand — and I assure you I did not wish to be nearer in spite of my intense curiosity — the creature, shall we say, which would make such footprints. And if the snow was not so dense, I could show you the place where I saw him."

He pointed straight out of the window, where across the valley lies the huge tower of the Ungeheuerhorn with the carved pinnacle of rock at the top like some gigantic rhinoceros-horn.

On one side only, as I knew, was the mountain practicable, and that for none but the finest climbers; on the other three a succession of ledges and precipices rendered it unscalable. Two thousand feet of sheer rock form the tower; below are five hundred feet of fallen boulders, up to the edge of which grow dense woods of larch and pine.

"Upon the Ungeheuerhorn?" I asked.

"Yes. Up till twenty years ago it had never been ascended, and I, like several others, spent a lot of time in trying to find a route up it. My guide and I sometimes spent three nights together at the hut beside the Blumen glacier, prowling round it, and it was by luck really that we found the route, for the mountain looks even more impracticable from the far side than it does from this.

"But one day we found a long, transverse fissure in the side which led to a negotiable ledge; then there came a slanting ice couloir which you could not see till you got to the foot of it. However, I need not go into that."

The big room where we sat was filling up with cheerful groups driven indoors by this sudden gale and snowfall, and the cackle of merry tongues grew loud. The band, too, that invariable appanage of tea-time at Swiss resorts, had begun to tune up for the usual potpourri from the works of Puccini. Next moment the sugary, sentimental melodies began.

"Strange contrast!" said Ingram. "Here are we sitting warm and cosy, our ears pleasantly tickled with these little baby tunes and outside is the great storm growing more violent every moment, and swirling round the austere cliffs of the Ungeheuerhorn: the Horror–Horn, as indeed it was to me."

"I want to hear all about it," I said. "Every detail: make a short story long, if it's short. I want to know why it's your Horror–Horn?"

"Well, Chanton and I (he was my guide) used to spend days prowling about the cliffs, making a little progress on one side and then being stopped, and gaining perhaps five hundred feet on another side and then being confronted by some insuperable obstacle, till the day when by luck we found the route. Chanton never liked the job, for some reason that I could not fathom.

"It was not because of the difficulty or danger of the climbing, for he was the most fearless man I have ever met when dealing with rocks and ice, but he was always insistent that we should get off the mountain and back to the Blumen hut before sunset. He was scarcely easy even when we had got back to shelter and locked and barred the door, and I well remember one night when, as we ate our supper, we heard some animal, a wolf probably, howling somewhere out in the night.

"A positive panic seized him, and I don't think he closed his eyes till morning. It struck me then that there might be some grisly legend about the mountain, connected possibly with its name, and next day I asked him why the peak was called the Horror–Horn. He put the question off at first, and said that, like the Schreckhorn, its name was due to its precipices and falling stones; but when I pressed him further he acknowledged that there was a legend about it, which his father had told him. There were creatures, so it was supposed, that lived in its caves, things human in shape, and covered, except for the face and hands, with long black hair. They were dwarfs in size, four feet high or thereabouts, but of prodigious strength and agility, remnants of some wild primeval race. It seemed that they were still in an upward stage of evolution, or so I guessed, for the story ran that sometimes girls had been carried off by them, not as prey, and not for any such fate as for those captured by cannibals, but to be bred from. Young men also had been raped by them, to be mated with the females of their tribe. All this looked as if the creatures, as I said, were tending towards humanity. But naturally I did not believe a word of it, as applied to the conditions of the present day. Centuries ago, conceivably, there may have been such beings, and, with the extraordinary tenacity of tradition, the news of this had been handed down and was still current round the hearths of the peasants. As for their numbers, Chanton told me that three had been once seen together by a man who owing to his swiftness on skis had escaped to tell the tale.

{212}

"This man, he averred, was no other than his grand-father, who had been benighted one winter evening as he passed through the dense woods below the Ungeheuerhorn, and Chanton supposed that they had been driven down to these lower altitudes in search of food during severe winter weather, for otherwise the recorded sights of them had always taken place among the rocks of the peak itself. They had pursued his grandfather, then a young man, at an extraordinarily swift canter, running sometimes upright as men run, sometimes on all-fours in the manner of beasts, and their howls were just such as that we had heard that night in the Blumen hut. Such at any rate was the story Chanton told me, and, like you, I regarded it as the very moonshine of superstition.

"But the very next day I had reason to reconsider my judgment about it.

"It was on that day that after a week of exploration we hit on the only route at present known to the top of our peak. We started as soon as there was light enough to climb by, for, as you may guess, on very difficult rocks it is impossible to climb by lantern or moonlight. We hit on the long fissure I have spoken of, we explored the ledge which from below seemed to end in nothingness, and with an hour's stepcutting ascended the couloir which led upwards from it.

"From there onwards it was a rock-climb, certainly of considerable difficulty, but with no heart-breaking discoveries ahead, and it was about nine in the morning that we stood on the top. We did not wait there long, for that side of the mountain is raked by falling stones loosened, when the sun grows hot, from the ice that holds them, and we made haste to pass the ledge where the falls are most frequent. After that there was the long fissure to descend, a matter of no great difficulty, and we were at the end of our work by midday, both of us, as you may imagine, in the state of the highest elation.

"A long and tiresome scramble among the huge boulders at the foot of the cliff then lay before us. Here the hill-side is very porous and great caves extend far into the mountain. We had unroped at the base of the fissure, and were picking our way as seemed good to either of us among these fallen rocks, many of them bigger than an ordinary house, when, on coming round the corner of one of these, I saw that which made it clear that the stories Chanton had told me were no figment of traditional superstition.

"Not twenty yards in front of me lay one of the beings of which he had spoken. There it sprawled naked and basking on its back with face turned up to the sun, which its narrow eyes regarded unwinking. In form it was completely human, but the growth of hair that covered limbs and trunk alike almost completely hid the sun-tanned skin beneath. But its face, save for the down on its cheeks and chin, was hairless, and I looked on a countenance the sensual and malevolent bestiality of which froze me with horror. Had the creature been an animal, one would have felt scarcely a shudder at the gross animalism of it; the horror lay in the fact that it was a man. There lay by it a couple of gnawed bones, and, its meal finished, it was lazily licking its protuberant lips, from which came a purring murmur of content. With one hand it scratched the thick hair on its belly, in the other it held one of these bones, which presently split in half beneath the pressure of its finger and thumb. But my horror was not based on the information of what happened to those men whom these creatures caught, it was due only to my proximity to a thing so human and so infernal. The peak, of which the ascent had a moment ago filled us with such elated satisfaction, became to me an Ungeheuerhorn indeed, for it was the home of beings more awful than the delirium of nightmare could ever have conceived.

"Chanton was a dozen paces behind me, and with a backward wave of my hand I caused him to halt. Then withdrawing myself with infinite precaution, so as not to attract the gaze of that basking creature, I slipped back round the rock, whispered to him what I had seen, and with blanched faces we made a long detour, peering round every corner, and crouching low, not knowing that at any step we might not come upon another of these beings, or that from the mouth of one of these caves in the mountain-side there might not appear another of those hairless and dreadful faces, with perhaps this time the breasts and insignia of womanhood. That would have been the worst of all.

"Luck favoured us, for we made our way among the boulders and shifting stones, the rattle of which might at any moment have betrayed us, without a repetition of my experience, and once among the trees we ran as if the Furies themselves were in pursuit. Well now did I understand, though I dare say I cannot convey, the qualms of Chanton's mind when he spoke to me of these creatures. Their very humanity was what made them so terrible, the fact that they were of the same race as ourselves, but of a type so abysmally degraded that the most brutal and inhuman of men would have seemed angelic in comparison."

The music of the small band was over before he had finished the narrative, and the chattering groups round the tea-table had dispersed. He paused a moment.

"There was a horror of the spirit," he said, "which I experienced then, from which, I verily believe, I have never entirely recovered. I saw then how terrible a living thing could be, and how terrible, in consequence, was life itself. In us all I suppose lurks some inherited germ of that ineffable bestiality, and who knows whether, sterile as it has apparently become in the course of centuries, it might not fructify again. When I saw that creature sun itself, I looked into the abyss out of which we have crawled. And these creatures are trying to crawl out of it now, if they exist any longer. Certainly for the last twenty years there has been no record of their being seen, until we come to this story of the footprint seen by the climbers on Everest. If that is authentic, if the party did not mistake the footprint of some bear, or what not, for a human tread, it seems as if still this bestranded remnant of mankind is in existence."

Now, Ingram, had told his story well; but sitting in this warm and civilised room, the horror which he had clearly felt had not communicated itself to me in any very vivid manner.

Intellectually, I agreed, I could appreciate his horror, but certainly my spirit felt no shudder of interior comprehension.

"But it is odd," I said, "that your keen interest in physiology did not disperse your qualms.

"You were looking, so I take it, at some form of man more remote probably than the earliest human remains. Did not something inside you say 'This is of absorbing significance'?"

He shook his head.

"No: I only wanted to get away," said he. "It was not, as I have told you, the terror of what according to Chanton's story, might — await us if we were captured; it was sheer horror at the creature itself. I quaked at it."

The snowstorm and the gale increased in violence that night, and I slept uneasily, plucked again and again from slumber by the fierce battling of the wind that shook my windows as if with an imperious demand for admittance. It came in billowy gusts, with strange noises intermingled with it as for a moment it abated, with flutings and moanings that rose to shrieks as the fury of it returned. These noises, no doubt, mingled themselves with my drowsed and sleepy consciousness, and once I tore myself out of nightmare, imagining that the creatures of the Horror–Horn had gained footing on my balcony and were rattling at the window-bolts. But before morning the gale had died away, and I awoke to see the snow falling dense and fast in a windless air. For three days it continued, without intermission, and with its cessation there came a frost such as I have never felt before. Fifty degrees were registered one night, and more the next, and what the cold must have been on the cliffs of the Ungeheuerborn I cannot imagine. Sufficient, so I thought, to have made an end altogether of its secret inhabitants: my cousin, on that day twenty years ago, had missed an opportunity for study which would probably never fall again either to him or another.

I received one morning a letter from a friend saying that he had arrived at the neighbouring winter resort of St. Luigi, and proposing that I should come over for a morning's skating and lunch afterwards. The place was not more than a couple of miles off, if one took the path over the low, pine-clad foot-hills above which lay the steep woods below the first rocky slopes of the Ungeheuerhorn; and accordingly, with a knapsack containing skates on my back, I went on skis over the wooded slopes and down by an easy descent again on to St. Luigi. The day was overcast, clouds entirely obscured the higher peaks though the sun was visible, pale and unluminous, through the mists. But as the morning went on, it gained the upper hand, and I slid down into St. Luigi beneath a sparkling firmament. We skated and lunched, and then, since it looked as if thick weather was coming up again, I set out early about three o'clock for my return journey.

Hardly had I got into the woods when the clouds gathered thick above, and streamers and skeins of them began to descend among the pines through which my path threaded its way. In ten minutes more their opacity had so increased that I could hardly see a couple of yards in front of me. Very soon I became aware that I must have got off the path, for snow-cowled shrubs lay directly in my way, and, casting back to find it again, I got altogether confused as to direction.

But, though progress was difficult, I knew I had only to keep on the ascent, and presently I should come to the brow of these low foot-hills, and descend into the open valley where Alhubel stood. So on I went, stumbling and sliding over obstacles, and unable, owing to the thickness of the snow, to take off my skis, for I should have sunk over the knees at each step. Still the ascent continued, and looking at my watch I saw that I had already been near an hour on my way from St. Luigi, a period more than sufficient to complete my whole journey. But still I stuck to my idea that though I had certainly strayed far from my proper route a few minutes more must surely see me over the top of the upward way, and I should find the ground declining into the next valley. About now, too, I noticed that the mists were growing suffused with rose-colour, and, though the inference was that it must be close on sunset, there was consolation in the fact that they were there and might lift at any moment and disclose to me my whereabouts. But the fact that night would soon be on me made it needful to bar my mind against that despair of loneliness which so eats out the heart of a man who is lost in woods or on mountain-side, that, though still there is plenty of vigour in his limbs, his nervous force is sapped, and he can do no more than lie down and abandon himself to whatever fate may await him . . . And then I heard that which made the thought of loneliness seem bliss indeed, for there was a worse fate than loneliness. What I heard resembled the howl of a wolf, and it came from not far in front of me where the ridge — was it a ridge? — still rose higher in vestment of pines.

From behind me came a sudden puff of wind, which shook the frozen snow from the drooping pine-branches, and swept away the mists as a broom sweeps the dust from the floor.

Radiant above me were the unclouded skies, already charged with the red of the sunset, and in front I saw that I had come to the very edge of the wood through which I had wandered so long.

But it was no valley into which I had penetrated, for there right ahead of me rose the steep slope of boulders and rocks soaring upwards to the foot of the Ungeheuerhorn. What, then, was that cry of a wolf which had made my heart stand still? I saw.

Not twenty yards from me was a fallen tree, and leaning against the trunk of it was one of the denizens of the Horror–Horn, and it was a woman. She was enveloped in a thick growth of hair grey and tufted, and from her head it streamed down over her shoulders and her bosom, from which hung withered and pendulous breasts. And looking on her face I comprehended not with my mind alone, but with a shudder of my spirit, what Ingram had felt. Never had nightmare fashioned so terrible a countenance; the beauty of sun and stars and of the beasts of the field and the kindly race of men could not atone for so hellish an incarnation of the spirit of life. A fathomless bestiality modelled the slavering mouth and the narrow eyes; I looked into the abyss itself and knew that out of that abyss on the edge of which I leaned the generations of men had climbed. What if that ledge crumbled in front of me and pitched me headlong into its nethermost depths? . . .

{216}

In one hand she held by the horns a chamois that kicked and struggled. A blow from its hindleg caught her withered thigh, and with a grunt of anger she seized the leg in her other hand, and, as a man may pull from its sheath a stem of meadow-grass, she plucked it off the body, leaving the torn skin hanging round the gaping wound. Then putting the red, bleeding member to her mouth she sucked at it as a child sucks a stick of sweetmeat. Through flesh and gristle her short, brown teeth penetrated, and she licked her lips with a sound of purring. Then dropping the leg by her side, she looked again at the body of the prey now quivering in its death-convulsion, and with finger and thumb gouged out one of its eyes. She snapped her teeth on it, and it cracked like a soft-shelled nut.

It must have been but a few seconds that I stood watching her, in some indescribable catalepsy of terror, while through my brain there pealed the panic-command of my mind to my stricken limbs "Begone, begone, while there is time." Then, recovering the power of my joints and muscles, I tried to slip behind a tree and hide myself from this apparition. But the woman — shall I say? — must have caught my stir of movement, for she raised her eyes from her living feast and saw me. She craned forward her neck, she dropped her prey, and half rising began to move towards me. As she did this, she opened her mouth, and gave forth a howl such as I had heard a moment before. It was answered by another, but faintly and distantly.

Sliding and slipping, with the toes of my skis tripping in the obstacles below the snow, I plunged forward down the hill between the pine-trunks. The low sun already sinking behind some rampart of mountain in the west reddened the snow and the pines with its ultimate rays. My knapsack with the skates in it swung to and fro on my back, one ski-stick had already been twitched out of my hand by a fallen branch of pine, but not a second's pause could I allow myself to recover it. I gave no glance behind, and I knew not at what pace my pursuer was on my track, or indeed whether any pursued at all, for my whole mind and energy, now working at full power again under the stress of my panic, was devoted to getting away down the hill and out of the wood as swiftly as my limbs could bear me. For a little while I heard nothing but the hissing snow of my headlong passage, and the rustle of the covered undergrowth beneath my feet, and then, from close at hand behind me, once more the wolf-howl sounded and I heard the plunging of footsteps other than my own.

The strap of my knapsack had shifted, and as my skates swung to and fro on my back it chafed and pressed on my throat, hindering free passage of air, of which, God knew, my labouring lungs were in dire need, and without pausing I slipped it free from my neck, and held it in the hand from which my ski-stick had been jerked. I seemed to go a little more easily for this adjustment, and now, not so far distant, I could see below me the path from which I had strayed.

If only I could reach that, the smoother going would surely enable me to outdistance my pursuer, who even on the rougher ground was but slowly overhauling me, and at the sight of that riband stretching unimpeded downhill, a ray of hope pierced the black panic of my soul. With that came the desire, keen and insistent, to see who or what it was that was on my tracks, and I spared a backward glance. It was she, the hag whom I had seen at her gruesome meal; her long grey hair flew out behind her, her mouth chattered and gibbered, her fingers made grabbing movements, as if already they closed on me.

But the path was now at hand, and the nearness of it I suppose made me incautious. A hump of snow-covered bush lay in my path, and, thinking I could jump over it, I tripped and fell, smothering myself in snow. I heard a maniac noise, half scream, half laugh, from close behind, and before I could recover myself the grabbing fingers were at my neck, as if a steel vice had closed there. But my right hand in which I held my knapsack of skates was free, and with a blind back-handed movement I whirled it behind me at the full length of its strap, and knew that my desperate blow had found its billet somewhere. Even before I could look round I felt the grip on my neck relax, and something subsided into the very bush which had entangled me. I recovered my feet and turned.

There she lay, twitching and quivering. The heel of one of my skates piercing the thin alpaca of the knapsack had hit her full on the temple, from which the blood was pouring, but a hundred yards away I could see another such figure coming downwards on my tracks, leaping and bounding. At that panic rose again within me, and I sped off down the white smooth path that led to the lights of the village already beckoning. Never once did I pause in my headlong going: there was no safety until I was back among the haunts of men. I flung myself against the door of the hotel, and screamed for admittance, though I had but to turn the handle and enter; and once more as when Ingram had told his tale, there was the sound of the band, and the chatter of voices, and there, too, was he himself, who looked up and then rose swiftly to his feet as I made my clattering entrance.

"I have seen them too," I cried. "Look at my knapsack. Is there not blood on it? It is the blood of one of them, a woman, a hag, who tore off the leg of a chamois as I looked, and pursued me through the accursed wood. I—".Whether it was I who spun round, or the room which seemed to spin round me, I knew not, but I heard myself falling, collapsed on the floor, and the next time that I was conscious at all I was in bed. There was Ingram there, who told me that I was quite safe, and another man, a stranger, who pricked my arm with the nozzle of a syringe, and reassured me . . .

A day or two later I gave a coherent account of my adventure, and three or four men, armed with guns, went over my traces. They found the bush in which I had stumbled, with a pool of blood which had soaked into the snow, and, still following my ski-tracks, they came on the body of a chamois, from which had been torn one of its hindlegs and one eye-socket was empty. That is all the corroboration of my story that I can give the reader, and for myself I imagine that the creature which pursued me was either not killed by my blow or that her fellows removed her body . . . Anyhow, it is open to the incredulous to prowl about the caves of the Ungeheuerhorn, and see if anything occurs that may convince them.

THE GLAMOUR OF THE SNOW
Algernon Blackwood

HIBBERT, always conscious of two worlds, was in this mountain village conscious of three. It lay on the slopes of the Valais Alps, and he had taken a room in the little post office, where he could be at peace to write his book, yet at the same time enjoy the winter sports and find companionship in the hotels when he wanted it.

The three worlds that met and mingled here seemed to his imaginative temperament very obvious, though it is doubtful if another mind less intuitively equipped would have seen them so well-defined. There was the world of tourist English, civilised, quasi-educated, to which he belonged by birth, at any rate; there was the world of peasants to which he felt himself drawn by sympathy — for he loved and admired their toiling, simple life; and there was this other — which he could only call the world of Nature. To this last, however, in virtue of a vehement poetic imagination, and a tumultuous pagan instinct fed by his very blood, he felt that most of him belonged. The others borrowed from it, as it were, for visits. Here, with the soul of Nature, hid his central life.

Between all three was conflict — potential conflict. On the skating-rink each Sunday the tourists regarded the natives as intruders; in the church the peasants plainly questioned: "Why do you come? We are here to worship; you to stare and whisper!" For neither of these two worlds accepted the other. And neither did Nature accept the tourists, for it took advantage of their least mistakes, and indeed, even of the peasant-world "accepted" only those who were strong and bold enough to invade her savage domain with sufficient skill to protect themselves from several forms of — death.

Now Hibbert was keenly aware of this potential conflict and want of harmony; he felt outside, yet caught by it — torn in the three directions because he was partly of each world, but wholly in only one. There grew in him a constant, subtle effort — or, at least, desire — to unify them and decide positively to which he should belong and live in. The attempt, of course, was largely subconscious. It was the natural instinct of a richly imaginative nature seeking the point of equilibrium, so that the mind could feel at peace and his brain be free to do good work.

Among the guests no one especially claimed his interest. The men were nice but undistinguished — athletic schoolmasters, doctors snatching a holiday, good fellows all; the women, equally various — the clever, the would-be-fast, the dare-to-be-dull, the women "who understood," and the usual pack of jolly dancing girls and "flappers." And Hibbert, with his forty odd years of thick experience behind him, got on well with the lot; he understood them all; they belonged to definite, predigested types that are the same the world over, and that he had met the world over long ago.

But to none of them did he belong. His nature was too "multiple" to subscribe to the set of shibboleths of any one class. And, since all liked him, and felt that

somehow he seemed outside of them — spectator, looker-on — all sought to claim him.

In a sense, therefore, the three worlds fought for him: natives, tourists, Nature. . .

It was thus began the singular conflict for the soul of Hibbert. In his own soul, however, it took place. Neither the peasants nor the tourists were conscious that they fought for anything. And Nature, they say, is merely blind and automatic.

The assault upon him of the peasants may be left out of account, for it is obvious that they stood no chance of success. The tourist world, however, made a gallant effort to subdue him to themselves. But the evenings in the hotel, when dancing was not in order, were — English. The provincial imagination was set upon a throne and worshipped heavily through incense of the stupidest conventions possible. Hibbert used to go back early to his room in the post office to work.

"It is a mistake on my part to have realised that there is any conflict at all," he thought, as he crunched home over the snow at midnight after one of the dances. "It would have been better to have kept outside it all and done my work. Better," he added, looking back down the silent village street to the church tower, "and — safer."

The adjective slipped from his mind before he was aware of it. He turned with an involuntary start and looked about him. He knew perfectly well what it meant — this thought that had thrust its head up from the instinctive region. He understood, without being able to express it fully, the meaning that betrayed itself in the choice of the adjective. For if he had ignored the existence of this conflict he would at the same time, have remained outside the arena. Whereas now he had entered the lists. Now this battle for his soul must have issue. And he knew that the spell of Nature was greater for him than all other spells in the world combined — greater than love, revelry, pleasure, greater even than study. He had always been afraid to let himself go. His pagan soul dreaded her terrific powers of witchery even while he worshipped.

The little village already slept. The world lay smothered in snow. The chalet roofs shone white beneath the moon, and pitch-black shadows gathered against the walls of the church. His eye rested a moment on the square stone tower with its frosted cross that pointed to the sky: then travelled with a leap of many thousand feet to the enormous mountains that brushed the brilliant stars. Like a forest rose the huge peaks above the slumbering village, measuring the night and heavens. They beckoned him. And something born of the snowy desolation, born of the midnight and the silent grandeur, born of the great listening hollows of the night, something that lay 'twixt terror and wonder, dropped from the vast wintry spaces down into his heart — and called him. Very softly, unrecorded in any word or thought his brain could compass, it laid its spell upon him. Fingers of snow brushed the surface of his heart. The power and quiet majesty of the winter's night appalled him. . . .

Fumbling a moment with the big unwieldy key, he let himself in and went upstairs to bed. Two thoughts went with him — apparently quite ordinary and sensible ones:

{221}

"What fools these peasants are to sleep through such a night!" And the other: "Those dances tire me. I'll never go again. My work only suffers in the morning." The claims of peasants and tourists upon him seemed thus in a single instant weakened.

The clash of battle troubled half his dreams. Nature had sent her Beauty of the Night and won the first assault. The others, routed and dismayed, fled far away.

II

"Don't go back to your dreary old post office. We're going to have supper in my room — something hot. Come and join us. Hurry up!"

There had been an ice carnival, and the last party, tailing up the snow-slope to the hotel, called him. The Chinese lanterns smoked and sputtered on the wires; the band had long since gone. The cold was bitter and the moon came only momentarily between high, driving clouds. From the shed where the people changed from skates to snow-boots he shouted something to the effect that he was "following"; but no answer came; the moving shadows of those who had called were already merged high up against the village darkness. The voices died away. Doors slammed. Hibbert found himself alone on the deserted rink.

And it was then, quite suddenly, the impulse came to — stay and skate alone. The thought of the stuffy hotel room, and of those noisy people with their obvious jokes and laughter, oppressed him. He felt a longing to be alone with the night; to taste her wonder all by himself there beneath the stars, gliding over the ice. It was not yet midnight, and he could skate for half an hour. That supper party, if they noticed his absence at all, would merely think he had changed his mind and gone to bed.

It was an impulse, yes, and not an unnatural one; yet even at the time it struck him that something more than impulse lay concealed behind it. More than invitation, yet certainly less than command, there was a vague queer feeling that he stayed because he had to, almost as though there was something he had forgotten, overlooked, left undone. Imaginative temperaments are often thus; and impulse is ever weakness. For with such ill-considered opening of the doors to hasty action may come an invasion of other forces at the same time — forces merely waiting their opportunity perhaps!

He caught the fugitive warning even while he dismissed it as absurd, and the next minute he was whirling over the smooth ice in delightful curves and loops beneath the moon. There was no fear of collision. He could take his own speed and space as he willed. The shadows of the towering mountains fell across the rink, and a wind of ice came from the forests, where the snow lay ten feet deep. The hotel lights winked and went out. The village slept. The high wire netting could not keep out the wonder of the winter night that grew about him like a presence. He skated on and on, keen exhilarating pleasure in his tingling blood, and weariness all forgotten.

And then, midway in the delight of rushing movement, he saw a figure gliding behind the wire netting, watching him. With a start that almost made him lose his balance — for the abruptness of the new arrival was so unlooked for — he paused and stared. Although the light was dim he made out that it was the figure of a woman and that she was feeling her way along the netting, trying to get in. Against the white background of the snow-field he watched her rather stealthy efforts as she passed with a silent step over the banked-up snow. She was tall and slim and graceful; he could see that even in the dark. And then, of course, he understood. It was another adventurous skater like himself, stolen down unawares from hotel or chalet, and searching for the opening. At once, making a sign and pointing with one hand, he turned swiftly and skated over to the little entrance on the other side.

But, even before he got there, there was a sound on the ice behind him and, with an exclamation of amazement he could not suppress, he turned to see her swerving up to his side across the width of the rink. She had somehow found another way in.

Hibbert, as a rule, was punctilious, and in these free-and-easy places, perhaps, especially so. If only for his own protection he did not seek to make advances unless some kind of introduction paved the way. But for these two to skate together in the semi-darkness without speech, often of necessity brushing shoulders almost, was too absurd to think of. Accordingly he raised his cap and spoke. His actual words he seems unable to recall, nor what the girl said in reply, except that she answered him in accented English with some commonplace about doing figures at midnight on an empty rink. Quite natural it was, and right. She wore grey clothes of some kind, though not the customary long gloves or sweater, for indeed her hands were bare, and presently when he skated with her, he wondered with something like astonishment at their dry and icy coldness.

And she was delicious to skate with — supple, sure, and light, fast as a man yet with the freedom of a child, sinuous and steady at the same time. Her flexibility made him wonder, and when he asked where she had learned she murmured — he caught the breath against his ear and recalled later that it was singularly cold — that she could hardly tell, for she had been accustomed to the ice ever since she could remember.

But her face he never properly saw. A muffler of white fur buried her neck to the ears, and her cap came over the eyes. He only saw that she was young. Nor could he gather her hotel or chalet, for she pointed vaguely, when he asked her, up the slopes. "Just over there —" she said, quickly taking his hand again. He did not press her; no doubt she wished to hide her escapade. And the touch of her hand thrilled him more than anything he could remember; even through his thick glove he felt the softness of that cold and delicate softness.

The clouds thickened over the mountains. It grew darker. They talked very little, and did not always skate together. Often they separated, curving about in corners by themselves, but always coming together again in the centre of the rink; and when she left him thus Hibbert was conscious of — yes, of missing her. He found a peculiar satisfaction, almost a fascination, in skating by her side. It was quite an adventure — these two strangers with the ice and snow and night!

Midnight had long since sounded from the old church tower before they parted. She gave the sign, and he skated quickly to the shed, meaning to find a seat and help her take her skates off. Yet when he turned — she had already gone. He saw her slim figure gliding away across the snow . . . and hurrying for the last time round the rink alone he searched in vain for the opening she had twice used in this curious way.

"How very queer!" he thought, referring to the wire netting. "She must have lifted it and wriggled under . . .!"

Wondering how in the world she managed it, what in the world had possessed him to be so free with her, and who in the world she was, he went up the steep slope to the post office and so to bed, her promise to come again another night still ringing delightfully in his ears. And curious were the thoughts and sensations that accompanied him. Most of all, perhaps, was the half suggestion of some dim memory that he had known this girl before, had met her somewhere, more — that she knew him. For in her voice — a low, soft, windy little voice it was, tender and soothing for all its quiet coldness — there lay some faint reminder of two others he had known, both long since gone: the voice of the woman he had loved, and — the voice of his mother.

But this time through his dreams there ran no clash of battle. He was conscious, rather, of something cold and clinging that made him think of sifting snowflakes climbing slowly with entangling touch and thickness round his feet. The snow, coming without noise, each flake so light and tiny none can mark the spot whereon it settles, yet the mass of it able to smother whole villages, wove through the very texture of his mind — cold, bewildering, deadening effort with its clinging network of ten million feathery touches.

III

In the morning Hibbert realised he had done, perhaps, a foolish thing. The brilliant sunshine that drenched the valley made him see this, and the sight of his work-table with its typewriter, books, papers, and the rest, brought additional conviction. To have skated with a girl alone at midnight, no matter how innocently the thing had come about, was unwise — unfair, especially to her. Gossip in these little winter resorts was worse than in a provincial town. He hoped no one had seen them. Luckily the night had been dark. Most likely none had heard the ring of skates.

Deciding that in future he would be more careful, he plunged into work, and sought to dismiss the matter from his mind.

But in his times of leisure the memory returned persistently to haunt him. When he "ski-d," "luged," or danced in the evenings, and especially when he skated on the little rink, he was aware that the eyes of his mind forever sought this strange companion of the night. A hundred times he fancied that he saw her, but always sight deceived him. Her face he might not know, but he could hardly fail to recognise her figure. Yet nowhere among the others did he catch a glimpse of that slim young creature he had skated with alone beneath the clouded stars. He searched in vain. Even his inquiries as to the occupants of the private chalets brought no results. He had lost her. But the queer thing was that he felt as though she were somewhere close; he knew she had not really gone. While people came and left with every day, it never once occurred to him that she had left. On the contrary, he felt assured that they would meet again.

This thought he never quite acknowledged. Perhaps it was the wish that fathered it only. And, even when he did meet her, it was a question how he would speak and claim acquaintance, or whether she would recognise himself. It might be awkward. He almost came to dread a meeting, though "dread," of course, was far too strong a word to describe an emotion that was half delight, half wondering anticipation.

Meanwhile the season was in full swing. Hibbert felt in perfect health, worked hard, ski-d, skated, luged, and at night danced fairly often — in spite of his decision. This dancing was, however, an act of subconscious surrender; it really meant he hoped to find her among the whirling couples. He was searching for her without quite acknowledging it to himself; and the hotel-world, meanwhile, thinking it had won him over, teased and chaffed him. He made excuses in a similar vein; but all the time he watched and searched and — waited.

For several days the sky held clear and bright and frosty, bitterly cold, everything crisp and sparkling in the sun; but there was no sign of fresh snow, and the ski-ers began to grumble. On the mountains was an icy crust that made "running" dangerous; they wanted the frozen, dry, and powdery snow that makes for speed, renders steering easier and falling less severe. But the keen east wind showed no signs of changing for a whole ten days. Then, suddenly, there came a touch of softer air and the weather-wise began to prophesy.

Hibbert, who was delicately sensitive to the least change in earth or sky, was perhaps the first to feel it. Only he did not prophesy. He knew through every nerve in his body that moisture had crept into the air, was accumulating, and that presently a fall would come. For he responded to the moods of Nature like a fine barometer.

And the knowledge, this time, brought into his heart a strange little wayward emotion that was hard to account for — a feeling of unexplained uneasiness and disquieting joy. For behind it, woven through it rather, ran a faint exhilaration that connected remotely somewhere with that touch of delicious alarm, that tiny anticipating "dread," that so puzzled him when he thought of his next meeting with his skating companion of the night. It lay beyond all words, all telling, this queer relationship between the two; but somehow the girl and snow ran in a pair across his mind.

Perhaps for imaginative writing-men, more than for other workers, the smallest change of mood betrays itself at once. His work at any rate revealed this slight shifting of emotional values in his soul. Not that his writing suffered, but that it altered, subtly as those changes of sky or sea or landscape that come with the passing of afternoon into evening — imperceptibly. A subconscious excitement sought to push outwards and express itself . . . and, knowing the uneven effect such moods produced in his work, he laid his pen aside and took instead to reading that he had to do.

Meanwhile the brilliance passed from the sunshine, the sky grew slowly overcast; by dusk the mountain tops came singularly close and sharp; the distant valley rose into absurdly near perspective. The moisture increased, rapidly approaching saturation point, when it must fall in snow. Hibbert watched and waited.

And in the morning the world lay smothered beneath its fresh white carpet. It snowed heavily till noon, thickly, incessantly, chokingly, a foot or more; then the sky cleared, the sun came out in splendour, the wind shifted back to the east, and frost came down upon the mountains with its keenest and most biting tooth. The drop in the temperature was tremendous, but the ski-ers were jubilant. Next day the "running" would be fast and perfect. Already the mass was settling, and the surface freezing into those moss-like, powdery crystals that make the ski run almost of their own accord with the faint "sishing" as of a bird's wings through the air.

IV

That night there was excitement in the little hotel-world, first because there was a *bal costume*, but chiefly because the new snow had come. And Hibbert went — felt drawn to go; he did not go in costume, but he wanted to talk about the slopes and skiing with the other men, and at the same time. . . .

Ah, there was the truth, the deeper necessity that called. For the singular connection between the stranger and the snow again betrayed itself, utterly beyond explanation as before, but vital and insistent. Some hidden instinct in his pagan soul — heaven knows how he phrased it even to himself, if he phrased it at all — whispered that with the snow the girl would be somewhere about, would emerge from her hiding place, would even look for him.

Absolutely unwarranted it was. He laughed while he stood before the little glass and trimmed his moustache, tried to make his black tie sit straight, and shook down his dinner jacket so that it should lie upon the shoulders without a crease. His brown eyes were very bright. "I look younger than I usually do," he thought. It was unusual, even significant, in a man who had no vanity about his appearance and certainly never questioned his age or tried to look younger than he was. Affairs of the heart, with one tumultuous exception that left no fuel for lesser subsequent fires, had never troubled him. The forces of his soul and mind not called upon for "work" and obvious duties, all went to Nature. The desolate, wild places of the earth were what he loved; night, and the beauty of the stars and snow. And this evening he felt their claims upon him mightily stirring. A rising wildness caught his blood, quickened his pulse, woke longing and passion too. But chiefly snow. The snow whirred softly through his thoughts like white, seductive dreams. . . . For

{226}

the snow had come; and She, it seemed, had somehow come with it — into his mind.

And yet he stood before that twisted mirror and pulled his tie and coat askew a dozen times, as though it mattered. "What in the world is up with me?" he thought. Then, laughing a little, he turned before leaving the room to put his private papers in order. The green morocco desk that held them he took down from the shelf and laid upon the table. Tied to the lid was the visiting card with his brother's London address "in case of accident." On the way down to the hotel he wondered why he had done this, for though imaginative, he was not the kind of man who dealt in presentiments. Moods with him were strong, but ever held in leash.

"It's almost like a warning," he thought, smiling. He drew his thick coat tightly round the throat as the freezing air bit at him. "Those warnings one reads of in stories sometimes . . .!"

A delicious happiness was in his blood. Over the edge of the hills across the valley rose the moon. He saw her silver sheet the world of snow. Snow covered all. It smothered sound and distance. It smothered houses, streets, and human beings. It smothered — life.

V

In the hall there was light and bustle; people were already arriving from the other hotels and chalets, their costumes hidden beneath many wraps. Groups of men in evening dress stood about smoking, talking "snow" and "skiing." The band was tuning up. The claims of the hotel-world clashed about him faintly as of old. At the big glass windows of the verandah, peasants stopped a moment on their way home from the cafe to peer. Hibbert thought laughingly of that conflict he used to imagine. He laughed because it suddenly seemed so unreal. He belonged so utterly to Nature and the mountains, and especially to those desolate slopes where now the snow lay thick and fresh and sweet, that there was no question of a conflict at all. The power of the newly fallen snow had caught him, proving it without effort. Out there, upon those lonely reaches of the moonlit ridges, the snow lay ready — masses and masses of it — cool, soft, inviting. He longed for it. It awaited him. He thought of the intoxicating delight of skiing in the moonlight. . . .

Thus, somehow, in vivid flashing vision, he thought of it while he stood there smoking with the other men and talking all the "shop" of skiing.

And, ever mysteriously blended with this power of the snow, poured also through his inner being the power of the girl. He could not disabuse his mind of the insinuating presence of the two together. He remembered that queer skating-impulse of ten days ago, the impulse that had let her in. That any mind, even an imaginative one, could pass beneath the sway of such a fancy was strange enough; and Hibbert, while fully aware of the disorder, yet found a curious joy in yielding to it. This insubordinate centre that drew him towards old pagan beliefs had assumed command. With a kind of sensuous pleasure he let himself be conquered.

{227}

And snow that night seemed in everybody's thoughts. The dancing couples talked of it; the hotel proprietors congratulated one another; it meant good sport and satisfied their guests; every one was planning trips and expeditions, talking of slopes and telemarks, of flying speed and distance, of drifts and crust and frost. Vitality and enthusiasm pulsed in the very air; all were alert and active, positive, radiating currents of creative life even into the stuffy atmosphere of that crowded ball-room. And the snow had caused it, the snow had brought it; all this discharge of eager sparkling energy was due primarily to the — Snow.

But in the mind of Hibbert, by some swift alchemy of his pagan yearnings, this energy became transmuted. It rarefied itself, gleaming in white and crystal currents of passionate anticipation, which he transferred, as by a species of electrical imagination, into the personality of the girl — the Girl of the Snow. She somewhere was waiting for him, expecting him, calling to him softly from those leagues of moonlit mountain. He remembered the touch of that cool, dry hand; the soft and icy breath against his cheek; the hush and softness of her presence in the way she came and the way she had gone again — like a flurry of snow the wind sent gliding up the slopes. She, like himself, belonged out there. He fancied that he heard her little windy voice come sifting to him through the snowy branches of the trees, calling his name . . . that haunting little voice that dived straight to the centre of his life as once, long years ago, two other voices used to do. . . .

But nowhere among the costumed dancers did he see her slender figure. He danced with one and all, distrait and absent, a stupid partner as each girl discovered, his eyes ever turning towards the door and windows, hoping to catch the luring face, the vision that did not come . . . and at length, hoping even against hope. For the ball-room thinned; groups left one by one, going home to their hotels and chalets; the band tired obviously; people sat drinking lemon-squashes at the little tables, the men mopping their foreheads, everybody ready for bed.

It was close on midnight. As Hibbert passed through the hall to get his overcoat and snow-boots, he saw men in the passage by the "sport-room," greasing their ski against an early start. Knapsack luncheons were being ordered by the kitchen swing doors. He sighed. Lighting a cigarette a friend offered him, he returned a confused reply to some question as to whether he could join their party in the morning. It seemed he did not hear it properly. He passed through the outer vestibule between the double glass doors, and went into the night.

The man who asked the question watched him go, an expression of anxiety momentarily in his eyes.

"Don't think he heard you," said another, laughing. "You've got to shout to Hibbert, his mind's so full of his work."
"He works too hard," suggested the first, "full of queer ideas and dreams."

But Hibbert's silence was not rudeness. He had not caught the invitation, that was all. The call of the hotel-world had faded. He no longer heard it. Another wilder call was sounding in his ears.

For up the street he had seen a little figure moving. Close against the shadows of the baker's shop it glided — white, slim, enticing.

VI

And at once into his mind passed the hush and softness of the snow — yet with it a searching, crying wildness for the heights. He knew by some incalculable, swift instinct she would not meet him in the village street. It was not there, amid crowding houses, she would speak to him. Indeed, already she had disappeared, melted from view up the white vista of the moonlit road. Yonder, he divined, she waited where the highway narrowed abruptly into the mountain path beyond the chalets.

It did not even occur to him to hesitate; mad though it seemed, and was — this sudden craving for the heights with her, at least for open spaces where the snow lay thick and fresh — it was too imperious to be denied. He does not remember going up to his room, putting the sweater over his evening clothes, and getting into the fur gauntlet gloves and the helmet cap of wool. Most certainly he has no recollection of fastening on his ski; he must have done it automatically. Some faculty of normal observation was in abeyance, as it were. His mind was out beyond the village — out with the snowy mountains and the moon.

Henri Défago, putting up the shutters over his cafe windows, saw him pass, and wondered mildly: "Un monsieur qui fait du ski a cette heure! Il est Anglais, done . . .!" He shrugged his shoulders, as though a man had the right to choose his own way of death. And Marthe Perotti, the hunchback wife of the shoemaker, looking by chance from her window, caught his figure moving swiftly up the road. She had other thoughts, for she knew and believed the old traditions of the witches and snow-beings that steal the souls of men. She had even heard, 'twas said, the dreaded "synagogue" pass roaring down the street at night, and now, as then, she hid her eyes. "They've called to him . . . and he must go," she murmured, making the sign of the cross.

But no one sought to stop him. Hibbert recalls only a single incident until he found himself beyond the houses, searching for her along the fringe of forest where the moonlight met the snow in a bewildering frieze of fantastic shadows. And the incident was simply this — that he remembered passing the church. Catching the outline of its tower against the stars, he was aware of a faint sense of hesitation. A vague uneasiness came and went — jarred unpleasantly across the flow of his excited feelings, chilling exhilaration. He caught the instant's discord, dismissed it, and — passed on. The seduction of the snow smothered the hint before he realised that it had brushed the skirts of warning.

And then he saw her. She stood there waiting in a little clear space of shining snow, dressed all in white, part of the moonlight and the glistening background, her slender figure just discernible.

"I waited, for I knew you would come," the silvery little voice of windy beauty floated down to him. "You had to come."

"I'm ready," he answered, "I knew it too."

The world of Nature caught him to its heart in those few words — the wonder and the glory of the night and snow. Life leaped within him. The passion of his pagan soul exulted, rose in joy, flowed out to her. He neither reflected nor considered, but let himself go like the veriest schoolboy in the wildness of first love.

"Give me your hand," he cried, "I'm coming . . .!"

"A little farther on, a little higher," came her delicious answer. "Here it is too near the village — and the church."

And the words seemed wholly right and natural; he did not dream of questioning them; he understood that, with this little touch of civilisation in sight, the familiarity he suggested was impossible. Once out upon the open mountains, 'mid the freedom of huge slopes and towering peaks, the stars and moon to witness and the wilderness of snow to watch, they could taste an innocence of happy intercourse free from the dead conventions that imprison literal minds.

He urged his pace, yet did not quite overtake her. The girl kept always just a little bit ahead of his best efforts. . . . And soon they left the trees behind and passed on to the enormous slopes of the sea of snow that rolled in mountainous terror and beauty to the stars. The wonder of the white world caught him away. Under the steady moonlight it was more than haunting. It was a living, white, bewildering power that deliciously confused the senses and laid a spell of wild perplexity upon the heart. It was a personality that cloaked, and yet revealed, itself through all this sheeted whiteness of snow. It rose, went with him, fled before, and followed after. Slowly it dropped lithe, gleaming arms about his neck, gathering him in. . . .

Certainly some soft persuasion coaxed his very soul, urging him ever forwards, upwards, on towards the higher icy slopes. Judgment and reason left their throne, it seemed, completely, as in the madness of intoxication. The girl, slim and seductive, kept always just ahead, so that he never quite came up with her. He saw the white enchantment of her face and figure, something that streamed about her neck flying like a wreath of snow in the wind, and heard the alluring accents of her whispering voice that called from time to time: "A little farther on, a little higher. . . . Then we'll run home together!"

Sometimes he saw her hand stretched out to find his own, but each time, just as he came up with her, he saw her still in front, the hand and arm withdrawn. They took a gentle angle of ascent. The toil seemed nothing. In this crystal, wine-like air fatigue vanished. The sishing of the ski through the powdery surface of the snow was the only sound that broke the stillness; this, with his breathing and the rustle of her skirts, was all he heard. Cold moonshine, snow, and silence held the world. The sky was black, and the peaks beyond cut into it like frosted wedges of iron and steel. Far below the valley slept, the village long since hidden out of sight. He felt that he could never tire. . . . The sound of the church clock rose from time to time faintly through the air — more and more distant.

"Give me your hand. It's time now to turn back."

{230}

"Just one more slope," she laughed. "That ridge above us. Then we'll make for home." And her low voice mingled pleasantly with the purring of their ski. His own seemed harsh and ugly by comparison.

"But I have never come so high before. It's glorious! This world of silent snow and moonlight — and you. You're a child of the snow, I swear. Let me come up — closer — to see your face — and touch your little hand."

Her laughter answered him.

"Come on! A little higher. Here we're quite alone together."

"It's magnificent," he cried. "But why did you hide away so long? I've looked and searched for you in vain ever since we skated —" he was going to say "ten days ago," but the accurate memory of time had gone from him; he was not sure whether it was days or years or minutes. His thoughts of earth were scattered and confused.

"You looked for me in the wrong places," he heard her murmur just above him. "You looked in places where I never go. Hotels and houses kill me. I avoid them." She laughed — a fine, shrill, windy little laugh.

"I loathe them too —"

He stopped. The girl had suddenly come quite close. A breath of ice passed through his very soul. She had touched him.

"But this awful cold!" he cried out, sharply, "this freezing cold that takes me. The wind is rising; it's a wind of ice. Come, let us turn . . .!"

But when he plunged forward to hold her, or at least to look, the girl was gone again. And something in the way she stood there a few feet beyond, and stared down into his eyes so steadfastly in silence, made him shiver. The moonlight was behind her, but in some odd way he could not focus sight upon her face, although so close. The gleam of eyes he caught, but all the rest seemed white and snowy as though he looked beyond her — out into space. . . .

The sound of the church bell came up faintly from the valley far below, and he counted the strokes — five. A sudden, curious weakness seized him as he listened. Deep within it was, deadly yet somehow sweet, and hard to resist. He felt like sinking down upon the snow and lying there. . . . They had been climbing for five hours. . . . It was, of course, the warning of complete exhaustion.

With a great effort he fought and overcame it. It passed away as suddenly as it came.

"We'll turn," he said with a decision he hardly felt. "It will be dawn before we reach the village again. Come at once. It's time for home."

The sense of exhilaration had utterly left him. An emotion that was akin to fear swept coldly through him. But her whispering answer turned it instantly to terror — a terror that gripped him horribly and turned him weak and unresisting.

"Our home is —here!" A burst of wild, high laughter, loud and shrill, accompanied the words. It was like a whistling wind. The wind had risen, and clouds obscured the moon. "A little higher — where we cannot hear the wicked bells," she cried, and for the first time seized him deliberately by the hand. She moved, was suddenly close against his face. Again she touched him.

{231}

And Hibbert tried to turn away in escape, and so trying, found for the first time that the power of the snow — that other power which does not exhilarate but deadens effort — was upon him. The suffocating weakness that it brings to exhausted men, luring them to the sleep of death in her clinging soft embrace, lulling the will and conquering all desire for life — this was awfully upon him. His feet were heavy and entangled. He could not turn or move.

The girl stood in front of him, very near; he felt her chilly breath upon his cheeks; her hair passed blindingly across his eyes; and that icy wind came with her. He saw her whiteness close; again, it seemed, his sight passed through her into space as though she had no face. Her arms were round his neck. She drew him softly downwards to his knees. He sank; he yielded utterly; he obeyed. Her weight was upon him, smothering, delicious. The snow was to his waist. . . . She kissed him softly on the lips, the eyes, all over his face. And then she spoke his name in that voice of love and wonder, the voice that held the accent of two others — both taken over long ago by Death — the voice of his mother, and of the woman he had loved.

He made one more feeble effort to resist. Then, realising even while he struggled that this soft weight about his heart was sweeter than anything life could ever bring, he let his muscles relax, and sank back into the soft oblivion of the covering snow. Her wintry kisses bore him into sleep.

<h2 style="text-align:center">VII</h2>

They say that men who know the sleep of exhaustion in the snow find no awakening on the hither side of death. . . . The hours passed and the moon sank down below the white world's rim. Then, suddenly, there came a little crash upon his breast and neck, and Hibbert — woke.

He slowly turned bewildered, heavy eyes upon the desolate mountains, stared dizzily about him, tried to rise. At first his muscles would not act; a numbing, aching pain possessed him. He uttered a long, thin cry for help, and heard its faintness swallowed by the wind. And then he understood vaguely why he was only warm — not dead. For this very wind that took his cry had built up a sheltering mound of driven snow against his body while he slept. Like a curving wave it ran beside him. It was the breaking of its over-toppling edge that caused the crash, and the coldness of the mass against his neck that woke him.

Dawn kissed the eastern sky; pale gleams of gold shot every peak with splendour; but ice was in the air, and the dry and frozen snow blew like powder from the surface of the slopes. He saw the points of his ski projecting just below him. Then he — remembered. It seems he had just strength enough to realise that, could he but rise and stand, he might fly with terrific impetus towards the woods and village far beneath. The ski would carry him. But if he failed and fell . . .!

How he contrived it Hibbert never knew; this fear of death somehow called out his whole available reserve force. He rose slowly, balanced a moment, then, taking the angle of an immense zigzag, started down the awful slopes like an arrow from a bow. And automatically the splendid muscles of the practised ski-er and athlete saved and guided him, for he was hardly conscious of controlling either speed or direction. The snow stung face and eyes like fine steel shot; ridge after ridge flew past; the summits raced across the sky; the valley leaped up with bounds to meet him. He scarcely felt the ground beneath his feet as the huge slopes and distance melted before the lightning speed of that descent from death to life.

He took it in four mile-long zigzags, and it was the turning at each corner that nearly finished him, for then the strain of balancing taxed to the verge of collapse the remnants of his strength.

Slopes that have taken hours to climb can be descended in a short half-hour on ski, but Hibbert had lost all count of time. Quite other thoughts and feelings mastered him in that wild, swift dropping through the air that was like the flight of a bird. For ever close upon his heels came following forms and voices with the whirling snow-dust. He heard that little silvery voice of death and laughter at his back. Shrill and wild, with the whistling of the wind past his ears, he caught its pursuing tones; but in anger now, no longer soft and coaxing. And it was accompanied; she did not follow alone. It seemed a host of these flying figures of the snow chased madly just behind him. He felt them furiously smite his neck and cheeks, snatch at his hands and try to entangle his feet and ski in drifts. His eyes they blinded, and they caught his breath away.

The terror of the heights and snow and winter desolation urged him forward in the maddest race with death a human being ever knew; and so terrific was the speed that before the gold and crimson had left the summits to touch the ice-lips of the lower glaciers, he saw the friendly forest far beneath swing up and welcome him.

And it was then, moving slowly along the edge of the woods, he saw a light. A man was carrying it. A procession of human figures was passing in a dark line laboriously through the snow. And — he heard the sound of chanting.

Instinctively, without a second's hesitation, he changed his course. No longer flying at an angle as before, he pointed his ski straight down the mountain-side. The dreadful steepness did not frighten him. He knew full well it meant a crashing tumble at the bottom, but he also knew it meant a doubling of his speed — with safety at the end. For, though no definite thought passed through his mind, he understood that it was the village curé who carried that little gleaming lantern in the dawn, and that he was taking the Host to a chalet on the lower slopes — to some peasant in extremis. He remembered her terror of the church and bells. She feared the holy symbols.

There was one last wild cry in his ears as he started, a shriek of the wind before his face, and a rush of stinging snow against closed eyelids — and then he dropped through empty space. Speed took sight from him. It seemed he flew off the surface of the world.

కు

Indistinctly he recalls the murmur of men's voices, the touch of strong arms that lifted him, and the shooting pains as the ski were unfastened from the twisted ankle . . . for when he opened his eyes again to normal life he found himself lying in his bed at the post office with the doctor at his side. But for years to come the story of "mad Hibbert's" skiing at night is recounted in that mountain village. He went, it seems, up slopes, and to a height that no man in his senses ever tried before. The tourists were agog about it for the rest of the season, and the very same day two of the bolder men went over the actual ground and photographed the slopes. Later Hibbert saw these photographs. He noticed one curious thing about them — though he did not mention it to any one:

There was only a single track.

THE TRANSITION
Algernon Blackwood

JOHN Mudbury was on his way home from the shops, his arms full of Christmas Presents. It was after six o'clock and the streets were very crowded. He was an ordinary man, lived in an ordinary suburban flat, with an ordinary wife and ordinary children. He did not think them ordinary, but everybody else did. He had ordinary presents for each one, a cheap blotter for his wife, a cheap air-gun for the boy, and so forth. He was over fifty, bald, in an office, decent in mind and habits, of uncertain opinions, uncertain politics, and uncertain religion. Yet he considered himself a decided, positive gentleman, quite unaware that the morning newspaper determined his opinions for the day. He just lived--from day to day. Physically, he was fit enough, except for a weak heart (which never troubled him); and his summer holiday was bad golf, while the children bathed and his wife read Garvice on the sands. Like the majority of men, he dreamed idly of the past, muddled away the present, and guessed vaguely--after imaginative reading on occasions--at the future.

'I'd like to survive all right,' he said, 'provided it's better than this,' surveying his wife and children, and thinking of his daily toil. 'Otherwise--!' and he shrugged his shoulders as a brave man should.

He went to church regularly. But nothing in church convinced him that he did survive, just as nothing in church enticed him into hoping that he would. On the other hand, nothing in life persuaded him that he didn't, wouldn't, couldn't. 'I'm an Evolutionist,' he loved to say to thoughtful cronies (over a glass), having never heard that Darwinism had been questioned.

And so he came home gaily, happily, with his bunch of Christmas Presents 'for the wife and little ones,' stroking himself upon their keen enjoyment and excitement. The night before he had taken 'the wife' to see Magic at a select London theatre where the Intellectuals went--and had been extraordinarily stirred. He had gone questioningly, yet expecting something out of the common. 'It's not musical,' he warned her, 'nor farce, nor comedy, so to speak'; and in answer to her question as to what the critics had said, he had wriggled, sighed, and put his gaudy neck-tie straight four times in quick succession. For no Man in the Street, with any claim to self-respect, could be expected to understand what the critics had said, even if he understood the Play. And John had answered truthfully: 'Oh, they just said things. But the theatre's always full--and that's the only test.'

And just now, as he crossed the crowded Circus to catch his 'bus, it chanced that his mind (having glimpsed an advertisement) was full of this particular Play, or rather, of the effect it had produced upon him at the time. For it had thrilled him--inexplicably: with its marvellous speculative hint, its big audacity, its alert and spiritual beauty...Thought plunged to find something--plunged after this bizarre suggestion of a bigger universe, after this quasi-jocular suggestion that man is not the only--then dashed full-tilt against a sentence that memory thrust beneath his nose: 'Science does not exhaust the Universe'--and at the same time dashed full-tilt against destruction of another kind as well...!

How it happened he never exactly knew. He saw a Monster glaring at him with eyes of blazing fire. It was horrible! It rushed upon him. He dodged...Another Monster met him round the corner. Both came at him simultaneously. He dodged again--a leap that might have cleared a hurdle easily, but was too late. Between the pair of them--his heart literally in his gullet--he was mercilessly caught. Bones crunched...There was a soft sensation, icy cold and hot as fire.

Horns and voices roared. Battering-rams he saw, and a carapace of iron...Then dazzling light...

'Always face the traffic!' he remembered with a frantic yell--and, by some extraordinary luck, escaped miraculously on to the opposite pavement.

There was no doubt about it. By the skin of his teeth he had dodged a rather ugly death. First...he felt for his Presents--all were safe. And then, instead of congratulating himself and taking breath, he hurried homewards--on foot, which proved that his mind had lost control a bit!--thinking only how disappointed the wife and children would have been if--well, if anything had happened. Another thing he realised, oddly enough, was that he no longer really loved his wife, but had only great affection for her. What made him think of that, Heaven only knows, but he did think of it. He was an honest man without pretence. This came as a discovery somehow. He turned a moment, and saw the crowd gathered about the entangled taxi-cabs, policemen's helmets gleaming in the lights of the shop windows...then hurried on again, his thoughts full of the joy his Presents would give...of the scampering children...and of his wife--bless her silly heart!--eyeing the mysterious parcels...

And, though he never could explain how, he presently stood at the door of the jail-like building that contained his flat, having walked the whole three miles. His thoughts had been so busy and absorbed that he had hardly noticed the length of weary trudge. 'Besides,' he reflected, thinking of the narrow escape, 'I've had a nasty shock. It was a d--d near thing, now I come to think of it...' He still felt a bit shaky and bewildered. Yet, at the same time, he felt extraordinarily jolly and lighthearted.

He counted his Christmas parcels.., hugged himself in anticipatory joy...and let himself in swiftly with his latchkey. 'I'm late,' he realised, 'but when she sees the brown-paper parcels, she'll forget to say a word. God bless the old faithful soul.' And he softly used the key a second time and entered his flat on tiptoe...In his mind was the master impulse of that afternoon--the pleasure these Christmas Presents would give his wife and children...

He heard a noise. He hung up hat and coat in the poky vestibule (they never called it 'hall') and moved softly towards the parlour door, holding the packages behind him. Only of them he thought, not of himself--of his family, that is, not of the packages. Pushing the door cunningly ajar, he peeped in slyly. To his amazement the room was full of people. He withdrew quickly, wondering what it meant. A party? And without his knowing about it! Extraordinary!...Keen

{236}

disappointment came over him. But, as he stepped back, the vestibule, he saw, was full of people too.

He was uncommonly surprised, yet somehow not surprised at all. People were congratulating him. There was a perfect mob of them. Moreover, he knew them all--vaguely remembered them, at least. And they all knew him.

'Isn't it a game?' laughed someone, patting him on the back. 'They haven't the least idea...!'

And the speaker--it was old John Palmer, the book-keeper at the office--emphasised the 'they.'

'Not the least idea,' he answered with a smile, saying something he didn't understand, yet knew was right.

His face, apparently, showed the utter bewilderment he felt. The shock of the collision had been greater than he realised evidently. His mind was wandering...Possibly! Only the odd thing was--he had never felt so clear-headed in his life. Ten thousand things grew simple suddenly.

But, how thickly these people pressed about him, and how--familiarly!

'My parcels,' he said, joyously pushing his way across the throng. 'These are Christmas Presents I've bought for them.' He nodded toward the room. 'I've saved for weeks--stopped cigars and billiards and--and several other good things--to buy them.'

'Good man!' said Palmer with a happy laugh. 'It's the heart that counts.'

Mudbury looked at him. Palmer had said an amazing truth, only--people would hardly understand and believe him...Would they?

'Eh?' he asked, feeling stuffed and stupid, muddied somewhere between two meanings, one of which was gorgeous and the other stupid beyond belief.

'If you please, Mr. Mudbury, step inside. They are expecting you,' said a kindly, pompous voice. And, turning sharply, he met the gentle, foolish eyes of Sir James Epiphany, a director of the Bank where he worked.

The effect of the voice was instantaneous from long habit. 'They are,' he smiled from his heart, and advanced as from the custom of many years. Oh, how happy and gay he felt! His affection for his wife was real. Romance, indeed, had gone, but he needed her--and she needed him. And the children--Milly, Bill, and Jean--he deeply loved them. Life was worth living indeed!

In the room was a crowd, but--an astounding silence. John Mudbury looked round him. He advanced towards his wife, who sat in the corner arm-chair with Milly on her knee. A lot people talked and moved about. Momentarily the crowd increased. He stood in front of them--in front of Milly and his wife. And he spoke--holding out his packages. 'It's Christmas Eve,' he whispered shyly, 'and I've--brought you something--something for everybody. Look!' He held the packages before their eyes.

'Of course, of course,' said a voice behind him, 'but you may hold them out like that for a century. They'll never see them!'

'Of course they won't. But I love to do the old, sweet thing,' replied John Mudbury--then wondered with a gasp of stark amazement why he said it.

'I think' whispered Milly, staring round her.

'Well, what do you think?' her mother asked sharply. 'You're always thinking something queer.'

'I think,' the girl continued dreamily, 'that Daddy's already here.' She paused, then added with a child's impossible conviction, 'I'm sure he is. I feel him.'

There was an extraordinary laugh. Sir James Epiphany laughed. The others--the whole crowd of them--also turned their heads and smiled. But the mother, thrusting the child away from her, rose up suddenly with a violent start. Her face had turned to chalk. She stretched her arms out--into the air before her. She gasped and shivered. There was anguish in her eyes.

'Look' repeated John, 'these are the Presents that I brought.'

But his voice apparently was soundless. And, with a spasm of icy pain, he remembered that Palmer and Sir James--some years ago--had died.

'It's magic,' he cried, 'but--I love you, Jinny--I love you--and--and I have always been true to you--as true as steel. We need each other--oh, can't you see--we go on together--you and I--for ever and ever--'

'Think,' interrupted an exquisitely tender voice, 'don't shout! They can't hear you--now.'

And, turning, John Mudbury met the eyes of Everard Minturn, their President of the year before.

Minturn had gone down with the Titanic.

He dropped his parcels then. His heart gave an enormous leap of joy.

He saw her face--the face of his wife--look through him.

But the child gazed straight into his eyes. She saw him..The next thing he knew was that he heard something tinkling...far, far away. It sounded miles below him--inside him--he was sounding himself--all utterly bewildering--like a bell. It was a bell.

Milly stooped down and picked the parcels up. Her face shone with happiness and laughter...

But a man came in soon after, a man with a ridiculous, solemn face, a pencil, and a notebook.

He wore a dark blue helmet. Behind him came a string of other men. They carried something...something...he could not see exactly what it was. But, when he pressed forward through the laughing throng to gaze upon it, he dimly made out two eyes, a nose, a chin, a deep red smear, and a pair of folded hands upon and overcoat. A woman's form fell down upon them then, and he heard soft sounds of children weeping strangely ...and other sounds...as of familiar voices laughing...laughing gaily.

'They'll join us presently. It goes like a flash...'

And, turning with great happiness in his heart, he saw that Sir James had said it, holding Palmer by the arm as with some natural yet unexpected love of sympathetic friendship.

'Come on,' said Palmer, smiling like a man who accepts a gift in universal fellowship, 'let's help 'em. They'll never understand...Still, we can always try.'

The entire throng moved up with laughter and amusement. It was a moment of hearty, genuine life at last. Delight and Joy and Peace were everywhere.

Then John Mudbury realised the truth--that he was dead.

THE MISTLETOE BOUGH; OR, THE LOST BRIDE
N. Thomas Haynes Bayly

THE mistletoe hung in the castle hall
The holly branch shone on the old oak wall.
The Baron's retainers were blithe and gay,
Keeping the Christmas holiday.
The Baron beheld with a father's pride
His beautiful child, Lord Lovell's bride.
And she, with her bright eyes seemed to be
The star of that goodly company.
   Oh, the mistletoe bough.
   Oh, the mistletoe bough.
"I'm weary of dancing, now," she cried;
"Here, tarry a moment, I'll hide, I'll hide,
And, Lovell, be sure you're the first to trace
The clue to my secret hiding place."
Away she ran, and her friends began
Each tower to search and each nook to scan.
And young Lovell cried, "Oh, where do you hide?
I'm lonesome without you, my own fair bride."
   Oh, the mistletoe bough.
   Oh, the mistletoe bough.
They sought her that night, they sought her next day,
They sought her in vain when a week passed away.
In the highest, the lowest, the loneliest spot,
Young Lovell sought wildly, but found her not.
The years passed by and their brief at last
Was told as a sorrowful tale long past.
When Lovell appeared, all the children cried,
"See the old man weeps for his fairy bride."
   Oh, the mistletoe bough.
   Oh, the mistletoe bough.
At length, an old chest that had long laid hid
Was found in the castle; they raised the lid.
A skeleton form lay mouldering there
In the bridal wreath of that lady fair.
How sad the day when in sportive jest
She hid from her lord in the old oak chest,
It closed with a spring and a dreadful doom,
And the bride lay clasped in a living tomb.
   Oh, the mistletoe bough.
   Oh, the mistletoe bough.

THE OTHER BED
E. F. Benson

I had gone out to Switzerland just before Christmas, expecting, from experience, a month of divinely renovating weather, of skating all day in brilliant sun, and basking in the hot frost of that windless atmosphere. Occasionally, as I knew, there might be a snowfall, which would last perhaps for forty-eight hours at the outside, and would be succeeded by another ten days of cloudless perfection, cold even to zero at night, but irradiated all day long by the unflecked splendour of the sun.

Instead the climatic conditions were horrible. Day after day a gale screamed through this upland valley that should have been so windless and serene, bringing with it a tornado of sleet that changed to snow by night. For ten days there was no abatement of it, and evening after evening, as I consulted my barometer, feeling sure that the black finger would show that we were coming to the end of these abominations, I found that it had sunk a little lower yet, till it stayed, like a homing pigeon, on the S of storm. I mention these things in depredation of the story that follows, in order that the intelligent reader may say at once, if he wishes, that all that occurred was merely a result of the malaise of nerves and digestion that perhaps arose from those storm-bound and disturbing conditions. And now to go back to the beginning again.

I had written to engage a room at the Hotel Beau Site, and had been agreeably surprised on arrival to find that for the modest sum of twelve francs a day I was allotted a room on the first floor with two beds in it. Otherwise the hotel was quite full. Fearing to be billeted in a twenty-two franc room, by mistake, I instantly confirmed my arrangements at the bureau. There was no mistake: I had ordered a twelve-franc room and had been given one. The very civil clerk hoped that I was satisfied with it, for otherwise there was nothing vacant. I hastened to say that I was more than satisfied, fearing the fate of Esau.

I arrived about three in the afternoon of a cloudless and glorious day, the last of the series. I hurried down to the rink, having had the prudence to put skates in the forefront of my luggage, and spent a divine but struggling hour or two, coming up to the hotel about sunset. I had letters to write, and after ordering tea to be sent up to my gorgeous apartment, No. 23, on the first floor, I went straight up there.

The door was ajar and--I feel certain I should not even remember this now except in the light of what followed--just as I got close to it, I heard some faint movement inside the room and instinctively knew that my servant was there unpacking. Next moment I was in the room myself, and it was empty. The unpacking had been finished, and everything was neat, orderly, and comfortable. My barometer was on the table, and I observed with dismay that it had gone down nearly half an inch. I did not give another thought to the movement I thought I had heard from outside.

Certainly I had a delightful room for my twelve francs a day. There were, as I have said, two beds in it, on one of which were already laid out my dress-clothes, while night-things were disposed on the other. There were two windows, between which stood a large washing-stand, with plenty of room on it; a sofa with its back to the light stood conveniently near the pipes of central heating, there were a couple of good arm-chairs, a writing table, and, rarest of luxuries, another table, so that every time one had breakfast it was not necessary to pile up a drift of books and papers to make room for the tray. My window looked east, and sunset still flamed on the western faces of the virgin snows, while above, in spite of the dejected barometer, the sky was bare of clouds, and a thin slip of pale crescent moon was swung high among the stars that still burned dimly in these first moments of their kindling. Tea came up for me without delay, and, as I ate, I regarded my surroundings with extreme complacency.

Then, quite suddenly and without cause, I saw that the disposition of the beds would never do; I could not possibly sleep in the bed that my servant had chosen for me, and without pause I jumped up, transferred my dress clothes to the other bed, and put my night things where they had been. It was done breathlessly almost, and not till then did I ask myself why I had done it. I found I had not the slightest idea. I had merely felt that I could not sleep in the other bed. But having made the change I felt perfectly content.

My letters took me an hour or so to finish, and I had yawned and blinked considerably over the last one or two, in part from their inherent dullness, in part from quite natural sleepiness. For I had been in the train for twenty-four hours, and was fresh to these bracing airs which so conduce to appetite, activity, and sleep, and as there was still an hour before I need dress, I lay down on my sofa with a book for excuse, but the intention to slumber as reason. And consciousness ceased as if a tap had been turned off.

Then--I dreamed. I dreamed that my servant came very quietly into the room, to tell me no doubt that it was time to dress. I supposed there were a few minutes to spare yet, and that he saw I was dozing, for, instead of rousing me, he moved quietly about the room, setting things in order. The light appeared to me to be very dim, for I could not see him with any distinctness, indeed, I only knew it was he because it could not be any body else. Then he paused by my washing-stand, which had a shelf for brushes and razors above it, and I saw him take a razor from its case and begin stropping it; the light was strongly reflected on the blade of the razor. He tried the edge once or twice on his thumb-nail, and then to my horror I saw him trying it on his throat. Instantaneously one of those deafening dream-crashes awoke me, and I saw the door half open, and my servant in the very act of coming in. No doubt the opening of the door had constituted the crash.

I had joined a previously-arrived party of five, all of us old friends, and accustomed to see each other often; and at dinner, and afterwards in intervals of bridge, the conversation roamed agreeably over a variety of topics, rocking-turns and the prospects of weather (a thing of vast importance in Switzerland, and not a commonplace subject) and the performances at the opera, and under what circumstances as revealed in dummy's hand, is it justifiable for a player to refuse to return his partner's original lead in no trumps. Then over whisky and soda and the repeated "last cigarette," it veered back via the Zantzigs to thought transference and the transference of emotion. Here one of the party, Harry Lambert, put forward the much discussed explanation of haunted houses based on this principle. He put it very concisely.

"Everything that happens," he said, "whether it is a step we take, or a thought that crosses our mind, makes some change in it, immediate material world. Now the most violent and concentrated emotion we can imagine is the emotion that leads a man to take so extreme a step as killing himself or somebody else. I can easily imagine such a deed so eating into the material scene, the room or the haunted heath, where it happens, that its mark lasts an enormous time. The air rings with the cry of the slain and still drips with his blood. It is not everybody who will perceive it, but sensitives will. By the way, I am sure that man who waits on us at dinner is a sensitive."

It was already late, and I rose.

"Let us hurry him to the scene of a crime," I said. "For myself I shall hurry to the scene of sleep."

Outside the threatening promise of the barometer was already finding fulfilment, and a cold ugly wind was complaining among the pines, and hooting round the peaks, and snow had begun to fall. The night was thickly overcast, and it seemed as if uneasy presences were going to and fro in the darkness. But there was no use in ill augury, and certainly if we were to be house-bound for a few days I was lucky in having so commodious a lodging. I had plenty to occupy myself with indoors, though I should vastly have preferred to be engaged outside, and in the immediate present how good it was to lie free in a proper bed after a cramped night in the train.

I was half-undressed when there came a tap at my door, and the waiter who had served us at dinner came in carrying a bottle of whisky. He was a tall young fellow, and though I had not noticed him at dinner, I saw at once now, as he stood in the glare of the electric light, what Harry had meant when he said he was sure he was a sensitive. There is no mistaking that look: it is exhibited in a peculiar "inlooking" of the eye. Those eyes, one knows, see further than the surface...

"The bottle of whisky for monsieur," he said putting it down on the table.

"But I ordered no whisky," said I. He looked puzzled.

"Number twenty-three?" he said. Then he glanced at the other bed.

"Ah, for the other gentleman, without doubt," he said.

"But there is no other gentleman," said I.

"I am alone here."

He took up the bottle again.

"Pardon, monsieur," he said. "There must be a mistake. I am new here; I only came today."

"But I thought--"

"Yes?" said I.

"I thought that number twenty-three had ordered a bottle of whisky," he repeated.

"Goodnight, monsieur, and pardon."

I got into bed, extinguished the light, and feeling very sleepy and heavy with the oppression, no doubt, of the snow that was coming, expected to fall asleep at once. Instead my mind would not quite go to roost, but kept sleepily stumbling about among the little events of the day, as some tired pedestrian in the dark stumbles over stones instead of lifting his feet. And as I got sleepier it seemed to me that my mind kept moving in a tiny little circle. At one moment it drowsily recollected how I had thought I had heard movement inside my room, at the next it remembered my dream of some figure going stealthily about and stropping a razor, at a third it wondered why this Swiss waiter with the eyes of a "sensitive" thought that number twenty-three had ordered a bottle of whisky. But at the time I made no guess as to any coherence between these little isolated facts; I only dwelt on them with drowsy persistence. Then a fourth fact came to join the sleepy circle, and I wondered why I had felt a repugnance against using the other bed.

But there was no explanation of this forthcoming, either, and the outlines of thought grew more blurred and hazy, until I lost consciousness altogether.

Next morning began the series of awful days, sleet and snow falling relentlessly with gusts of chilly wind, making any out-of-door amusement next to impossible. The snow was too soft for tobogganning, it balled on the skis, and as for the rink it was but a series of pools of slushy snow.

This in itself, of course, was quite enough to account for any ordinary depression and heaviness of spirit, but all the time I felt there was something more than that to which I owed the utter blackness that hung over those days. I was beset too by fear that at first was only vague, but which gradually became more definite, until it resolved itself into a fear of number twenty-three and in particular a terror of the other bed. I had no notion why or how I was afraid of it, the thing was perfectly causeless, but the shape and the outline of it grew slowly clearer, as detail after detail of ordinary life, each minute and trivial in itself, carved and moulded this fear, till it became definite. Yet the whole thing was so causeless and childish that I could speak to no one of it; I could but assure myself that it was all a figment of nerves disordered by this unseemly weather.

However, as to the details, there were plenty of them. Once I woke up from strangling nightmare, unable at first to move, but in a panic of terror, believing that I was sleeping in the other bed. More than once, too, awaking before I was called, and getting out of bed to look at the aspect of the morning, I saw with a sense of dreadful misgiving that the bed-clothes on the other bed were strangely disarranged, as if some one had slept there, and smoothed them down afterwards, but not so well as not to give notice of the occupation. So one night I laid a trap, so to speak, for the intruder of which the real object was to calm my own nervousness (for I still told myself that I was frightened of nothing), and tucked in the sheet very carefully, laying the pillow on the top of it. But in the morning it seemed as if my interference had not been to the taste of the occupant, for there was more impatient disorder than usual in the bed-clothes, and on the pillow was an indentation, round and rather deep, such as we may see any morning in our own beds. Yet by day these things did not frighten me, but it was when I went to bed at night that I quaked at the thought of further developments.

It happened also from time to time that I wanted something brought me, or wanted my servant. On three or four of these occasions my bell was answered by the "Sensitive," as we called him, but the Sensitive, I noticed, never came into the room. He would open the door a chink to receive my order and on returning would again open it a chink to say that my boots, or whatever it was, were at the door. Once I made him come in, but I saw him cross himself as, with a face of icy terror, he stepped into the room, and the sight somehow did not reassure me. Twice also he came up in the evening, when I had not rung at all, even as he came up the first night, and opened the door a chink to say that my bottle of whisky was outside. But the poor fellow was in a state of such bewilderment when I went out and told him that I had not ordered whisky, that I did not press for an explanation. He begged my pardon profusely; he thought a bottle of whisky had been ordered for number twenty-three. It was his mistake, entirely--I should not be charged for it; it must have been the other gentleman. Pardon again; he remembered there was no other gentleman, the other bed was unoccupied.

It was on the night when this happened for the second time that I definitely began to wish that I too was quite certain that the other bed was unoccupied. The ten days of snow and sleet were at an end, and to-night the moon once more, grown from a mere slip to a shining shield, swung serenely among the stars. But though at dinner everyone exhibited an extraordinary change of spirit, with the rising of the barometer and the discharge of this huge snow-fall, the intolerable gloom which had been mine so long but deepened and blackened. The fear was to me now like some statue, nearly finished, modelled by the carving hands of these details, and though it still stood below its moistened sheet, any moment, I felt, the sheet might be twitched away, and I be confronted with it. Twice that evening I had started to go to the bureau, to ask to have a bed made up for me, anywhere, in the billiard-room or the smoking-room, since the hotel was full, but the intolerable childishness of the proceeding revolted me. What was I afraid of? A dream of my own, a mere nightmare? Some fortuitous disarrangement of bed linen? The fact that a Swiss waiter made mistakes about bottles of whisky? It was an impossible cowardice.

But equally impossible that night were billiards or bridge, or any form of diversion. My only salvation seemed to lie in downright hard work, and soon after dinner I went to my room (in order to make my first real counter-move against fear) and sat down solidly to several hours of proof-correcting, a menial and monotonous employment, but one which is necessary, and engages the entire attention. But first I looked thoroughly round the room, to reassure myself, and found all modern and solid; a bright paper of daisies on the wall, a floor parquetted, the hot-water pipes chuckling to themselves in the corner, my bed-clothes turned down for the night, the other bed--The electric light was burning brightly, and there seemed to me to be a curious stain, as of a shadow, on the lower part of the pillow and the top of the sheet, definite and suggestive, and for a

{244}

moment I stood there again throttled by a nameless terror. Then taking my courage in my hands I went closer and looked at it. Then I touched it; the sheet, where the stain or shadow was, seemed damp to the hand, so also was the pillow. And then I remembered; I had thrown some wet clothes on the bed before dinner. No doubt that was the reason. And fortified by this extremely simple dissipation of my fear, I sat down and began on my proofs. But my fear had been this, that the stain had not in that first moment looked like the mere greyness of water-moistened linen.

From below, at first came the sound of music, for they were dancing to-night, but I grew absorbed in my work, and only recorded the fact that after a time there was no more music. Steps went along the passages, and I heard the buzz of conversation on landings, and the closing of doors till by degrees the silence became noticeable. The loneliness of night had come.

It was after the silence had become lonely that I made the first pause in my work, and by the watch on my table saw that it was already past midnight. But I had little more to do; another half-hour would see the end of the business, but there were certain notes I had to make for future reference, and my stock of paper was already exhausted. However, I had bought some in the village that afternoon, and it was in the bureau downstairs, where I had left it, when I came in and had subsequently forgotten to bring it upstairs. It would be the work of a minute only to get it.

The electric light had brightened considerably during the last hour, owing no doubt to many burners being put out in the hotel, and as I left the room I saw again the stain on the pillow and sheet of the other bed. I had really forgotten all about it for the last hour, and its presence there came as an unwelcome surprise. Then I remembered the explanation of it, which had struck me before, and for purposes of self-reassurement I again touched it. It was still damp, but--Had I got chilly with my work? For it was warm to the hand. Warm, and surely rather sticky. It did not seem like the touch of the water-damp. And at the same moment I knew I was not alone in the room. There was something there, something silent as yet, and as yet invisible. But it was there.

Now for the consolation of persons who are inclined to be fearful, I may say at once that I am in no way brave, but that terror which, God knows, was real enough, was yet so interesting, that interest overruled it. I stood for a moment by the other bed, and, half-consciously only, wiped the hand that had felt the stain, for the touch of it, though all the time I told myself that it was but the touch of the melted snow on the coat I had put there, was unpleasant and unclean. More than that I did not feel, because in the presence of the unknown and the perhaps awful, the sense of curiosity, one of the strongest instincts we have, came to the fore. So, rather eager to get back to my room again, I ran downstairs to get the packet of paper. There was still a light in the bureau, and the Sensitive, on night-duty, I suppose, was sitting there dozing. My entrance did not disturb him, for I had on noiseless felt slippers, and seeing at once the package I was in search of, I took it, and left him still unawakened. That was somehow of a fortifying nature. The Sensitive anyhow could sleep in his hard chair; the occupant of the unoccupied bed was not calling to him to-night.

I closed my door quietly, as one does at night when the house is silent, and sat down at once to open my packet of paper and finish my work. It was wrapped up in an old news-sheet, and struggling with the last of the string that bound it, certain words caught my eye. Also the date at the top of the paper caught my eye, a date nearly a year old, or, to be quite accurate, a date fifty-one weeks old. It was an American paper and what it recorded was this:

"The body of Mr. Silas R. Hume, who committed suicide last week at the Hotel Beau Site, Moulin sur Chalons, is to be buried at his house in Boston, Mass. The inquest held in Switzerland showed that he cut his throat with a razor, in an attack of delirium tremens induced by drink. In the cupboard of his room were found three dozen empty bottles of Scotch whisky..."

So far I had read when without warning the electric light went out, and I was left in, what seemed for the moment, absolute darkness. And again I knew I was not alone, and I knew now who it was who was with me in the room.

Then the absolute paralysis of fear seized me. As if a wind had blown over my head, I felt the hair of it stir and rise a little. My eyes also, I suppose, became accustomed to the sudden darkness, for they could now perceive the shape of the furniture in the room from the light of the starlit sky outside. They saw more too than the mere furniture. There was standing by the wash-stand between the two windows a figure, clothed only in night-garments, and its hands moved among the objects on the shelf above the basin. Then with two steps it made a sort of dive for the other bed, which was in shadow. And then the sweat poured on to my forehead.

Though the other bed stood in shadow I could still see dimly, but sufficiently, what was there. The shape of a head lay on the pillow, the shape of an arm lifted its hand to the electric bell that was close by on the wall, and I fancied I could hear it distantly ringing. Then a moment later came hurrying feet up the stairs and along the passage outside, and a quick rapping at my door.

"Monsieur's whisky, monsieur's whisky," said a voice just outside. "Pardon, monsieur, I brought it as quickly as I could."

The impotent paralysis of cold terror was still on me. Once I tried to speak and failed, and still the gentle tapping went on at the door, and the voice telling some one that his whisky was there. Then at a second attempt, I heard a voice which was mine saying hoarsely:

"For God's sake come in; I am alone with it."

There was the click of a turned door-handle, and as suddenly as it had gone out a few seconds before, the electric light came back again, and the room was in full illumination. I saw a face peer round the corner of the door, but it was at another face I looked, the face of a man sallow and shrunken, who lay in the other bed, staring at me with glazed eyes. He lay high in bed, and his throat was cut from ear to ear; and the lower part of the pillow was soaked in blood, and the sheet streamed with it.

Then suddenly that hideous vision vanished, and there was only a sleepy-eyed waiter looking into the room. But below the sleepiness terror was awake, and his voice shook when he spoke.

"Monsieur rang?" he asked.

No, monsieur had not rung. But monsieur made himself a couch in the billiard-room.

A STRANGE CHRISTMAS GAME
Mrs J. H. Riddell

WHEN, through the death of a distant relative, I, John Lester, succeeded to the Martingdale Estate, there could not have been found in the length and breadth of England a happier pair than myself and my only sister Clare.

We were not such utter hypocrites as to affect sorrow for the loss of our kinsman, Paul Lester, a man whom we had never seen, of whom we had heard but little, and that little unfavourable, at whose hands we had never received a single benefit - who was, in short, as great a stranger to us as the then Prime Minister, the Emperor of Russia, or any other human being utterly removed from our extremely humble sphere of life.

His loss was very certainly our gain. His death represented to us, not a dreary parting from one long loved and highly honoured, but the accession of lands, houses, consideration, wealth, to myself - John Lester, artist and second-floor lodger at 32, Great Smith Street, Bloomsbury.

Not that Martingdale was much of an estate as country properties go. The Lesters who had succeeded to that domain from time to time during the course of a few hundred years, could by no stretch of courtesy have been called prudent men. In regard of their posterity they were, indeed, scarcely honest, for they parted with manors and farms, with common rights and advowsons, in a manner at once so baronial and so unbusiness-like, that Martingdale at length in the hands of Jeremy Lester, the last resident owner, melted to a mere little dot in the map of Bedfordshire.

Concerning this Jeremy Lester there was a mystery. No man could say what had become of him. He was in the oak parlour at Martingdale one Christmas Eve, and before the next morning he had disappeared - to reappear in the flesh no more.

Over night, one Mr Wharley, a great friend and boon companion of Jeremy's, had sat playing cards with him until after twelve o'clock chimes, then he took leave of his host and rode home under the moonlight. After that no person, as far as could be ascertained, ever saw Jeremy Lester alive.

His ways of life had not been either the most regular, or the most respectable, and it was not until a new year had come in without any tidings of his whereabouts reaching the house, that his servants became seriously alarmed concerning his absence.

Then enquiries were set on foot concerning him - enquiries which grew more urgent as weeks and months passed by without the slightest clue being obtained as to his whereabouts. Rewards were offered, advertisements inserted, but still Jeremy made no sign; and so in course of time the heir-at-law, Paul Lester, took possession of the house, and went down to spend the summer months at Martingdale with his rich wife, and her four children by a first husband. Paul Lester was a barrister - an over-worked barrister, who everyone supposed would be glad enough to leave the bar and settle at Martingdale, where his wife's money and

{248}

the fortune he had accumulated could not have failed to give him a good standing even among the neighbouring country families; and perhaps it was with such intention that he went down into Bedfordshire.

If this were so, however, he speedily changed his mind, for with the January snows he returned to London, let off the land surrounding the house, shut up the Hall, put in a caretaker, and never troubled himself further about his ancestral seat.

Time went on, and people began to say the house was haunted, that Paul Lester had 'seen something', and so forth - all which stories were duly repeated for our benefit when, forty-one years after the disappearance of Jeremy Lester, Clare and I went down to inspect our inheritance.

I say 'our', because Clare had stuck bravely to me in poverty - grinding poverty, and prosperity was not going to part us now. What was mine was hers, and that she knew, God bless her, without my needing to tell her so.

The transition from rigid economy to comparative wealth was in our case the more delightful also, because we had not in the least degree anticipated it. We never expected Paul Lester's shoes to come to us, and accordingly it was not upon our consciences that we had ever in our dreariest moods wished him dead.

Had he made a will, no doubt we never should have gone to Martingdale, and I, consequently, never written this story; but, luckily for us, he died intestate, and the Bedfordshire property came to me.

As for the fortune, he had spent it in travelling, and in giving great entertainments at his grand house in Portman Square. Concerning his effects, Mrs Lester and I came to a very amicable arrangement, and she did me the honour of inviting me to call upon her occasionally, and, as I heard, spoke of me as a very worthy and presentable young man 'for my station', which, of course, coming from so good an authority, was gratifying. Moreover, she asked me if I intended residing at Martingdale, and on my replying in the affirmative, hoped I should like it.

It struck me at the time that there was a certain significance in her tone, and when I went down to Martingdale and heard the absurd stories which were afloat concerning the house being haunted, I felt confident that if Mrs Lester had hoped much, she had feared more.

People said Mr Jeremy 'walked' at Martingdale. He had been seen, it was averred, by poachers, by gamekeepers, by children who had come to use the park as a near cut to school, by lovers who kept their tryst under the elms and beeches.

As for the caretaker and his wife, the third in residence since Jeremy Lester's disappearance, the man gravely shook his head when questioned, while the woman stated that wild horses, or even wealth untold, should not draw her into the red bedroom, nor into the oak parlour, after dark.

'I have heard my mother tell, sir - it was her as followed old Mrs Reynolds, the first caretaker - how there were things went on in these self same rooms as might make any Christian's hair stand on end. Such stamping, and swearing, and knocking about on furniture; and then tramp, tramp, up the great staircase; and along the corridor and so into the red bedroom, and then bang, and tramp, tramp again. They do say, sir, Mr Paul Lester met him once, and from that time the oak parlour has never been opened. I never was inside it myself.'

Upon hearing which fact, the first thing I did was to proceed to the oak parlour, open the shutters, and let the August sun stream in upon the haunted chamber. It was an old-fashioned, plainly furnished apartment, with a large table in the centre, a smaller in a recess by the fire-place, chairs ranged against the walls, and a dusty moth-eaten carpet upon the floor. There were dogs on the hearth, broken and rusty; there was a brass fender, tarnished and battered; a picture of some sea-fight over the mantel-piece, while another work of art about equal in merit hung between the windows. Altogether, an utterly prosaic and yet not uncheerful apartment, from out of which the ghosts flitted as soon as daylight was let into it, and which I proposed, as soon as I 'felt my feet', to redecorate, refurnish, and convert into a pleasant morning-room. I was still under thirty, but I had learned prudence in that very good school, Necessity; and it was not my intention to spend much money until I had ascertained for certain what were the actual revenues derivable from the lands still belonging to the Martingdale estates, and the charges upon them. In fact, I wanted to know what I was worth before committing myself to any great extravagances, and the place had for so long been neglected, that I experienced some difficulty in arriving at the state of my real income.

But in the meanwhile, Clare and I found great enjoyment in exploring every nook and corner of our domain, in turning over the contents of old chests and cupboards, in examining the faces of our ancestors looking down on us from the walls, in walking through the neglected gardens, full of weeds, overgrown with shrubs and birdweed, where the boxwood was eighteen feet high, and the shoots of the rosetrees yards long. I have put the place in order since then; there is no grass on the paths, there are no trailing brambles over the ground, the hedges have been cut and trimmed, and the trees pruned and the boxwood clipped. But I often say nowadays that in spite of all my improvements, or rather, in consequence of them, Martingdale does not look one half so pretty as it did in its pristine state of uncivilised picturesqueness.

Although I determined not to commence repairing and decorating the house till better informed concerning the rental of Martingdale, still the state of my finances was so far satisfactory that Clare and I decided on going abroad to take our long-talked-of holiday before the fine weather was past. We could not tell what a year might bring forth, as Clare sagely remarked; it was wise to take our pleasure while we could; and accordingly, before the end of August arrived we were wandering about the continent, loitering at Rouen, visiting the galleries at Paris, and talking of extending our one month of enjoyment into three. What decided me on this course was the circumstance of our becoming acquainted with an English family who intended wintering in Rome. We met accidentally, but discovering that we were near neighbours in England - in fact that Mr Cronson's property lay close beside Martingdale - the slight acquaintance soon ripened into intimacy, and ere long we were travelling in company.

From the first, Clare did not much like this arrangement. There was 'a little girl' in England she wanted me to marry, and Mr Cronson had a daughter who certainly was both handsome and attractive. The little girl had not despised John Lester, artist, while Miss Cronson indisputably set her cap at John Lester of Martingdale, and would have turned away her pretty face from a poor man's admiring glance - all this I can see plainly enough now, but I was blind then and should have proposed for Maybel - that was her name - before the winter was over, had news not suddenly arrived of the illness of Mrs Cronson, senior. In a moment the programme was changed; our pleasant days of foreign travel were at an end. The Cronsons packed up and departed, while Clare and I returned more slowly to England, a little out of humour, it must be confessed, with each other.

It was the middle of November when we arrived at Martingdale, and we found the place anything but romantic or pleasant. The walks were wet and sodden, the trees were leafless, there were no flowers save a few late pink roses blooming in the garden.

It had been a wet season, and the place looked miserable. Clare would not ask Alice down to keep her company in the winter months, as she had intended; and for myself, the Cronsons were still absent in Norfolk, where they meant to spend Christmas with old Mrs Cronson, now recovered.

Altogether, Martingdale seemed dreary enough, and the ghost stories we had laughed at while sunshine flooded the rooms became less unreal when we had nothing but blazing fires and wax candles to dispel the gloom. They became more real also when servant after servant left us to seek situations elsewhere; when 'noises' grew frequent in the house; when we ourselves, Clare and I, with our own ears heard the tramp, tramp, the banging and the clattering which had been described to us.

My dear reader, you are doubtless free from superstitious fancies. You pooh-pooh the existence of ghosts, and only 'wish you could find a haunted house in which to spend a night', which is all very brave and praiseworthy, but wait till you are left in a dreary, desolate old country mansion, filled with the most unaccountable sounds, without a servant, with no one save an old caretaker and his wife, who, living at the extremest end of the building, heard nothing of the tramp, tramp, bang, bang, going on at all hours of the night.

At first I imagine the noises were produced by some evil-disposed persons who wished, for purposes of their own, to keep the house uninhabited; but by degrees Clare and I came to the conclusion the visitation must be supernatural, and Martingdale by consequence untenantable. Still being practical people, and unlike our predecessors, not having money to live where and how we liked, we decided to watch and see whether we could trace any human influence in the matter. If not, it was agreed we were to pull down the right wing of the house and the principal staircase.

For nights and nights we sat up till two or three o'clock in the morning; but just to test the matter, I determined on Christmas-eve, the anniversary of Mr Jeremy Lester's disappearance, to keep watch by myself in the red bed-chamber. Even to Clare I never mentioned my intention.

About ten, tired out with our previous vigils, we each retired to rest. Somewhat ostentatiously, perhaps, I noisily shut the door of my room, and when I opened it half an hour afterwards, no mouse could have pursued its way along the corridor with greater silence and caution than myself.

Quite in the dark I sat in the red room. For over an hour I might as well have been in my grave for anything I could see in the apartment; but at the end of that time the moon rose and cast strange lights across the floor and upon the wall of the haunted chamber.

Hitherto I had kept my watch opposite the window; now I changed my place to a corner near the door, where I was shaded from observation by the heavy hangings of the bed, and an antique wardrobe.

Still I sat on, but still no sound broke the silence. I was weary with many nights' watching; and tired of my solitary vigil, I dropped at last into a slumber from which I was awakened by hearing the door softly opened.

'John,' said my sister, almost in a whisper; 'John, are you here?'

'Yes, Clare,' I answered; 'but what are you doing up at this hour?'

'Come downstairs,' she replied; 'they are in the oak parlour.' I did not need any explanation as to whom she meant, but crept downstairs, after her, warned by an uplifted hand of the necessity for silence and caution.

By the door - by the open door of the oak parlour, she paused, and we both looked in.

There was the room we left in darkness overnight, with a bright wood fire blazing on the hearth, candles on the chimney-piece, the small table pulled out from its accustomed corner, and two men seated beside it, playing at cribbage.

We could see the face of the younger player; it was that of a man of about five-and-twenty, of a man who had lived hard and wickedly; who had wasted his substance and his health; who had been while in the flesh, Jeremy Lester. It would be difficult for me to say how I knew this, how in a moment I identified the features of the player with those of a man who had been missing for forty-one years - forty-one years that very night. He was dressed in the costume of a bygone period; his hair was powdered, and round his wrists there were ruffles of lace.

He looked like one who, having come from some great party had sat down after his return home to play at cards with an intimate friend. On his little finger there sparkled a ring, in the front of his shirt there gleamed a valuable diamond. There were diamond buckles in his shoes, and, according to the fashion of his time, he wore knee-breeches and silk stockings, which showed off advantageously the shape of a remarkably good leg and ankle.

He sat opposite to the door, but never once lifted his eyes to it. His attention seemed concentrated on the cards.

For a time there was utter silence in the room, broken only by the monotonous counting of the game.

In the doorway we stood, holding our breath, terrified, and yet fascinated by the scene which was being acted before us.

The ashes dropped on the hearth softly and like the snow; we could hear the rustle of the cards as they were dealt out and fell upon the table: we listened to the count - fifteen-one, fifteen-two, and so forth - but there was no other word spoken till at length the player whose face we could not see, exclaimed, 'I win; the game is mine.'

Then his opponent took up the cards, sorted them over negligently in his hand, put them close together, and flung the whole pack in his guest's face, exclaiming, 'Cheat! Liar! Take that!'

There was a bustle and a confusion - a flinging over of chairs, and fierce gesticulation, and such a noise of passionate voices mingling, that we could not hear a sentence which was uttered.

All at once, however, Jeremy Lester strode out of the room in so great a hurry that he almost touched us where we stood; out of the room, and tramp, tramp up the staircase, to the red room, whence he descended in a few minutes with a couple of rapiers under his arm.

When he re-entered the room he gave, as it seemed to us, the other man his choice of the weapons, and then he flung open the window, and after ceremoniously giving place to his opponent to pass out first, he walked forth into the night-air, Clare and I following.

We went through the garden and down a narrow winding walk to a smooth piece of turf sheltered from the north by a plantation of young fir-trees. It was a bright moonlit night by this time, and we could distinctly see Jeremy Lester measuring off the ground.

'When you say "three",' he said to the man whose back was still toward us. They had drawn lots for the ground, and the lot had fallen against Mr Lester. He stood thus with the moonbeams falling full upon him, and a handsomer fellow I would never desire to behold.

'One,' began the other; 'two', and before our kinsman hd the slightest suspicion of his design, he was upon him, and his rapier through Jeremy Lester's breast. At the sight of that cowardly treachery, Clare screamed aloud. In a moment the combatants had disappeared, the moon was obscured behind a cloud, and we were standing in the shadow of the fir-plantation, shivering with cold and terror.

But we knew at last what had become of the late owner of Martingdale: that he had fallen, not in fair fight, but foully murdered by a false friend.

When, late on Christmas morning, I awoke, it was to see a white world, to behold the ground, and trees, and shrubs all laden and covered with snow. There was snow everywhere, such snow as no person could remember having fallen for forty-one years.

'It was on just such a Christmas as this that Mr Jeremy disappeared,' remarked the old sexton to my sister, who had insisted on dragging me through the snow to church, whereupon Clare fainted away and was carried into the vestry, where I made a full confession to the Vicar of all we had beheld the previous night.

At first that worthy individual rather inclined to treat the matter lightly, but when a fortnight after, the snow melted away and the fir-plantation came to be examined, he confessed there might be more things in heaven and earth than his limited philosophy had dreamed of.

In a little clear space just within the plantation, Jeremy Lester's body was found. We knew it by the ring and the diamond buckles, and the sparkling breast-pin; and Mr Cronson, who in his capacity as magistrate came over to inspect these relics, was visibly perturbed at my narrative.

'Pray, Mr Lester, did you in your dream see the face of - of the gentleman - your kinsman's opponent?'

'No,' I answered, 'he sat and stood with his back to us all the time.'

'There is nothing more, of course, to be done in the matter,' observed Mr Cronson.

'Nothing,' I replied; and there the affair would doubtless have terminated, but that a few days afterwards when we were dining at Cronson Park, Clare all of a sudden dropped the glass of water she was carrying to her lips, and exclaiming, 'Look, John, there he is!' rose from her seat, and with a face as white as the tablecloth, pointed to a portrait hanging on the wall.

'I saw him for an instant when he turned his head towards the door as Jeremy Lester left it,' she exclaimed; 'that is he.'

Of what followed after this identification I have only the vaguest recollection. Servants rushed hither and thither; Mrs Cronson dropped off her chair into hysterics; the young ladies gathered round their mamma; Mr Cronson, trembling like one in an ague fit, attempted some kind of explanation, while Clare kept praying to be taken away - only to be taken away.

I took her away, not merely from Cronson Park, but from Martingdale. Before we left the latter place, however, I had an interview with Mr Cronson, who said the portrait Clare had identified was that of his wife's father, the last person who saw Jeremy Lester alive.

'He is an old man now,' finished Mr Cronson, 'a man of over eighty, who has confessed everything to me. You won't bring further sorrow and disgrace upon us by making this matter public?'

I promised him I would keep silence, but the story gradually oozed out, and the Cronsons left the country.

My sister never returned to Martingdale; she married and is living in London. Though I assure her there are no strange noises now in my house, she will not visit Bedfordshire, where the 'little girl' she wanted me so long ago to 'think seriously of', is now my wife and the mother of my children.

NUMBER 17
E. Nesbit

I yawned. I could not help it. But the flat, inexorable voice went on.

"Speaking from the journalistic point of view—I may tell you, gentlemen, that I once occupied the position of advertisement editor to the *Bradford Woollen Goods Journal*—and speaking from that point of view, I hold the opinion that all the best ghost stories have been written over and over again; and if I were to leave the road and return to a literary career I should never be led away by ghosts. Realism's what's wanted nowadays, if you want to be up-to-date."

The large commercial paused for breath.

"You never can tell with the public," said the lean, elderly traveller; "it's like in the fancy business. You never know how it's going to be. Whether it's a clockwork ostrich or Sometite silk or a particular shape of shaded glass novelty or a tobacco-box got up to look like a raw chop, you never know your luck."

"That depends on who you are," said the dapper man in the corner by the fire. "If you've got the right push about you, you can make a thing go, whether it's a clockwork kitten or imitation meat, and with stories, I take it, it's just the same—realism or ghost stories. But the best ghost story would be the realest one, *I* think."

The large commercial had got his breath.

"I don't believe in ghost stories, myself," he was saying with earnest dullness; "but there was a rather a queer thing happened to a second cousin of an aunt of mine by marriage—a very sensible woman with no nonsense about her. And the soul of truth and honour. I shouldn't have believed it if she had been one of your flighty, fanciful sort."

"Don't tell us the story," said the melancholy man who travelled in hardware; "you'll make us afraid to go to bed."

The well-meant effort failed. The large commercial went on, as I had known he would; his words overflowed his mouth, as his person overflowed his chair. I turned my mind to my own affairs, coming back to the commercial room in time to hear the summing up.

"The doors were all locked, and she was quite certain she saw a tall, white figure glide past her and vanish. I wouldn't have believed it if——" And so on *da capo*, from "if she hadn't been the second cousin" to the "soul of truth and honour."

I yawned again.

"Very good story," said the smart little man by the fire. He was a traveller, as the rest of us were; his presence in the room told us that much. He had been rather silent during dinner, and afterwards, while the red curtains were being drawn and the red and black cloth laid between the glasses and the decanters and the mahogany, he had quietly taken the best chair in the warmest corner. We had got our letters written and the large traveller had been boring for some time before I even noticed that there was a best chair and that this silent, bright-eyed, dapper, fair man had secured it.

{256}

"Very good story," he said; "but it's not what I call realism. You don't tell us half enough, sir. You don't say when it happened or where, or the time of year, or what colour your aunt's second cousin's hair was. Nor yet you don't tell us what it was she saw, nor what the room was like where she saw it, nor why she saw it, nor what happened afterwards. And I shouldn't like to breathe a word against anybody's aunt by marriage's cousin, first or second, but I must say I like a story about what a man's seen *himself*."

"So do I," the large commercial snorted, "when I hear it."

He blew his nose like a trumpet of defiance.

"But," said the rabbit-faced man, "we know nowadays, what with the advance of science and all that sort of thing, we know there aren't any such things as ghosts. They're hallucinations; that's what they are—hallucinations."

"Don't seem to matter what you call them," the dapper one urged. "If you see a thing that looks as real as you do yourself, a thing that makes your blood run cold and turns you sick and silly with fear—well, call it ghost, or call it hallucination, or call it Tommy Dodd; it isn't the *name* that matters."

The elderly commercial coughed and said, "You might call it another name. You might call it——"

"No, you mightn't," said the little man, briskly; "not when the man it happened to had been a teetotal Bond of Joy for five years and is to this day."

"Why don't you tell us the story?" I asked.

"I might be willing," he said, "if the rest of the company were agreeable. Only I warn you it's not that sort-of-a-kind-of-a-somebody-fancied-they-saw-a-sort-of-a-kind-of-a-something-sort of story. No, sir. Everything I'm going to tell you is plain and straightforward and as clear as a time-table—clearer than some. But I don't much like telling it, especially to people who don't believe in ghosts."

Several of us said we did believe in ghosts. The heavy man snorted and looked at his watch. And the man in the best chair began.

"Turn the gas down a bit, will you? Thanks. Did any of you know Herbert Hatteras? He was on this road a good many years. No? well, never mind. He was a good chap, I believe, with good teeth and a black whisker. But I didn't know him myself. He was before my time. Well, this that I'm going to tell you about happened at a certain commercial hotel. I'm not going to give it a name, because that sort of thing gets about, and in every other respect it's a good house and reasonable, and we all have our living to get. It was just a good ordinary old-fashioned commercial hotel, as it might be this. And I've often used it since, though they've never put me in that room again. Perhaps they shut it up after what happened.

"Well, the beginning of it was, I came across an old schoolfellow; in Boulter's Lock one Sunday it was, I remember. Jones was his name, Ted Jones. We both had canoes. We had tea at Marlow, and we got talking about this and that and old times and old mates; and do you remember Jim, and what's become of Tom, and so on. Oh, you know. And I happened to ask after his brother, Fred by name. And Ted turned pale and almost dropped his cup, and he said, 'You don't mean to say you haven't heard?' 'No,' says I, mopping up the tea he'd slopped over with my handkerchief. 'No, what?' I said.

"'It was horrible,' he said. 'They wired for me, and I saw him afterwards. Whether he'd done it himself or not, nobody knows; but they'd found him lying on the floor with his throat cut.' No cause could be assigned for the rash act, Ted told me. I asked him where it had happened, and he told me the name of this hotel— I'm not going to name it. And when I'd sympathised with him and drawn him out about old times and poor old Fred being such a good old sort and all that, I asked him what the room was like. I always like to know what the places look like where things happen.

"No, there wasn't anything specially rum about the room, only that it had a French bed with red curtains in a sort of alcove; and a large mahogany wardrobe as big as a hearse, with a glass door; and, instead of a swing-glass, a carved, black-framed glass screwed up against the wall between the windows, and a picture of 'Belshazzar's Feast' over the mantelpiece. I beg your pardon?" He stopped, for the heavy commercial had opened his mouth and shut it again.

"I thought you were going to say something," the dapper man went on. "Well, we talked about other things and parted, and I thought no more about it till business brought me to—but I'd better not name the town either—and I found my firm had marked this very hotel—where poor Fred had met his death, you know— for me to put up at. And I had to put up there too, because of their addressing everything to me there. And, anyhow, I expect I should have gone there out of curiosity.

"No. I didn't believe in ghosts in those days. I was like you, sir." He nodded amiably to the large commercial.

"The house was very full, and we were quite a large party in the room—very pleasant company, as it might be to-night; and we got talking of ghosts—just as it might be us. And there was a chap in glasses, sitting just over there, I remember— an old hand on the road, he was; and he said, just as it might be any of you, 'I don't believe in ghosts, but I wouldn't care to sleep in Number Seventeen, for all that'; and, of course, we asked him why. 'Because,' said he, very short, 'that's why.'

"But when we'd persuaded him a bit, he told us.

"'Because that's the room where chaps cut their throats,' he said. "There was a chap called Bert Hatteras began it. They found him weltering in his gore. And since that every man that's slept there's been found with his throat cut.'

"I asked him how many had slept there. 'Well, only two beside the first,' he said; 'they shut it up then.' 'Oh, did they?' said I. 'Well, they've opened it again. Number Seventeen's my room!'

"I tell you those chaps looked at me.

"'But you aren't going to *sleep* in it?' one of them said. And I explained that I didn't pay half a dollar for a bedroom to keep awake in.

"'I suppose it's press of business has made them open it up again,' the chap in spectacles said. 'It's a very mysterious affair. There's some secret horror about that room that we don't understand,' he said, 'and I'll tell you another queer thing.

{258}

Every one of those poor chaps was a commercial gentleman. That's what I don't like about it. There was Bert Hatteras—he was the first, and a chap called Jones—Frederick Jones, and then Donald Overshaw—a Scotchman he was, and travelled in children's underclothing.'

"Well, we sat there and talked a bit, and if I hadn't been a Bond of Joy, I don't know that I mightn't have exceeded, gentlemen—yes, positively exceeded; for the more I thought about it the less I liked the thought of Number Seventeen. I hadn't noticed the room particularly, except to see that the furniture had been changed since poor Fred's time. So I just slipped out, by and by, and I went out to the little glass case under the arch where the booking-clerk sits—just like here, that hotel was—and I said:—

"'Look here, miss; haven't you got another room empty except seventeen?'

"'No,' she said; 'I don't think so.'"

"'Then what's that?' I said, and pointed to a key hanging on the board, the only one left.

"'Oh,' she said, 'that's sixteen.'

"'Anyone in sixteen?' I said. 'Is it a comfortable room?'

"'No,' said she. 'Yes; quite comfortable. It's next door to yours—much the same class of room.'

"'Then I'll have sixteen, if you've no objection,' I said, and went back to the others, feeling very clever.

"When I went up to bed I locked my door, and, though I didn't believe in ghosts, I wished seventeen wasn't next door to me, and I wished there wasn't a door between the two rooms, though the door was locked right enough and the key on my side. I'd only got the one candle besides the two on the dressing-table, which I hadn't lighted; and I got my collar and tie off before I noticed that the furniture in my new room was the furniture out of Number Seventeen; French bed with red curtains, mahogany wardrobe as big as a hearse, and the carved mirror over the dressing-table between the two windows, and 'Belshazzar's Feast' over the mantelpiece. So that, though I'd not got the *room* where the commercial gentlemen had cut their throats, I'd got the *furniture* out of it. And for a moment I thought that was worse than the other. When I thought of what that furniture could tell, if it could speak——

"It was a silly thing to do—but we're all friends here and I don't mind owning up—I looked under the bed and I looked inside the hearse-wardrobe and I looked in a sort of narrow cupboard there was, where a body could have stood upright——"

"A body?" I repeated.

"A man, I mean. You see, it seemed to me that either these poor chaps had been murdered by someone who hid himself in Number Seventeen to do it, or else there was something there that frightened them into cutting their throats; and upon my soul, I can't tell you which idea I liked least!"

He paused, and filled his pipe very deliberately. "Go, on," someone said. And he went on.

{259}

"Now, you'll observe," he said, "that all I've told you up to the time of my going to bed that night's just hearsay. So I don't ask you to believe it—though the three coroners' inquests would be enough to stagger most chaps, I should say. Still, what I'm going to tell you now's *my* part of the story—what happened to me myself in that room."

He paused again, holding the pipe in his hand, unlighted.

There was a silence, which I broke.

"Well, what *did* happen?" I asked.

"I had a bit of a struggle with myself," he said. "I reminded myself it was not *that* room, but the next one that it had happened in. I smoked a pipe or two and read the morning paper, advertisements and all. And at last I went to bed. I left the candle burning, though, I own that."

"Did you sleep?" I asked.

"Yes. I slept. Sound as a top. I was awakened by a soft tapping on my door. I sat up. I don't think I've ever been so frightened in my life. But I made myself say, 'Who's there?' in a whisper. Heaven knows I never expected any one to answer. The candle had gone out and it was pitch-dark. There was a quiet murmur and a shuffling sound outside. And no one answered. I tell you I hadn't expected any one to. But I cleared my throat and cried out, 'Who's there?' in a real out-loud voice. And 'Me, sir,' said a voice. 'Shaving-water, sir; six o'clock, sir.'"

"It was the chambermaid."

A movement of relief ran round our circle.

"I don't think much of your story," said the large commercial.

"You haven't heard it yet," said the story-teller, dryly. "It was six o'clock on a winter's morning, and pitch-dark. My train went at seven. I got up and began to dress. My one candle wasn't much use. I lighted the two on the dressing-table to see to shave by. There wasn't any shaving-water outside my door, after all. And the passage was as black as a coal-hole. So I started to shave with cold water; one has to sometimes, you know. I'd gone over my face and I was just going lightly round under my chin, when I saw something move in the looking-glass. I mean something that moved was reflected in the looking-glass. The big door of the wardrobe had swung open, and by a sort of double reflection I could see the French bed with the red curtains. On the edge of it sat a man in his shirt and trousers—a man with black hair and whiskers, with the most awful look of despair and fear on his face that I've ever seen or dreamt of. I stood paralyzed, watching him in the mirror. I could not have turned round to save my life. Suddenly he laughed. It was a horrid, silent laugh, and showed all his teeth. They were very white and even. And the next moment he had cut his throat from ear to ear, there before my eyes. Did you ever see a man cut his throat? The bed was all white before."

The story-teller had laid down his pipe, and he passed his hand over his face before he went on.

"When I could look around I did. There was no one in the room. The bed was as white as ever. Well, that's all," he said, abruptly, "except that now, of course, I

{260}

understood how these poor chaps had come by their deaths. They'd all seen this horror—the ghost of the first poor chap, I suppose—Bert Hatteras, you know; and with the shock their hands must have slipped and their throats got cut before they could stop themselves. Oh! by the way, when I looked at my watch it was two o'clock; there hadn't been any chambermaid at all. I must have dreamed that. But I didn't dream the other. Oh! And one thing more. It was the same room. They hadn't changed the room, they'd only changed the number. *It was the same room!*"

"Look here," said the heavy man; "the room you've been talking about. *My* room's sixteen. And it's got that same furniture in it as what you describe, and the same picture and all."

"Oh, has it?" said the story-teller, a little uncomfortable, it seemed. "I'm sorry. But the cat's out of the bag now, and it can't be helped. Yes, it *was* this house I was speaking of. I suppose they've opened the room again. But you don't believe in ghosts; *you'll* be all right."

"Yes," said the heavy man, and presently got up and left the room.

"He's gone to see if he can get his room changed. You see if he hasn't," said the rabbit-faced man; "and I don't wonder."

The heavy man came back and settled into his chair.

"I could do with a drink," he said, reaching to the bell.

"I'll stand some punch, gentlemen, if you'll allow me," said our dapper story-teller. "I rather pride myself on my punch. I'll step out to the bar and get what I need for it."

"I thought he said he was a teetotaller," said the heavy traveller when he had gone. And then our voices buzzed like a hive of bees. When our story-teller came in again we turned on him—half-a-dozen of us at once—and spoke.

"One at a time," he said, gently. "I didn't quite catch what you said."

"We want to know," I said, "how it was—if seeing that ghost made all those chaps cut their throats by startling them when they were shaving—how was it *you* didn't cut *your* throat when you saw it?"

"I should have," he answered, gravely, "without the slightest doubt—I should have cut my throat, only," he glanced at our heavy friend, "I always shave with a safety razor. I travel in them," he added, slowly, and bisected a lemon.

"But—but," said the large man, when he could speak through our uproar, "I've gone and given up my room."

"Yes," said the dapper man, squeezing the lemon; "I've just had my things moved into it. It's the best room in the house. I always think it worth while to take a little pains to secure it."

Jerry Bundler
W. W. Jacobs

IT wanted a few nights to Christmas, a festival for which the small market town of Torchester was making extensive preparations. The narrow streets which had been thronged with people were now almost deserted; the cheap-jack from London, with the remnant of breath left him after his evening's exertions, was making feeble attempts to blow out his naphtha lamp, and the last shops open were rapidly closing for the night.

In the comfortable coffee-room of the old Boar's Head, half a dozen guests, principally commercial travellers, sat talking by the light of the fire. The talk had drifted from trade to politics, from politics to religion, and so by easy stages to the supernatural. Three ghost stories, never known to fail before, had fallen flat; there was too much noise outside, too much light within. The fourth story was told by an old hand with more success; the streets were quiet, and he had turned the gas out. In the flickering light of the fire, as it shone on the glasses and danced with shadows on the walls, the story proved so enthralling that George, the waiter, whose presence had been forgotten, created a very disagreeable sensation by suddenly starting up from a dark corner and gliding silently from the room. "That's what I call a good story," said one of the men, sipping his hot whisky. "Of course it's an old idea that spirits like to get into the company of human beings. A man told me once that he travelled down the Great Western with a ghost and hadn't the slightest suspicion of it until the inspector came for tickets. My friend said the way that ghost tried to keep up appearances by feeling for it in all its pockets and looking on the floor was quite touching. Ultimately it gave it up and with a faint groan vanished through the ventilator."

"That'll do, Hirst," said another man.

"It's not a subject for jesting," said a little old gentleman who had been an attentive listener. "I've never seen an apparition myself, but I know people who have, and I consider that they form a very interesting link between us and the afterlife. There's a ghost story connected with this house, you know."

"Never heard of it," said another speaker, "and I've been here some years now."

"It dates back a long time now," said the old gentleman. "You've heard about Jerry Bundler, George?"

"Well, I've just 'eard odds and ends, sir," said the old waiter, "but I never put much count to 'em. There was one chap 'ere what said 'e saw it, and the gov'ner sacked 'im prompt."

"My father was a native of this town," said the old gentleman, "and knew the story well. He was a truthful man and a steady churchgoer, but I've heard him declare that once in his life he saw the appearance of Jerry Bundler in this house.".

"And who was this Bundler?" inquired a voice.

"A London thief, pickpocket, highwayman—anything he could turn his dishonest hand to," replied the old gentleman; "and he was run to earth in this

house one Christmas week some eighty years ago. He took his last supper in this very room, and after he had gone up to bed a couple of Bow Street runners, who had followed him from London but lost the scent a bit, went upstairs with the landlord and tried the door. It was stout oak, and fast, so one went into the yard, and by means of a short ladder got onto the window-sill, while the other stayed outside the door. Those below in the yard saw the man crouching on the sill, and then there was a sudden smash of glass, and with a cry he fell in a heap on the stones at their feet. Then in the moonlight they saw the white face of the pickpocket peeping over the sill, and while some stayed in the yard, others ran into the house and helped the other man to break the door in. It was difficult to obtain an entrance even then, for it was barred with heavy furniture, but they got in at last, and the first thing that met their eyes was the body of Jerry dangling from the top of the bed by his own handkerchief."

"Which bedroom was it?" asked two or three voices together.

The narrator shook his head. "That I can't tell you; but the story goes that Jerry still haunts this house, and my father used to declare positively that the last time he slept here the ghost of Jerry Bundler lowered itself from the top of his bed and tried to strangle him."

"That'll do," said an uneasy voice. "I wish you'd thought to ask your father which bedroom it was."

"What for?" inquired the old gentleman.

"Well, I should take care not to sleep in it, that's all," said the voice, shortly.

"There's nothing to fear," said the other. "I don't believe for a moment that ghosts could really-hurt one. In fact my father used to confess that it was only the unpleasantness of the thing that upset him, and that for all practical purposes Jerry's fingers might have been made of cottonwool for all the harm they could do."

"That's all very fine," said the last speaker again; "a ghost story is a ghost story, sir; but when a gentleman tells a tale of a ghost in the house in which one is going to sleep, I call it most ungentlemanly!"

"Pooh! Nonsense!" said the old gentleman, rising; "ghosts can't hurt you. For my own part, I should rather like to see one. Good night, gentlemen."

"Good night," said the others. "And I only hope Jerry'll pay you a visit," added the nervous man as the door closed.

"Bring some more whisky, George," said a stout commercial; "I want keeping up when the talk turns this way."

"Shall I light the gas, Mr. Malcolm?" said George.

"No; the fire's very comfortable," said the traveller. "Now, gentlemen, any of you know any more?"

"I think we've had enough," said another man; "we shall be thinking we see spirits next, and we're not all like the old gentleman who's just gone."

"Old humbug!" said Hirst. "I should like to put him to the test. Suppose I dress up as Jerry Bundler and go and give him a chance of displaying his courage?"

"Bravo!" said Malcolm, huskily, drowning one or two faint "Noes." "Just for the joke, gentlemen."

"No, no! Drop it, Hirst," said another man.

"Only for the joke," said Hirst, somewhat eagerly. "I've got some things upstairs in which I am going to play in the *Rivals*—knee-breeches, buckles, and all that sort of thing. It's a rare chance. If you'll wait a bit I'll give you a full-dress rehearsal, entitled, 'Jerry Bundler; or, The Nocturnal Strangler.'"

"You won't frighten us," said the commercial, with a husky laugh.

"I don't know that," said Hirst, sharply; "it's a question of acting, that's all. I'm pretty good, ain't I, Somers?"

"Oh, you're all right—for an amateur," said his friend, with a laugh.

"I'll bet you a level sov' you don't frighten me," said the stout traveller.

"Done!" said Hirst. "I'll take the bet to frighten you first and the old gentleman afterwards. These gentlemen shall be the judges."

"You won't frighten us, sir," said another man, "because we're prepared for you; but you'd better leave the old man alone. It's dangerous play."

"Well, I'll try you first," said Hirst, springing up. "No gas, mind."

He ran lightly upstairs to his room, leaving the others, most of whom had been drinking somewhat freely, to wrangle about his proceedings. It ended in two of them going to bed.

"He's crazy on acting," said Somers, lighting his pipe. "Thinks he's the equal of anybody almost. It doesn't matter with us, but I won't let him go to the old man. And he won't mind so long as he gets an opportunity of acting to us."

"Well, I hope he'll hurry up," said Malcolm, yawning; "it's after twelve now."

Nearly half an hour passed. Malcolm drew his watch from his pocket and was busy winding it, when George, the waiter, who had been sent on an errand to the bar, burst suddenly into the room and rushed towards them.

"'E's comin', gentlemen," he said breathlessly.

"Why, you're frightened, George," said the stout commercial, with a chuckle.

"It was the suddenness of it," said George, sheepishly; "and besides, I didn't look for seein' 'im in the bar. There's only a glimmer of light there, and 'e was sitting on the floor behind the bar. I nearly trod on 'im."

"Oh, you'll never make a man, George," said Malcolm.

"Well, it took me unawares," said the waiter. "Not that I'd have gone to the bar by myself if I'd known 'e was there, and I don't believe you would either, sir."

"Nonsense!" said Malcolm. "I'll go and fetch him in."

"You don't know what it's like, sir," said George, catching him by the sleeve. "It ain't fit to look at by yourself, it ain't, indeed. It's got the—*What's that*?"

They all started at the sound of a smothered cry from the staircase and the sound of somebody running hurriedly along the passage. Before anybody could speak, the door flew open and a figure bursting into the room flung itself gasping and shivering upon them.

{265}

"What is it? What's the matter?" demanded Malcolm. "Why, it's Mr. Hirst." He shook him roughly and then held some spirit to his lips. Hirst drank it greedily and with a sharp intake of his breath gripped him by the arm.

"Light the gas, George," said Malcolm.

The waiter obeyed hastily. Hirst, a ludicrous but pitiable figure in knee-breeches and coat, a large wig all awry and his face a mess of grease paint, clung to him, trembling.

"Now, what's the matter?" asked Malcolm.

"I've seen it," said Hirst, with a hysterical sob. "O Lord, I'll never play the fool again, never!"

"Seen what?" said the others.

"Him—it—the ghost—anything!" said Hirst, wildly.

"Rot!" said Malcolm, uneasily.

"I was coming down the stairs," said Hirst. "Just capering down—as I thought—it ought to do. I felt a tap—"

He broke off suddenly and peered nervously through the open door into the passage.

"I thought I saw it again," he whispered.

"Look—at the foot of the stairs. Can you see anything?"

"No, there's nothing there," said Malcolm, whose own voice shook a little. "Go on. You felt a tap on your shoulder—"

"I turned round and saw it—a little wicked head and a white dead face. Pah!"

"That's what I saw in the bar," said George. "'Orrid it was—devilish!"

Hirst shuddered, and, still retaining his nervous grip of Malcolm's sleeve, dropped into a chair.

"Well, it's a most unaccountable thing," said the dumbfounded Malcolm, turning round to the others. "It's the last time I come to this house."

"I leave to-morrow," said George. "I wouldn't go down to that bar again by myself, no, not for fifty pounds!"

"It's talking about the thing that's caused it, I expect," said one of the men; "we've all been talking about this and having it in our minds. Practically we've been forming a spiritualistic circle without knowing it."

"Hang the old gentleman!" said Malcolm, heartily. "Upon my soul, I'm half afraid to go to bed. It's odd they should both think they saw something."

"I saw it as plain as I see you, sir," said George, solemnly. "P'raps if you keep your eyes turned up the passage you'll see it for yourself."

They followed the direction of his finger, but saw nothing, although one of them fancied that a head peeped round the corner of the wall.

"Who'll come down to the bar?" said Malcolm, looking round.

"You can go, if you like," said one of the others, with a faint laugh; "we'll wait here for you."

The stout traveller walked towards the door and took a few steps up the passage. Then he stopped. All was quite silent, and he walked slowly to the end and looked down fearfully towards the glass partition which shut off the bar. Three times he made as though to go to it; then he turned back, and, glancing over his shoulder, came hurriedly back to the room.

"Did you see it, sir?" whispered George.

"Don't know," said Malcolm, shortly. "I fancied I saw something, but it might have been fancy. I'm in the mood to see anything just now. How are you feeling now, sir?"

"Oh, I feel a bit better now," said Hirst, somewhat brusquely, as all eyes were turned upon him.

"I dare say you think I'm easily scared, but you didn't see it."

"Not at all," said Malcolm, smiling faintly despite himself.

"I'm going to bed," said Hirst, noticing the smile and resenting it. "Will you share my room with me, Somers?"

"I will with pleasure," said his friend, "provided you don't mind sleeping with the gas on full all night."

He rose from his seat, and bidding the company a friendly good-night, left the room with his crestfallen friend. The others saw them to the foot of the stairs, and having heard their door close, returned to the coffee-room.

"Well, I suppose the bet's off?" said the stout commercial, poking the fire and then standing with his legs apart on the hearthrug; "though, as far as I can see, I won it. I never saw a man so scared in all my life. Sort of poetic justice about it, isn't there?"

"Never mind about poetry or justice," said one of his listeners; "who's going to sleep with me?"

"I will," said Malcolm, affably.

"And I suppose we share a room together, Mr. Leek?" said the third man, turning to the fourth.

"No, thank you," said the other, briskly; "I don't believe in ghosts. If anything comes into my room I shall shoot it."

"That won't hurt a spirit, Leek," said Malcolm, decisively.

"Well the noise'll be like company to me," said Leek, "and it'll wake the house too. But if you're nervous, sir," he added, with a grin, to the man who had suggested sharing his room, "George'll be only too pleased to sleep on the door-mat inside your room, I know."

"That I will, sir," said George, fervently; "and if you gentlemen would only come down with me to the bar to put the gas out, I could never be sufficiently grateful."

They went out in a body, with the exception of Leek, peering carefully before them as they went George turned the light out in the bar and they returned unmolested to the coffee-room, and, avoiding the sardonic smile of Leek, prepared to separate for the night.

"Give me the candle while you put the gas out, George," said the traveller.

The waiter handed it to him and extinguished the gas, and at the same moment all distinctly heard a step in the passage outside. It stopped at the door, and as they watched with bated breath, the door creaked and slowly opened. Malcolm fell back open-mouthed, as a white, leering face, with sunken eyeballs and close-cropped bullet head, appeared at the opening.

For a few seconds the creature stood regarding them, blinking in a strange fashion at the candle. Then, with a sidling movement, it came a little way into the room and stood there as if bewildered.

Not a man spoke or moved, but all watched with a horrible fascination as the creature removed its dirty neckcloth and its head rolled on its shoulder. For a minute it paused, and then, holding the rag before it, moved towards Malcolm.

The candle went out suddenly with a flash and a bang. There was a smell of powder, and something writhing in the darkness on the floor. A faint, choking cough, and then silence. Malcolm was the first to speak. "Matches," he said, in a strange voice. George struck one. Then he leapt at the gas and a burner flamed from the match. Malcolm touched the thing on the floor with his foot and found it soft. He looked at his companions. They mouthed inquiries at him, but he shook his head. He lit the candle, and, kneeling down, examined the silent thing on the floor. Then he rose swiftly, and dipping his handkerchief in the water-jug, bent down again and grimly wiped the white face. Then he sprang back with a cry of incredulous horror, pointing at it. Leek's pistol fell to the floor and he shut out the sight with his hands, but the others, crowding forward, gazed spell-bound at the dead face of Hirst.

Before a word was spoken the door opened and Somers hastily entered the room. His eyes fell on the floor. "Good God!" he cried. "You didn't—"

Nobody spoke.

"I told him not to," he said, in a suffocating voice. "I told him not to. I told him—"

He leaned against the wall, deathly sick, put his arms out feebly, and fell fainting into the traveller's arms.

THE PHANTOM COACH
Amelia B. Edwards

THE circumstances I am about to relate to you have truth to recommend them. They happened to myself, and my recollection of them is as vivid as if they had taken place only yesterday. Twenty years, however, have gone by since that night. During those twenty years I have told the story to but one other person. I tell it now with a reluctance which I find it difficult to overcome. All I entreat, meanwhile, is that you will abstain from forcing your own conclusions upon me. I want nothing explained away. I desire no arguments. My mind on this subject is quite made up, and, having the testimony of my own senses to rely upon, I prefer to abide by it.

Well! It was just twenty years ago, and within a day or two of the end of the grouse season. I had been out all day with my gun, and had had no sport to speak of. The wind was due east; the month, December; the place, a bleak wide moor in the far north of England. And I had lost my way. It was not a pleasant place in which to lose one's way, with the first feathery flakes of a coming snowstorm just fluttering down upon the heather, and the leaden evening closing in all around. I shaded my eyes with my hand, and staled anxiously into the gathering darkness, where the purple moorland melted into a range of low hills, some ten or twelve miles distant. Not the faintest smoke-wreath, not the tiniest cultivated patch, or fence, or sheep-track, met my eyes in any direction. There was nothing for it but to walk on, and take my chance of finding what shelter I could, by the way. So I shouldered my gun again, and pushed wearily forward; for I had been on foot since an hour after daybreak, and had eaten nothing since breakfast.

Meanwhile, the snow began to come down with ominous steadiness, and the wind fell. After this, the cold became more intense, and the night came rapidly up. As for me, my prospects darkened with the darkening sky, and my heart grew heavy as I thought how my young wife was already watching for me through the window of our little inn parlour, and thought of all the suffering in store for her throughout this weary night. We had been married four months, and, having spent our autumn in the Highlands, were now lodging in a remote little village situated just on the verge of the great English moorlands. We were very much in love, and, of course, very happy. This morning, when we parted, she had implored me to return before dusk, and I had promised her that I would. What would I not have given to have kept my word!

Even now, weary as I was, I felt that with a supper, an hour's rest, and a guide, I might still get back to her before midnight, if only guide and shelter could be found.

And all this time, the snow fell and the night thickened. I stopped and shouted every now and then, but my shouts seemed only to make the silence deeper. Then a vague sense of uneasiness came upon me, and I began to remember stories of travellers who had walked on and on in the falling snow until, wearied out, they

were fain to lie down and sleep their lives away. Would it be possible, I asked myself, to keep on thus through all the long dark night? Would there not come a time when my limbs must fail, and my resolution give way? When I, too, must sleep the sleep of death. Death! I shuddered. How hard to die just now, when life lay all so bright before me! How hard for my darling, whose whole loving heart but that thought was not to be borne! To banish it, I shouted again, louder and longer, and then listened eagerly. Was my shout answered, or did I only fancy that I heard a far-off cry? I halloed again, and again the echo followed. Then a wavering speck of light came suddenly out of the dark, shifting, disappearing, growing momentarily nearer and brighter. Running towards it at full speed, I found myself, to my great joy, face to face with an old man and a lantern.

"Thank God!" was the exclamation that burst involuntarily from my lips. Blinking and frowning, he lifted his lantern and peered into my face. "What for?" growled he, sulkily.

"Well—for you. I began to fear I should be lost in the snow."

"Eh, then, folks do get cast away hereabouts fra' time to time, an' what's to hinder you from bein' cast away likewise, if the Lord's so minded?"

"If the Lord is so minded that you and I shall be lost together, friend, we must submit," I replied; "but I don't mean to be lost without you. How far am I now from Dwolding?"

"A gude twenty mile, more or less." "And the nearest village?"

"The nearest village is Wyke, an' that's twelve mile t'other side." "Where do you live, then?"

"Out yonder," said he, with a vague jerk of the lantern. "You're going home, I presume?"

"Maybe I am."

"Then I'm going with you."

The old man shook his head, and rubbed his nose reflectively with the handle of the lantern.

"It ain't o' no use," growled he. "He 'ont let you in—not he."

"We'll see about that," I replied, briskly. "Who is He?"

"The master."

"Who is the master?"

"That's nowt to you," was the unceremonious reply.

"Well, well; you lead the way, and I'll engage that the master shall give me shelter and a supper to-night."

"Eh, you can try him!" muttered my reluctant guide; and, still shaking his head, he hobbled, gnome-like, away through the falling snow. A large mass loomed up presently out of the darkness, and a huge dog rushed out, barking furiously.

"Is this the house?" I asked.

"Ay, it's the house. Down, Bey!"

And he fumbled in his pocket for the key. I drew up close behind him, prepared to lose no chance of entrance, and saw in the little circle of light shed by the lantern that the door was heavily studded with iron nails, like the door of a prison.

In another minute he had turned the key and I had pushed past him into the house.

Once inside, I looked round with curiosity, and found myself in a great raftered hall, which served, apparently, a variety of uses. One end was piled to the roof with corn, like a barn. The other was stored with flour-sacks, agricultural implements, casks, and all kinds of miscellaneous lumber; while from the beams overhead hung rows of hams, flitches, and bunches of dried herbs for winter use. In the centre of the floor stood some huge object gauntly dressed in a dingy wrapping-cloth, and reaching half way to the rafters. Lifting a corner of this cloth, I saw, to my surprise, a telescope of very considerable size, mounted on a rude movable platform, with four small wheels. The tube was made of painted wood, bound round with bands of metal rudely fashioned; the speculum, so far as I could estimate its size in the dim light, measured at least fifteen inches in diameter. While I was yet examining the instrument, and asking myself whether it was not the work of some self-taught optician, a bell rang sharply.

"That's for you," said my guide, with a malicious grin. "Yonder's his room." He pointed to a low black door at the opposite side of the hall. I crossed over, rapped somewhat loudly, and went in, without waiting for an invitation. A huge, white-haired old man rose from a table covered with books and papers, and confronted me sternly.

"Who are you?" said he. "How came you here? What do you want?" "James Murray, barrister-at-law. On foot across the moor. Meat, drink, and sleep."

He bent his bushy brows into a portentous frown.

"Mine is not a house of entertainment," he said, haughtily. "Jacob, how dared you admit this stranger?"

"I didn't admit him," grumbled the old man. "He followed me over the muir, and shouldered his way in before me. I'm no match for six foot two."

"And pray, sir, by what right have you forced an entrance into my house?" "The same by which I should have clung to your boat, if I were drowning. The right of self-preservation." "Self-preservation?"

"There's an inch of snow on the ground already," I replied, briefly; "and it would be deep enough to cover my body before daybreak."

He strode to the window, pulled aside a heavy black curtain, and looked out.

"It is true," he said. "You can stay, if you choose, till morning. Jacob, serve the supper."

With this he waved me to a seat, resumed his own, and became at once absorbed in the studies from which I had disturbed him.

I placed my gun in a corner, drew a chair to the hearth, and examined my quarters at leisure. Smaller and less incongruous in its arrangements than the hall, this room contained, nevertheless, much to awaken my curiosity. The floor was carpetless. The whitewashed walls were in parts scrawled over with strange diagrams, and in others covered with shelves crowded with philosophical instruments, the uses of many of which were unknown to me. On one side of the fireplace, stood a bookcase filled with dingy folios; on the other, a small organ, fantastically decorated with painted carvings of mediæval saints and devils. Through the half-opened door of a cupboard at the further end of the room, I saw a long array of geological specimens, surgical preparations, crucibles, retorts, and jars of chemicals; while on the mantelshelf beside me, amid a number of small objects, stood a model of the solar system, a small galvanic battery, and a microscope. Every chair had its burden. Every corner was heaped high with books. The very floor was littered over with maps, casts, papers, tracings, and learned lumber of all conceivable kinds.

I stared about me with an amazement increased by every fresh object upon which my eyes chanced to rest. So strange a room I had never seen; yet seemed it stranger still, to find such a room in a lone farmhouse amid those wild and solitary moors! Over and over again, I looked from my host to his surroundings, and from his surroundings back to my host, asking myself who and what he could be? His head was singularly fine; but it was more the head of a poet than of a philosopher. Broad in the temples, prominent over the eyes, and clothed with a rough profusion of perfectly white hair, it had all the ideality and much of the ruggedness that characterises the head of Louis von Beethoven. There were the same deep lines about the mouth, and the same stern furrows in the brow. There was the same concentration of expression. While I was yet observing him, the door opened, and Jacob brought in the supper. His master then closed his book, rose, and with more courtesy of manner than he had yet shown, invited me to the table.

A dish of ham and eggs, a loaf of brown bread, and a bottle of admirable sherry, were placed before me.

"I have but the homeliest farmhouse fare to offer you, sir," said my entertainer. "Your appetite, I trust, will make up for the deficiencies of our larder."

I had already fallen upon the viands, and now protested, with the enthusiasm of a starving sportsman, that I had never eaten anything so delicious.

He bowed stiffly, and sat down to his own supper, which consisted, primitively, of a jug of milk and a basin of porridge. We ate in silence, and, when we had done, Jacob removed the tray. I then drew my chair back to the fireside. My host, somewhat to my surprise, did the same, and turning abruptly towards me, said:

"Sir, I have lived here in strict retirement for three-and-twenty years. During that time, I have not seen as many strange faces, and I have not read a single newspaper. You are the first stranger who has crossed my threshold for more than four years. Will you favour me with a few words of information respecting that outer world from which I have parted company so long?"

"Pray interrogate me," I replied. "I am heartily at your service."

He bent his head in acknowledgment; leaned forward, with his elbows resting on his knees and his chin supported in the palms of his hands; stared fixedly into the fire; and proceeded to question me.

His inquiries related chiefly to scientific matters, with the later progress of which, as applied to the practical purposes of life, he was almost wholly unacquainted. No student of science myself, I replied as well as my slight information permitted; but the task was far from easy, and I was much relieved when, passing from interrogation to discussion, he began pouring forth his own conclusions upon the facts which I had been attempting to place before him. He talked, and I listened spellbound. He talked till I believe he almost forgot my presence, and only thought aloud. I had never heard anything like it then; I have never heard anything like it since. Familiar with all systems of all philosophies, subtle in analysis, bold in generalisation, he poured forth his thoughts in an uninterrupted stream, and, still leaning forward in the same moody attitude with his eyes fixed upon the fire, wandered from topic to topic, from speculation to speculation, like an inspired dreamer. From practical science to mental philosophy; from electricity in the wire to electricity in the nerve; from Watts to Mesmer, from Mesmer to Reichenbach, from Reichenbach to Swedenborg, Spinoza, Condillac, Descartes, Berkeley, Aristotle, Plato, and the Magi and mystics of the East, were transitions which, however bewildering in their variety and scope, seemed easy and harmonious upon his lips as sequences in music. By-and-by—I forget now by what link of conjecture or illustration—he passed on to that field which lies beyond the boundary line of even conjectural philosophy, and reaches no man knows whither. He spoke of the soul and its aspirations; of the spirit and its powers; of second sight; of prophecy; of those phenomena which, under the names of ghosts, spectres, and supernatural appearances, have been denied by the sceptics and attested by the credulous, of all ages.

"The world," he said, "grows hourly more and more sceptical of all that lies beyond its own narrow radius; and our men of science foster the fatal tendency. They condemn as fable all that resists experiment. They reject as false all that cannot be brought to the test of the laboratory or the dissecting-room. Against what superstition have they waged so long and obstinate a war, as against the belief in apparitions? And yet what superstition has maintained its hold upon the minds of men so long and so firmly? Show me any fact in physics, in history, in archæology, which is supported by testimony so wide and so various. Attested by all races of men, in all ages, and in all climates, by the soberest sages of antiquity, by the rudest savage of to-day, by the Christian, the Pagan, the Pantheist, the Materialist, this phenomenon is treated as a nursery tale by the philosophers of our century. Circumstantial evidence weighs with them as a feather in the balance. The comparison of causes with effects, however valuable in physical science, is put aside as worthless and unreliable. The evidence of competent witnesses, however conclusive in a court of justice, counts for nothing. He who pauses before he pronounces, is condemned as a trifler. He who believes, is a dreamer or a fool."

He spoke with bitterness, and, having said thus, relapsed for some minutes into silence. Presently he raised his head from his hands, and added, with an altered voice and manner, "I, sir, paused, investigated, believed, and was not ashamed to state my convictions to the world. I, too, was branded as a visionary, held up to ridicule by my contemporaries, and hooted from that field of science in which I had laboured with honour during all the best years of my life. These things happened just three-and-twenty years ago. Since then, I have lived as you see me living now, and the world has forgotten me, as I have forgotten the world. You have my history."

"It is a very sad one," I murmured, scarcely knowing what to answer. "It is a very common one," he replied. "I have only suffered for the truth, as many a better and wiser man has suffered before me."

He rose, as if desirous of ending the conversation, and went over to the window.

"It has ceased snowing," he observed, as he dropped the curtain, and came back to the fireside.

"Ceased!" I exclaimed, starting eagerly to my feet. "Oh, if it were only possible--but no! it is hopeless. Even if I could find my way across the moor, I could not walk twenty miles to-night."

"Walk twenty miles to-night!" repeated my host. "What are you thinking of?"

"Of my wife," I replied, impatiently. "Of my young wife, who does not know that I have lost my way, and who is at this moment breaking her heart with suspense and terror."

"Where is she?"

"At Dwolding, twenty miles away."

"At Dwolding," he echoed, thoughtfully. "Yes, the distance, it is true, is twenty miles; but—are you so very anxious to save the next six or eight hours?"

"So very, very anxious, that I would give ten guineas at this moment for a guide and a horse."

"Your wish can be gratified at a less costly rate," said he, smiling. "The night mail from the north, which changes horses at Dwolding, passes within five miles of this spot, and will be due at a certain cross-road in about an hour and a quarter. If Jacob were to go with you across the moor, and put you into the old coach-road, you could find your way, I suppose, to where it joins the new one?"

"Easily—gladly."

He smiled again, rang the bell, gave the old servant his directions, and, taking a bottle of whisky and a wineglass from the cupboard in which he kept his chemicals, said:

"The snow lies deep, and it will be difficult walking to-night on the moor. A glass of usquebaugh before you start?"

I would have declined the spirit, but he pressed it on me, and I drank it. It went down my throat like liquid flame, and almost took my breath away.

"It is strong," he said; "but it will help to keep out the cold. And now you have no moments to spare. Good night!"

I thanked him for his hospitality, and would have shaken hands, but that he had turned away before I could finish my sentence. In another minute I had traversed the hall, Jacob had locked the outer door behind me, and we were out on the wide white moor.

Although the wind had fallen, it was still bitterly cold. Not a star glimmered in the black vault overhead. Not a sound, save the rapid crunching of the snow beneath our feet, disturbed the heavy stillness of the night. Jacob, not too well pleased with his mission, shambled on before in sullen silence, his lantern in his hand, and his shadow at his feet. I followed, with my gun over my shoulder, as little inclined for conversation as himself. My thoughts were full of my late host. His voice yet rang in my ears. His eloquence yet held my imagination captive. I remember to this day, with surprise, how my over-excited brain retained whole sentences and parts of sentences, troops of brilliant images, and fragments of splendid reasoning, in the very words in which he had uttered them. Musing thus over what I had heard, and striving to recall a lost link here and there, I strode on at the heels of my guide, absorbed and unobservant. Presently—at the end, as it seemed to me, of only a few minutes—he came to a sudden halt, and said:

"Yon's your road. Keep the stone fence to your right hand, and you can't fail of the way."

"This, then, is the old coach-road?" "Ay, 'tis the old coach-road."

"And how far do I go, before I reach the crossroads?" "Nigh upon three mile."

I pulled out my purse, and he became more communicative.

"The road's a fair road enough," said he, "for foot passengers; but 'twas over steep and narrow for the northern traffic. You'll mind where the parapet's broken away, close again the sign-post. It's never been mended since the accident."

"What accident?"

"Eh, the night mail pitched right over into the valley below—a gude fifty feet an' more—just at the worst bit o' road in the whole county."

"Horrible! Were many lives lost?"

"All. Four were found dead, and t'other two died next morning."

"How long is it since this happened?"

"Just nine year."

"Near the sign-post, you say? I will bear it in mind. Good night."

"Gude night, sir, and thankee." Jacob pocketed his half-crown, made a faint pretence of touching his hat, and trudged back by the way he had come.

I watched the light of his lantern till it quite disappeared, and then turned to pursue my way alone. This was no longer matter of the slightest difficulty, for, despite the dead darkness overhead, the line of stone fence showed distinctly enough against the pale gleam of the snow. How silent it seemed now, with only my footsteps to listen to; how silent and how solitary! A strange disagreeable sense of loneliness stole over me. I walked faster. I hummed a fragment of a tune. I cast up enormous sums in my head, and accumulated them at compound interest. I did my best, in short, to forget the startling speculations to which I had but just been listening, and, to some extent, I succeeded.

Meanwhile the night air seemed to become colder and colder, and though I walked fast I found it impossible to keep myself warm. My feet were like ice. I lost sensation in my hands, and grasped my gun mechanically. I even breathed with difficulty, as though, instead of traversing a quiet north country highway, I were scaling the uppermost heights of some gigantic Alp. This last symptom became presently so distressing, that I was forced to stop for a few minutes, and lean against the stone fence. As I did so, I chanced to look back up the road, and there, to my infinite relief, I saw a distant point of light, like the gleam of an approaching lantern. I at first concluded that Jacob had retraced his steps and followed me; but even as the conjecture presented itself, a second light flashed into sight—a light evidently parallel with the first, and approaching at the same rate of motion. It needed no second thought to show me that these must be the carriage-lamps of some private vehicle, though it seemed strange that any private vehicle should take a road professedly disused and dangerous

There could be no doubt, however, of the fact, for the lamps grew larger and brighter every moment, and I even fancied I could already see the dark outline of the carriage between them. It was coming up very fast, and quite noiselessly, the snow being nearly a foot deep under the wheels.

And now the body of the vehicle became distinctly visible behind the lamps. It looked strangely lofty. A sudden suspicion flashed upon me. Was it possible that I had passed the cross-roads in the dark without observing the sign-post, and could this be the very coach which I had come to meet?

No need to ask myself that question a second time, for here it came round the bend of the road, guard and driver, one outside passenger, and four steaming greys, all wrapped in a soft haze of light, through which the lamps blazed out, like a pair of fiery meteors.

I jumped forward, waved my hat, and shouted. The mail came down at full speed, and passed me. For a moment I feared that I had not been seen or heard, but it was only for a moment. The coachman pulled up; the guard, muffled to the eyes in capes and comforters, and apparently sound asleep in the rumble, neither answered my hail nor made the slightest effort to dismount; the outside passenger did not even turn his head. I opened the door for myself, and looked in. There were but three travellers inside, so I stepped in, shut the door, slipped into the vacant corner, and congratulated myself on my good fortune.

The atmosphere of the coach seemed, if possible, colder than that of the outer air, and was pervaded by a singularly damp and disagreeable smell. I looked round at my fellow-passengers. They were all three, men, and all silent. They did not seem to be asleep, but each leaned back in his corner of the vehicle, as if absorbed in his own reflections. I attempted to open a conversation.

"How intensely cold it is to-night," I said, addressing my opposite neighbour.

He lifted his head, looked at me, but made no reply.

"The winter," I added, "seems to have begun in earnest."

Although the corner in which he sat was so dim that I could distinguish none of his features very clearly, I saw that his eyes were still turned full upon me. And yet he answered never a word.

At any other time I should have felt, and perhaps expressed, some annoyance, but at the moment I felt too ill to do either. The icy coldness of the night air had struck a chill to my very marrow, and the strange smell inside the coach was affecting me with an intolerable nausea. I shivered from head to foot, and, turning to my left-hand neighbour, asked if he had any objection to an open window?

He neither spoke nor stirred.

I repeated the question somewhat more loudly, but with the same result. Then I lost patience, and let the sash down. As I did so, the leather strap broke in my hand, and I observed that the glass was covered with a thick coat of mildew, the accumulation, apparently, of years. My attention being thus drawn to the condition of the coach, I examined it more narrowly, and saw by the uncertain light of the outer lamps that it was in the last stage of dilapidation. Every part of it was not only out of repair, but in a condition of decay. The sashes splintered at a touch. The leather fittings were crusted over with mould, and literally rotting from the woodwork. The floor was almost breaking away beneath my feet. The whole machine, in short, was foul with damp, and had evidently been dragged from some outhouse in which it had been mouldering away for years, to do another day or two of duty on the road.

I turned to the third passenger, whom I had not yet addressed, and hazarded one more remark.

"This coach," I said, "is in a deplorable condition. The regular mail, I suppose, is under repair?"

He moved his head slowly, and looked me in the face, without speaking a word. I shall never forget that look while I live. I turned cold at heart under it. I turn cold at heart even now when I recall it. His eyes glowed with a fiery unnatural lustre. His face was livid as the face of a corpse. His bloodless lips were drawn back as if in the agony of death, and showed the gleaming teeth between.

The words that I was about to utter died upon my lips, and a strange horror—a dreadful horror—came upon me. My sight had by this time become used to the gloom of the coach, and I could see with tolerable distinctness. I turned to my opposite neighbour. He, too, was looking at me, with the same startling pallor in his face, and the same stony glitter in his eyes. I passed my hand across my brow. I turned to the passenger on the seat beside my own, and saw—oh Heaven! how shall I describe what I saw? I saw that he was no living man—that none of them were living men, like myself! A pale phosphorescent light—the light of putrefaction—played upon their awful faces; upon their hair, dank with the dews of the grave; upon their clothes, earth-stained and dropping to pieces; upon their hands, which were as the hands of corpses long buried. Only their eyes, their terrible eyes, were living; and those eyes were all turned menacingly upon me!

A shriek of terror, a wild unintelligible cry for help and mercy; burst from my lips as I flung myself against the door, and strove in vain to open it.

In that single instant, brief and vivid as a landscape beheld in the flash of summer lightning, I saw the moon shining down through a rift of stormy cloud— the ghastly sign-post rearing its warning finger by the wayside— the broken parapet—the plunging horses—the black gulf below. Then, the coach reeled like a ship at sea. Then, came a mighty crash—a sense of crushing pain—and then, darkness.

ട

It seemed as if years had gone by when I awoke one morning from a deep sleep, and found my wife watching by my bedside I will pass over the scene that ensued, and give you, in half a dozen words, the tale she told me with tears of thanksgiving. I had fallen over a precipice, close against the junction of the old coach-road and the new, and had only been saved from certain death by lighting upon a deep snowdrift that had accumulated at the foot of the rock beneath. In this snowdrift I was discovered at daybreak, by a couple of shepherds, who carried me to the nearest shelter, and brought a surgeon to my aid. The surgeon found me in a state of raving delirium, with a broken arm and a compound fracture of the skull. The letters in my pocket-book showed my name and address; my wife was summoned to nurse me; and, thanks to youth and a fine constitution, I came out of danger at last. The place of my fall, I need scarcely say, was precisely that at which a frightful accident had happened to the north mail nine years before.

I never told my wife the fearful events which I have just related to you. I told the surgeon who attended me; but he treated the whole adventure as a mere dream born of the fever in my brain. We discussed the question over and over again, until we found that we could discuss it with temper no longer, and then we dropped it. Others may form what conclusions they please—I know that twenty years ago I was the fourth inside passenger in that Phantom Coach.

THE HOSTEL
Guy de Maupassant

LIKE all the wooden inns in the higher Alps, which are situated in the rocky and bare gorges which intersect the white summits of the mountains, the inn of Schwarenbach stands as a refuge for travelers who are crossing the Gemmi.

It remains open for six months in the year, and is inhabited by the family of Jean Hauser; then, as soon as the snow begins to fall, and fills the valley so as to make the road down to Loëche impassable, the father and his three sons go away, and leave the house in charge of the old guide, Gaspard Hari, with the young guide, Ulrich Kunzi, and Sam, the great mountain dog.

The two men and the dog remained till the spring in their snowy prison, with nothing before their eyes except the immense, white slopes of the Balmhorn; they were surrounded by light, glistening summits, and shut up, blocked up and buried by the snow which rose around them, and which enveloped, bound and crushed the little house, which lay piled on the roof, reached to the windows and blocked up the door.

It was the day on which the Hauser family were going to return to Loëche, as winter was approaching, and the descent was becoming dangerous. Three mules started first, laden with baggage and led by the three sons. Then the mother, Jean Hauser and her daughter Louise mounted a fourth mule, and set off in their turn, and the father followed them, accompanied by the two men in charge, who were to escort the family as far as the brow of the descent. First of all they passed round the small lake, which was now frozen over, at the bottom of the mass of rocks which stretched in front of the inn, and then they followed the valley, which was dominated on all sides by the snow covered summits.

A ray of sunlight fell into that little white, glistening, frozen desert, and illuminated it with a cold and dazzling flame; no living thing appeared among this ocean of hills; there was nothing more in this immeasurable solitude, and no noise disturbed the profound silence.

By degrees the young guide Ulrich Kunzi, a tall, long legged Swiss, left daddy Hauser and old Gaspard behind, in order to catch up to the mule, which carried the two women. The younger one looked at him as he approached, and appeared to be calling him, with her sad eyes. She was a young, light haired peasant girl, whose milk white cheeks and pale hair looked as if they had lost their color by their long abode amidst the ice. When he had got up with the animal which carried them, he put his hand on the crupper, and relaxed his speed. Mother Hauser began to talk to him, and enumerated with the minutest details all that he would have to attend to during the winter. It was the first time that he was going to stop up there, while old Hari had already spent fourteen winters amidst the snow, at the inn of Schwarenbach.

Ulrich Kunzi listened, without appearing to understand, and looked incessantly at the girl. From time to time he replied: "Yes, Madame Hauser;" but his thoughts seemed far away, and his calm features remained unmoved.

They reached Lake Daube, whose broad, frozen surface extended to the bottom of the valley. On the right, the Daubenhorn showed its black rocks, rising up in a peak above the enormous moraines of the Lömmeon glacier, which rose above the Wildstrubel. As they approached the neck of the Gemmi, where the descent to Loëche begins, they suddenly beheld the immense horizon of the Alps of the Valais, from which the broad, deep valley of the Rhone separated them.

In the distance, there was a group of white, unequal flat or pointed mountain summits, which glistened in the sun; the Mischabel with its two peaks, the huge group of the Weisshorn, the heavy Brunegghorn, the lofty and formidable pyramid of Mont Cervin, that slayer of men, and the Dent–Blanche, that terrible coquette.

Then, beneath them, in a tremendous hole, at the bottom of a terrible abyss, they perceived Loëche, where houses looked as grains of sand which had been thrown in that enormous crevice, which finishes and closes the Gemmi, and which opens, down below, onto the Rhone.

The mule stopped at the edge of the path, which goes turning and twisting continually, and which comes back fantastically and strangely, along the side of the mountain, as far as the almost invisible little village at its feet. The women jumped into the snow, and the two old men joined them. "Well," father Hauser said, "good-bye, and keep up your spirits till next year, my friends," and old Hari replied: "Till next year."

They embraced each other, and then Madame Hauser in her turn, offered her cheek, and the girl did the same.

When Ulrich Kunzi's turn came, he whispered in Louise's ear: "Do not forget those up yonder," and she replied: "no," in such a low voice, that he guessed what she had said, without hearing it. "Well, adieu," Jean Hauser repeated, "and don't fall ill." And going before the two women, he commenced the descent, and soon all three disappeared at the first turn in the road, while the two men returned to the inn at Schwarenbach.

They walked slowly, side by side, without speaking. It was over, and they would be alone together for four or five months. Then Gaspard Bari began to relate his life last winter. He had remained with Michael Canol, who was too old now to stand it; for an accident might happen during that long solitude. They had not been dull, however; the only thing was to make up one's mind to it from the first, and in the end one would find plenty of distraction, games and other means of whiling away the time.

Ulrich Kunzi listened to him with his eyes on the ground, for in his thoughts he was following those who were descending to the village. They soon came in sight of the inn, which was, however, scarcely visible, so small did it look, a black speck at the foot of that enormous billow of snow, and when they opened the door, Sam, the great curly dog, began to romp round them.

"Come, my boy," old Gaspard said, "we have no women now, so we must get our own dinner ready. Go and peel the potatoes." And they both sat down on wooden stools, and began to put the bread into the soup.

The next morning seemed very long to Kunzi. Old Hari smoked and spat onto the hearth, while the young man looked out of the window at the snow-covered mountain opposite the house.

In the afternoon he went out, and going over yesterday's ground again, he looked for the traces of the mule that had carried the two women; then when he had reached the neck of the Gemmi, he laid himself down on his stomach and looked at Loëche.

The village, in its rocky pit, was not yet buried under the snow, although it came quite close to it, but it was stopped short by the pine woods which protected it. Its low houses looked like paving stones in a large meadow, from up there. Hauser's little daughter was there now, in one of those gray colored houses. In which? Ulrich Kunzi was too far away to be able to make them out separately. How he would have liked to go down, while he was yet able!

But the sun had disappeared behind the lofty crest of the Wildstrubel, and the young man returned to the chalet. Daddy Hari was smoking, and when he saw his mate come in, he proposed a game of cards to him, and they sat down opposite each other, on either side of the table. They played for a long time, a simple game called *brisque*, and then they had supper and went to bed.

The following days were like the first, bright and cold, without any more snow. Old Gaspard spent his afternoons in watching the eagles and other rare birds which ventured onto those frozen heights, while Ulrich returned regularly to the neck of the Gemmi to look at the village. Then they played at cards, dice or dominoes, and lost and won a trifle, just to create an interest in the game.

One morning Hari, who was up first, called his companion. A moving deep and light cloud of white spray was falling on them noiselessly, and was by degrees burying them under a thick, dark coverlet of foam, and that lasted four days and four nights. It was necessary to free the door and the windows, to dig out a passage and to cut steps to get over this frozen powder, which a twelve hours frost had made as hard as the granite of the moraines.

They lived like prisoners, and did not venture outside their abode. They had divided their duties, which they performed regularly. Ulrich Kunzi undertook the scouring, washing, and everything that belonged to cleanliness. He also chopped up the wood, while Gaspard Hari did the cooking and attended to the fire. Their regular and monotonous work was interrupted by long games at cards or dice, and they never quarreled, but were always calm and placid. They were never even impatient or ill-humored, nor did they ever use hard words, for they had laid in a stock of patience for their wintering on the top of the mountain.

Sometimes old Gaspard took his rifle and went after chamois, and occasionally he killed one. Then there was a feast in the inn at Schwarenbach, and they reveled in fresh meat. One morning he went out as usual. The thermometer outside marked eighteen degrees of frost, and as the sun had not yet risen, the hunter hoped to surprise the animals at the approaches to the Wildstrubel, and Ulrich, being alone, remained in bed until ten o'clock. He was of a sleepy nature, but he would not have dared to give way like that to his inclination in the presence of the old guide, who was ever an early riser. He breakfasted leisurely with Sam, who also spent his days and nights in sleeping in front of the fire; then he felt low-spirited and even frightened at the solitude, and was seized by a longing for his daily game of cards, as one is by the desire of an invincible habit, and so he went out to meet his companion, who was to return at four o'clock.

The snow had leveled the whole deep valley, filled up the *crevasses*, obliterated all signs of the two lakes and covered the rocks, so that between the high summits there was nothing but an immense, white, regular, dazzling and frozen surface. For three weeks, Ulrich had not been to the edge of the precipice, from which he had looked down onto the village, and he wanted to go there before climbing the slopes which led to Wildstrubel. Loëche was now also covered by the snow, and the houses could scarcely be distinguished, covered as they were by that white cloak.

Then turning to the right, he reached the Lämmern glacier. He went along with a mountaineer's long strides, striking the snow, which was as hard as a rock, with his iron-shod stick, and with his piercing eyes, he looked for the little black, moving speck in the distance, on that enormous, white expanse.

When he reached the end of the glacier he stopped and asked himself whether the old man had taken that road, and then he began to walk along the moraines with rapid and uneasy steps. The day was declining; the snow was assuming a rosy tint, and a dry, frozen wind blew in rough gusts over its crystal surface. Ulrich uttered a long, shrill, vibrating call; his voice sped through the deathlike silence in which the mountains were sleeping; it reached the distance, over profound and motionless waves of glacial foam, like the cry of a bird over the waves of the sea; then it died away and nothing answered him.

He set to walk again. The sun had sunk yonder behind the mountain tops, which were still purple with the reflection from the sky; but the depths of the valley were becoming gray, and suddenly the young man felt frightened. It seemed to him as if the silence, the cold, the solitude, the winter death of these mountains were taking possession of him, were going to stop and to freeze his blood, to make his limbs grow stiff, and to turn him into a motionless and frozen object; and he set off running, fleeing towards his dwelling. The old man, he thought, would have returned during his absence. He had taken another road; he would, no doubt, be sitting before the fire, with a dead chamois at his feet.

He soon came in sight of the inn, but no smoke rose from it. Ulrich walked faster and opened the door; Sam ran up to him to greet him, but Gaspard Hari had not returned. Kunzi, in his alarm, turned round suddenly, as if he had expected to find his comrade hidden in a corner. Then he re-lighted the fire and made the soup; hoping every moment to see the old man come in. From time to time he went out, to see if he were not coming in. It was quite night now, that wan night of the mountains, a livid night, with the crescent moon, yellow and dim and just disappearing behind the mountain tops, lit up on the edge of the horizon.

Then the young man went in and sat down to warm his hands and his feet, while he pictured to himself every possible accident. Gaspard might have broken a leg, have fallen into a crevasse, taken a false step and dislocated his ankle. And perhaps he was lying on the snow, overcome and stiff with the cold, in agony of mind, lost and perhaps shouting for help, calling with all his might, in the silence of the night.

But where? The mountain was so vast, so rugged, so dangerous in places, especially at that time of the year, that it would have required ten or twenty guides to walk for a week in all directions, to find a man in that immense space. Ulrich Kunzi, however, made up his mind to set out with Sam, if Gaspard did not return by one in the morning; and he made his preparations.

He put provisions for two days into a bag, took his steel climbing irons, tied a long, thin, strong rope round his waist and looked to see that his iron-shod stick and his axe, which served to cut steps in the ice, were in order. Then he waited. The fire was burning on the hearth and the great dog was snoring in front of it, and the clock was ticking as regularly as a heart beating, in its case of resounding wood.

He waited, with his ears on the alert for distant sounds, and he shivered when the wind blew against the roof and the walls. It struck twelve, and he trembled. Then, as he felt frightened and shuddering, he put some water on the fire, so that he might have some hot coffee before starting, and when the clock struck one he got up, woke Sam, opened the door and went off in the direction of the Wildstrubel. For five hours he mounted, scaling the rocks by means of his climbing irons, cutting into the ice, advancing continually and occasionally hauling up the dog, who remained below at the foot of some slope that was too steep for him, by means of the rope. It was about six o'clock when he reached one of the summits to which old Gaspard often came after chamois, and he waited till it should be daylight.

The sky was growing pale over head, and suddenly a strange light, springing, nobody could tell whence, illuminated the immense ocean of pale mountain summits, which stretched for a thousand leagues around him. One might have said that this vague brightness arose from the snow itself, in order to spread itself into space. By degrees the highest, distant summits assumed a delicate, fleshlike rose color, and the red sun appeared behind the ponderous giants of the Bernese Alps.

Ulrich Kunzi set off again, walking like a hunter, bent and looking for any traces, and saying to his dog: "Seek, old fellow, seek!"

He was descending the mountain now, scanning the depths closely, and from time to time shouting, uttering a loud, prolonged cry, which soon died away in that silent vastness. Then, he put his ear to the ground, to listen; he thought he could distinguish a voice, and so he began to run, and shouted again, but he heard nothing more and sat down, worn out and in despair. Towards midday, he breakfasted and gave Sam, who was as tired as himself, something to eat also, and then he recommenced his search.

When evening came he was still walking, and he had walked more than thirty miles over the mountains. As he was too far away to return home, and too tired to drag himself along any further, he dug a hole in the snow and crouched in it with his dog, under a blanket which he had brought with him. And the man and the dog lay side by side, warming themselves one against the other, but frozen to the marrow, nevertheless. Ulrich scarcely slept, his mind haunted by visions and his limbs shaking with cold.

Day was breaking when he got up. His legs were as stiff as iron bars, and his spirits so low that he was ready to cry with grief, while his heart was beating so that he almost fell with excitement, when he thought he heard a noise.

Suddenly he imagined that he also was going to die of cold in the midst of this vast solitude, and the terror of such a death roused his energies and gave him renewed vigor. He was descending towards the inn, falling down and getting up again, and followed at a distance by Sam, who was limping on three legs, and they did not reach Schwarenbach until four o'clock in the afternoon. The house was empty, and the young man made a fire, had something to eat and went to sleep, so worn out that he did not think of anything more.

He slept for a long time, for a very long time, an unconquerable sleep. But suddenly a voice, a cry, a name: "Ulrich," aroused him from his profound torpor and made him sit up in bed. Had he been dreaming? Was it one of those strange appeals which cross the dreams of disquieted minds? No, he heard it still, that reverberating cry, — which had entered at his ears and remained in his flesh, — to the tips of his sinewy fingers. Certainly, somebody had cried out, and called: "Ulrich!" There was somebody there, near the house, there could be no doubt of that, and he opened the door and shouted: "Is it you, Gaspard?" with all the strength of his lungs. But there was no reply, no murmur, no groan, nothing. It was quite dark, and the snow looked wan.

The wind had risen, that icy wind that cracks the rocks, and leaves nothing alive on those deserted heights, and it came in sudden gusts, which were more parching and more deadly than the burning wind of the desert, and again Ulrich shouted: "Gaspard! Gaspard! Gaspard!" And then he waited again. Everything was silent on the mountain! Then he shook with terror and with a bound he was inside the inn, when he shut and bolted the door, and then he fell into a chair, trembling all over, for he felt certain that his comrade had called him, at the moment he was expiring.

He was sure of that, as sure as one is of being alive, or of eating a piece of bread. Old Gaspard Hari had been dying for two days and three nights somewhere, in some hole, in one of those deep, untrodden ravines whose whiteness is more sinister than subterranean darkness. He had been dying for two days and three nights and he had just then died, thinking of his comrade. His soul, almost before it was released, had taken its flight to the inn where Ulrich was sleeping, and it had called him by that terrible and mysterious power which the spirits of the dead have, to haunt the living. That voiceless soul had cried to the wornout soul of the sleeper; it had uttered its last farewell, or its reproach, or its curse on the man who had not searched carefully enough.

And Ulrich felt that it was there, quite close to him, behind the wall, behind the door which he had just fastened. It was wandering about, like a night bird, which lightly touches a lighted window with his wings, and the terrified young man was ready to scream with horror. He wanted to run away, but did not dare to go out; he did not dare, and he should never dare to do it in the future, for that phantom would remain there day and night, round the inn, as long as the old man's body was not recovered and had not been deposited in the consecrated earth of a churchyard.

{285}

When it was daylight, Kunzi recovered some of his courage at the return of the bright sun. He prepared his meal, gave his dog some food, and then remained motionless on a chair, tortured at heart as he thought of the old man lying on the snow, and then, as soon as night once more covered the mountains, new terrors assailed him. He now walked up and down the dark kitchen, which was scarcely lighted by the flame of one candle, and he walked from one end of it to the other with great strides, listening, listening whether the terrible cry of the other night would again break the dreary silence outside. He felt himself alone, unhappy man, as no man had ever been alone before! He was alone in this immense desert of snow, alone five thousand feet above the inhabited earth, above human habitations, above that stirring, noisy, palpitating life, alone under an icy sky! A mad longing impelled him to run away, no matter where, to get down to Loëche by flinging himself over the precipice; but he did not even dare to open the door, as he felt sure that the other, the dead man, would bar his road, so that he might not be obliged to remain up there alone.

Towards midnight, tired with walking, wornout by grief and fear, he at last fell into a doze in his chair, for he was as afraid of his bed, as one is of a haunted spot. But suddenly the strident cry of the other evening pierced his ears, and it was so shrill that Ulrich stretched out his arms to repulse the ghost, and he fell onto his back with his chair.

Sam, who was awakened by the noise, began to howl, like frightened dogs do howl, and he walked all about the house, trying to find out where the danger came from; but when he got to the door, he sniffed beneath it, smelling vigorously, with his coat bristling and his tail stiff, while he growled angrily. Kunzi, who was terrified, jumped up, and holding his chair by one leg, he cried: "Don't come in, don't come in, or I shall kill you." And the dog, excited by this threat, barked angrily at that invisible enemy who defied his master's voice. By degrees, however, he quieted down and came back and stretched himself in front of the fire, but he was uneasy, and kept his head up, and growled between his teeth.

Ulrich, in turn, recovered his senses, but as he felt faint with terror, he went and got a bottle of brandy out of the sideboard, and he drank off several glasses, one after another, at a gulp. His ideas became vague, his courage revived, and a feverish glow ran through his veins.

He ate scarcely anything the next day, and limited himself to alcohol, and so he lived for several days, like a drunken brute. As soon as he thought of Gaspard Hari, he began to drink again, and went on drinking until he fell onto the ground, overcome by intoxication. And there he remained on his face, dead drunk, his limbs benumbed, and snoring, with his face to the ground. But scarcely had he digested the maddening and burning liquor, than the same cry, "Ulrich," woke him like a bullet piercing his brain, and he got up, still staggering, stretching out his hands to save himself from falling, and calling to Sam to help him. And the dog, who appeared to be going mad, like his master, rushed to the door, scratched it with his claws, and gnawed it with his long white teeth, while the young man, with his neck thrown back, and his head in the air, drank the brandy in draughts, as if it had been cold water, so that it might by and by send his thoughts, his frantic terror and his memory, to sleep again.

In three weeks he had consumed all his stock of ardent spirits, but his continual drunkenness only lulled his terror, which awoke more furiously than ever, as soon as it was impossible for him to calm it. His fixed idea then, which had been intensified by a month of drunkenness, and which was continually increasing in his absolute solitude, penetrated him like a gimlet. He now walked about his house like a wild beast in its cage, putting his ear to the door to listen if the other were there, and defying him through the wall. Then, as soon as he dozed, overcome by fatigue, he heard the voice which made him leap to his feet.

At last one night, like cowards do when driven to extremities, he sprang to the door and opened it, to see who was calling him, and to force him to keep quiet, but such a gust of cold wind blew into his face that it chilled him to the bone, and he closed and bolted the door again immediately, without noticing that Sam had rushed out. Then, as he was shivering with cold, he threw some wood on the fire, and sat down in front of it to warm himself, but suddenly he started, for somebody was scratching at the wall, and crying. In desperation he called out: "Go away!" but was answered by another long, sorrowful wail.

Then, all his remaining senses forsook him, from sheer fright. He repeated: "Go away!" and turned round to try to find some corner in which to hide, while the other person went round the house, still crying and rubbing against the wall. Ulrich went to the oak sideboard, which was full of plates and dishes and of provisions, and lifting it up with superhuman strength, he dragged it to the door, so as to form a barricade. Then piling up all the rest of the furniture, the mattresses, palliasses and chairs, he stopped up the windows like one does when assailed by an enemy.

But the person outside now uttered long, plaintive, mournful groans, to which the young man replied by similar groans, and thus days and nights passed, without their ceasing to howl at each other. The one was continually walking round the house, and scraped the walls with his nails so vigorously that it seemed as if he wished to destroy them, while the other, inside, followed all his movements, stooping down, and holding his ear to the walls, and replying to all his appeals with terrible cries. One evening, however, Ulrich heard nothing more, and he sat down, so overcome by fatigue, that he went to sleep immediately, and awoke in the morning without a thought, without any recollection of what had happened, just as if his head had been emptied during his heavy sleep, but he felt hungry, and he ate.

The winter was over, and the Gemmi pass was practicable again, so the Hauser family started off to return to their inn. As soon as they had reached the top of the ascent, the women mounted their mule, and spoke about the two men who they would meet again shortly. They were, indeed, rather surprised that neither of them had come down a few days before, as soon as the road became usable, in order to tell them all about their long winter sojourn. At last, however, they saw the inn, still covered with snow, like a quilt. The door and the window were closed, but a little smoke was coming out of the chimney, which reassured old Hauser; on going up to the door, however, he saw the skeleton of an animal which had been torn to pieces by the eagles, a large skeleton lying on its side.

They all looked closely at it, and the mother said: "That must be Sam," and then she shouted: "Hi! Gaspard!" A cry from the interior of the house answered her, and a sharp cry, that one might have thought some animal had uttered it. Old Hauser repeated: "Hi! Gaspard!" and they heard another cry, similar to the first.

Then the three men, the father and the two sons, tried to open the door, but it resisted their efforts. From the empty cow-stall they took a beam to serve as a battering-ram, and hurled it against the door with all their might. The wood gave way, and the boards flew into splinters; then the house was shaken by a loud voice, and inside, behind the sideboard, which was overturned, they saw a man standing upright, with his hair falling onto his shoulders, and a beard descending to his breast, with shining eyes and nothing but rags to cover him. They did not recognize him, but Louise Hauser exclaimed: "It is Ulrich, mother." And her mother declared that it was Ulrich, although his hair was white.

He allowed them to go up to him, and to touch him, but he did not reply to any of their questions, and they were obliged to take him to Loëche, where the doctors found that he was mad, and nobody ever knew what had become of his companion.

Little Louise Hauser nearly died that summer of decline, which the medical men attributed to the cold air of the mountains.

In the Vault

H. P. Lovecraft

THERE is nothing more absurd, as I view it, than that conventional association of the homely and the wholesome which seems to pervade the psychology of the multitude. Mention a bucolic Yankee setting, a bungling and thick-fibred village undertaker, and a careless mishap in a tomb, and no average reader can be brought to expect more than a hearty albeit grotesque phase of comedy. God knows, though, that the prosy tale which George Birch's death permits me to tell has in it aspects beside which some of our darkest tragedies are light.

Birch acquired a limitation and changed his business in 1881, yet never discussed the case when he could avoid it. Neither did his old physician Dr. Davis, who died years ago. It was generally stated that the affliction and shock were results of an unlucky slip whereby Birch had locked himself for nine hours in the receiving tomb of Peck Valley Cemetery, escaping only by crude and disastrous mechanical means; but while this much was undoubtedly true, there were other and blacker things which the man used to whisper to me in his drunken delirium toward the last. He confided in me because I was his doctor, and because he probably felt the need of confiding in someone else after Davis died. He was a bachelor, wholly without relatives.

Birch, before 1881, had been the village undertaker of Peck Valley; and was a very calloused and primitive specimen even as such specimens go. The practices I heard attributed to him would be unbelievable today, at least in a city; and even Peck Valley would have shuddered a bit had it known the easy ethics of its mortuary artist in such debatable matters as the ownership of costly "laying-out" apparel invisible beneath the casket's lid, and the degree of dignity to be maintained in posing and adapting the unseen members of lifeless tenants to containers not always calculated with sublimest accuracy. Most distinctly Birch was lax, insensitive, and professionally undesirable; yet I still think he was not an evil man. He was merely crass of fibre and function — thoughtless, careless, and liquorish, as his easily avoidable accident proves, and without that modicum of imagination which holds the average citizen within certain limits fixed by taste.

Just where to begin Birch's story I can hardly decide, since I am no practiced teller of tales. I suppose one should start in the cold December of 1880, when the ground froze and the cemetery delvers found they could dig no more graves till spring. Fortunately the village was small and the death rate low, so that it was possible to give all of Birch's inanimate charges a temporary haven in the single antiquated receiving tomb. The undertaker grew doubly lethargic in the bitter weather, and seemed to outdo even himself in carelessness. Never did he knock together flimsier and ungainlier caskets, or disregard more flagrantly the needs of the rusty lock on the tomb door which he slammed open and shut with such nonchalant abandon.

At last the spring thaw came, and graves were laboriously prepared for the nine silent harvests of the grim reaper which waited in the tomb. Birch, though dreading the bother of removal and interment, began his task of transference one disagreeable April morning, but ceased before noon because of a heavy rain that seemed to irritate his horse, after having laid but one mortal tenant to its permanent rest. That was Darius Peck, the nonagenarian, whose grave was not far from the tomb. Birch decided that he would begin the next day with little old Matthew Fenner, whose grave was also near by; but actually postponed the matter for three days, not getting to work till Good Friday, the 15th. Being without superstition, he did not heed the day at all; though ever afterward he refused to do anything of importance on that fateful sixth day of the week. Certainly, the events of that evening greatly changed George Birch.

On the afternoon of Friday, April 15th, then, Birch set out for the tomb with horse and wagon to transfer the body of Matthew Fenner. That he was not perfectly sober, he subsequently admitted; though he had not then taken to the wholesale drinking by which he later tried to forget certain things. He was just dizzy and careless enough to annoy his sensitive horse, which as he drew it viciously up at the tomb neighed and pawed and tossed its head, much as on that former occasion when the rain had vexed it. The day was clear, but a high wind had sprung up; and Birch was glad to get to shelter as he unlocked the iron door and entered the side-hill vault. Another might not have relished the damp, odorous chamber with the eight carelessly placed coffins; but Birch in those days was insensitive, and was concerned only in getting the right coffin for the right grave. He had not forgotten the criticism aroused when Hannah Bixby's relatives, wishing to transport her body to the cemetery in the city whither they had moved, found the casket of Judge Capwell beneath her headstone.

The light was dim, but Birch's sight was good, and he did not get Asaph Sawyer's coffin by mistake, although it was very similar. He had, indeed, made that coffin for Matthew Fenner; but had cast it aside at last as too awkward and flimsy, in a fit of curious sentimentality aroused by recalling how kindly and generous the little old man had been to him during his bankruptcy five years before. He gave old Matt the very best his skill could produce, but was thrifty enough to save the rejected specimen, and to use it when Asaph Sawyer died of a malignant fever. Sawyer was not a lovable man, and many stories were told of his almost inhuman vindictiveness and tenacious memory for wrongs real or fancied. To him Birch had felt no compunction in assigning the carelessly made coffin which he now pushed out of the way in his quest for the Fenner casket.

It was just as he had recognised old Matt's coffin that the door slammed to in the wind, leaving him in a dusk even deeper than before. The narrow transom admitted only the feeblest of rays, and the overhead ventilation funnel virtually none at all; so that he was reduced to a profane fumbling as he made his halting way among the long boxes toward the latch. In this funereal twilight he rattled the rusty handles, pushed at the iron panels, and wondered why the massive portal had grown so suddenly recalcitrant. In this twilight too, he began to realise the truth and to shout loudly as if his horse outside could do more than neigh an unsympathetic reply. For the long-neglected latch was obviously broken, leaving the careless undertaker trapped in the vault, a victim of his own oversight.

The thing must have happened at about three-thirty in the afternoon. Birch, being by temperament phlegmatic and practical, did not shout long; but proceeded to grope about for some tools which he recalled seeing in a corner of the tomb. It is doubtful whether he was touched at all by the horror and exquisite weirdness of his position, but the bald fact of imprisonment so far from the daily paths of men was enough to exasperate him thoroughly. His day's work was sadly interrupted, and unless chance presently brought some rambler hither, he might have to remain all night or longer. The pile of tools soon reached, and a hammer and chisel selected, Birch returned over the coffins to the door. The air had begun to be exceedingly unwholesome; but to this detail he paid no attention as he toiled, half by feeling, at the heavy and corroded metal of the latch. He would have given much for a lantern or bit of candle; but lacking these, bungled semi-sightlessly as best he might.

When he perceived that the latch was hopelessly unyielding, at least to such meagre tools and under such tenebrous conditions as these, Birch glanced about for other possible points of escape. The vault had been dug from a hillside, so that the narrow ventilation funnel in the top ran through several feet of earth, making this direction utterly useless to consider. Over the door, however, the high, slit-like transom in the brick facade gave promise of possible enlargement to a diligent worker; hence upon this his eyes long rested as he racked his brains for means to reach it. There was nothing like a ladder in the tomb, and the coffin niches on the sides and rear — which Birch seldom took the trouble to use — afforded no ascent to the space above the door. Only the coffins themselves remained as potential stepping-stones, and as he considered these he speculated on the best mode of transporting them. Three coffin-heights, he reckoned, would permit him to reach the transom; but he could do better with four. The boxes were fairly even, and could be piled up like blocks; so he began to compute how he might most stably use the eight to rear a scalable platform four deep. As he planned, he could not but wish that the units of his contemplated staircase had been more securely made. Whether he had imagination enough to wish they were empty, is strongly to be doubted.

Finally he decided to lay a base of three parallel with the wall, to place upon this two layers of two each, and upon these a single box to serve as the platform. This arrangement could be ascended with a minimum of awkwardness, and would furnish the desired height. Better still, though, he would utilise only two boxes of the base to support the superstructure, leaving one free to be piled on top in case the actual feat of escape required an even greater altitude. And so the prisoner toiled in the twilight, heaving the unresponsive remnants of mortality with little ceremony as his miniature Tower of Babel rose course by course. Several of the coffins began to split under the stress of handling, and he planned to save the stoutly built casket of little Matthew Fenner for the top, in order that his feet might have as certain a surface as possible. In the semi-gloom he trusted mostly to touch to select the right one, and indeed came upon it almost by accident, since it tumbled into his hands as if through some odd volition after he had unwittingly placed it beside another on the third layer.

The tower at length finished, and his aching arms rested by a pause during which he sat on the bottom step of his grim device, Birch cautiously ascended with his tools and stood abreast of the narrow transom. The borders of the space were entirely of brick, and there seemed little doubt but that he could shortly chisel away enough to allow his body to pass. As his hammer blows began to fall, the horse outside whinnied in a tone which may have been encouraging and to others may have been mocking. In either case it would have been appropriate; for the unexpected tenacity of the easy-looking brickwork was surely a sardonic commentary on the vanity of mortal hopes, and the source of a task whose performance deserved every possible stimulus.

Dusk fell and found Birch still toiling. He worked largely by feeling now, since newly gathered clouds hid the moon; and though progress was still slow, he felt heartened at the extent of his encroachments on the top and bottom of the aperture. He could, he was sure, get out by midnight — though it is characteristic of him that this thought was untinged with eerie implications. Undisturbed by oppressive reflections on the time, the place, and the company beneath his feet, he philosophically chipped away the stony brickwork; cursing when a fragment hit him in the face, and laughing when one struck the increasingly excited horse that pawed near the cypress tree. In time the hole grew so large that he ventured to try his body in it now and then, shifting about so that the coffins beneath him rocked and creaked. He would not, he found, have to pile another on his platform to make the proper height; for the hole was on exactly the right level to use as soon as its size might permit.

It must have been midnight at least when Birch decided he could get through the transom. Tired and perspiring despite many rests, he descended to the floor and sat a while on the bottom box to gather strength for the final wriggle and leap to the ground outside. The hungry horse was neighing repeatedly and almost uncannily, and he vaguely wished it would stop. He was curiously unelated over his impending escape, and almost dreaded the exertion, for his form had the indolent stoutness of early middle age. As he remounted the splitting coffins he felt his weight very poignantly; especially when, upon reaching the topmost one, he heard that aggravated crackle which bespeaks the wholesale rending of wood. He had, it seems, planned in vain when choosing the stoutest coffin for the platform; for no sooner was his full bulk again upon it than the rotting lid gave way, jouncing him two feet down on a surface which even he did not care to imagine. Maddened by the sound, or by the stench which billowed forth even to the open air, the waiting horse gave a scream that was too frantic for a neigh, and plunged madly off through the night, the wagon rattling crazily behind it.

Birch, in his ghastly situation, was now too low for an easy scramble out of the enlarged transom; but gathered his energies for a determined try. Clutching the edges of the aperture, he sought to pull himself up, when he noticed a queer retardation in the form of an apparent drag on both his ankles. In another moment he knew fear for the first time that night; for struggle as he would, he could not shake clear of the unknown grasp which held his feet in relentless captivity. Horrible pains, as of savage wounds, shot through his calves; and in his mind was a vortex of fright mixed with an unquenchable materialism that suggested splinters, loose nails, or some other attribute of a breaking wooden box. Perhaps he screamed. At any rate he kicked and squirmed frantically and automatically whilst his consciousness was almost eclipsed in a half-swoon.

Instinct guided him in his wriggle through the transom, and in the crawl which followed his jarring thud on the damp ground. He could not walk, it appeared, and the emerging moon must have witnessed a horrible sight as he dragged his bleeding ankles toward the cemetery lodge; his fingers clawing the black mould in brainless haste, and his body responding with that maddening slowness from which one suffers when chased by the phantoms of nightmare. There was evidently, however, no pursuer; for he was alone and alive when Armington, the lodge-keeper, answered his feeble clawing at the door.

Armington helped Birch to the outside of a spare bed and sent his little son Edwin for Dr. Davis. The afflicted man was fully conscious, but would say nothing of any consequence; merely muttering such things as "Oh, my ankles!", "Let go!", or "Shut in the tomb". Then the doctor came with his medicine-case and asked crisp questions, and removed the patient's outer clothing, shoes, and socks. The wounds — for both ankles were frightfully lacerated about the Achilles' tendons — seemed to puzzle the old physician greatly, and finally almost to frighten him. His questioning grew more than medically tense, and his hands shook as he dressed the mangled members; binding them as if he wished to get the wounds out of sight as quickly as possible.

For an impersonal doctor, Davis' ominous and awestruck cross-examination became very strange indeed as he sought to drain from the weakened undertaker every least detail of his horrible experience. He was oddly anxious to know if Birch were sure — absolutely sure — of the identity of that top coffin of the pile; how he had chosen it, how he had been certain of it as the Fenner coffin in the dusk, and how he had distinguished it from the inferior duplicate coffin of vicious Asaph Sawyer. Would the firm Fenner casket have caved in so readily? Davis, an old-time village practitioner, had of course seen both at the respective funerals, as indeed he had attended both Fenner and Sawyer in their last illnesses. He had even wondered, at Sawyer's funeral, how the vindictive farmer had managed to lie straight in a box so closely akin to that of the diminutive Fenner.

After a full two hours Dr. Davis left, urging Birch to insist at all times that his wounds were caused entirely by loose nails and splintering wood. What else, he added, could ever in any case be proved or believed? But it would be well to say as little as could be said, and to let no other doctor treat the wounds. Birch heeded this advice all the rest of his life till he told me his story; and when I saw the scars — ancient and whitened as they then were — I agreed that he was wise in so doing. He always remained lame, for the great tendons had been severed; but I think the greatest lameness was in his soul. His thinking processes, once so phlegmatic and logical, had become ineffaceably scarred; and it was pitiful to note his response to certain chance allusions such as "Friday", "Tomb", "Coffin", and words of less obvious concatenation. His frightened horse had gone home, but his frightened wits never quite did that. He changed his business, but something always preyed upon him. It may have been just fear, and it may have been fear mixed with a queer belated sort of remorse for bygone crudities. His drinking, of course, only aggravated what it was meant to alleviate.

When Dr. Davis left Birch that night he had taken a lantern and gone to the old receiving tomb. The moon was shining on the scattered brick fragments and marred facade, and the latch of the great door yielded readily to a touch from the outside. Steeled by old ordeals in dissecting rooms, the doctor entered and looked about, stifling the nausea of mind and body that everything in sight and smell induced. He cried aloud once, and a little later gave a gasp that was more terrible than a cry. Then he fled back to the lodge and broke all the rules of his calling by rousing and shaking his patient, and hurling at him a succession of shuddering whispers that seared into the bewildered ears like the hissing of vitriol.

"It was Asaph's coffin, Birch, just as I thought! I knew his teeth, with the front ones missing on the upper jaw — never, for God's sake, show those wounds! The body was pretty badly gone, but if ever I saw vindictiveness on any face — or former face . . . You know what a fiend he was for revenge — how he ruined old Raymond thirty years after their boundary suit, and how he stepped on the puppy that snapped at him a year ago last August . . . He was the devil incarnate, Birch, and I believe his eye-for-an-eye fury could beat old Father Death himself. God, what a rage! I'd hate to have it aimed at me!

"Why did you do it, Birch? He was a scoundrel, and I don't blame you for giving him a cast-aside coffin, but you always did go too damned far! Well enough to skimp on the thing some way, but you knew what a little man old Fenner was.

"I'll never get the picture out of my head as long as I live. You kicked hard, for Asaph's coffin was on the floor. His head was broken in, and everything was tumbled about. I've seen sights before, but there was one thing too much here. An eye for an eye! Great heavens, Birch, but you got what you deserved. The skull turned my stomach, but the other was worse — those ankles cut neatly off to fit Matt Fenner's cast-aside coffin!"

THE SILVER HATCHET
Sir Arthur Conan Doyle

ON the 3rd of December 1861, Dr. Otto von Hopstein, Regius Professor of Comparative Anatomy of the University of Budapest, and Curator of the Academical Museum, was foully and brutally murdered within a stone-throw of the entrance to the college quadrangle.

Besides the eminent position of the victim and his popularity amongst both students and towns-folk, there were other circumstances which excited public interest very strongly, and drew general attention throughout Austria and Hungary to this murder. The *Peshter Abendblatt* of the following day had an article upon it, which may still be consulted by the curious, and from which I translate a few passages giving a succinct account of the circumstances under which the crime was committed, and the peculiar features in the case which puzzled the Hungarian police.

"It appears," said that very excellent paper, "that Professor von Hopstein left the University about half-past four in the afternoon, in order to meet the train which is due from Vienna at three minutes after five. He was accompanied by his old and dear friend, Herr Wilhelm Schlessinger, sub-Curator of the Museum and Privat-docent of Chemistry. The object of these two gentlemen in meeting this particular train was to receive the legacy bequeathed by Graf von Schulling to the University of Budapest. It is well known that this unfortunate nobleman, whose tragic fate is still fresh in the recollection of the public, left his unique collection of mediaeval weapons, as well as several priceless black-letter editions, to enrich the already celebrated museum of his Alma Mater. The worthy Professor was too much of an enthusiast in such matters to intrust the reception or care of this valuable legacy to any subordinate; and, with the assistance of Herr Schlessinger, he succeeded in removing the whole collection from the train, and stowing it away in a light cart which had been sent by the University authorities. Most of the books and more fragile articles were packed in cases of pine-wood, but many of the weapons were simply done round with straw, so that considerable labour was involved in moving them all. The Professor was so nervous, however, lest any of them should be injured, that he refused to allow any of the railway employes (Eisenhahndiener) to assist. Every article was carried across the platform by Herr Schlessinger, and handed to Professor von Hopstein in the cart, who packed it away. When everything was in, the two gentlemen, still faithful to their charge, drove back to the University, the Professor being in excellent spirits, and not a little proud of the physical exertion which he had shown himself capable of. He made some joking allusion to it to Reinmaul, the janitor, who, with his friend Schiffer, a Bohemian Jew, met the cart on its return and unloaded the contents. Leaving his curiosities safe in the storeroom, and locking the door, the Professor handed the key to his sub-curator, and, bidding every one good evening, departed in the direction of his lodgings. Schlessinger took a last look to reassure himself that all was right, and

also went off, leaving Reinmaul and his friend Schiffer smoking in the janitor's lodge.

"At eleven o'clock, about an hour and a half after Von Hopstein's departure, a soldier of the 14th regiment of Jager, passing the front of the University on his way to barracks, came upon the lifeless body of the Professor lying a little way from the side of the road. He had fallen upon his face, with both hands stretched out. His head was literally split in two halves by a tremendous blow, which, it is conjectured, must have been struck from behind, there remaining a peaceful smile upon the old man's face, as if he had been still dwelling upon his new archaeological acquisition when death had overtaken him. There is no other mark of violence upon the body, except a bruise over the left patella, caused probably by the fall. The most mysterious part of the affair is that the Professor's purse, containing forty-three gulden, and his valuable watch have been untouched. Robbery cannot, therefore, have been the incentive to the deed, unless the assassins were disturbed before they could complete their work.

"This idea is negatived by the fact that the body must have lain at least an hour before any one discovered it. The whole affair is wrapped in mystery. Dr. Langemann, the eminent medico-jurist, has pronounced that the wound is such as might have been inflicted by a heavy sword-bayonet wielded by a powerful arm. The police are extremely reticent upon the subject, and it is suspected that they are in possession of a clue which may lead to important results."

Thus far the Pesther Abendblatt. The researches of the police failed, however, to throw the least glimmer of light upon the matter. There was absolutely no trace of the murderer, nor could any amount of ingenuity invent any reason which could have induced any one to commit the dreadful deed. The deceased Professor was a man so wrapped in his own studies and pursuits that he lived apart from the world, and had certainly never raised the slightest animosity in any human breast. It must have been some fiend, some savage, who loved blood for its own sake, who struck that merciless blow.

Though the officials were unable to come to any conclusions upon the matter, popular suspicion was not long in pitching upon a scapegoat. In the first published accounts of the murder the name of one Schiffer had been mentioned as having remained with the janitor after the Professor's departure. This man was a Jew, and Jews have never been popular in Hungary. A cry was at once raised for Schiffer's arrest; but as there was not the slightest grain of evidence against him, the authorities very properly refused to consent to so arbitrary a proceeding. Reinmaul, who was an old and most respected citizen, declared solemnly that Schiffer was with him until the startled cry of the soldier had caused them both to run out to the scene of the tragedy. No one ever dreamed of implicating Reinmaul in such a matter; but still, it was rumoured that his ancient and well-known friendship for Schiffer might have induced him to tell a falsehood in order to screen him. Popular feeling ran very high upon the subject, and there seemed a danger of Schiffer's being mobbed in the street, when an incident occurred which threw a very different light upon the matter.

{297}

On the morning of the 12th of December, just nine days after the mysterious murder of the Professor, Schiffer the Bohemian Jew was found lying in the north-western corner of the Grand Platz stone dead, and so mutilated that he was hardly recognisable. His head was cloven open in very much the same way as that of Von Hopstein, and his body exhibited numerous deep gashes, as if the murderer had been so carried away and transported with fury that he had continued to hack the lifeless body. Snow had fallen heavily the day before, and was lying at least a foot deep all over the square; some had fallen during the night, too, as was evidenced by a thin layer lying like a winding-sheet over the murdered man. It was hoped at first that this circumstance might assist in giving a clue by enabling the footsteps of the assassin to be traced; but the crime had been committed, unfortunately, in a place much frequented during the day, and there were innumerable tracks in every direction. Besides, the newly-fallen snow had blurred the footsteps to such an extent that it would have been impossible to draw trustworthy evidence from them.

In this case there was exactly the same impenetrable mystery and absence of motive which had characterised the murder of Professor von Hopstein. In the dead man's pocket there was found a notebook containing a considerable sum in gold and several very valuable bills, but no attempt had been made to rifle him. Supposing that any one to whom he had lent money (and this was the first idea which occurred to the police) had taken this means of evading his debt, it was hardly conceivable that he would have left such a valuable spoil untouched. Schiffer lodged with a widow named Gruga, at 49 Marie Theresa Strasse, and the evidence of his landlady and her children showed that he had remained shut up in his room the whole of the preceding day in a state of deep dejection, caused by the suspicion which the populace had fastened upon him. She had heard him go out about eleven o'clock at night for his last and fatal walk, and as he had a latch-key she had gone to bed without waiting for him. His object in choosing such a late hour for a ramble obviously was that he did not consider himself safe if recognised in the streets.

The occurrence of this second murder so shortly after the first threw not only the town of Budapest, but the whole of Hungary, into a terrible state of excitement, and even of terror. Vague dangers seemed to hang over the head of every man. The only parallel to this intense feeling was to be found in our own country at the time of the Williams murders described by De Quincey. There were so many resemblances between the cases of Von Hopstein and of Schiffer that no one could doubt that there existed a connection between the two. The absence of object and of robbery, the utter want of any clue to the assassin, and, lastly, the ghastly nature of the wounds, evidently inflicted by the same or a similar weapon, all pointed in one direction. Things were in this state when the incidents which I am now about to relate occurred, and in order to make them intelligible I must lead up to them from a fresh point of departure.

Otto von Schlegel was a younger son of the old Silesian family of that name. His father had originally destined him for the army, but at the advice of his teachers, who saw the surprising talent of the youth, had sent him to the University of Budapest to be educated in medicine. Here young Schlegel carried everything before him, and promised to be one of the most brilliant graduates turned out for many a year. Though a hard reader, he was no bookworm, but an active, powerful young fellow, full of animal spirits and vivacity, and extremely popular among his fellow-students.

The New Year examinations were at hand, and Schlegel was working hard—so hard that even the strange murders in the town, and the general excitement in men's minds, failed to turn his thoughts from his studies. Upon Christmas Eve, when every house was illuminated, and the roar of drinking songs came from the Bierkeller in the Student-quartier, he refused the many invitations to roystering suppers which were showered upon him, and went off with his books under his arm to the rooms of Leopold Strauss, to work with him into the small hours of the morning.

Strauss and Schlegel were bosom friends. They were both Silesians, and had known each other from boyhood. Their affection had become proverbial in the University. Strauss was almost as distinguished a student as Schlegel, and there had been many a tough struggle for academic honours between the two fellow-countrymen, which had only served to strengthen their friendship by a bond of mutual respect. Schlegel admired the dogged pluck and never-failing good temper of his old playmate; while the latter considered Schlegel, with his many talents and brilliant versatility, the most accomplished of mortals.

The friends were still working together, the one reading from a volume on anatomy, the other holding a skull and marking off the various parts mentioned in the text, when the deep-toned bell of St. Gregory's church struck the hour of midnight.

"Hark to that!" said Schlegel, snapping up the book and stretching out his long legs towards the cheery fire. "Why, it's Christmas morning, old friend! May it not be the last that we spend together!"

"May we have passed all these confounded examinations before another one comes!" answered Strauss. "But see here, Otto, one bottle of wine will not be amiss. I have laid one up on purpose;" and with a smile on his honest South German face, he pulled out a long-necked bottle of Rhenish from amongst a pile of books and bones in the corner.

"It is a night to be comfortable indoors," said Otto von Schlegel, looking out at the snowy landscape, "for 'tis bleak and bitter enough outside. Good health, Leopold!"

"Lebe hoch!" replied his companion. "It is a comfort indeed to forget sphenoid bones and ethmoid bones, if it be but for a moment. And what is the news of the corps, Otto? Has Graube fought the Swabian?"

"They fight to-morrow," said Von Schlegel. "I fear that our man will lose his beauty, for he is short in the arm. Yet activity and skill may do much for him. They say his hanging guard is perfection."

"And what else is the news amongst the students?" asked Strauss.

"They talk, I believe, of nothing but the murders. But I have worked hard of late, as you know, and hear little of the gossip."

"Have you had time," inquired Strauss, "to look over the books and the weapons which our dear old Professor was so concerned about the very day he met his death? They say they are well worth a visit."

"I saw them to-day," said Schlegel, lighting his pipe. "Reinmaul, the janitor, showed me over the store-room, and I helped to label many of them from the original catalogue of Graf Schulling's museum. As far as we can see, there is but one article missing of all the collection."

"One missing!" exclaimed Strauss. "That would grieve old Von Hopstein's ghost. Is it anything of value?"

"It is described as an antique hatchet, with a head of steel and a handle of chased silver. We have applied to the railway company, and no doubt it will be found."

"I trust so," echoed Strauss; and the conversation drifted off into other channels. The fire was burning low and the bottle of Rhenish was empty before the two friends rose from their chairs, and Von Schlegel prepared to depart.

"Ugh! It's a bitter night!" he said, standing on the doorstep and folding his cloak round him. "Why, Leopold, you have your cap on. You are not going out, are you?"

"Yes, I am coming with you," said Strauss, shutting the door behind him. "I feel heavy," he continued, taking his friend's arm, and walking down the street with him. "I think a walk as far as your lodgings, in the crisp frosty air, is just the thing to set me right."

The two students went down Stephen Strasse together and across Julien Platz, talking on a variety of topics. As they passed the corner of the Grand Platz, however, where Schiffer had been found dead, the conversation turned naturally upon the murder.

"That's where they found him," remarked Von Schlegel, pointing to the fatal spot

"Perhaps the murderer is near us now," said Strauss. "Let us hasten on."

They both turned to go, when Von Schlegel gave a sudden cry of pain and stooped down.

"Something has cut through my boot!" he cried; and feeling about with his hand in the snow, he pulled out a small glistening battle-axe, made apparently entirely of metal. It had been lying with the blade turned slightly upwards, so as to cut the foot of the student when he trod upon it.

"The weapon of the murderer!" he ejaculated.

"The silver hatchet from the museum!" cried Strauss in the same breath.

There could be no doubt that it was both the one and the other. There could not be two such curious weapons, and the character of the wounds was just such as would be inflicted by a similar instrument. The murderer had evidently thrown it aside after committing the dreadful deed, and it had lain concealed in the snow some twenty metres from the spot ever since. It was extraordinary that of all the

{300}

people who had passed and repassed none had discovered it; but the snow was deep, and it was a little off the beaten track.

"What are we to do with it? said Von Schlegel, holding it in his hand. He shuddered as he noticed by the light of the moon that the head of it was all dabbled with dark-brown stains.

"Take it to the Commissary of Police," suggested Strauss.

"He'll be in bed now. Still, I think you are right. But it is nearly four o'clock. I will wait until morning, and take it round before breakfast Meanwhile, I must carry it with me to my lodgings."

"That is the best plan," said his friend; and the two walked on together talking of the remarkable find which they had made. When they came to Schlegel's door, Strauss said good-bye, refusing an invitation to go in, and walked briskly down the street in the direction of his own lodgings.

Schlegel was stooping down putting the key into the lock, when a strange change came over him. He trembled violently, and dropped the key from his quivering fingers. His right hand closed convulsively round the handle of the silver hatchet, and his eye followed the retreating figure of his friend with a vindictive glare. In spite of the coldness of the night the perspiration streamed down his face. For a moment he seemed to struggle with himself, holding his hand up to his throat as if he were suffocating. Then, with crouching body and rapid, noiseless steps, he crept after his late companion.

Strauss was plodding sturdily along through the snow, humming snatches of a student song, and little dreaming of the dark figure which pursued him. At the Grand Platz it was forty yards behind him; at the Julien Platz it was but twenty; in Stephen Strasse it was ten, and gaining on him with panther-like rapidity. Already it was almost within arm's length of the unsuspecting man, and the hatchet glittered coldly in the moonlight, when some slight noise must have reached Strauss's ears, for he faced suddenly round upon his pursuer. He started and uttered an exclamation as his eye met the white set face, with flashing eyes and clenched teeth, which seemed to be suspended in the air behind him.

"What, Otto!" he exclaimed, recognising his friend. "Art thou ill? You look pale. Come with me to my Ah! hold, you madman, hold! Drop that axe! Drop it, I say, or by heaven I'll choke you!"

Von Schlegel had thrown himself upon him with a wild cry and uplifted weapon; but the student was stout-hearted and resolute. He rushed inside the sweep of the hatchet and caught his assailant round the waist, narrowly escaping a blow which would have cloven his head. The two staggered for a moment in, a deadly wrestle, Schlegel endeavouring to shorten his weapon; but Strauss with a desperate wrench managed to bring him to the ground, and they rolled together in the snow, Strauss clinging to the other's right arm and shouting frantically for assistance. It was as well that he did so, for Schlegel would certainly have succeeded in freeing his arm had it not been for the arrival of two stalwart gendarmes, attracted by the uproar. Even then the three of them found it difficult to overcome the maniacal strength of Schlegel, and they were utterly unable to wrench the silver hatchet from his grasp. One of the gendarmes, however, had a coil of rope round his waist, with which he rapidly secured the

{301}

student's arms to his sides. In this way, half pushed, half dragged, he was conveyed, in spite of furious cries and frenzied struggles, to the central police station.

Strauss assisted in coercing his former friend, and accompanied the police to the station; protesting loudly at the same time against any unnecessary violence, and giving it as his opinion that a lunatic asylum would be a more fitting place for the prisoner. The events of the last half-hour had been so sudden and inexplicable that he felt quite dazed himself. What did it all mean? It was certain that his old friend from boyhood had attempted to murder him, and had nearly succeeded. Was Von Schlegel then the murderer of Professor von Hopstein and of the Bohemian Jew? Strauss felt that it was impossible, for the Jew was not even known to him, and the Professor had been his especial favourite. He followed mechanically to the police station, lost in grief and amazement.

Inspector Baumgarten, one of the most energetic and best known of the police officials, was on duty in the absence of the Commissary. He was a wiry little active man, quiet and retiring in his habits, but possessed of great sagacity and a vigilance which never relaxed. Now, though he had had a six hours' vigil, he sat as erect as ever, with his pen behind his ear, at his official desk, while his friend, Sub-inspector Winkel, snored in a chair at the side of the stove. Even the inspector's usually immovable features betrayed surprise, however, when the door was flung open and Von Schlegel was dragged in with pale face and disordered clothes, the silver hatchet still grasped firmly in his hand. Still more surprised was he when Strauss and the gendarmes gave their account, which was duly entered in the official register.

"Young man, young man," said Inspector Baumgarten, laying down his pen and fixing his eyes sternly upon the prisoner, "this is pretty work for Christmas morning; why have you done this thing?"

"God knows!" cried Von Schlegel, covering his face with his hands and dropping the hatchet. A change had come over him, his fury and excitement were gone, and he seemed utterly prostrated with grief.

"You have rendered yourself liable to a strong suspicion of having committed the other murders which have disgraced our city."

"No, no, indeed!" said Von Schlegel earnestly. "God forbid!"

"At least you are guilty of attempting the life of Herr Leopold Strauss."

"The dearest friend I have in the world," groaned the student. "Oh, how could I! How could I!"

"His being your friend makes your crime ten times more heinous," said the inspector severely. "Remove him for the remainder of the night to the But steady! Who comes here?"

The door was pushed open, and a man came into the room, so haggard and careworn that he looked more like a ghost than a human being. He tottered as he walked, and had to clutch at the backs of the chairs as he approached the inspector's desk. It was hard to recognise in this miserable-looking object the once cheerful and rubicund sub-curator of the museum and privat-docent of chemistry, Herr Wilhelm Schlessinger. The practised eye of Baumgarten, however, was not to be baffled by any change.

"Good morning, mein herr," he said; "you are up early. No doubt the reason is that you have heard that one of your students, Von Schlegel, is arrested for attempting the life of Leopold Strauss?"

"No; I have come for myself," said Schlessinger, speaking huskily, and putting his hand up to his throat. "I have come to ease my soul of the weight of a great sin, though, God knows, an unmeditated one. It was I who— But, merciful heavens! there it is—the horrid thing! Oh, that I had never seen it!"

He shrank back in a paroxysm of terror, glaring at the silver hatchet where it lay upon the floor, and pointing at it with his emaciated hand.

"There it lies!" he yelled. "Look at it! It has come to condemn me. See that brown rust on it! Do you know what that is? That is the blood of my dearest, best friend. Professor von Hopstein. I saw it gush over the very handle as I drove the blade through his brain. Mein Gott, I see it now!"

"Sub-inspector Winkel," said Baumgarten, endeavouring to preserve his official austerity, "you will arrest this man, charged on his own confession with the murder of the late Professor. I also deliver into your hands Von Schlegel here, charged with a murderous assault upon Herr Strauss. You will also keep this hatchet"—here he picked it from the floor—"which has apparently been used for both crimes."

Wilhelm Schlessinger had been leaning against the table, with a face of ashy paleness. As the inspector ceased speaking, he looked up excitedly.

"What did you say?" he cried. "Von Schlegel attack Strauss! The two dearest friends in the college! I slay my old master! It is magic, I say; it is a charm! There is a spell upon us! It is—Ah, I have it! It is that hatchet—that thrice accursed hatchet!" and he pointed convulsively at the weapon which Inspector Baumgarten still held in his hand.

The inspector smiled contemptuously.

"Restrain yourself, mein herr," he said. "You do but make your case worse by such wild excuses for the wicked deed you confess to. Magic and charms are not known in the legal vocabulary, as my friend Winkel will assure you."

"I know not," remarked his sub-inspector, shrugging his broad shoulders. "There are many strange things in the world. Who knows but that—"

"What!" roared Inspector Baumgarten furiously. "You would undertake to contradict me! You would set up your opinion! You would be the champion of these accursed murderers! Fool, miserable fool, your hour has come!" and rushing at the astounded Winkel, he dealt a blow at him with the silver hatchet which would certainly have justified his last assertion had it not been that, in his fury, he overlooked the lowness of the rafters above his head. The blade of the hatchet struck one of these, and remained there quivering, while the handle was splintered into a thousand pieces.

"What have I done?" gasped Baumgarten, falling back into his chair. "What have I done?"

"You have proved Herr Schlessinger's words to be correct," said Von Schlegel, stepping forward, for the astonished policemen had let go their grasp of him. "That is what you have done. Against reason, science, and everything else though it be, there is a charm at work. There must be! Strauss, old boy, you know I would not, in my right senses, hurt one hair of your head. And you, Schlessinger, we both know you loved the old man who is dead. And you, Inspector Baumgarten, you would not willingly have struck your friend the sub-inspector?"

"Not for the whole world," groaned the inspector, covering his face with his hands.

"Then is it not clear? But now, thank Heaven, the accursed thing is broken, and can never do harm again. But see, what is that?"

Right in the centre of the room was lying a thin brown cylinder of parchment. One glance at the fragments of the handle of the weapon showed that it had been hollow. This roll of paper had apparently been hidden away inside the metal case thus formed, having been introduced through a small hole, which had been afterwards soldered up. Von Schlegel opened the document. The writing upon it was almost illegible from age; but as far as they could make out it stood thus, in mediaeval German—

"*Diese Waffe benutzte Max von Erlichingen, um Joanna Bodeck zu ermorden; deshalb beschuldige ich, Johann Bodeck, mittelst der Macht, welche mir als Mitglied des Concils des rothen Kreuzes verliehen wurde, dieselbe mit dieser Unthat. Mag sie anderen denselben Schmerz verursachen, den sie mir verursacht hat. Mag jede Hand, die sie ergreift, mit dem Blut eines Freundes geröthet sein.*

"*Immer übel, niemals gut, Geröthet mit des Freundes Blut.'*"

Which may be roughly translated—

"*This weapon was used by Max von Erlichingen for the murder of Joanna Bodeck. Therefore do I, Johann Bodeck, accuse it by the power which has been bequeathed to me as one of the Council of the Rosy Cross. May it deal to others the grief which it has dealt to me! May every hand that grasps it be reddened in the blood of a friend! "'Ever evil, never good, Reddened with a loved one's blood.'*"

There was a dead silence in the room when Von Schlegel had finished spelling out this strange document. As he put it down Strauss laid his hand affectionately upon his arm.

"No such proof is needed by me, old friend," he said. "At the very moment that you struck at me I forgave you in my heart. I well know that if the poor Professor were in the room he would say as much to Herr Wilhelm Schlessinger."

"Gentlemen," remarked the inspector, standing up and resuming his official tones, "this affair, strange as it is, must be treated according to rule and precedent Sub-inspector Winkel, as your superior officer, I command you to arrest me upon a charge of murderously assaulting you. You will commit me to prison for the night, together with Herr von Schlegel and Herr Wilhelm Schlessinger. We shall take our trial at the coming sitting of the judges. In the meantime take care of that piece of evidence —pointing to the piece of parchment—"and, while I am away, devote your time and energy to utilising the clue you have obtained in discovering who it was who slew Herr Schiffer, the Bohemian Jew."

The one missing link in the chain of evidence was soon supplied. On the 28th of December the wife of Reinmaul the janitor, coming into the bedroom after a short absence, found her husband hanging lifeless from a hook in the wall. He had tied a long bolster-case round his neck and stood upon a chair in order to commit the fatal deed. On the table was a note in which he confessed to the murder of Schiffer the Jew, adding that the deceased had been his oldest friend, and that he had slain him without premeditation, in obedience to some incontrollable impulse. Remorse and grief, he said, had driven him to self-destruction; and he wound up his confession by commending his soul to the mercy of Heaven.

The trial which ensued was one of the strangest which ever occurred in the whole history of jurisprudence. It was in vain that the prosecuting council urged the improbability of the explanation offered by the prisoners, and deprecated the introduction of such an element as magic into a nineteenth-century law-court. The chain of facts was too strong, and the prisoners were unanimously acquitted. "This silver hatchet," remarked the judge in his summing up, "has hung untouched upon the wall in the mansion of the Graf von Schulling for nearly two hundred years. The shocking manner in which he met his death at the hands of his favourite house steward is still fresh in your recollection. It has come out in evidence that, a few days before the murder, the steward had overhauled the old weapons and cleaned them. In doing this he must have touched the handle of this hatchet. Immediately afterwards he slew his master, whom he had served faithfully for twenty years. The weapon then came, in conformity with the Count's will, to Budapest, where, at the station, Herr Wilhelm Schlessinger grasped it, and, within two hours, used it against the person of the deceased Professor. The next man whom we find touching it is the janitor Reinmaul, who helped to remove the weapons from the cart to the store-room. At the first opportunity he buried it in the body of his friend Schiffer. We then have the attempted murder of Strauss by Schlegel, and of Winkel by Inspector Baumgarten, all immediately following the taking of the hatchet into the hand. Lastly, comes the providential discovery of the extraordinary document which has been read to you by the clerk of the court. I invite your most careful consideration, gentlemen of the jury, to this chain of facts, knowing that you will find a verdict according to your consciences without fear and without favour."

Perhaps the most interesting piece of evidence to the English reader, though it found few supporters among the Hungarian audience, was that of Dr. Langemann, the eminent medico-jurist, who has written text-books upon metallurgy and toxicology. He said—

"I am not so sure, gentlemen, that there is need to fall back upon necromancy or the black art for an explanation of what has occurred. What I say is merely a hypothesis, without proof of any sort, but in a case so extraordinary every suggestion may be of value. The Rosicrucians, to whom allusion is made in this paper, were the most profound chemists of the early Middle Ages, and included the principal alchemists whose names have descended to us. Much as chemistry has advanced, there are some points in which the ancients were ahead of us, and in none more so than in the manufacture of poisons of subtle and deadly action. This man Bodeck, as one of the elders of the Rosicrucians, possessed, no doubt, the recipe of many such mixtures, some of which, like the aqua tofana of the Medicis, would poison by penetrating through the pores of the skin. It is conceivable that the handle of this silver hatchet has been anointed by some preparation which is a diffusible poison, having the effect upon the human body of bringing on sudden and acute attacks of homicidal mania. In such attacks it is well known that the madman's rage is turned against those whom he loved best when sane. I have, as I remarked before, no proof to support me in my theory, and simply put it forward for what it is worth."

With this extract from the speech of the learned and ingenious professor, we may close the account of this famous trial.

The broken pieces of the silver hatchet were thrown into a deep pond, a clever poodle being employed to carry them in his mouth, as no one would touch them for fear some of the infection might still hang about them. The piece of parchment was preserved in the museum of the University. As to Strauss and Schlegel, Winkel and Baumgarten, they continued the best of friends, and are so still for all I know to the contrary. Schlessinger became surgeon of a cavalry regiment; and was shot at the battle of Sadowa five years later, while rescuing the wounded under a heavy fire. By his last injunctions his little patrimony was to be sold to erect a marble obelisk over the grave of Professor von Hopstein.

THE STORY OF A DISAPPEARANCE AND AN APPEARANCE

M. R. James

THE letters which I now publish were sent to me recently by a person who knows me to be interested in ghost stories. There is no doubt about their authenticity. The paper on which they are written, the ink, and the whole external aspect put their date beyond the reach of question.

The only point which they do not make clear is the identity of the writer. He signs with initials only, and as none of the envelopes of the letters are preserved, the surname of his correspondent — obviously a married brother — is as obscure as his own. No further preliminary explanation is needed, I think. Luckily the first letter supplies all that could be expected.

LETTER I

GREAT CHRISHALL, *Dec. 22, 1837.*

MY DEAR ROBERT — It is with great regret for the enjoyment I am losing, and for a reason which you will deplore equally with myself, that I write to inform you that I am unable to join your circle for this Christmas: but you will agree with me that it is unavoidable when I say that I have within these few hours received a letter from Mrs. Hunt at B— — to the effect that our Uncle Henry has suddenly and mysteriously disappeared, and begging me to go down there immediately and join the search that is being made for him. Little as I, or you either, I think, have ever seen of Uncle, I naturally feel that this is not a request that can be regarded lightly, and accordingly I propose to go to B—— by this afternoon's mail, reaching it late in the evening. I shall not go to the Rectory, but put up at the King's Head, and to which you may address letters. I enclose a small draft, which you will please make use of for the benefit of the young people. I shall write you daily (supposing me to be detained more than a single day) what goes on, and you may be sure, should the business be cleared up in time to permit of my coming to the Manor after all, I shall present myself. I have but a few minutes at disposal. With cordial greetings to you all, and many regrets, believe me, your affectionate Bro.,

W. R.

LETTER II

KING'S HEAD, *Dec. 23, '37.*

MY DEAR ROBERT — In the first place, there is as yet no news of Uncle H., and I think you may finally dismiss any idea — I won't say hope — that I might after all "turn up" for Xmas. However, my thoughts will be with you, and you have my best wishes for a really festive day. Mind that none of my nephews or nieces expend any fraction of their guineas on presents for me.

Since I got here I have been blaming myself for taking this affair of Uncle H. too easily. From what people here say, I gather that there is very little hope that he can still be alive; but whether it is accident or design that carried him off I cannot judge. The facts are these. On Friday the 19th, he went as usual shortly before five o'clock to read evening prayers at the Church; and when they were over the clerk brought him a message, in response to which he set off to pay a visit to a sick person at an outlying cottage the better part of two miles away. He paid the visit, and started on his return journey at about half-past six. This is the last that is known of him. The people here are very much grieved at his loss; he had been here many years, as you know, and though, as you also know, he was not the most genial of men, and had more than a little of the *martinet* in his composition, he seems to have been active in good works, and unsparing of trouble to himself.

Poor Mrs. Hunt, who has been his housekeeper ever since she left Woodley, is quite overcome: it seems like the end of the world to her. I am glad that I did not entertain the idea of taking quarters at the Rectory; and I have declined several kindly offers of hospitality from people in the place, preferring as I do to be independent, and finding myself very comfortable here.

You will, of course, wish to know what has been done in the way of inquiry and search. First, nothing was to be expected from investigation at the Rectory; and to be brief, nothing has transpired. I asked Mrs. Hunt — as others had done before — whether there was either any unfavourable symptom in her master such as might portend a sudden stroke, or attack of illness, or whether he had ever had reason to apprehend any such thing: but both she, and also his medical man, were clear that this was not the case. He was quite in his usual health. In the second place, naturally, ponds and streams have been dragged, and fields in the neighbourhood which he is known to have visited last, have been searched — without result. I have myself talked to the parish clerk and — more important — have been to the house where he paid his visit.

There can be no question of any foul play on these people's part. The one man in the house is ill in bed and very weak: the wife and the children of course could do nothing themselves, nor is there the shadow of a probability that they or any of them should have agreed to decoy poor Uncle H. out in order that he might be attacked on the way back. They had told what they knew to several other inquirers already, but the woman repeated it to me. The Rector was looking just as usual: he wasn't very long with the sick man —"He ain't," she said, "like some what has a gift in prayer; but there, if we was all that way, 'owever would the chapel people get their living?" He left some money when he went away, and one of the children saw him cross the stile into the next field. He was dressed as he always was: wore his bands — I gather he is nearly the last man remaining who does so — at any rate in this district.

You see I am putting down everything. The fact is that I have nothing else to do, having brought no business papers with me; and, moreover, it serves to clear my own mind, and may suggest points which have been overlooked. So I shall continue to write all that passes, even to conversations if need be — you may read or not as you please, but pray keep the letters. I have another reason for writing so fully, but it is not a very tangible one.

You may ask if I have myself made any search in the fields near the cottage. Something — a good deal — has been done by others, as I mentioned; but I hope to go over the ground tomorrow. Bow Street has now been informed, and will send down by to-night's coach, but I do not think they will make much of the job. There is no snow, which might have helped us. The fields are all grass. Of course I was on the *qui vive* for any indication today both going and returning; but there was a thick mist on the way back, and I was not in trim for wandering about unknown pastures, especially on an evening when bushes looked like men, and a cow lowing in the distance might have been the last trump. I assure you, if Uncle Henry had stepped out from among the trees in a little copse which borders the path at one place, carrying his head under his arm, I should have been very little more uncomfortable than I was. To tell you the truth, I was rather expecting something of the kind. But I must drop my pen for the moment: Mr. Lucas, the curate, is announced.

Later. Mr. Lucas has been, and gone, and there is not much beyond the decencies of ordinary sentiment to be got from him. I can see that he has given up any idea that the Rector can be alive, and that, so far as he can be, he is truly sorry. I can also discern that even in a more emotional person than Mr. Lucas, Uncle Henry was not likely to inspire strong attachment.

Besides Mr. Lucas, I have had another visitor in the shape of my Boniface — mine host of the "King's Head"— who came to see whether I had everything I wished, and who really requires the pen of a Boz to do him justice. He was very solemn and weighty at first. "Well, sir," he said, "I suppose we must bow our 'ead beneath the blow, as my poor wife had used to say. So far as I can gather there's been neither hide nor yet hair of our late respected incumbent scented out as yet; not that he was what the Scripture terms a hairy man in any sense of the word."

I said — as well as I could — that I supposed not, but could not help adding that I had heard he was sometimes a little difficult to deal with. Mr. Bowman looked at me sharply for a moment, and then passed in a flash from solemn sympathy to impassioned declamation. "When I think," he said, "of the language that man see fit to employ to me in this here parlour over no more a matter than a cask of beer — such a thing as I told him might happen any day of the week to a man with a family — though as it turned out he was quite under a mistake, and that I knew at the time, only I was that shocked to hear him I couldn't lay my tongue to the right expression."

He stopped abruptly and eyed me with some embarrassment. I only said, "Dear me, I'm sorry to hear you had any little differences; I suppose my uncle will be a good deal missed in the parish?" Mr. Bowman drew a long breath. "Ah, yes!" he said; "your uncle! You'll understand me when I say that for the moment it had slipped my remembrance that he was a relative; and natural enough, I must say, as it should, for as to you bearing any resemblance to — to him, the notion of any such a thing is clean ridiculous. All the same, 'ad I 'ave bore it in my mind, you'll be among the first to feel, I'm sure, as I should have abstained my lips, or rather I should *not* have abstained my lips with no such reflections."

I assured him that I quite understood, and was going to have asked him some further questions, but he was called away to see after some business. By the way, you need not take it into your head that he has anything to fear from the inquiry into poor Uncle Henry's disappearance — though, no doubt, in the watches of the night it will occur to him that *I* think he has, and I may expect explanations tomorrow.

I must close this letter: it has to go by the late coach.

LETTER III

Dec. 25, '37.

MY DEAR ROBERT — This is a curious letter to be writing on Christmas Day, and yet after all there is nothing much in it. Or there may be — you shall be the judge. At least, nothing decisive. The Bow Street men practically say that they have no clue. The length of time and the weather conditions have made all tracks so faint as to be quite useless: nothing that belonged to the dead man — I'm afraid no other word will do — has been picked up.

As I expected, Mr. Bowman was uneasy in his mind this morning; quite early I heard him holding forth in a very distinct voice — purposely so, I thought — to the Bow Street officers in the bar, as to the loss that the town had sustained in their Rector, and as to the necessity of leaving no stone unturned (he was very great on this phrase) in order to come at the truth. I suspect him of being an orator of repute at convivial meetings.

When I was at breakfast he came to wait on me, and took an opportunity when handing a muffin to say in a low tone, "I 'ope, sir, you reconize as my feelings towards your relative is not actuated by any taint of what you may call melignity — you can leave the room, Eliza, I will see the gentleman 'as all he requires with my own hands — I ask your pardon, sir, but you must be well aware a man is not always master of himself: and when that man has been 'urt in his mind by the application of expressions which I will go so far as to say 'ad not ought to have been made use of (his voice was rising all this time and his face growing redder); no, sir; and 'ere, if you will permit of it, I should like to explain to you in a very few words the exact state of the bone of contention. This cask — I might more truly call it a firkin — of beer —"

I felt it was time to interpose, and said that I did not see that it would help us very much to go into that matter in detail. Mr. Bowman acquiesced, and resumed more calmly:

"Well, sir, I bow to your ruling, and as you say, be that here or be it there, it don't contribute a great deal, perhaps, to the present question. All I wish you to understand is that I am prepared as you are yourself to lend every hand to the business we have afore us, and — as I took the opportunity to say as much to the Orficers not three-quarters of an hour ago — to leave no stone unturned as may throw even a spark of light on this painful matter."

In fact, Mr. Bowman did accompany us on our exploration, but though I am sure his genuine wish was to be helpful, I am afraid he did not contribute to the serious side of it. He appeared to be under the impression that we were likely to meet either Uncle Henry or the person responsible for his disappearance, walking about the fields — and did a great deal of shading his eyes with his hand and calling our attention, by pointing with his stick, to distant cattle and labourers. He

{310}

held several long conversations with old women whom we met, and was very strict and severe in his manner — but on each occasion returned to our party saying, "Well, I find she don't seem to 'ave no connexion with this sad affair. I think you may take it from me, sir, as there's little or no light to be looked for from that quarter; not without she's keeping somethink back intentional."

We gained no appreciable result, as I told you at starting; the Bow Street men have left the town, whether for London or not, I am not sure.

This evening I had company in the shape of a bagman, a smartish fellow. He knew what was going forward, but though he has been on the roads for some days about here, he had nothing to tell of suspicious characters — tramps, wandering sailors or gipsies. He was very full of a capital Punch and Judy Show he had seen this same day at W— — and asked if it had been here yet, and advised me by no means to miss it if it does come. The best Punch and the best Toby dog, he said, he had ever come across. Toby dogs, you know, are the last new thing in the shows. I have only seen one myself, but before long all the men will have them.

Now why, you will want to know, do I trouble to write all this to you? I am obliged to do it, because it has something to do with another absurd trifle (as you will inevitably say), which in my present state of rather unquiet fancy — nothing more, perhaps — I have to put down. It is a dream, sir, which I am going to record, and I must say it is one of the oddest I have had. Is there anything in it beyond what the bagman's talk and Uncle Henry's disappearance could have suggested? You, I repeat, shall judge: I am not in a sufficiently cool and judicial frame to do so.

It began with what I can only describe as a pulling aside of curtains: and I found myself seated in a place — I don't know whether in doors or out. There were people — only a few — on either side of me, but I did not recognize them, or indeed think much about them. They never spoke, but, so far as I remember, were all grave and pale-faced and looked fixedly before them. Facing me there was a Punch and Judy Show, perhaps rather larger than the ordinary ones, painted with black figures on a reddish-yellow ground. Behind it and on each side was only darkness, but in front there was a sufficiency of light. I was "strung up" to a high degree of expectation and listened every moment to hear the panpipes and the Roo-too-too-it. Instead of that there came suddenly an enormous — I can use no other word — an enormous single toll of a bell, I don't know from how far off — somewhere behind. The little curtain flew up and the drama began.

I believe someone once tried to re-write Punch as a serious tragedy; but whoever he may have been, this performance would have suited him exactly. There was something Satanic about the hero. He varied his methods of attack: for some of his victims he lay in wait, and to see his horrible face — it was yellowish white, I may remark — peering round the wings made me think of the Vampyre in Fuseli's foul sketch. To others he was polite and carneying — particularly to the unfortunate alien who can only say *Shallabalah* — though what Punch said I never could catch. But with all of them I came to dread the moment of death. The crack of the stick on their skulls, which in the ordinary way delights me, had here a crushing sound as if the bone was giving way, and the victims quivered and kicked as they lay. The baby — it sounds more ridiculous as I go on — the baby, I am sure, was alive. Punch wrung its neck, and if the choke or squeak which it gave were not real, I know nothing of reality.

The stage got perceptibly darker as each crime was consummated, and at last there was one murder which was done quite in the dark, so that I could see nothing of the victim, and took some time to effect. It was accompanied by hard breathing and horrid muffled sounds, and after it Punch came and sat on the foot-board and fanned himself and looked at his shoes, which were bloody, and hung his head on one side, and sniggered in so deadly a fashion that I saw some of those beside me cover their faces, and I would gladly have done the same. But in the meantime the scene behind Punch was clearing, and showed, not the usual house front, but something more ambitious — a grove of trees and the gentle slope of a hill, with a very natural — in fact, I should say a real — moon shining on it. Over this there rose slowly an object which I soon perceived to be a human figure with something peculiar about the head — what, I was unable at first to see. It did not stand on its feet, but began creeping or dragging itself across the middle distance towards Punch, who still sat back to it; and by this time, I may remark (though it did not occur to me at the moment) that all pretence of this being a puppet show had vanished. Punch was still Punch, it is true, but, like the others, was in some sense a live creature, and both moved themselves at their own will.

When I next glanced at him he was sitting in malignant reflection; but in another instant something seemed to attract his attention, and he first sat up sharply and then turned round, and evidently caught sight of the person that was approaching him and was in fact now very near. Then, indeed, did he show unmistakable signs of terror: catching up his stick, he rushed towards the wood, only just eluding the arm of his pursuer, which was suddenly flung out to intercept him. It was with a revulsion which I cannot easily express that I now saw more or less clearly what this pursuer was like. He was a sturdy figure clad in black, and, as I thought, wearing bands: his head was covered with a whitish bag.

The chase which now began lasted I do not know how long, now among the trees, now along the slope of the field, sometimes both figures disappearing wholly for a few seconds, and only some uncertain sounds letting one know that they were still afoot. At length there came a moment when Punch, evidently exhausted, staggered in from the left and threw himself down among the trees. His pursuer was not long after him, and came looking uncertainly from side to side. Then, catching sight of the figure on the ground, he too threw himself down — his back was turned to the audience — with a swift motion twitched the covering from his head, and thrust his face into that of Punch. Everything on the instant grew dark.

There was one long, loud, shuddering scream, and I awoke to find myself looking straight into the face of — what in all the world do you think? — but a large owl, which was seated on my window-sill immediately opposite my bed-foot, holding up its wings like two shrouded arms. I caught the fierce glance of its yellow eyes, and then it was gone. I heard the single enormous bell again — very likely, as you are saying to yourself, the church clock; but I do not think so — and then I was broad awake.

All this, I may say, happened within the last half-hour. There was no probability of my getting to sleep again, so I got up, put on clothes enough to keep me warm, and am writing this rigmarole in the first hours of Christmas Day. Have I left out anything? Yes, there was no Toby dog, and the names over the front of the Punch and Judy booth were Kidman and Gallop, which were certainly not what the bagman told me to look out for.

By this time, I feel a little more as if I could sleep, so this shall be sealed and wafered.

LETTER IV

Dec. 26, '37.

MY DEAR ROBERT — All is over. The body has been found. I do not make excuses for not having sent off my news by last night's mail, for the simple reason that I was incapable of putting pen to paper. The events that attended the discovery bewildered me so completely that I needed what I could get of a night's rest to enable me to face the situation at all. Now I can give you my journal of the day, certainly the strangest Christmas Day that ever I spent or am likely to spend.

The first incident was not very serious. Mr. Bowman had, I think, been keeping Christmas Eve, and was a little inclined to be captious: at least, he was not on foot very early, and to judge from what I could hear, neither men or maids could do anything to please him. The latter were certainly reduced to tears; nor am I sure that Mr. Bowman succeeded in preserving a manly composure. At any rate, when I came downstairs, it was in a broken voice that he wished me the compliments of the season, and a little later on, when he paid his visit of ceremony at breakfast, he was far from cheerful: even Byronic, I might almost say, in his outlook on life.

"I don't know," he said, "if you think with me, sir; but every Christmas as comes round the world seems a hollerer thing to me. Why, take an example now from what lays under my own eye. There's my servant Eliza — been with me now for going on fifteen years. I thought I could have placed my confidence in Elizar, and yet this very morning — Christmas morning too, of all the blessed days in the year — with the bells a ringing and — and — all like that — I say, this very morning, had it not have been for Providence watching over us all, that girl would have put — indeed I may go so far to say, 'ad put the cheese on your breakfast table ——" He saw I was about to speak, and waved his hand at me. "It's all very well for you to say, 'Yes, Mr. Bowman, but you took away the cheese and locked it up in the cupboard,' which I did, and have the key here, or if not the actual key one very much about the same size. That's true enough, sir, but what do you think is the effect of that action on me? Why it's no exaggeration for me to say that the ground is cut from under my feet. And yet when I said as much to Eliza, not nasty, mind you, but just firm like, what was my return? 'Oh,' she says: 'Well,' she says, 'there wasn't no bones broke, I suppose.' Well, sir, it 'urt me, that's all I can say: it 'urt me, and I don't like to think of it now."

There was an ominous pause here, in which I ventured to say something like, "Yes, very trying," and then asked at what hour the church service was to be. "Eleven o'clock," Mr. Bowman said with a heavy sigh. "Ah, you won't have no such discourse from poor Mr. Lucas as what you would have done from our late Rector. Him and me may have had our little differences, and did do, more's the pity."

I could see that a powerful effort was needed to keep him off the vexed question of the cask of beer, but he made it. "But I will say this, that a better preacher, nor yet one to stand faster by his rights, or what he considered to be his rights — however, that's not the question now — I for one, never set under. Some might say, 'Was he a eloquent man?' and to that my answer would be: 'Well, there you've a better right per'aps to speak of your own uncle than what I have.' Others might ask, 'Did he keep a hold of his congregation?' and there again I should reply, 'That depends.' But as I say — Yes, Eliza, my girl, I'm coming — eleven o'clock, sir, and you inquire for the King's Head pew." I believe Eliza had been very near the door, and shall consider it in my vail.

The next episode was church: I felt Mr. Lucas had a difficult task in doing justice to Christmas sentiments, and also to the feeling of disquiet and regret which, whatever Mr. Bowman might say, was clearly prevalent. I do not think he rose to the occasion. I was uncomfortable. The organ wolved — you know what I mean: the wind died — twice in the Christmas Hymn, and the tenor bell, I suppose owing to some negligence on the part of the ringers, kept sounding faintly about once in a minute during the sermon. The clerk sent up a man to see to it, but he seemed unable to do much. I was glad when it was over. There was an odd incident, too, before the service. I went in rather early, and came upon two men carrying the parish bier back to its place under the tower. From what I overheard them saying, it appeared that it had been put out by mistake, by some one who was not there. I also saw the clerk busy folding up a moth-eaten velvet pall — not a sight for Christmas Day.

I dined soon after this, and then, feeling disinclined to go out, took my seat by the fire in the parlour, with the last number of *Pickwick*, which I had been saving up for some days. I thought I could be sure of keeping awake over this, but I turned out as bad as our friend Smith. I suppose it was half-past two when I was roused by a piercing whistle and laughing and talking voices outside in the market-place. It was a Punch and Judy — I had no doubt the one that my bagman had seen at W——. I was half delighted, half not — the latter because my unpleasant dream came back to me so vividly; but, anyhow, I determined to see it through, and I sent Eliza out with a crown-piece to the performers and a request that they would face my window if they could manage it.

The show was a very smart new one; the names of the proprietors, I need hardly tell you, were Italian, Foresta and Calpigi. The Toby dog was there, as I had been led to expect. All B—— turned out, but did not obstruct my view, for I was at the large first-floor window and not ten yards away.

The play began on the stroke of a quarter to three by the church clock. Certainly it was very good; and I was soon relieved to find that the disgust my dream had given me for Punch's onslaughts on his ill-starred visitors was only transient. I laughed at the demise of the Turncock, the Foreigner, the Beadle, and even the baby. The only drawback was the Toby dog's developing a tendency to howl in the wrong place. Something had occurred, I suppose, to upset him, and something considerable: for, I forget exactly at what point, he gave a most lamentable cry, leapt off the foot board, and shot away across the market-place and down a side street. There was a stage-wait, but only a brief one. I suppose the men decided that it was no good going after him, and that he was likely to turn up again at night.

We went on. Punch dealt faithfully with Judy, and in fact with all comers; and then came the moment when the gallows was erected, and the great scene with Mr. Ketch was to be enacted. It was now that something happened of which I can certainly not yet see the import fully. You have witnessed an execution, and know what the criminal's head looks like with the cap on. If you are like me, you never wish to think of it again, and I do not willingly remind you of it. It was just such a head as that, that I, from my somewhat higher post, saw in the inside of the show-box; but at first the audience did not see it. I expected it to emerge into their view, but instead of that there slowly rose for a few seconds an uncovered face, with an expression of terror upon it, of which I have never imagined the like. It seemed as if the man, whoever he was, was being forcibly lifted, with his arms somehow pinioned or held back, towards the little gibbet on the stage. I could just see the nightcapped head behind him. Then there was a cry and a crash. The whole show-box fell over backwards; kicking legs were seen among the ruins, and then two figures — as some said; I can only answer for one — were visible running at top speed across the square and disappearing in a lane which leads to the fields.

Of course everybody gave chase. I followed; but the pace was killing, and very few were in, literally, at the death. It happened in a chalk pit: the man went over the edge quite blindly and broke his neck. They searched everywhere for the other, until it occurred to me to ask whether he had ever left the market-place. At first everyone was sure that he had; but when we came to look, he was there, under the show-box, dead too.

But in the chalk pit it was that poor Uncle Henry's body was found, with a sack over the head, the throat horribly mangled. It was a peaked corner of the sack sticking out of the soil that attracted attention. I cannot bring myself to write in greater detail.

I forgot to say the men's real names were Kidman and Gallop. I feel sure I have heard them, but no one here seems to know anything about them.

I am coming to you as soon as I can after the funeral. I must tell you when we meet what I think of it all.

ABOUT *the* EDITOR.

Michael Grant Kellermeyer (b. 1987) edits, illustrates, and owns Oldstyle Tales Press. He grew up in Berne, Indiana where he cut his teeth on Walt Disney's *The Legend of Sleepy Hollow* at the age of five, a startling vision of humor and horror that began his love affair with speculative fiction. First earning his B.A. in English at Anderson University, Michael wrote his Master's thesis on dialectics of national identity in the 18th century novel of sympathy at nearby Ball State University, before pursuing a career teaching writing at the college level.

Michael's literary interests range from dark romanticism, Transcendentalism, the Scottish, English, and American Enlightenments, the British Romantics, the Gothic novel, and German and Russian 19th century literature. He is also deeply interested in early modern European history, American colonial history, and Western history at large 1521 – 1921, comparative mythology, philosophy, psychology, psychoanalysis, religion, anthropology, and world art. By definition, Michael's critical viewpoint is a combination of Jungian and Freudian psychoanalysis, comparative mythology, and new historicism. He is also strongly influenced by feminist, Marxist, and structuralist criticism methods. His favorite non-horror authors include Hawthorne, Irving, Melville, the Brontës, Dostoyevsky, Dante, Graham Greene, Goethe, Hermann Hesse, Steinbeck, Hemingway, Dickens, and Milton.

On a more basic, human level, Michael plays violin, paints and draws, cooks fairly basic, fairly tasty food, enjoys spats of archery and hiking, and takes pleasure in air-dried laundry, lemon wedges in ice water, mint tea, gin tonics, straight razors, sandalwood shaving cream, strong pipe tobacco, the films of Stanley Kubrick, and a hodgepodge of music ranging from sea shanties, the Delta Blues, and John Coltrane to The Decemberists, Fleet Foxes, and Classical music of all eras and types.

20914798R00175

Made in the USA
Lexington, KY
07 December 2018